W9-BSY-442

MODELS FOR WRITERS
SHORT ESSAYS FOR COMPOSITION

MODELS FOR WRITERS

SHORT ESSAYS FOR COMPOSITION

Editors

Alfred Rosa
Paul Eschholz
University of Vermont

ST. MARTIN'S PRESS NEW YORK

Library of Congress Catalog Card Number: 81–51841

Manufactured in the United States of America.
5
f
For Information, write St. Martin's Press, Inc.,
175 Fifth Avenue, New York, N.Y. 10010

cover design: Melissa Tardiff
cover art: "Gestalt III, 1969" by Victor Vasarely. From VASARELY, by Gaston Diehl, QLP Art Series. Crown Publishers, Inc., New York. Used by permission of Madeleine Ledivelec-Gloeckner.
typography: Avis Epstein-Larson

ISBN: 0–312–53590–2

Acknowledgments

I. The Elements of an Essay

1. Thesis

"I'd Rather Be Black Than Female" by Shirley Chisholm and reprinted with her permission. Originally appeared in *McCall's* August 1970.

"Politics: Never Satisfactory, Always Necessary" from pp. 158–160, THROUGH THE COMMUNICATION BARRIER by S. I. Hayakawa. Copyright © 1979 by S. I. Hayakawa. Reprinted by permission of Harper & Row, Publishers, Inc.

2. Unity

"Over-Generalization" from pp. 39–40 and 48 in GUIDES TO STRAIGHT THINKING by Stuart Chase. ©1956 by Stuart Chase. Reprinted by permission of Harper & Row, Publishers, Inc.

"Does a Finger Fing?" by Nedra Newkirk Lamar. Reprinted by permission from THE CHRISTIAN SCIENCE MONITOR. © 1981 The Christian Science Monitor Publishing Society. All rights reserved.

"Intelligence" by Isaac Asimov. (original title "What Is Intelligence, Anyway?") Reprinted courtesy of Isaac Asimov.

"Don't Let Stereotypes Warp Your Judgments" by Robert Heilbroner and reprinted with his permission.

Acknowledgments and copyrights continue at the back of the book on pages 351–354, which constitute an extension of the copyright page.

Table of Contents

II. The Language of the Essay

III. Types of Essays

Preface

Models for Writers offers sixty-two short, lively essays that have been selected for their appropriateness as models for use by the beginning college writer. Most of the selections are shorter than 1,000 words, like the essays students themselves are commonly asked to write. Each essay clearly illustrates a basic rhetorical element, principle, or pattern. The essays deal with subjects that we know from our own classroom experience are of interest to college students. We have sought a level of readability that is neither so easy as to be condescending nor so difficult as to distract the reader's attention from the rhetorical issue under study. Although we have included a few older classics, most of the essays have been written in the last ten years. They are drawn from a wide range of sources and represent a variety of contemporary prose styles.

The essays are grouped in eighteen chapters, each devoted to a particular element or principle. Chapters 1–6 focus on the concepts of thesis, unity, organization, the paragraph, transitions, and effective sentences. Chapters 7–9 illustrate some uses and effects of language: diction, tone, figurative language. Chapters 10–18 explore the various types of writing most often required of college students: illustration, narration, description, process analysis, definition, division and classification, comparison and contrast, cause and effect, and argument. The arrangement of the chapters suggests a logical teaching sequence, moving from the elements of the essay to its language to the different types of essays. An alternative teaching strategy might be to structure the course around chapters 10–18, bringing in the other chapters as necessary. Each chapter is self-contained, so that instructors may easily devise their own sequences, omitting or emphasizing particular chapters according to the needs of a particular group of students. Whatever sequence is followed, thematic comparisons among the selections will be facilitated by the *Thematic Table of Contents* at the end of the book.

The chapters all follow a similar pattern. Each opens with an explanation of the element or principle to be considered. We then present three or four essays, each of which has its own brief introduction providing information about the author and directing the student's attention to rhetorical features. Every essay is followed by study materials in three parts: *Questions for Study and Discussion, Vocabulary,* and *Suggested Writing Assignments.*

The *Questions for Study and Discussion* focus, in sequence, on the content, the author's purpose, and the rhetorical strategy used to achieve that purpose. Some questions allow brief answers, but most are designed to stimulate more searching analysis and to promote lively classroom discussion. In order to reinforce the lessons of other chapters and remind students that good writing is never one-dimensional, at least one question at the end of each series focuses on a writing concern other than the one highlighted in the chapter at hand. Whenever it seemed helpful, we have included references to the *Glossary of Useful Terms,* which provides concise definitions of rhetorical and other terms. The *Vocabulary* exercise draws from each reading several words that students will find worth adding to their active vocabularies. The exercise asks them to define each word as it is used in the context of the selection and then to use the word in a new sentence of their own. The *Suggested Writing Assignments* always focus on the rhetorical concerns illustrated in the essays they follow; some assignments are based on the content of the essays as well.

We are indebted to many people for their criticism and advice as we prepared *Models for Writers.* We are especially grateful to Ruth Bradley, Diablo Valley College; A. Patricia Burnes, University of Maine at Orono; H. Ramsey Fowler, Memphis State University; Maxine Hairston, University of Texas; Francis Hubbard, University of Wisconsin—Milwaukee; and Eugene P. Wright, North Texas State University. It has been our special pleasure to work with John W. N. Francis, our knowledgeable and genial editor at St. Martin's Press. Judy Cota typed our manuscript with efficiency and patience. Our greatest debt, as always, is to our students, for all that they have taught us.

Alfred Rosa
Paul Eschholz

I

THE ELEMENTS OF AN ESSAY

1

THESIS

The thesis of an essay is its main idea, the point it is trying to make. The thesis is often expressed in a one- or two-sentence statement, although sometimes it is implied or suggested rather than stated directly. The thesis statement controls and directs the content of the essay: everything that the writer says must be logically related to the thesis statement.

Usually the thesis is presented early in an essay, sometimes in the first sentence. Here are some thesis statements that begin essays:

> New York is a city of things unnoticed.
>
> Gay Talese

> Most Americans are in terrible shape.
>
> James F. Fixx

> One of the most potent elements in body language is eye behavior.
>
> Flora Davis

Each of these sentences does what a good thesis statement should do—it identifies the topic and makes an assertion about it.

Often writers prepare readers for a thesis statement with one or several sentences that establish a context. Notice, in the following example, how the author eases the reader into his thesis about television instead of presenting it abruptly in the first sentence:

> With the advent of television, for the first time in history, all aspects of animal and human life and death, of societal and individual behavior have been condensed on the average to a 19 inch diagonal screen and a 30 minute time slot. Television, a unique medium, claiming to be neither a reality nor art, has become

> reality for many of us, particularly for our children who are growing up in front of it.
>
> Jerzy Kosinski

On occasion a writer may even purposefully delay the presentation of a thesis until the middle or end of an essay. If the thesis is controversial or needs extended discussion and illustration, the writer might present it later to make it easier for the reader to understand and accept it. Appearing near or at the end of an essay, a thesis also gains prominence.

Some kinds of writing do not need thesis statements. These include descriptions, narratives, and personal writing such as letters and diaries. But any essay that seeks to explain or prove a point has a thesis that is usually set forth in a thesis statement.

The Most Important Day

Helen Keller

Helen Keller (1880–1968) was afflicted by a disease that left her blind and deaf at the age of eighteen months. With the aid of her teacher Anne Sullivan, she was able to overcome her severe handicaps, to graduate from Radcliffe College, and to lead a productive and challenging adult life. In the following selection from her autobiography The Story of My Life *(1902), Keller tells of the day she first met Anne Sullivan, a day she regarded as the most important in her life. Notice that Keller states her thesis in the first paragraph and that it serves to direct and unify the remaining paragraphs.*

1 The most important day I remember in all my life is the one on which my teacher, Anne Mansfield Sullivan, came to me. I am filled with wonder when I consider the immeasurable contrast between the two lives which it connects. It was the third of March, 1887, three months before I was seven years old.

2 On the afternoon of that eventful day, I stood on the porch, dumb, expectant. I guessed vaguely from my mother's signs and from the hurrying to and fro in the house that something unusual was about to happen, so I went to the door and waited on the steps. The afternoon sun penetrated the mass of honeysuckle that covered the porch and fell on my upturned face. My fingers lingered almost unconsciously on the familiar leaves and blossoms which had just come forth to greet the sweet southern spring. I did not know what the future held of marvel or surprise for me. Anger and bitterness had preyed upon me continually for weeks and a deep languor had succeeded this passionate struggle.

3 Have you ever been at sea in a dense fog, when it seemed

as if a tangible white darkness shut you in, and the great ship, tense and anxious, groped her way toward the shore with plummet and sounding-line, and you waited with beating heart for something to happen? I was like that ship before my education began, only I was without compass or sounding-line, and had no way of knowing how near the harbor was. "Light! give me light!" was the wordless cry of my soul, and the light of love shone on me in that very hour.

I felt approaching footsteps. I stretched out my hand as I supposed to my mother. Someone took it, and I was caught up and held close in the arms of her who had come to reveal all things to me, and, more than all things else, to love me.

The morning after my teacher came she led me into her room and gave me a doll. The little blind children at the Perkins Institution had sent it and Laura Bridgman had dressed it; but I did not know this until afterward. When I had played with it a little while, Miss Sullivan slowly spelled into my hand the word "d-o-l-l." I was at once interested in this finger play and tried to imitate it. When I finally succeeded in making the letters correctly I was flushed with childish pleasure and pride. Running downstairs to my mother I held up my hand and made the letters for doll. I did not know that I was spelling a word or even that words existed; I was simply making my fingers go in monkeylike imitation. In the days that followed I learned to spell in this uncomprehending way a great many words, among them *pin, hat, cup* and a few verbs like *sit, stand* and *walk*. But my teacher had been with me several weeks before I understood that everything has a name.

One day, while I was playing with my new doll, Miss Sullivan put my big rag doll into my lap also, spelled "d-o-l-l" and tried to make me understand that "d-o-l-l" applied to both. Earlier in the day we had had a tussle over the words "m-u-g" and "w-a-t-e-r." Miss Sullivan had tried to impress it upon me that "m-u-g" is *mug* and that "w-a-t-e-r" is *water*, but I persisted in confounding the two. In despair she had dropped the subject for the time, only to renew it at the first opportunity. I became impatient at her repeated attempts and, seizing the new doll, I dashed it upon the floor. I was keenly delighted when I felt the fragments of the broken doll at my feet. Neither sorrow nor regret followed my passionate outburst. I had not loved the doll. In the still, dark world in which I lived there was no strong sentiment or tenderness. I felt my teacher sweep the fragments to one side of the hearth, and I had a sense of satisfaction that the cause of my discomfort was removed. She brought me my hat, and I knew I was going out into the warm sunshine. This thought, if a wordless sensation may be called a thought, made me hop and skip with pleasure.

7 We walked down the path to the well-house, attracted by the fragrance of the honeysuckle with which it was covered. Some one was drawing water and my teacher placed my hand under the spout. As the cool stream gushed over one hand she spelled into the other the word *water,* first slowly, then rapidly. I stood still, my whole attention fixed upon the motions of her fingers. Suddenly I felt a misty consciousness as of something forgotten—a thrill of returning thought; and somehow the mystery of language was revealed to me. I knew then that "w-a-t-e-r" meant the wonderful cool something that was flowing over my hand. The living word awakened my soul, gave it light, hope, joy, set it free! There were barriers still, it is true, but barriers that could in time be swept away.

8 I left the well-house eager to learn. Everything had a name, and each name gave birth to a new thought. As we returned to the house every object which I touched seemed to quiver with life. That was because I saw everything with the strange, new sight that had come to me. On entering the door I remembered the doll I had broken. I felt my way to the hearth and picked up the pieces. I tried vainly to put them together. Then my eyes filled with tears; for I realized what I had done, and for the first time I felt repentance and sorrow.

9 I learned a great many new words that day. I do not remember what they all were; but I do know that *mother, father, sister, teacher* were among them—words that were to make the world blossom for me, "like Aaron's rod, with flowers." It would have been difficult to find a happier child than I was as I lay in my crib at the close of that eventful day and lived over the joys it had brought me, and for the first time longed for a new day to come.

Questions for Study and Discussion

1. What is Helen Keller's thesis in this essay?
2. What is Helen Keller's purpose in this essay? (Glossary: *Purpose*)
3. Helen Keller narrates the events of the day Anne Sullivan arrived (2–4), the morning after she arrived (5), and one day several weeks after her arrival (6–9). Describe what happens on each day, and explain how these separate incidents support her thesis.
4. Identify the figure of speech that Helen Keller uses in paragraph 3. Why is it effective? (Glossary: *Figures of Speech*)

Vocabulary

Refer to your dictionary to define the following words as they are used in this selection. Then use each word in a sentence of your own.

dumb (2)
preyed (2)
languor (2)
passionate (2)
plummet (3)
tussle (6)
vainly (8)

Suggested Writing Assignment

Think about an important day in your own life. Using the thesis statement "The most important day of my life was ______," write an essay in which you show the significance of that day by recounting and explaining the events that took place.

I'd Rather Be Black Than Female

Shirley Chisholm

Shirley Chisholm is a member of the United States House of Representatives serving Brooklyn, New York. She is an outspoken advocate of the rights of all minorities, an authority on child welfare, and an educational consultant. Her books Unbought and Unbossed *(1970) and* The Good Fight *(1973) are records of her experiences as a black female politician. In the following essay, first published in the August 1970* McCall's, *it is Chisholm's thesis that in America today it is less of a disadvantage to be black than to be female.*

Being the first black woman elected to Congress has made me some kind of phenomenon. There are nine other blacks in Congress; there are ten other women. I was the first to overcome both handicaps at once. Of the two handicaps, being black is much less of a drawback than being female. 1

If I said that being black is a greater handicap than being a woman, probably no one would question me. Why? Because "we all know" there is prejudice against black people in America. That there is prejudice against women is an idea that still strikes nearly all men—and, I am afraid, most women—as bizarre. 2

Prejudice against blacks was invisible to most white Americans for many years. When blacks finally started to "mention" it, with sit-ins, boycotts, and freedom rides, Americans were incredulous. "Who, us?" they asked in injured tones. "*We're* prejudiced?" It was the start of a long, 3 painful reeducation for white America. It will take years for whites—including those who think of themselves as liberals—to discover and eliminate the racist attitudes they all actually have.

How much harder will it be to eliminate the prejudice against women? I am sure it will be a longer struggle. Part of the problem is that women in America are much more brainwashed and content with their roles as second-class citizens than blacks ever were.

Let me explain. I have been active in politics for more than twenty years. For all but the last six, I have done the work—all the tedious details that make the difference between victory and defeat on election day—while men reaped the rewards, which is almost invariably the lot of women in politics.

It is still women—about three million volunteers—who do most of this work in the American political world. The best any of them can hope for is the honor of being district or county vice-chairman, a kind of separate-but-equal position with which a woman is rewarded for years of faithful envelope stuffing and card-party organizing. In such a job, she gets a number of free trips to state and sometimes national meetings and conventions, where her role is supposed to be to vote the way her male chairman votes.

When I tried to break out of that role in 1963 and run for the New York State Assembly seat from Brooklyn's Bedford-Stuyvesant, the resistance was bitter. From the start of that campaign, I faced undisguised hostility because of my sex.

But it was four years later, when I ran for Congress, that the question of my sex became a major issue. Among members of my own party, closed meetings were held to discuss ways of stopping me.

My opponent, the famous civil rights leader James Farmer, tried to project a black, masculine image; he toured the neighborhood with sound trucks filled with young men wearing Afro haircuts, dashikis, and beards. While the television crews ignored me, they were not aware of a very important statistic, which both I and my campaign manager, Wesley MacD. Holder, knew. In my district there are 2.5

women for every man registered to vote. And those women are organized—in PTAs, church societies, card clubs, and other social and service groups. I went to them and asked their help. Mr. Farmer still doesn't quite know what hit him.

When a bright young woman graduate starts looking for a job, why is the first question always: "Can you type?" A history of prejudice lies behind that question. Why are women thought of as secretaries, not administrators? Librarians and teachers, but not doctors and lawyers? Because they are thought of as different and inferior. The happy homemaker and the contented darky are both stereotypes produced by prejudice. 10

Women have not even reached the level of tokenism that blacks are reaching. No women sit on the Supreme Court. Only two have held Cabinet rank, and none do at present. Only two women hold ambassadorial rank. But women predominate in the lower-paying, menial, unrewarding, dead-end jobs, and when they do reach better positions, they are invariably paid less than a man gets for the same job. 11

If that is not prejudice, what would you call it? 12

A few years ago, I was talking with a political leader about a promising young woman as a candidate. "Why invest time and effort to build the girl up?" he asked me. "You know she'll only drop out of the game to have a couple of kids just about the time we're ready to run her for mayor." 13

Plenty of people have said similar things about me. Plenty of others have advised me, every time I tried to take another upward step, that I should go back to teaching, a woman's vocation, and leave politics to the men. I love teaching, and I am ready to go back to it as soon as I am convinced that this country no longer needs a woman's contribution. 14

When there are no children going to bed hungry in this rich nation, I may be ready to go back to teaching. When there is a good school for every child, I may be ready. When we do not spend our wealth on hardware to murder people, when we no longer tolerate prejudice against minorities, and when the laws against unfair housing and unfair employment practices are enforced instead of evaded, then there may be nothing more for me to do in politics. 15

But until that happens—and we all know it will not be this year or next—what we need is more women in politics, because we have a very special contribution to make. I hope that the example of my success will convince other women to get into politics—and not just to stuff envelopes, but to run for office.

It is women who can bring empathy, tolerance, insight, patience, and persistence to government—the qualities we naturally have or have had to develop because of our suppression by men. The women of a nation mold its morals, its religion, and its politics by the lives they live. At present, our country needs women's idealism and determination, perhaps more in politics than anywhere else.

Questions for Study and Discussion

1. Where does Chisholm state her thesis?
2. Chisholm's purpose is to convince the reader that there is more prejudice against women than against blacks. How successful is she in convincing you?
3. Discuss Chisholm's use of comparison and contrast in this essay. (Glossary: *Comparison and Contrast*)
4. A *rhetorical question* is a question that requires no answer; it is often used for emphasis. In the context of the essay, what is the function of paragraph 12?

Vocabulary

Refer to your dictionary to define the following words as they are used in this selection. Then use each word in a sentence of your own.

bizarre (2)	menial (11)
incredulous (3)	vocation (14)
tedious (5)	empathy (17)
tokenism (11)	persistence (17)

Suggested Writing Assignment

Write an essay in which you use as your thesis the formula "I'd rather be _____ than _____." You may use one of the following topics or create one of your own:

I'd rather be honest than successful.
I'd rather be a spectator than an athlete.
I'd rather be a worker than a supervisor.
I'd rather take chances than lead a boring life.

Politics: Never Satisfactory, Always Necessary

S. I. Hayakawa

S. I. Hayakawa, former president of San Francisco State University and currently a United States Senator from California, is one of the leading semanticists in this country. In this excerpt from Through the Communication Barrier *(1979), Hayakawa wants us to understand the role that language plays in the political process, and to see that the political process, while not satisfying to everyone all the time, is nonetheless the very essence of a civilized society.*

The language scholar Benjamin Lee Whorf once said, "Whenever agreement or assent is reached in human affairs, this agreement is reached by linguistic processes, or else it is not reached." By linguistic processes he meant, of course, discussion, argument, persuasion; definitions and judgments; promises and contracts—all those exchanges of words by means of which human beings interact with each other.

Without language—without words—there is no such thing as the future. "Mary and John are married" is a statement about the present and also the future; it points to the obligations that Mary and John have toward each other in the days and years ahead. The future is real to us because it is formulated into words. Society is a network of agreements about future conduct. Here, let us say, are two tribes, the Blues and the Reds. Both tribes want exclusive access to the fish in Clearwater Bay. If the two tribes are equally strong, they will fight and fight and kill each other—until someone has the good sense to say, "Since we can't lick them and they can't lick us, let's call a conference and see what we can work out."

What Benjamin Lee Whorf calls linguistic processes are initiated. Delegates from the two tribes argue and shout and scream, but ultimately they come to an agreement. The Reds will fish the bay Mondays, Wednesdays, and Fridays; the Blues on Tuesdays, Thursdays, and Saturdays; no fishing on Sundays. 3

People who work out agreements of this kind are known as politicians. Politicians are people who resolve through linguistic processes conflicts that would otherwise have to be solved by force. But politicians are rarely thanked for their efforts. Many of the Blues are disappointed. "Look at what the politicians gave away to the Reds," they say. "What a sellout! They must have been bribed." The Reds are equally critical of their delegates. "Everyone knows," they say, "that God intended the bay for the exclusive use of us Reds, but now the Blues act as if they had equal rights to it. What we need are delegates who are men of principle, not compromisers." 4

The results of a political process are never satisfactory to all concerned. Give the Arabs what they want, and the Israelis are enraged. Give the employers what they want, and the unions are furious. Introduce a measure of gun control, and the National Rifle Association is apoplectic. If the political process is successful, all get only part of what they want, and none gets all he wants. And everyone blames the politicians for their disappointments. It often seems that the political process is far too subtle, far too complex, for men of words—intellectuals and journalists—to understand. Intellectuals, with their passion for logic and order, often disdain the democratic process. They are fascinated by Plato's perfect republic governed by philosopher kings.* Imagining themselves to be the "gold" of Plato's classification of human beings, intellectuals are easily seduced by Marxism, which insists that government should be in the hands of those who understand such arcane matters as dialectical materialism and historic necessity—that is, intellectuals. 5

---

*Refers to an aristocratic utopia described in *The Republic*, by the ancient Greek philosopher Plato. The absolute rulers would be philosophers, lovers of perfect truth who would therefore not be corrupted by their high office.

This is no doubt the reason that there are more Marxists than Democrats and Republicans combined in so many university departments of philosophy.

Mike Royko of the Chicago *Daily News*, a characteristic journalistic critic of politics, wrote a book entitled *Boss*, which attacked and criticized the late Mayor Richard Daley of Chicago as corrupt, venal, ruthless, and given to making shady alliances with the underworld and ridiculous mistakes in English grammar. The book has become quite a favorite in college courses in political science as required and recommended reading.

However, not long after the publication of Royko's book, Richard Daley was returned to office as mayor of Chicago, at the age of seventy-three and no longer in the best of health, with the biggest majority of his long political career. Apparently there is something about politics that neither Mr. Royko nor political science teachers quite understand—and that is how successful practitioners of the art of politics like Mayor Daley earn the trust and affection of so many people.

Disgusted with politicians, people from time to time yearn for government without politics. Sometimes, to their dismay, they get it, as in Soviet Russia, China, Poland, and North Korea, where the political process has been abolished, or as in Northern Ireland, where the political process has failed.

As Americans we need more than ever today to understand and cherish the political process. It is admittedly untidy. It is confusing. But it is the very essence of civilization.

Questions for Study and Discussion

1. What, according to Hayakawa, do intellectuals unrealistically expect of the democratic process?
2. Hayakawa presents his thesis in the last paragraph of the essay. What would be gained or lost if he had made his last paragraph the first one of the essay?
3. What three points does Hayakawa illustrate with his example of the two tribes, the Blues and the Reds? (Glossary: *Illustration*)

4. In order not to be misunderstood, writers often define terms that they feel readers will not readily understand or terms that they are using in a particular way. Identify two terms that Hayakawa defines, and explain why you think Hayakawa defined each one.
5. Do you agree with Hayakawa's argument? Why or why not?

Vocabulary

Refer to your dictionary to define the following words as they are used in this selection. Then use each word in a sentence of your own.

linguistic (1)
apoplectic (5)
arcane (5)
venal (6)
cherish (9)

Suggested Writing Assignment

Select one of the following quotations from Hayakawa's essay to use as your thesis statement in a brief essay:

> "Society is a network of agreements about future conduct."
>
> "Politicians are rarely thanked for their efforts."
>
> "The results of a political process are never satisfactory to all concerned."
>
> "As Americans we need more than ever today to understand and cherish the political process."

Use examples from your own experience and reading to illustrate and substantiate your thesis. Using Hayakawa's essay as a model, present your thesis statement at the conclusion of your essay.

2

UNITY

A well-written essay should be unified; that is, everything in it should be related to its thesis, or main idea. The first requirement for unity is that the thesis itself be clear, either through a direct statement, called the thesis statement, or by implication. The second requirement is that there be no digressions, no discussion or information that is not shown to be logically related to the thesis. A unified essay stays within the limits of its thesis.

Here, for example, is a short essay called "Over-Generalizing" about the dangers of making generalizations. As you read, notice how carefully author Stuart Chase sticks to his point.

> One swallow does not make a summer, nor can two or three cases often support a dependable generalization. Yet all of us, including the most polished eggheads, are constantly falling into this mental mantrap. It is the commonest, probably the most seductive, and potentially the most dangerous, of all the fallacies. 1
>
> You drive through a town and see a drunken man on the sidewalk. A few blocks further on you see another. You turn to your companion: "Nothing but drunks in this town!" Soon you are out in the country, bowling along at fifty. A car passes you as if you were parked. On a curve a second whizzes by. Your companion turns to you: "All the drivers in this state are crazy!" Two thumping generalizations, each built on two cases. If we stop to think, we usually recognize the exaggeration and the unfairness of such generalizations. Trouble comes when we do not stop to think—or when we build them on a prejudice. 2
>
> This kind of reasoning has been around for a long time. Aristotle was aware of its dangers and called it "reasoning by example," meaning too few examples. What it boils down to is failing to count your swallows 3

before announcing that summer is here. Driving from my home to New Haven the other day, a distance of about forty miles, I caught myself saying: "Every time I look around I see a new ranch-type house going up." So on the return trip I counted them; there were exactly five under construction. And how many times had I "looked around"? I suppose I had glanced to right and left—as one must at side roads and so forth in driving—several hundred times.

4 In this fallacy we do not make the error of neglecting facts altogether and rushing immediately to the level of opinion. We start at the fact level properly enough, but *we do not stay there.* A case of two and up we go to a rousing over-simplification about drunks, speeders, ranch-style houses—or, more seriously, about foreigners, Negroes, labor leaders, teen-agers.

5 Why do we over-generalize so often and sometimes so disastrously? One reason is that the human mind is a generalizing machine. We would not be men without this power. The old academic crack: "All generalizations are false, including this one," is only a play on words. We *must* generalize to communicate and to live. But we should beware of beating the gun; of not waiting until enough facts are in to say something useful. Meanwhile it is a plain waste of time to listen to arguments based on a few hand-picked examples.

Everything in the essay relates to Chase's thesis statement, which is included in the essay's first sentence: ". . . nor can two or three cases often support a dependable generalization." Paragraphs 2 and 3 document the thesis with examples; paragraph 4 explains how over-generalizing occurs; paragraph 5 analyzes why people over-generalize; and, for a conclusion, Chase restates his thesis in different words. An essay may be longer, more complex, and more wide-ranging than this one, but to be effective it must also avoid digressions and remain close to the author's main idea.

Does a Finger Fing?

Nedra Newkirk Lamar

Nedra Newkirk Lamar is a free-lance writer and teacher of reading. Her articles have appeared in numerous magazines, and she is a frequent contributor to the Christian Science Monitor, *from which the following selection was taken. Notice the close relationship between Lamar's thesis and the examples she uses—a relationship that results in a well-unified essay.*

Everybody knows that a tongue-twister is something that twists the tongue, and a skyscraper is something that scrapes the sky, but is an eavesdropper someone who drops eaves? A thinker is someone who thinks but is a tinker someone who tinks? Is a clabber something that goes around clabbing?

Somewhere along the way we all must have had an English teacher who gave us the fascinating information that words that end in ER mean something or somebody who *does* something, like trapper, designer, or stopper.

A stinger is something that stings, but is a finger something that fings? Fing fang fung. Today I fing. Yesterday I fang. Day before yesterday I had already fung.

You'd expect eyes, then, to be called seers and ears to be hearers. We'd wear our shoes on our walkers and our sleeves on our reachers. But we don't. The only parts of the body that sound as if they might indicate what they're supposed to do are our fingers, which we've already counted out, our livers, and our shoulders. And they don't do what they sound as if they might. At least, I've never seen anyone use his shoulders for shoulding. You shoulder your way through a crowd, but you don't should your way. It's only in slang that we follow the pattern, when we smell with our smellers and kiss with our kissers.

The animal pattern seems to have more of a feeling for this formation than people do, because insects actually do feel with their feelers. But do cats use their whiskers for whisking? 5

I've seen people mend socks and knit socks, but I've never seen anyone dolage a sock. Yet there must be people who do, else how could we have sock-dolagers? 6

Is a humdinger one who dings hums? And what is a hum anyway, and how would one go about dinging it? Maybe Winnie the Pooh could have told us. He was always humming hums, but A. A. Milne never tells us whether he also was fond of dinging them. He sang them but do you suppose he ever dang them? 7

Sometimes occupational names do reveal what the worker does, though. Manufacturers manufacture, miners mine, adjusters adjust—or at least try to. But does a grocer groce? Does a fruiterer fruiter? Does a butler buttle? 8

No, you just can't trust the English language. You can love it because it's your mother tongue. You can take pride in it because it's the language Shakespeare was dramatic in. You can thrill to it because it's the language Browning and Tennyson were poetic in. You can have fun with it because it's the language Dickens and Mark Twain and Lewis Carroll were funny in. You can revere it because it's the language Milton was majestic in. You can be grateful to it because it's the language the Magna Carta and the Declaration of Independence were expressed in. 9

But you just can't trust it! 10

Questions for Study and Discussion

1. What is Lamar's main idea, or thesis? (Glossary: *Thesis*)
2. How does she support her thesis? (Glossary: *Illustration*)
3. Does Lamar at any point digress from her thesis?
4. Why, do you suppose, Lamar has chosen "Does a Finger Fing?" as a title for her essay? (Glossary: *Title*)

Vocabulary

Refer to your dictionary to define the following words as they are used in this selection. Then use each word in a sentence of your own.

slang (4)
butler (8)
revere (9)
majestic (9)

Suggested Writing Assignment

Lamar makes the generalization that "you just can't trust the English language" and supports it with numerous examples. Make a generalization about a topic of your choice and write an essay in which you use multiple examples to support it. Make sure that your essay is unified; choose your examples carefully and relate them to your thesis.

Intelligence

Isaac Asimov

Isaac Asimov was born in the Soviet Union in 1920 and came to the United States in 1923. Author of more than 200 books, he is internationally recognized as a great popularizer of science. In addition to his writings on science, he has written much science fiction as well as books on history, Shakespeare, and the Bible. Whatever kind of writing Asimov undertakes, he is both entertaining and lucid, as can be seen in the following selection. As you read the essay, notice how every paragraph is related to Asimov's thesis that intelligence is a relative matter.

What is intelligence, anyway? When I was in the army I received a kind of aptitude test that all soldiers took and, against a normal of 100, scored 160. No one at the base had ever seen a figure like that, and for two hours they made a big fuss over me. (It didn't mean anything. The next day I was still a buck private with KP as my highest duty.) 1

All my life I've been registering scores like that, so that I have the complacent feeling that I'm highly intelligent, and I expect other people to think so, too. Actually, though, don't such scores simply mean that I am very good at answering the type of academic questions that are considered worthy of answers by the people who make up the intelligence tests—people with intellectual bents similar to mine? 2

For instance, I had an auto-repair man once, who, on these intelligence tests, could not possibly have scored more than 80, by my estimate. I always took it for granted that I was far more intelligent than he was. Yet, when anything went wrong with my car I hastened to him with it, watched him anxiously as he explored its vitals, and listened to his pronouncements as though they were divine oracles—and he always fixed my car. 3

Well, then, suppose my auto-repair man devised questions for an intelligence test. Or suppose a carpenter did, or a farmer, or, indeed, almost anyone but an academician. By every one of those tests, I'd prove myself a moron. And I'd *be* a moron, too. In a world where I could not use my academic training and my verbal talents but had to do something intricate or hard, working with my hands, I would do poorly. My intelligence, then, is not absolute but is a function of the society I live in and of the fact that a small subsection of that society has managed to foist itself on the rest as an arbiter of such matters.

Consider my auto-repair man, again. He had a habit of telling me jokes whenever he saw me. One time he raised his head from under the automobile hood to say: "Doc, a deaf-and-dumb guy went into a hardware store to ask for some nails. He put two fingers together on the counter and made hammering motions with the other hand. The clerk brought him a hammer. He shook his head and pointed to the two fingers he was hammering. The clerk brought him nails. He picked out the sizes he wanted, and left. Well, doc, the next guy who came in was a blind man. He wanted scissors. How do you suppose he asked for them?"

Indulgently, I lifted my right hand and made scissoring motions with my first two fingers. Whereupon my auto-repair man laughed raucously and said, "Why, you dumb jerk, he used his *voice* and asked for them." Then he said, smugly, "I've been trying that on all my customers today." "Did you catch many?" I asked. "Quite a few," he said, "but I knew for sure I'd catch *you*." "Why is that?" I asked. "Because you're so goddamned educated, doc, I *knew* you couldn't be very smart."

And I have an uneasy feeling he had something there.

Questions for Study and Discussion

1. The main point of this essay is that intelligence is a relative matter. How is each paragraph in the essay related to this thesis?

2. Discuss how Asimov achieves coherence in this essay by using transitions to link paragraphs. (Glossary: *Transitions*)
3. What is the author's purpose in telling the auto-repair man's joke? What distinction does the auto-repair man make between "educated" and "smart"?
4. Why, in your opinion, does Asimov make the final sentence a separate paragraph instead of including it in the preceding one?

Vocabulary

Refer to your dictionary to define the following words as they are used in this selection. Then use each word in a sentence of your own.

aptitude (1)	foist (4)
complacent (2)	indulgently (6)
oracles (3)	raucously (6)

Suggested Writing Assignment

Write an essay in which you attempt to come to an understanding of intelligence or of another elusive abstract term. Make sure that your essay, like Asimov's, is unified; that is, your examples and discussions must relate to your thesis.

DON'T LET STEREOTYPES WARP YOUR JUDGMENTS

Robert L. Heilbroner

The economist Robert L. Heilbroner was educated at Harvard and at the New School for Social Research, where he has been the Norman Thomas Professor of Economics since 1972. He has written The Future as History *(1960),* A Primer of Government Spending: Between Capitalism and Socialism *(1970), and* An Inquiry into the Human Prospect *(1974). "Don't Let Stereotypes Warp Your Judgments" first appeared in* Reader's Digest. *As you read this essay, pay particular attention to its unity—the relationships of the paragraphs to the thesis.*

Is a girl called Gloria apt to be better-looking than one called Bertha? Are criminals more likely to be dark than blond? Can you tell a good deal about someone's personality from hearing his voice briefly over the phone? Can a person's nationality be pretty accurately guessed from his photograph? Does the fact that someone wears glasses imply that he is intelligent?

The answer to all these questions is obviously, "No."

Yet, from all the evidence at hand, most of us believe these things. Ask any college boy if he'd rather take his chances with a Gloria or a Bertha, or ask a college girl if she'd rather blind-date a Richard or a Cuthbert. In fact, you don't have to ask: college students in questionnaires have revealed that names conjure up the same images in their minds as they do in yours—and for as little reason.

Look into the favorite suspects of persons who report "suspicious characters" and you will find a large percentage of them to be "swarthy" or "dark and foreign-looking"—

despite the testimony of criminologists that criminals do *not* tend to be dark, foreign or "wild-eyed." Delve into the main asset of a telephone stock swindler and you will find it to be a marvelously confidence-inspiring telephone "personality." And whereas we all think we know what an Italian or a Swede looks like, it is the sad fact that when a group of Nebraska students sought to match faces and nationalities of 15 European countries, they were scored wrong in 93 percent of their identifications. Finally, for all the fact that horn-rimmed glasses have now become the standard television sign of an "intellectual," optometrists know that the main thing that distinguishes people with glasses is just bad eyes.

Stereotypes are a kind of gossip about the world, a gossip that makes us prejudge people before we ever lay eyes on them. Hence it is not surprising that stereotypes have something to do with the dark world of prejudice. Explore most prejudices (note that the word means prejudgment) and you will find a cruel stereotype at the core of each one. 5

For it is the extraordinary fact that once we have typecast the world, we tend to see people in terms of our standardized pictures. In another demonstration of the power of stereotypes to affect our vision, a number of Columbia and Barnard students were shown 30 photographs of pretty but unidentified girls, and asked to rate each in terms of "general liking," "intelligence," "beauty" and so on. Two months later, the same group were shown the same photographs, this time with fictitious Irish, Italian, Jewish and "American" names attached to the pictures. Right away the ratings changed. Faces which were now seen as representing a national group went down in looks and still farther down in likability, while the "American" girls suddenly looked decidedly prettier and nicer. 6

Why is it that we stereotype the world in such irrational and harmful fashion? In part, we begin to type-cast people in our childhood years. Early in life, as every parent whose child has watched a TV Western knows, we learn to spot the Good Guys from the Bad Guys. Some years ago, a social psychologist showed very clearly how powerful these stereotypes of childhood vision are. He secretly asked the most 7 popular youngsters in an elementary school to make errors in their morning gym exercises. Afterwards, he asked the class if anyone had noticed any mistakes during gym period. Oh, yes, said the children. But it was the *unpopular* members of the class—the "bad guys"—they remembered as being out of step.

We not only grow up with standardized pictures forming inside of us, but as grown-ups we are constantly having them thrust upon us. Some of them, like the half-joking, half-serious stereotypes of mothers-in-law, or country yokels, or psychiatrists, are dinned into us by the stock jokes we hear and repeat. In fact, without such stereotypes, there would be a lot fewer jokes. Still other stereotypes are perpetuated by the advertisements we read, the movies we see, the books we read.

And finally, we tend to stereotype because it helps us make sense out of a highly confusing world, a world which William James once described as "one great, blooming, buzzing confusion." It is a curious fact that if we don't *know* what we're looking at, we are often quite literally unable to *see* what we're looking at. People who recover their sight after a lifetime of blindness actually cannot at first tell a triangle from a square. A visitor to a factory sees only noisy chaos where the superintendent sees a perfectly synchronized flow of work. As Walter Lippmann has said, "For the most part we do not first see, and then define; we define first, and then we see."

Stereotypes are one way in which we "define" the world in order to see it. They classify the infinite variety of human beings into a convenient handful of "types" towards whom we learn to act in stereotyped fashion. Life would be a wearing process if we had to start from scratch with each and every human contact. Stereotypes economize on our mental effort by covering up the blooming, buzzing confusion with big recognizable cut-outs. They save us the "trouble" of finding out what the world is like—they give it its accustomed look.

Thus the trouble is that stereotypes make us mentally lazy. As S. I. Hayakawa, the authority on semantics, has written: "The danger of stereotypes lies not in their existence, but in the fact that they become for all people some of the time, and for some people all the time, *substitutes for observation*." Worse yet, stereotypes get in the way of our judgment, even when we do observe the world. Someone who has formed rigid preconceptions of all Latins as "excitable," or all teenagers as "wild," doesn't alter his point of view when he meets a calm and deliberate Genoese, or a serious-minded high school student. He brushes them aside as "exceptions that prove the rule." And, of course, if he meets someone true to type, he stands triumphantly vindicated. "They're all like that," he proclaims, having encountered an excited Latin, an ill-behaved adolescent.

12 Hence, quite aside from the injustice which stereotypes do to others, they impoverish ourselves. A person who lumps the world into simple categories, who type-casts all labor leaders as "racketeers," all businessmen as "reactionaries," all Harvard men as "snobs," and all Frenchmen as "sexy," is in danger of becoming a stereotype himself. He loses his capacity to be himself—which is to say, to see the world in his own absolutely unique, inimitable and independent fashion.

13 Instead, he votes for the man who fits his standardized picture of what a candidate "should" look like or sound like, buys the goods that someone in his "situation" in life "should" own, lives the life that others define for him. The mark of the stereotype person is that he never surprises us, that we do indeed have him "typed." And no one fits this strait-jacket so perfectly as someone whose opinions about *other people* are fixed and inflexible.

14 Impoverishing as they are, stereotypes are not easy to get rid of. The world we type-cast may be no better than a Grade B movie, but at least we know what to expect of our stock characters. When we let them act for themselves in the strangely unpredictable way that people do act, who knows but that many of our fondest convictions will be proved wrong?

15 Nor do we suddenly drop our standardized pictures for a blinding vision of the Truth. Sharp swings of ideas about people often just substitute one stereotype for another. The true process of change is a slow one that adds bits and pieces of reality to the pictures in our heads, until gradually they

take on some of the blurriness of life itself. Little by little, we learn not that Jews and Negroes and Catholics and Puerto Ricans are "just like everybody else"—for that, too, is a stereotype—but that each and every one of them is unique, special, different and individual. Often we do not even know that we have let a stereotype lapse until we hear someone saying, "all so-and-so's are like such-and-such," and we hear ourselves saying, "Well—maybe."

Can we speed the process along? Of course we can.

First, we can become *aware* of the standardized pictures in our heads, in other peoples' heads, in the world around us.

Second, we can become suspicious of all judgments that we allow exceptions to "prove." There is no more chastening thought than that in the vast intellectual adventure of science, it takes but one tiny exception to topple a whole edifice of ideas.

Third, we can learn to be chary of generalizations about people. As F. Scott Fitzgerald once wrote: "Begin with an individual, and before you know it you have created a type; begin with a type, and you find you have created—nothing."

Most of the time, when we type-cast the world, we are not in fact generalizing about people at all. We are only revealing the embarrassing facts about the pictures that hang in the gallery of stereotypes in our own heads.

Questions for Study and Discussion

1. What is Heilbroner's main point, or thesis, in this essay? (Glossary: *Thesis*)
2. Study paragraphs 6, 8, and 15. Each paragraph illustrates Heilbroner's thesis. How? What does each paragraph contribute to support the thesis?
3. Transitional devices indicate relationships between paragraphs and thus help to unify the essay. Identify three transitions in this essay. Explain how they help to unify the essay. (Glossary: *Transitions*)

4. Heilbroner uses the word *picture* in his discussion of stereotypes. Why is this an appropriate word in this discussion? (Glossary: *Diction*)

Vocabulary

Refer to your dictionary to define the following words as they are used in this selection. Then use each word in a sentence of your own.

irrational (7)
perpetuated (8)
infinite (10)
preconceptions (11)
vindicated (11)
impoverish (12)
chastening (18)
edifice (18)
chary (19)

Suggested Writing Assignment

Write an essay in which you attempt to convince your readers that it is not in their best interests to perform a particular act—for example, smoke, take stimulants to stay awake, go on a crash diet, make snap judgments. In writing your essay, follow Heilbroner's lead: First identify the issue; then explain why it is a problem; and, finally, offer a solution or some advice. Remember to unify the various parts of your essay.

3

ORGANIZATION

In an essay, ideas and information cannot be presented all at once; they have to be arranged in some order. That order is the essay's organization.

The pattern of organization in an essay should be suited to the writer's subject and purpose. For example, if you are writing about your experience working in a fast-food restaurant, and your purpose is to tell about the activities of a typical day, you might present those activities in chronological order. If, on the other hand, you wish to argue that working in a bank is an ideal summer job, you might proceed from the least rewarding to the most rewarding aspect of this job; this is called "climactic" order.

Some often-used patterns of organization are time order, space order, and logical order. Time order, or chronological order, is used to present events as they occurred. A personal narrative, a report of a campus incident, or an account of a historical event can be most naturally and easily related in chronological order. The description of a process, such as the refinishing of a table, the building of a stone wall, or the way to serve a tennis ball, almost always calls for a chronological organization. Of course, the order of events can sometimes be rearranged for special effect. For example, an account of an auto accident may begin with the collision itself and then go back in time to tell about the events leading up to it. Essays that are models of chronological order include Dick Gregory's "Shame" and Bernard Gladstone's "How to Build a Fire in a Fireplace."

Space order is used when describing a person, place, or thing. This organizational pattern begins at a particular point and moves in some direction, such as left to right, top to bottom, east to west, outside to inside, front to back, near to far, around, or over. In describing a house, for example, a writer could move from top to bottom, from outside to inside, or in a circle around the outside. Gilbert Highet's "Subway Station" (p. 190) is an essay in which space is used as the organizing principle.

Logical order can take many forms depending on the writer's purpose. These include: general to specific, most familiar to least familiar, and smallest to biggest. Perhaps the most common type of logical order is order of importance. Notice how the writer uses this order in the following paragraph.

> The Egyptians have taught us many things. They were excellent farmers. They knew all about irrigation. They built temples which were afterwards copied by the Greeks and which served as the earliest models for the churches in which we worship nowadays. They invented a calendar which proved such a useful instrument for the purpose of measuring time that it has survived with a few changes until today. But most important of all, the Egyptians learned how to preserve speech for the benefit of future generations. They invented the art of writing.

By organizing the material according to the order of increasing importance, the writer places special emphasis on the final sentence. In writing a descriptive essay you can move from the least striking to the most striking detail, so as to keep your reader interested and involved in the description. In an explanatory essay you can start with the point that readers will find least difficult to understand, and move on to the most difficult; that's how teachers organize many courses. Or, in writing an argumentative essay, you can move from your least controversial point to the most controversial, preparing your reader gradually to accept your argument.

Bugs Bunny Says They're Yummy

Dawn Ann Kurth

In 1972 eleven-year-old Dawn Ann Kurth was a surprise witness at a Senate subcommittee hearing on television advertising. She believes that television commercials, especially those shown on Saturday-morning television, take unfair advantage of children. The following is a transcript of her statement to the committee. As you read it, pay particular attention to the way her examples of television advertising are arranged.

Mr. Chairman:

My name is Dawn Ann Kurth. I am 11 years old and in the fifth grade at Meadowlane Elementary School in Melbourne, Florida. This year I was one of the 36 students chosen by the teachers out of 20,000 5th-through-8th graders to do a project in the Talented Student Program in Brevard County. We were allowed to choose a project in any field we wanted. It was difficult to decide. There seem to be so many problems in the world today. What could I do?

A small family crisis solved my problem. My sister Martha, who is 7, had asked my mother to buy a box of Post Raisin Bran so that she could get the free record that was on the back of the box. It had been advertised several times on Saturday morning cartoon shows. My mother bought the cereal, and we all (there are four children in our family) helped Martha eat it so she could get the record. It was after the cereal was eaten and she had the record that the crisis occurred. There was no way the record would work.

Martha was very upset and began crying and I was angry too. It just didn't seem right to me that something could be shown on TV that worked fine and people were listening and dancing to the record and when you bought the cereal, instead of laughing and dancing, we were crying and angry. Then I realized that perhaps here was a problem I could do something about or, if I couldn't change things, at least I could make others aware of deceptive advertising practices to children.

4 To begin my project I decided to keep a record of the number of commercials shown on typical Saturday morning TV shows. There were 25 commercial messages during one hour, from 8 to 9 A.M., not counting ads for shows coming up or public service ads. I found there were only 10 to 12 commercials during shows my parents like to watch. For the first time, I really began to think about what the commercials were saying. I had always listened before and many times asked my mother to buy certain products I had seen advertised, but now I was listening and really thinking about what was being said. Millions of kids are being told:

5 "Make friends with Kool-Aid. Kool-Aid makes good friends."

6 "People who love kids have to buy Fritos."

7 "Hershey chocolate makes milk taste like a chocolate bar." Why should milk taste like a chocolate bar anyway?

8 "Cheerios make you feel groovy all day long." I eat them sometimes and I don't feel any different.

9 "Libby frozen dinners have fun in them." Nothing is said about the food in them.

10 "Cocoa Krispies taste like a chocolate milk shake only they are crunchy."

11 "Lucky Charms are magically delicious with sweet surprises inside." Those sweet surprises are marshmallow candy.

12 I think the commercials I just mentioned are examples of deceptive advertising practices.

13 Another type of commercial advertises a free bonus gift if you buy a certain product. The whole commercial tells about the bonus gift and says nothing about the product they want you to buy. Many times, as in the case of the record, the bonus gift appears to be worthless junk or isn't in the package. I wrote to the TV networks and found it costs about $4,000 for a 30-second commercial. Many of those ads

appeared four times in each hour. I wonder why any company would spend $15,000 or $20,000 an hour to advertise worthless junk.

The ads that I have mentioned I consider deceptive. However, I've found others I feel are dangerous.

Bugs Bunny vitamin ads say their vitamins "taste yummy" and taste good.

Chocolate Zestabs says their product is "delicious" and compare taking it with eating a chocolate cookie.

If my mother were to buy those vitamins, and my little sister got to the bottles, I'm sure she would eat them just as if they were candy.

I do not know a lot about nutrition, but I do know that my mother tries to keep our family from eating so many sweets. She says they are bad for our teeth. Our dentist says so too. If they are bad, why are companies allowed to make children want them by advertising on TV? Almost all of the ads I have seen during children's programs are for candy, or sugar-coated cereal, or even sugar-coated cereal with candy in it.

I know people who make these commercials are not bad. I know the commercials pay for TV shows and I like to watch TV. I just think that it would be as easy to produce a good commercial as a bad one. If there is nothing good that can be said about a product that is the truth, perhaps the product should not be sold to kids on TV in the first place.

I do not know all the ways to write a good commercial, but I think commercials would be good if they taught kids something that was true. They could teach about good health, and also about where food is grown. If my 3-year-old sister can learn to sing, "It takes two hands to handle a whopper 'cause the burgers are better at Burger King," from a commercial, couldn't a commercial also teach her to recognize the letters of the alphabet, numbers, and colors? I am sure that people who write commercials are much smarter than I and they should be able to think of many ways to write a commercial that tells the truth about a product without telling kids they should eat it because it is sweeter or "shaped like fun" (what shape *is* fun, anyway?) or because Tony Tiger says so.

I also think kids should not be bribed to buy a product by commercials telling of the wonderful free bonus gift inside.

I think kids should not be told to eat a certain product because a well-known hero does. If this is a reason to eat something, then, when a well-known person uses drugs, should kids try drugs for the same reason? 22

Last of all, I think vitamin companies should never, never be allowed to advertise their product as being delicious, yummy, or in any way make children think they are candy. Perhaps these commercials could teach children the dangers of taking drugs or teach children that, if they do find a bottle of pills, or if the medicine closet is open, they should run and tell a grown-up, and never, never eat the medicine. 23

I want to thank the Committee for letting me appear. When I leave Washington, the thing that I will remember for the rest of my life is that some people *do* care what kids think. I know I could have led a protest about commercials through our shopping center and people would have laughed at me or thought I needed a good spanking or wondered what kind of parents I had that would let me run around in the streets protesting. I decided to gather my information and write letters to anyone I thought would listen. Many of them didn't listen, but some did. That is why I am here today. Because some people cared about what I thought. I hope now that I can tell every kid in America that when they see a wrong, they shouldn't just try to forget about it and hope it will go away. They should begin to do what they can to change it. 24

People will listen. I know, because you're listening to me. 25

Questions for Study and Discussion

1. What disturbs Kurth about advertisements directed at children?
2. Why does the writer include the incident about her sister and the Post Raisin Bran record?
3. Which of the three patterns of organization does she use in presenting her examples of TV advertising? Support your answers with examples.
4. Where is the writer's argument summarized?

Vocabulary

Refer to your dictionary to define the following words as they are used in this selection. Then use each word in a sentence of your own.

deceptive (3)
bonus (13)
nutrition (18)
bribed (21)

Suggested Writing Assignment

Advertisers rely on a very calculated use of language to sell their products. Analyze the language in three or more advertisements for any one of the following products, and write an essay in which you discuss the nature of the appeals made to consumers. Before writing, consider the most effective way to organize your ideas.

deodorants	detergents
cigarettes	automobiles
aspirins	soft drinks

DUST

Gale Lawrence

Gale Lawrence was born in Springfield, Vermont. A free-lance writer, teacher, and naturalist, Lawrence writes a weekly column on nature and has published The Beginning Naturalist *(1979). As the following selection illustrates, she is fascinated by everyday subjects that people tend to take for granted. Intrigued by the dust in her own house, Lawrence stops to consider the various types of dust. As you read, pay attention to the way in which she has organized her discussion.*

Recently I was expecting a visit from friends who had never been to my house. In anticipation of their arrival I decided to clean at least the surfaces of all the rooms they'd see. As I moved from room to room surveying the job, I was amazed at the amount of dust everywhere I looked. Under beds and sofas I found huge dust balls. My rarely-used dining room table was covered with a fine gray film that I could write in. Some of my windowsills were coated with a darker, grittier substance. By the time I started upstairs I was noticing dust in the heating grates, dust on the moldings, and even dust clinging to old spider webs. 1

Instead of attacking the dust as I should have, I plopped down in my comfortable reading chair to think about it. Up flew more dust, which I could see as fine particles floating in the sunbeam that was shining in the window. Rationalizing that I was a naturalist, not a housecleaner, I decided to examine my house dust to see exactly what it was made of. If I knew what it was, maybe I could prevent it at its source rather than having to vacuum, sweep, and wipe it up so often. 2

But dust—even house dust—is not a simple substance. It varies from house to house, from neighborhood to neighbor- 3 hood, from lifestyle to lifestyle. Much of it enters from outdoors, and the dust that floats around in the atmosphere differs with the environment, the time of day, the season, the altitude, and other variables. Beyond household and local dusts are such fine and pervasive particles as volcanic and meteoric dusts, and, finally that dust which we will never have to vacuum out of our household corners—cosmic dust.

My own household dust reflects the way I live. Much of it is fine particles of dirt that are tracked indoors on my work shoes. Because I live on a dirt road, a lot of those fine particles don't even need my shoes to carry them indoors. In the summer, many of my windows are wide open, and every car that drives by creates a cloud of dust, some of which will settle at random throughout my house. In the winter my wood-burning furnace and fireplaces add fine bits of ash to my house dust. The clothes I wear add small fibers of wool and cotton, my cat adds her short hairs and her dander, and I was surprised to see how many of the dust balls I collected were held together by my own long hairs. Once I started paying attention to the composition of my household dust, I saw myself creating it in everything I did. Even my pencil sharpenings and eraser rubbings are components of my personal dust.

A country house located on a dirt road and heated with wood might seem dustier on a day to day basis than a city apartment, but there's a significant difference in both the content and overall quantity of rural and urban dust. Urban dust includes many more particles that are byproducts of industrial processes. More cars also contribute more byproducts of internal combustion. In some cities, the particulate counts—the number of particles floating in a measured volume of air—drop considerably on Sundays when factories are closed and the twice-a-day rush hours are not in operation. In studies conducted all over the world it was determined that cities had more condensation nuclei—small particles of matter that cause water vapor to condense into water drops—than country areas. The difference was as much as 147,000 nuclei per cubic centimeter in the city compared to 9,500 in the country. Over the open ocean and on the tops of high mountains, the count drops to about 950. It is estimated that 43,000,000 tons of dust fall on the U.S. in a year's time, greater proportions of it landing around industrialized and urban areas.

6 Some dusts are directly related to human activities, but some are independent of what we do. For instance, when a volcano erupts, fine volcanic dust drifts into the atmosphere where it sometimes stays for long periods before settling back to earth. Krakatoa, which erupted in 1883, dispersed about 4 cubic miles of dust into the atmosphere and much of it continued to float around for three years. Meteoric dust is even less observable than volcanic dust. When a volcano erupts we hear about it, and if we live close by we can see the dust on cars and buildings. But we have to be lucky to notice a shooting star, which tells us that a meteoric particle has just entered our atmosphere. What's left of the particle after much of its energy has been dissipated as heat will eventually settle to the earth's surface as dust, but chances are we'll never see those meteoric particles, or even if we do, we probably won't perceive them as anything different from the particles of dust that originated on earth.

7 Cosmic dust is almost an abstraction. It exists, but it can be measured only as it reflects light or alters the light of distant stars. No one has ever seen it, and what it is made of is still a matter of speculation. Some say it's made of metals, graphite, or silicates, while others argue that it's more like ice. All I know is that cosmic dust is one of the few dusts I don't have to apologize for when friends come knocking at my door.

Questions for Study and Discussion

1. What types of dust does Lawrence discuss in this essay?
2. What principle of organization does Lawrence use to give order to her discussion? Would any other principle of organization be appropriate? Why or why not?
3. The last sentence in paragraph 3 helps to organize the essay. How?

4. How is the concluding paragraph related to the beginning of the essay? (Glossary: *Beginnings/Endings*)

Vocabulary

Refer to your dictionary to define the following words as they are used in this selection. Then use each word in a sentence of your own.

anticipation (1)	dissipated (6)
rationalizing (2)	abstraction (7)
pervasive (3)	speculation (7)

Suggested Writing Assignment

Think of a commonplace subject that people might take for granted, but that you find interesting. Write an essay on that subject, using one of the following types of logical order:

least important to most important
most familiar to least familiar
smallest to biggest
oldest to newest
easiest to understand to most difficult to understand
good news to bad news
general to specific

Bunkerisms: The Language of Archie Bunker

Alfred Rosa and Paul Eschholz

Alfred Rosa and Paul Eschholz are both professors of English at the University of Vermont, where they teach courses in composition, the English language, and American literature. The authors have long been interested in language used in the media, particularly television. In this essay they analyze Archie Bunker's use of language in the series All in the Family. *As you read the essay, note the order in which the authors present the three types of language devices used in the show for humor and social commentary.*

On January 12, 1971, American television viewers were first introduced to "All in the Family." It was not long before the Bunker family became an American institution. This award-winning show reaches an estimated 50 million to 100 million viewers weekly. It has spawned a huge commercial enterprise offering such items as sweatshirts, T-shirts, posters, ashtrays, beer mugs, and "Bunker Stickers." Another item in this commercial bonanza is *The Wit & Wisdom of Archie Bunker*, a book containing the most humorous lines and sequences from the show. Indeed, the book demonstrates that the humor of the show derives not only from the fact that it is a situational comedy but also from Archie's use of language. Archie's command of the language is "legionary"; viewers have witnessed him criticizing Mike for reacting "on the sperm of the moment," castigating Edith for taking things "out of contest," and telling his family that his prejudice is a "pigment of their imaginations." Archie's use of malapropisms and barbarisms, and especially of his unique creation, "Bunkerisms," deserves to be examined. These expressions are a major element in distin- 1 guishing "All in the Family" from other television situational comedies.

The malapropism—the inappropriate use of a word in place of another that has some similarity to it—has a long tradition among writers of comedy. Malapropisms indicate not only the ignorance but also the vanity and affectation of the characters who speak them. Shakespeare's Dogberry, for instance, states his belief that "comparisons are odorous." The name comes from Richard Sheridan's infamous Mrs. Malaprop who was given to this type of inappropriate usage. One recalls that in *The Rivals* she implores Lydia to "promise to forget this fellow—to illiterate him quite from [her] memory." In "All in the Family," Archie uses many malapropisms:

> What is this, the United Nations? We gotta have a whole addenda?
> I come home and tell you one o' the great antidotes of all times . . . and you sit there like you're in a comma.
> You gotta grab the bull by the corns and heave-ho.
> We don't want people thinking we live in no pig's eye.
> He's comin' over to claim his pound of fish.
> Them eggs are starting to foment.
> And position is nine-tenths of the law, right?
> Call it a father's intermission . . . but I smell a rat.
> Cold enough to freeze a witch's mitt.
> It's some of that Morgan David wine.
> You been standing on that phone like a pillow of salt.
> Rudy and me was as close as two peas in a pot.
> Whoever sent 'em obviously wanted to remain unanimous.

Several of the mistakes that Archie makes such as confusing *antidote* and *anecdote* and *ferment* and *foment* excite nervous laughter because we have all fallen into the trap at one time or another. Archie's penchant for name dropping betrays his ignorance and his inner desire to be more than the average American breadwinner. Although he is very funny, much of his humor is the product of dramatic irony; his use of clichés, humorous because of their inaccuracies, displays his lack of true wit and imagination.

If Archie is a modern master of the malapropism, he is

also a prolific creator of barbarisms—made-up or malformed words produced by false analogy with other, legitimate words. Like malapropisms, barbarisms reflect ignorance and often pretentiousness on the part of the person who uses them. Here are some of Archie's:

> It's gonna take a lotta thinkin' and it's gonna take all my consecretion.
> That makes you an excessity after the fact!
> One of these days I will probably dehead myself.
> It's a regular facsamile of the Apollo 14.
> Like the Presidential, the Senatorial, the Governororial, the Mayorororial . . . .
> What do you mean by that insinuendo?
> Back to the groinocologist!
> She's hangin' around my neck like an Albacross!
> Make this meathead take the literaracy test.
> Now lay off the social menuneties.
> And then write yourself a little note—you know, like a reminderandum.
> You didn't go and do something unlegal, you big dumb Polack?
> You've got a warfed sense of humor.

5 The analogies by which Archie creates these barbarisms are of two kinds, conceptual and structural. In the conceptual analogy, Archie remembers *accessory* because it is "something extra," and so he creates *excessity*; *facsimile* because it is "the same as," and so he creates *facsamile*; and *memorandum* because it "reminds," and so he creates *reminderandum.* In the structural analogy, Archie incorporates erroneous prefixes, suffixes, or extra syllables that occur legitimately in other words because of the way those words happen to have developed historically. Thus he creates *dehead, Governororial,* and *unlegal.* This structural analogy process is commonly found among children who are trying to cope with the complexities of the English language. Archie's usages are funny because he is trying to apply logic where tradition holds sway.

6 As humorous as Archie's malapropisms and barbarisms are, the comedy of "All in the Family" relies heavily on a third type of expression—the Bunkerism. Although closely

akin to the malapropisms and barbarisms we have been examining, Bunkerisms are unique. More than just comical ignorance and pretentiousness is involved in the Bunkerism. The essence of the Bunkerism is that it both expresses and, because it is an absurd usage, simultaneously undermines one or another of Archie's many prejudices. Expressions such as "Englebum Hunkerdunk," "dem bamboons," "like the immaculate connection," "pushy imported ricans," "welfare incipients," and "a regular Marco Polish," are Bunkerisms. In *The Wit & Wisdom of Archie Bunker*, Archie's comic usages are referred to as "Archieisms." While this label recognizes the unique quality of Archie's speech, it does not effectively label his coinages. After all, Archie is the arch-conservative and arch-debunker, and all his remarks are in one way or another "suppository." In a conversation with Edith, Archie says:

> You think he's a nice boy after he did what he did? Comin' in here, makin' suppository remarks about our country. And calling me prejudiced, while I was singin' "God Bless America," a song written by a well-known and respected Jewish guy, Milton Berlin.

Although Archie is objecting to someone else's derogatory remarks, the comment in this context says more about Archie's own bigoted attitude.

Certain types of situations within the show give rise to the Bunkerism. When Archie is trapped by logic, usually by Mike, has an audience and wishes to appear a "know-it-all," is embarrassed by or impatient with Edith, is nervous when confronted by a member of a minority group, or is forced to talk about taboo subjects, he loses control of the language and produces Bunkerisms. As we have noted, these are akin to either malapropisms or barbarisms. Here are some Bunkerisms of which Mrs. Malaprop could be proud:

> It's a proven fact that Capital Punishment is a known detergent for crime.
>
> And who are you supposed to be—Blackberry Finn?
>
> And you don't need to draw me any diaphragms neither!
>
> They weren't fortunate enough to be born with the same natural endorsements.

We've got the world's grossest national product.
Don't take everything so liberally.
I call Chinese food chinks 'cause that's what it is . . . chinks. There was no slurp intended against the Chinese.
Smells like a house of ill refute if ya ask me.
Lady, you wanna stoop this conversation down to the gutter level, that's your derogative.

Bunkerisms that are akin to barbarisms—words made up or malformed by analogy with legitimate words—include the following: 8

He wouldn't be related to me for complexionary reasons.
If you two malinjerers want anything . . . .
Your mother ain't got no preconscrewed ideas.
You ain't gonna sell me none of your pregressive pinko welfare ideas . . . .
The man don't have one regleaming feature.
In my day we used to keep things in their proper suspective.
Don't you never read the papers about all them unflocked priests running around?

Laura Hobson, in an article for *The New York Times* entitled "As I Listened to Archie Say 'Hebe' . . . ," criticizes the show for its implicit claims of "complete and honest bigotry" and what to her appears to be a very subtle manipulation of language. She claims that the show's producers have managed to make a distinction between "acceptable" terms of ethnic abuse and those which would be truly offensive. This, she contends, falsely permits Archie to be a lovable bigot and bigotry itself to be not so bad after all. Although Hobson recognizes the subtlety of the ethnic terms used on the show, she fails to see the full import of the self-debunking Bunkerism. There is a general impression that Archie is only "done out" in the waning moments of the show; however, the unintentional self-deprecating nature of the Bunkerism serves to undermine Archie's bigotry throughout the whole show. The writers have successfully employed age-old comic devices—together with a new creation, the Bunkerism—to fulfill their satiric intentions. 9

Questions for Study and Discussion

1. Into what main categories are Archie's expressions grouped? Are any of these categories further divided? Give examples.
2. How have the authors arranged the categories of Archie's expressions?
3. What are *malapropisms, barbarisms,* and *Bunkerisms*? How do they differ?
4. The authors include four lists of words misused by Archie to illustrate certain comic devices. Reread the examples in each list and be prepared to discuss and correct each expression.

Vocabulary

Refer to your dictionary to define the following words as they are used in this selection. Then use each word in a sentence of your own.

institution (1)
prejudice (1)
vanity (2)
affectation (2)
prolific (4)
pretentiousness (4)
bigoted (6)
taboo (7)
implicit (8)

Suggested Writing Assignment

Write an essay on one of the following topics:

local restaurants
reading materials
television shows
ways of financing a college education
types of summer jobs

Be sure to use an organizational pattern that is well suited to both your material and your purpose.

4

PARAGRAPHS

Within an essay, the paragraph is the most important unit of thought. Like the essay, it has its own main idea, often stated directly in a topic sentence. Like a good essay, a good paragraph is unified: It avoids digressions and develops its main idea. Paragraphs use many of the rhetorical techniques that essays use, techniques such as classification, comparison and contrast, and cause and effect. In fact, many writers find it helpful to think of the paragraph as a very small, compact essay.

Here is a paragraph from an essay on testing:

> Multiple-choice questions distort the purposes of education. Picking one answer among four is very different from thinking a question through to an answer of one's own, and far less useful in life. Recognition of vocabulary and isolated facts makes the best kind of multiple-choice questions, so these dominate the tests, rather than questions that test the use of knowledge. Because schools want their children to perform well, they are often tempted to teach the limited sorts of knowledge most useful on the tests.

This paragraph, like all well-written paragraphs, has several distinguishing characteristics: It is unified, coherent, and adequately developed. It is unified in that every sentence and every idea relate to the main idea, stated in the topic sentence, "Multiple-choice questions distort the purposes of education." It is coherent in that the sentences and ideas are arranged logically and the relationships among them are made clear by the use of effective transitions. Finally, the paragraph is adequately developed in that it presents a short but persuasive argument supporting its main idea.

How much development is "adequate" development? The answer depends on many things: how complicated or controversial the main idea is; what readers already know and believe; how much space the writer is permitted. Everyone, or nearly everyone, agrees that the earth circles around the sun; a single sentence would be enough to make that point. A writer trying to prove that the earth does *not* circle the sun, however, would need many sentences, indeed many paragraphs, to develop that idea convincingly.

Here is another model of an effective paragraph. As you read this paragraph about the resourcefulness of pigeons in evading attempts to control them, pay particular attention to its controlling idea, unity, development, and coherence.

> Pigeons [and their human friends] have proved remarkably resourceful in evading nearly all the controls, from birth-control pellets to carbide shells to pigeon apartment complexes, that pigeon-haters have devised. One of New York's leading museums once put large black rubber owls on its wide ledges to discourage the large number of pigeons that roosted there. Within the day the pigeons had gotten over their fear of owls and were back perched on the owls' heads. A few years ago San Francisco put a sticky coating on the ledges of some public buildings, but the pigeons got used to the goop and came back to roost. The city then tried trapping, using electric owls, and periodically exploding carbide shells outside a city building, hoping the noise would scare the pigeons away. It did, but not for long, and the program was abandoned. More frequent explosions probably would have distressed the humans in the area more than the birds. Philadelphia tried a feed that makes pigeons vomit, and then, they hoped, go away. A New York firm claimed it had a feed that made a pigeon's nervous system send "danger signals" to the other members of its flock.

The controlling idea is stated at the beginning in a topic sentence. Other sentences in the paragraph support the controlling idea with examples. Since all the separate examples illustrate how pigeons have evaded attempts to control them, the paragraph is unified. Since there are enough examples to convince the reader of the truth of the topic statement, the paragraph is adequately developed. Finally, the regular use of transitional words and phrases such as *once, within the day, a few years ago,* and *then,* lends the paragraph coherence.

How long should a paragraph be? In modern essays most paragraphs range from 50 to 250 words, but some run a full page or more and others may be only a few words long. The best answer is that a paragraph should be long enough to develop its main idea adequately. Some authors, when they find a paragraph running very long, may break it into two or more paragraphs so that readers can pause and catch their breath. Other writers forge ahead, relying on the unity and coherence of their paragraph to keep their readers from getting lost.

Articles and essays that appear in magazines and newspapers often have relatively short paragraphs, some of only one or two sentences. This is because they are printed in very narrow columns, which make paragraphs of average length appear very long. But often you will find that these journalistic "paragraphs" could be joined together into a few, longer, more normal paragraphs. Longer, more normal paragraphs are the kind you should use in all but journalistic writing.

Claude Fetridge's Infuriating Law

H. Allen Smith

H. Allen Smith (1907–1976) wrote many humorous books, among them Low Man on the Totem Pole *(1941),* Life in a Putty Knife Factory *(1943), and* Larks in the Popcorn *(1948). As can be seen in the following selection, Smith perceived the humor in everyday life and captured this humor in his writing. Notice the way in which Smith's topic sentences serve to control and focus the material in each of the essay's five paragraphs.*

Fetridge's Law, in simple language, states that important things that are supposed to happen do not happen, especially when people are looking; or, conversely, things that are supposed not to happen do happen, especially when people are looking. Thus a dog that will jump through a hoop a thousand times a day for his owner will not jump through a hoop when a neighbor is called in to watch; and a baby that will say "Dada" in the presence of its proud parents will, when friends are summoned, either clam up or screech like a jaybird.

Fetridge's Law takes its name from a onetime radio engineer named Claude Fetridge. Back in 1936, Mr. Fetridge thought up the idea of broadcasting the flight of the famous swallows from San Juan de Capistrano mission in Southern California. As is well known, the swallows depart from the mission each year on St. John's Day, October 23, and return on March 19, St. Joseph's Day. Claude Fetridge conceived the idea of broadcasting the flutter of wings of the departing swallows on October 23. His company went to considerable expense to set up its equipment at the mission; then, with the whole nation waiting anxiously for the soul-stirring event, it was discovered that this year the swallows, out of sheer orneriness, had departed a day ahead of schedule. Thus did a flock of birds lend immortality to Claude Fetridge.

3 Television sets, of course, are often subject to the workings of Fetridge's Law. If a friend tells me he is going to appear on a television show and asks me to watch it, I groan inwardly, knowing this is going to cost me money. The moment his show comes on the air, my screen will snow up or acquire the look of an old-school-tie pattern. I turn it off and call the repairman. He travels three miles to my house and turns the set on. The picture emerges bright and clear, the contrast exactly right, a better picture than I've ever had before. It's that way always and forever, days without end.

4 An attractive woman neighbor of mine drives her husband to the railroad station every morning. On rare occasions she has been late getting her backfield in motion, and hasn't had time to get dressed. These times she has thrown a coat over her nightgown and, wearing bedroom slippers, headed for the depot. Fetridge's Law always seems to give her trouble. Once she clashed fenders with another car on the highway and had to go to the police station in her night shift. Twice she has had motor trouble in the depot plaza, requiring that she get out of her car in robe and slippers and pincurlers. The last I heard, she was considering sleeping in her street clothes.

5 Fetridge's Law operates fiercely in the realm of dentistry. In my own case, I have often noted that whenever I develop a raging toothache it is a Sunday and the dentists are all on the golf course. Not long ago, my toothache hung on through the weekend, and Monday morning it was still throbbing and pulsating like a diesel locomotive. I called my dentist, proclaimed an emergency, and drove to his office. As I was going up the stairway, the ache suddenly vanished. By the time I got into his chair, I was confused and embarrassed and unable to tell him with certainty which tooth it was that had been killing me. The X ray showed no shady spots, though it would have several if he had pointed the thing at my brain. Claude Fetridge's law clearly has its good points; it can exasperate, but it can also cure toothaches.

Questions for Study and Discussion

1. How does Fetridge's Law work?
2. Identify the topic sentences in paragraphs 1, 3, and 5 of the essay. (Glossary: *Topic Sentence*)
3. How, specifically, do the other sentences in each paragraph support and/or develop the topic sentence?
4. Explain how Smith achieves coherence in paragraph 2. (Glossary: *Coherence*)
5. Briefly describe the organization of the essay. Would the essay be as effective if the paragraphs were arranged in a different order? Explain. (Glossary: *Organization*)
6. Do you think that the last sentence is an effective ending for the essay? Why or why not? (Glossary: *Beginnings/Endings*)

Vocabulary

Refer to your dictionary to define the following words as they are used in this selection. Then use each word in a sentence of your own.

conversely (1)
orneriness (2)
pulsating (5)
exasperate (5)

Suggested Writing Assignment

Using several examples from your own experience, write a short essay illustrating the validity of Fetridge's Law. Make sure that each of your paragraphs has a clearly identifiable topic sentence.

Americans and Physical Fitness

James F. Fixx

James F. Fixx is one of the country's best-known authorities on running. The Complete Book of Running *(1977) is an international bestseller and is in part responsible for popularizing running as a healthy everyday activity. In the following essay, taken from* The Complete Book of Running, *Fixx offers a series of well-developed paragraphs to support his thesis that "Most Americans are in terrible shape."*

Most Americans are in terrible shape. We smoke and drink too much, weigh too much, exercise too little and eat too many of the wrong things. A California pathologist, Thomas J. Bassler, says on the basis of autopsies he has performed that two out of every three deaths are premature; they are related to what he calls loafer's heart, smoker's lung and drinker's liver. Thomas K. Cureton, a professor at the University of Illinois Physical Fitness Laboratory, has said, "The average American young man has a middle-aged body. He can't run the length of a city block, he can't climb a flight of stairs without getting breathless. In his twenties, he has the capacity that a man is expected to have in his forties." 1

What about people who aren't so young? Cureton goes on: "The average middle-aged man in this country is close to death. He is only one emotional shock or one sudden exertion away from a serious heart attack." If that strikes you as overdramatic, for the next few days notice the ages in the obituary columns. 2

But isn't there a contradiction here? Participation in sports has been increasing since World War II: from 1946 to 1963 the numbers of participants doubled, and a glance at any tennis court or golf course is enough to suggest that the 3 rate of growth since then has accelerated. Unfortunately, only a fraction of the population does most of the participating. The rest of us are spectators. Certainly more than half of all Americans do not exercise enough to do themselves any good, and fifty million adult Americans never exercise at all.

The experience of Neil Carver, a Philadelphia criminal lawyer, is typical. Carver is tall, rangy and sturdily built, but at thirty-three he was out of shape. "I was carrying my two kids upstairs one night to put them to bed," he told me. "I got so winded I could hardly breathe. I said to myself, I've got to do something about this." Carver started running. Today, seven or eight years later, he has not only competed in an eight-mile race but spends part of every summer climbing with his wife and children in New Hampshire's rugged Presidential Range.

Even American kids are out of shape. In one Massachusetts school only eight fifth-graders out of a class of fifty-two were fit enough to earn presidential physical fitness awards. In a class in Connecticut, only two students out of forty qualified. Not long ago a study at Massachusetts General Hospital showed that 15 percent of 1,900 seventh-graders had high cholesterol levels and 8 percent had high blood pressure. (Both conditions are associated with an increased likelihood of heart attacks and strokes.) Nor, despite our growing interest in sports, is our children's physical fitness getting any better. When 12,000,000 youngsters ten to seventeen years old were tested by the University of Michigan for the U.S. Office of Education, strength, agility and speed showed no improvement over a ten-year period. (The one exception: Girls had slightly more endurance.)

The very people we might reasonably look to for guidance—physicians—are in no better shape than the rest of us. In Southern California not long ago, fifty-eight doctors were given physical exams. Most were found to be in poor physical condition. One out of five smoked; two out of three were overweight; one in four had high blood pressure; one in five had an abnormal electrocardiogram while exercising; more than half had high serum lipid levels. Their condition may reflect the attitude of a young physician friend of mine who smokes heavily. "I don't worry about lung cancer," he told me. "By the time I get it they'll have a cure for it."

The fact that our doctors often don't offer the rest of us a very inspiring example may be because, as John F. Moe, a thoughtful Indianapolis physician, put it, "The problem of physician ignorance and physician apathy are closely tied together. To compound the situation, there has been a great lack of impetus from the medical schools. When I was in school ten years ago, very little (if any) time was devoted to the serious study of physical fitness in the sense that you and I know it. I strongly suspect that the situation has not changed much. 7

"The underexercised, coronary-prone physician sees himself as the authority on health matters. He tends to reflect to others his own life style and thinks he is giving good, sound advice. Because he views himself as an authority figure, he finds it difficult to accept ideas foreign to his own concepts, especially when they differ radically from what he believes to be sound, conservative practice." 8

Can the federal government help make us fit? It's not likely, despite the example of several European countries. Although the government undeniably takes an interest in our health—to the tune of about a billion and a quarter dollars a year—it doesn't in truth do much good. "Health problems today are an instructive paradigm of the limits of government . . . ," George F. Will wrote in *Newsweek*. "It is to be prayerfully hoped, but not reasonably expected, that some political leader will find the gumption to blurt out the melancholy truth: each additional dollar spent on medical care is producing a declining marginal benefit." 9

If neither our doctors nor the government can be expected to bring us good health, to whom can we look? The answer is plain: to ourselves. 10

Questions for Study and Discussion

1. According to Fixx, in what ways are most Americans out of shape?
2. Identify the topic sentences in paragraphs 1, 5, and 6. (Glossary: *Topic Sentence*) How does Fixx develop these topic sentences?

3. How does Fixx achieve coherence in paragraph 6? (Glossary: *Coherence*)
4. Paragraphs 2, 3, 9, and 10 begin with rhetorical questions. How does Fixx use these questions to emphasize his points? (Glossary: *Coherence*)
5. In the context of the whole essay, what is the function of paragraph 4?

Vocabulary

Refer to your dictionary to define the following words as they are used in this selection. Then use each word in a sentence of your own.

obituary (2)	impetus (7)
agility (5)	paradigm (9)
apathy (7)	gumption (9)

Suggested Writing Assignment

Select one of the following statements as the thesis for a short essay. Make sure that each paragraph of your essay is unified, coherent, and adequately developed.

Car pooling is beneficial but makes demands of people.
Social activities for freshmen are limited.
A college is a community, just like a city or a town.
College is expensive.

What Makes a Leader?

Michael Korda

Michael Korda is the author of such bestsellers as Male Chauvinism *(1979),* Power *(1975), and* Charmed Lives *(1979). In this essay, which first appeared in* Newsweek, *Korda discusses the qualities that all good leaders have in common. Notice how Korda uses the topic sentence in each paragraph to focus our attention on these qualities.*

Not every President is a leader, but every time we elect a President we hope for one, especially in times of doubt and crisis. In easy times we are ambivalent—the leader, after all, makes demands, challenges the status quo, shakes things up. 1

Leadership is as much a question of timing as anything else. The leader must appear on the scene at a moment when people are looking for leadership, as Churchill did in 1940, as Roosevelt did in 1933, as Lenin did in 1917. And when he comes, he must offer a simple, eloquent message. 2

Great leaders are almost always great simplifiers, who cut through argument, debate and doubt to offer a solution everybody can understand and remember. Churchill warned the British to expect "blood, toil, tears and sweat"; FDR told Americans that "the only thing we have to fear is fear itself"; Lenin promised the war-weary Russians peace, land and bread. Straightforward but potent messages. 3

We have an image of what a leader ought to be. We even recognize the physical signs: leaders may not necessarily be tall, but they must have bigger-than-life, commanding features—LBJ's nose and ear lobes, Ike's broad grin. A trademark also comes in handy: Lincoln's stovepipe hat, JFK's rocker. We expect our leaders to stand out a little, not to be like ordinary men. Half of President Ford's trouble lay in the fact that, if you closed your eyes for a moment, you couldn't 4 remember his face, figure or clothes. A leader should have an unforgettable identity, instantly and permanently fixed in people's minds.

It also helps for a leader to be able to do something most of us can't: FDR overcame polio; Mao swam the Yangtze River at the age of 72. We don't want our leaders to be "just like us." We want them to be like us but better, special, more so. Yet if they are *too* different, we reject them. Adlai Stevenson was too cerebral. Nelson Rockefeller, too rich.

Even television, which comes in for a lot of knocks as an image-builder that magnifies form over substance, doesn't altogether obscure the qualities of leadership we recognize, or their absence. Television exposed Nixon's insecurity, Humphrey's fatal infatuation with his own voice.

A leader must know how to use power (that's what leadership is about), but he also has to have a way of showing that he does. He has to be able to project firmness—no physical clumsiness (like Ford), no rapid eye movements (like Carter).

A Chinese philosopher once remarked that a leader must have the grace of a good dancer, and there is a great deal of wisdom to this. A leader should know how to appear relaxed and confident. His walk should be firm and purposeful. He should be able, like Lincoln, FDR, Truman, Ike and JFK, to give a good, hearty, belly laugh, instead of the sickly grin that passes for good humor in Nixon or Carter. Ronald Reagan's training as an actor showed to good effect in the debate with Carter, when by his easy manner and apparent affability, he managed to convey the impression that in fact he was the President and Carter the challenger.

If we know what we're looking for, why is it so difficult to find? The answer lies in a very simple truth about leadership. *People can only be led where they want to go.* The leader follows, though a step ahead. Americans *wanted* to climb out of the Depression and needed someone to tell them they could do it, and FDR did. The British believed that they could still win the war after the defeats of 1940, and Churchill told them they were right.

A leader rides the waves, moves with the tides, understands the deepest yearnings of his people. He cannot make a nation that wants peace at any price go to war, or stop a nation determined to fight from doing so. His purpose must match the national mood. His task is to focus the people's energies and desires, to define them in simple terms, to inspire, the make what people already want seem attainable, important, within their grasp.

Above all, he must dignify our desires, convince us that we are taking part in the making of great history, give us a sense of glory about ourselves. Winston Churchill managed, by sheer rhetoric, to turn the British defeat and the evacuation of Dunkirk in 1940 into a major victory. FDR's words turned the sinking of the American fleet at Pearl Harbor into a national rallying cry instead of a humiliating national scandal. A leader must stir our blood, not appeal to our reason. . . . 11

A great leader must have a certain irrational quality, a stubborn refusal to face facts, infectious optimism, the ability to convince us that all is not lost even when we're afraid it is. Confucius suggested that, while the advisers of a great leader should be as cold as ice, the leader himself should have fire, a spark of divine madness. 12

He won't come until we're ready for him, for the leader is like a mirror, reflecting back to us our own sense of purpose, putting into words our own dreams and hopes, transforming our needs and fears into coherent policies and programs. 13

Our strength makes him strong; our determination makes him determined; our courage makes him a hero; he is, in the final analysis, the symbol of the best in us, shaped by our own spirit and will. And when these qualities are lacking in us, we can't produce him; and even with all our skill at image-building, we can't fake him. He is, after all, merely the sum of us. 14

Questions for Study and Discussion

1. What is Korda's main idea, or thesis, in this essay and where is it stated? Why do you suppose he states his thesis where he does instead of elsewhere in the essay? (Glossary: *Thesis*)
2. Identify the topic sentence in paragraph 4. What

would be gained or lost if the topic sentence were placed elsewhere in the paragraph?

3. Korda's knowledge of history and great leaders is reflected in the examples he uses to support his topic sentences. Using paragraphs 2, 4, 8, and 11 explain how Korda's examples develop his topic sentences. (Glossary: *Example*)
4. What would be gained or lost if paragraphs 13 and 14 were combined?
5. At the beginning of paragraph 9 Korda asks a rhetorical question, one that requires no answer and that is often used for emphasis. What is the purpose of this question in the context of his essay?

Vocabulary

Refer to your dictionary to define the following words as they are used in this selection. Then use each word in a sentence of your own.

ambivalent (1)	cerebral (5)
status quo (1)	affability (8)
eloquent (2)	infectious (12)

Suggested Writing Assignment

Select one of the following topics for a short essay:

What makes a good teacher?
What makes a good student?
What makes a good team captain?
What makes a good parent?

Make sure that your topic sentences are clear and effectively placed.

5

TRANSITIONS

Transitions are words and phrases that are used to signal the relationships between ideas in an essay and to join the various parts of an essay together. Writers use transitions to relate ideas within sentences, between sentences, and between paragraphs. Perhaps the most common type of transition is the so-called transitional expression. Following is a list of transitional expressions categorized according to their functions.

ADDITION: and, again, too, also, in addition, further, furthermore, moreover, besides

CAUSE AND EFFECT: therefore, consequently, thus, accordingly, as a result, hence, then, so

COMPARISON: similarly, likewise, by comparison

CONCESSION: to be sure, granted, of course, it is true, to tell the truth, certainly, with the exception of, although this may be true, even though, naturally

CONTRAST: but, however, in contrast, on the contrary, on the other hand, yet, nevertheless, after all, in spite of

EXAMPLE: for example, for instance

PLACE: elsewhere, here, above, below, farther on, there, beyond, nearby, opposite to, around

RESTATEMENT: that is, as I have said, in other words, in simpler terms, to put it differently, simply stated

SEQUENCE: first, second, third, next, finally

SUMMARY: in conclusion, to conclude, to summarize, in brief, in short

TIME: afterward, later, earlier, subsequently, at the same time, simultaneously, immediately, this time, until now, before, meanwhile, shortly, soon, currently, when, lately, in the meantime, formerly

Besides transitional expressions, there are two other important ways to make transitions: by using pronoun reference, and by repeating key words and phrases. This paragraph begins with the phrase "Besides transitional expressions": the phrase contains the transitional word *besides* and also repeats an earlier idea. Thus the reader knows that this discussion is moving toward a new but related idea. Repetition can also give a word or idea emphasis: "Foreigners look to America as a land of freedom. Freedom, however, is not something all Americans enjoy."

Pronoun reference avoids monotonous repetition of nouns and phrases. Without pronouns, these two sentences are wordy and tiring to read: "Jim went to the concert, where he heard some of Beethoven's music. Afterwards, Jim bought a recording of some of Beethoven's music." A more graceful and readable passage results if two pronouns are substituted in the second sentence: "Afterwards, he bought a recording of it." The second version has another advantage in that it is now more tightly related to the first sentence. The transition between the two sentences is smoother.

In the following example, notice how Rachel Carson uses transitional expressions, repetition of words and ideas, and pronoun reference:

> Under primitive agricultural conditions the farmer had few insect problems. *These* arose with the intensification of agriculture—the devotion of immense acreages to a single crop. *Such a system* set the stage for explosive increases in specific insect populations. Single-crop farming does not take advantage of the principles by which nature works; *it* is agriculture as an engineer might conceive it to be. Nature has introduced great variety into the landscape, but man has displayed a passion for

pronoun reference

repeated key idea

pronoun reference

pronoun reference | *repeated key word*

simplifying *it*. *Thus he* undoes the built-in checks and balances by which nature holds the species within bounds. One important natural *check* is a limit on the amount of suitable habitat for each species. *Obviously then*, an insect that lives on wheat can build up its population to much higher levels on a farm devoted to wheat than on one in which wheat is intermingled with other crops to which the insect is not adapted.

transitional expression; pronoun reference | *transitional expression*

repeated key idea

The same thing happens in other situations. A generation or more ago, the towns of large areas of the United States lined their streets with the noble elm tree. *Now* the beauty *they* hopefully created is threatened with complete destruction as disease sweeps through the elms, carried by a beetle that would have only limited chance to build up large populations and to spread from tree to tree if the elms were only occasional trees in a richly diversified planting.

transitional expression; pronoun reference

Carson's transitions in this passage enhance its *coherence*—that quality of good writing that results when all sentences, paragraphs, and longer divisions of an essay are effectively and naturally connected.

WALKING

Aaron Sussman and Ruth Goode

Aaron Sussman began his career as a reporter for the Brooklyn Eagle *and the New York* Daily News. *A frequent contributor to popular magazines, he has also written* The Amateur Photographer's Handbook *(1941), a classic in its field. Ruth Goode is a senior staff writer for* MD, *a leading medical magazine, and has written many books on medicine and psychiatry. Sussman and Goode, enthusiastic walkers themselves, collaborated on* The Magic of Walking *(1967), from which this selection was taken. Notice how the authors use transitions to connect sentences within paragraphs as well as to link paragraphs to each other.*

Walking gives us back our senses. We see, hear, smell the world as we never can when we ride. No matter what the vehicle, it is the vehicle that is moving, not ourselves. We are trapped inside its fixed environment, and once we have taken in its sensory aspects—mainly in terms of comfort or discomfort—we turn off our perceptions and either go to sleep or open a magazine and begin dozing awake.

But when we walk, the environment changes every moment and our senses are continuously being alerted. Around each corner of a city block, around each bend in a country road, there is something new to greet the eyes, the ears, the nose. Even the same walk, the one we may take every day, is never the same from one day to another, from one week and season to another.

This is true not only in the country, but anywhere at all. In New York City, a group of executives meets every weekday morning to walk from their homes in Brooklyn Heights to their offices in downtown Manhattan. Their way takes them through quiet streets of old brownstones, one of the oldest neighborhoods in the city, then up and over the Brooklyn Bridge with its cathedral arches supporting the weblike drapery of cables, then down into the tight skyscraper canyons of the financial district.

4 On their daily route they see, hear, smell the city in all its seasonal changes, under bright and cloudy skies. Only the most inclement weather stops them—suitably dressed, they can walk with pleasure in spring rains, autumn drizzles, the sunlight of a summer morning or a soft winter snowfall. The river waters roll by below their feet, sullen or sparkling. Tugboats chug past, shoving and hauling their variously laden barges; on a shrouded morning, foghorns hoot and moan. The famous skyline of lower Manhattan rises before them, glittering in sun, afloat in mist, against a backdrop of sky never twice the same.

Questions for Study and Discussion

1. Why do Sussman and Goode feel that every walk is a new experience?
2. Identify the transitions that the authors use in paragraphs 1 and 2 to give those paragraphs coherence.
3. What transitions link the paragraphs of the essay? Discuss one of the transitions between paragraphs, telling how you think it functions.

Vocabulary

Refer to your dictionary to define the following words as they are used in this selection. Then use each word in a sentence of your own.

sensory (1)
perceptions (1)
inclement (4)
sullen (4)
shrouded (4)

Suggested Writing Assignment

In *The New York Times Complete Manual of Home Repair*, Bernard Gladstone gives directions for applying blacktop sealer to a driveway. His directions appear below in scrambled order. First, carefully read all of Gladstone's sentences. Next, arrange the sentences in what seems to you the correct sequence, paying attention to transitional devices. Be prepared to explain the reasons for your particular arrangement of the sentences.

1. A long-handled pushbroom or roofing brush is used to spread the coating evenly over the entire area.
2. Care should be taken to make certain the entire surface is uniformly wet, though puddles should be swept away if water collects in low spots.
3. Greasy areas and oil slicks should be scraped up, then scrubbed thoroughly with a detergent solution.
4. With most brands there are just three steps to follow.
5. In most cases one coat of sealer will be sufficient.
6. The application of blacktop sealer is best done on a day when the weather is dry and warm, preferably while the sun is shining on the surface.
7. This should not be applied until the first coat is completely dry.
8. First sweep the surface absolutely clean to remove all dust, dirt and foreign material.
9. To simplify spreading and to assure a good bond, the surface of the driveway should be wet down thoroughly by sprinkling with a hose.
10. However, for surfaces in poor condition a second coat may be required.
11. The blacktop sealer is next stirred thoroughly and poured on while the surface is still damp.
12. The sealer should be allowed to dry overnight (or longer if recommended by the manufacturer) before normal traffic is resumed.

More Than Meets the Eye

Leo Rosten

Leo Rosten was educated at the University of Chicago and at the London School of Economics and Political Science. As a university lecturer, he has had many academic affiliations. Among his writings are The Education of H*Y*M*A*N K*A*P*L*A*N *(1937) and* The Joys of Yiddish *(1968). In "More Than Meets the Eye," taken from his book* The Story Behind the Painting *(1961), Rosten considers the view that there is no absolute reality. Notice how Rosten uses transitions to signal logical relationships among the ideas he discusses.*

The process we call seeing, which we all take for granted, is unbelievably complicated. We see not "what is there" but what we have been taught to see there—not what is "real" but what we have been conditioned to think of as real. The human eye is a lens that only *receives* images; these images are referred to the brain, where they must be patterned and given meaning. And meaning is a convention that stems from our education and our expectations. What we call "reality" is not much more than those perceptions that pass through the filters at our conditioning. We see things as *we* are, not as *they* are. 1

Does this idea seem preposterous? The brilliant art authority E.H. Gombrich reminds us that ancient artists used to draw eyelashes on the lower lids of horses. There are not lashes on the lower eyelids of the horses. Still, the artists "saw" them there—because they were accustomed to seeing lashes on men's lower lids. 2

But perhaps you believe in a realness, an absoluteness of things visible to anyone and everyone alike. Perhaps you are 3 thinking, "But reality is simple enough. Just press the trigger of a camera—and that will record exactly 'what is there'!"

To test that, suppose you take a camera and set out to photograph a house. Consider the decisions you will make—consciously or unconsciously. From what distance shall the house be photographed? Then, at what angle? How high? How low? All these depend on what kind of picture you want. If the house is seen from a low angle, that will emphasize its height. If seen from a hill looking down, it will look different.

"Just straight on," you say? Very well. Is the sycamore to the left to be included? The azalea on the right? The ridge beyond? Will you include the rail fence there, the rock here, and the curving path? Each position, each view, gives a different impression or atmosphere.

And all this is but the beginning. What kind of film will you use? Different films give different effects. Consider the light. Shall it come from the left, the right, overhead, from behind? How much light do you want? You can choose the time of day in which to shoot; you can use reflectors to diminish shadows, or floodlights to highlight a feature. You can manipulate light by varying the opening of your lens. You can also . . . but perhaps this is enough. The fact is that no two photographers take precisely the same picture of an identical subject—even if they try to—because there are different emotions and mentalities behind the lenses.

If what we have said here is true of photography, consider how much more powerfully it applies to painting. It is the great, revolutionary role of the artist to liberate us from the bonds of the familiar. An artist can draw what no camera can photograph—the images in a human's mind. No camera contains the flexibility, the resourcefulness, of the human hand, to say nothing of the immense imaginative possibilities of the human brain.

The artist gives us new eyes, eyes with which we can see aspects of reality we did not dream were there. They *were* not, in fact, there—until the artist created them out of his vision, his active transformation of reality. A Japanese master was once asked, "What is the most difficult part of a picture?" He answered, "The part that is to be left out."

Questions for Study and Discussion

1. State in your own words Rosten's main idea, or thesis, in this essay. (Glossary: *Thesis*)
2. Identify the transitions that Rosten uses to give coherence to paragraph 1. (Glossary: *Coherence*)
3. How does Rosten make the transition from paragraph 1 to paragraph 2? From 2 to 3?
4. How do the first sentences of paragraphs 4–7 give coherence to those paragraphs as a unit?
5. Rosten's tone in this essay is informal; he seems to be talking directly to the reader. How has he created this informality? (Glossary: *Tone*)

Vocabulary

Refer to your dictionary to define the following words as they are used in this selection. Then use each word in a sentence of your own.

preposterous (2)
manipulate (6)

Suggested Writing Assignment

Using examples from your own experience, support or dispute Rosten's argument in "More Than Meets the Eye." Remember to use transitions wherever necessary to connect your ideas logically and lend coherence to your essay.

AUTO SUGGESTION

Russell Baker

After graduating from Johns Hopkins University in 1947, Russell Baker joined the staff of the Baltimore Sun *and later worked in the Washington bureau of* The New York Times. *Since 1962 he has written a syndicated column for the* Times *for which he was awarded a Pulitzer Prize in 1979. "Auto Suggestion," first published in the* Times *on April 1, 1979, presents Baker's techniques for not buying a car. As you read, notice how the author's transitions give coherence to the essay.*

Many persons have written asking the secret of my technique for not buying a new car. Aware that it could destroy the American economy and reduce the sheiks of OPEC to prowling the streets with pleas for baksheesh, I divulge it here with the greatest reluctance.

In extenuation, let me explain that my power to resist buying a new car does not derive from a resentment of new cars. In fact, I bought a new car 10 years ago and would buy another at any moment if the right new car came along.

When seized by new-car passion, however, I do not deal with it as most people do. To conquer the lust and escape without a new car, you must have a program. The first step is to face the philosophical question: Is a new car really going to give you less trouble than your old car?

In most cases the notion that a new car will free its owner of auto headache will not hold water. Common experience shows that all cars, old or new, are trouble. The belief that a change of vintage will relieve the headache is a mental exercise in willful self-deception.

A new car simply presents a new set of troubles, which may be more disturbing than the beloved, familiar old troubles the old car presented. With your old car, strange troubles do not take you by surprise, but a new car's troubles are invariably terrifying for being strange and unexpected.

6 Before entering the new-car bazaar, I always remind myself that I am about to acquire an entirely new set of troubles and that it is going to take me months, maybe years, to learn to live happily with them.

7 Step Two is to place a sensible limit on the amount you will pay for a new car. As a guide to value, I use the price my parents paid for the house in which I grew up. To own a car that costs more than a house is vulgar and reflects an alarming disproportion in one's sense of values. Wheels may be splendid but they should not be valued more highly than four bedrooms, dining room, bath and cellar.

8 The price of my parents' house, purchased in 1940, was $5,900. This becomes my limit, effectively ruling out the kind of new car you have to drive to get to a business appointment in Los Angeles, as well as most other new cars on the market today.

9 After setting a price limit, the next step is to study the car's capacity to perform its duties. For this purpose I always go to the car dealer's place with two large children, a wife, a grandmother, two cats, six suitcases, an ice chest and a large club suitable for subduing quarrelsome children on the turnpike.

10 Loading all the paraphernalia and people into the car under study, I then ask myself whether I could drive 400 miles in this environment without suffering mental breakdown.

11 Since most cars within the $5,900 price limit nowadays are scarcely commodious enough to transport two persons and a strand of spaghetti, I am now approaching very close to the goal I despise, which is to avoid buying a new car.

12 Suppose, however, that you pack everything inside—children, wife, cats, club and grandmother—and it seems just barely possible that you might cover 400 miles despite the knees from the back seat grinding into your kidneys. Now is the time to take out your checkoff list.

13 Can you slide in behind the wheel without denting the skull against the door frame? Will you be able to do it at

night when you have had a drink and aren't thinking about it?

If the car passes this test, which is unlikely unless you're getting an incredible deal on a pickup truck—and cats and grandmothers, remember, don't much like riding in the open beds of pickup trucks, especially when it rains—if the car passes this test, you must give it the cascading rainwater test.

For this purpose I take a garden hose to the car lot, spray the top of the car heavily and then, upon opening the door try to slide in without being drenched in a cascade of water pouring into the driver's seat. If the car soaks you with hose water, imagine what it will do with a heavy dose of rain.

If the car passes this examination, the final test is to slip a fingernail under the plastic sheathing on the dashboard and see if the entire piece peels away easily. If it does not, I buy the new car immediately. The last time I had to do so was in 1969.

Questions for Study and Discussion

1. What are the steps in Baker's program for not buying a car? Give examples of transitions he uses to move from one step to the next.
2. In explaining how not to buy a new car, Baker pokes fun at the economy and at the auto industry. What aspects of each does he criticize?
3. What transitional device does Baker use to link paragraphs 7, 8, and 9?
4. Baker's essay provides an interesting combination of diction. It is colloquial as well as sophisticated and urbane. Cite several examples of each type of diction. (Glossary: *Diction*)

Vocabulary

Refer to your dictionary to define the following words as they are used in this selection. Then use each word in a sentence of your own.

divulge (1)
extenuation (2)
lust (3)
vintage (4)
vulgar (7)
paraphernalia (10)
commodious (11)
cascading (14)

Suggested Writing Assignment

Write a short essay in which you describe the steps a person ought to take when making a major decision, such as determining where to go to school. Be sure to use transitions wherever necessary, both to make the sequence of your ideas clear and to give your essay coherence.

6

EFFECTIVE SENTENCES

Each of the following paragraphs describes the city of Vancouver. Although the content of both paragraphs is essentially the same, the first paragraph is written in sentences of nearly the same length and pattern and the second paragraph in sentences of varying length and pattern.

> Water surrounds Vancouver on three sides. The snow-crowned Coast Mountains ring the city on the northeast. Vancouver has a floating quality of natural loveliness. There is a curved beach at English Bay. This beach is in the shape of a half moon. Residential high rises stand behind the beach. They are in pale tones of beige, blue, and ice-cream pink. Turn-of-the-century houses of painted wood frown upward at the glitter of office towers. Any urban glare is softened by folds of green lawns, flowers, fountains, and trees. Such landscaping appears to be unplanned. It links Vancouver to her ultimate treasure of greenness. That treasure is thousand-acre Stanley Park. Surrounding stretches of water dominate. They have image-evoking names like False Creek and Lost Lagoon. Sailboats and pleasure craft skim blithely across Burrard Inlet. Foreign freighters are out in English Bay. They await their turn to take on cargoes of grain.

> Surrounded by water on three sides and ringed to the northeast by the snow-crowned Coast Mountains, Vancouver has a floating quality of natural loveliness. At English Bay, the half-moon curve of beach is backed by high rises in pale tones of beige, blue, and ice-cream pink. Turn-of-the-century houses of painted wood frown upward at the glitter of office towers. Yet any urban glare is quickly softened by folds of green lawns, flowers, fountains, and trees that in a seemingly unplanned fashion link Vancouver to her ultimate trea-

> sure of greenness—thousand-acre Stanley Park. And always it is the surrounding stretches of water that dominate, with their image-evoking names like False Creek and Lost Lagoon. Sailboats and pleasure craft skim blithely across Burrard Inlet, while out in English Bay foreign freighters await their turn to take on cargoes of grain.

The difference between these two paragraphs is dramatic. The first is monotonous because of the sameness of the sentences and because the ideas are not related to one another in a meaningful way. The second paragraph is much more interesting and readable; its sentences vary in length and are structured to clarify the relationships among the ideas. Sentence variety, an important aspect of all good writing, should not be used for its own sake, but rather to express ideas precisely and to emphasize the most important ideas within each sentence. Sentence variety includes the use of subordination, the periodic and loose sentence, the dramatically short sentence, the active and passive voice, and coordination.

SUBORDINATION, the process of giving one idea less emphasis than another in a sentence, is one of the most important characteristics of an effective sentence and a mature prose style. Writers subordinate ideas by introducing them either with subordinating conjunctions (*because, if, as though, while, when, after, in order that*) or with relative pronouns (*that, which, who, whomever, what*). Subordination not only deemphasizes some ideas, but also highlights others that the writer feels are more important.

Of course, there is nothing about an idea—*any* idea—that automatically makes it primary or secondary in importance. The writer decides what to emphasize, and he or she may choose to emphasize the less profound or noteworthy of two ideas. Consider, for example, the following sentence: "Jane was reading a novel the day that Mount St. Helens erupted." Everyone, including the author of the sentence, knows that the Mount St. Helens eruption is a more noteworthy event than Jane's reading a novel. But the sentence concerns Jane, not the volcano, and so her reading is stated in the main clause, while the eruption is subordinated in a dependent clause.

Generally, writers place the ideas they consider important in main clauses, and other ideas go into dependent clauses. For example:

> When she was thirty years old, she made her first solo flight across the Atlantic.
>
> When she made her first solo flight across the Atlantic, she was thirty years old.

The first sentence emphasizes the solo flight; in the second, the emphasis is on the pilot's age.

Another way to achieve emphasis is to place the most important words, phrases, and clauses at the beginning or end of a sentence. The ending is the most emphatic part of a sentence; the beginning is less emphatic; and the middle is the least emphatic of all. The two sentences about the pilot put the main clause at the end, achieving special emphasis. The same thing occurs in a much longer kind of sentence, called a PERIODIC SENTENCE. Here is an example from John Updike:

> On the afternoon of the first day of spring, when the gutters were still heaped high with Monday's snow but the sky itself had been swept clean, we put on our galoshes and walked up the sunny side of Fifth Avenue to Central Park.

By holding the main clause back, Updike keeps his readers in suspense, and so puts the most emphasis possible on his main idea.

A LOOSE SENTENCE, on the other hand, states its main idea at the beginning and then adds details in subsequent phrases and clauses. Rewritten as a loose sentence, Updike's sentence might read like this:

> We put on our galoshes and walked up the sunny side of Fifth Avenue to Central Park on the afternoon of the first day of spring, when the gutters were still heaped high with Monday's snow but the sky itself had been swept clean.

The main idea still gets plenty of emphasis, since it is contained in a main clause at the beginning of the sentence. Yet a loose sentence resembles the way people talk: It flows naturally and is easy to understand.

Another way to create emphasis is to use a DRAMATICALLY SHORT SENTENCE. Especially following a long and involved sentence, a short declarative sentence helps drive a point home. Here are two examples, the first from Edwin Newman and the second from David Wise:

> Meaning no disrespect, I suppose there is, if not general rejoicing, at least some sense of relief when the football season ends. It's a long season.

> The executive suite on the thirty-fifth floor of the Columbia Broadcasting System skyscraper in Manhattan is a tasteful blend of dark wood paneling, expensive abstract paintings, thick carpets, and pleasing colors. It has the quiet look of power.

Finally, since the subject of a sentence is automatically emphasized, writers may choose to use the ACTIVE VOICE when they want to emphasize the doer of an action, and the PASSIVE VOICE when they want to downplay or omit the doer completely. Here are two examples:

> High winds pushed our sailboat onto the rocks, where the force of the waves tore it to pieces.

> Our sailboat was pushed by high winds onto the rocks, where it was torn to pieces by the force of the waves.

The first sentence emphasizes the natural forces that destroyed the boat, while the second sentence focuses attention on the boat itself. The passive voice may be useful in placing emphasis, but it has important disadvantages. As the examples show, and as the terms suggest, active-voice verbs are more vigorous and vivid than the same verbs in the passive voice. Then, too, some writers use the passive voice to hide or evade responsibility. "It has been decided" conceals who did the deciding, whereas "I have decided" makes all clear. So the passive voice should be used only when necessary—as it is in this sentence.

Often, a writer wants to place equal emphasis on several

facts or ideas. One way to do this is to give each its own sentence. For example:

> Tom Watson selected his club. He lined up his shot. He chipped the ball to within a foot of the pin.

But a long series of short, simple sentences quickly becomes tedious. Many writers would combine these three sentences by using COORDINATION. The coordinating conjunctions *and, but, or, nor, for, so,* and *yet* connect words, phrases, and clauses of equal importance:

> Tom Watson selected his club, lined up his shot, *and* chipped the ball to within a foot of the pin.

By coordinating three sentences into one, the writer not only makes the same words easier to read, but also shows that Watson's three actions are equally important parts of a single process.

When parts of a sentence are not only coordinated but also grammatically the same, they are *parallel*. Parallelism in a sentence is created by balancing a word with a word, a phrase with a phrase, or a clause with a clause. Parallelism is often used in speeches, for example in the last sentence of Lincoln's *Gettysburg Address* (p. 99). Here is another example, from the beginning of Mark Twain's *The Adventures of Huckleberry Finn:*

> Persons attempting to find a motive in this narrative will be prosecuted; persons attempting to find a moral in it will be banished; persons attempting to find a plot in it will be shot.

An Eye-Witness Account of the San Francisco Earthquake

Jack London

Jack London (1876–1916) was born in San Francisco and attended school only until the age of fourteen. A prolific and popular fiction writer, he is perhaps best remembered for his novels The Call of the Wild *(1903),* The Sea Wolf *(1904), and* White Fang *(1906). London was working near San Francisco when the great earthquake hit that city in the early morning of April 16, 1906. Notice how, in this account of the quake's aftermath, London uses a variety of sentence structures to capture the feelings that this disaster evoked in him.*

The earthquake shook down in San Francisco hundreds of thousands of dollars' worth of walls and chimneys. But the conflagration that followed burned up hundreds of millions of dollars' worth of property. There is no estimating within hundreds of millions the actual damage wrought. Not in history has a modern imperial city been so completely destroyed. San Francisco is gone! Nothing remains of it but memories and a fringe of dwelling houses on its outskirts. Its industrial section is wiped out. Its social and residential section is wiped out. The factories and warehouses, the great stores and newspaper buildings, the hotels and the palaces of the nabobs, are all gone. Remains only the fringe of dwelling houses on the outskirts of what was once San Francisco. 1

Within an hour after the earthquake shock the smoke of San Francisco's burning was a lurid tower visible a hundred miles away. And for three days and nights this lurid tower swayed in the sky, reddening the sun, darkening the day, and filling the land with smoke. 2

On Wednesday morning at a quarter past five came the earthquake. A minute later the flames were leaping upward. In a dozen different quarters south of Market Street, in the working-class ghetto, and in the factories, fires started. There was no opposing the flames. There was no organization, no communication. All the cunning adjustments of a twentieth-century city had been smashed by the earthquake. The streets were humped into ridges and depressions and piled with debris of fallen walls. The steel rails were twisted into perpendicular and horizontal angles. The telephone and telegraph systems were disrupted. And the great water mains had burst. All the shrewd contrivances and safeguards of man had been thrown out of gear by thirty seconds' twitching of the earth crust.

By Wednesday afternoon, inside of twelve hours, half the heart of the city was gone. At that time I watched the vast conflagration from out on the bay. It was dead calm. Not a flicker of wind stirred. Yet from every side wind was pouring in upon the city. East, west, north, and south, strong winds were blowing upon the doomed city. The heated air rising made an enormous suck. Thus did the fire of itself build its own colossal chimney through the atmosphere. Day and night, this dead calm continued, and yet, near to the flames, the wind was often half a gale, so mighty was the suck. . . .

Wednesday night saw the destruction of the very heart of the city. Dynamite was lavishly used, and many of San Francisco's proudest structures were crumbled by man himself into ruins, but there was no withstanding the onrush of the flames. Time and again successful stands were made by the fire fighters, and every time the flames flanked around on either side, or came up from the rear, and turned to defeat the hard-won victory.

An enumeration of the buildings destroyed would be a directory of San Francisco. An enumeration of the buildings undestroyed would be a line and several addresses. An enumeration of the deeds of heroism would stock a library and bankrupt the Carnegie medal fund.* An enumeration of

---

*Fund established by the philanthropist Andrew Carnegie in 1905 for the recognition of heroic deeds.

the dead—will never be made. All vestiges of them were destroyed by the flames. The number of the victims of the earthquake will never be known.

Questions for Study and Discussion

1. Why do you suppose London does not make one sentence out of his first two sentences? What effect does he gain by using two sentences?
2. If the third sentence in paragraph 3 were rewritten as follows, how would its impact differ from that of the original: "Fires started in a dozen different quarters south of Market Street, in the working-class ghetto, and in the factories"?
3. What is the effect of the short sentences "San Francisco is gone!" and "It was dead calm." in paragraphs 1 and 4?
4. Why do you suppose London uses the passive voice instead of the active voice in paragraph 3? (Glossary: *Voice*)
5. Point out examples of parallelism in paragraphs 1, 2, and 6. How does London add emphasis through the use of this rhetorical device? (Glossary: *Parallelism*)
6. In paragraph 4 London says that "the fire of itself [built] its own colossal chimney through the atmosphere." What does he mean?

Vocabulary

Refer to your dictionary to define the following words as they are used in this selection. Then use each word in a sentence of your own.

conflagration (1)
nabobs (1)
lurid (2)
contrivances (3)
vestiges (6)

Suggested Writing Assignment

Write a brief essay using one of the following sentences to focus and control the descriptive details you select. Place the sentence in the essay wherever it will have the greatest emphasis.

It was a strange party.
He was nervous.
I was shocked.
Music filled the air.
Dirt was everywhere.

Terror at Tinker Creek

Annie Dillard

Annie Dillard was born in Pittsburgh, and now makes her home in the Pacific Northwest. A poet, journalist, and contributing editor to Harper's *magazine, Dillard has written* Tickets for a Prayer Wheel *(1975) and* Holy the Firm *(1977). In 1974 she published* Pilgrim at Tinker Creek, *a fascinating collection of natural observations for which she was awarded the Pulitzer Prize for nonfiction. As you read the following selection from that work, notice how the varied structures of Dillard's sentences enhance her descriptions of her experience.*

A couple of summers ago I was walking along the edge of the island to see what I could see in the water, and mainly to scare frogs. Frogs have an inelegant way of taking off from invisible positions on the bank just ahead of your feet, in dire panic, emitting a froggy "Yike!" and splashing into the water. Incredibly, this amused me, and incredibly, it amuses me still. As I walked along the grassy edge of the island, I got better and better at seeing frogs both in and out of the water. I learned to recognize, slowing down, the difference in texture of the light reflected from mudbank, water, grass, or frog. Frogs were flying all around me. At the end of the island I noticed a small green frog. He was exactly half in and half out of the water, looking like a schematic diagram of an amphibian, and he didn't jump. 1

He didn't jump; I crept closer. At last I knelt on the island's winterkilled grass, lost, dumbstruck, staring at the frog in the creek just four feet away. He was a very small frog with wide, dull eyes. And just as I looked at him, he slowly crumpled and began to sag. The spirit vanished from his eyes as if snuffed. His skin emptied and drooped; his very 2 skull seemed to collapse and settle like a kicked tent. He was shrinking before my eyes like a deflating football. I watched the taut, glistening skin on his shoulders ruck, and rumple, and fall. Soon, part of his skin, formless as a pricked balloon, lay in floating folds like bright scum on top of the water: it was a monstrous and terrifying thing. I gaped bewildered, appalled. An oval shadow hung in the water behind the drained frog; then the shadow glided away. The frog skin bag started to sink.

I had read about the giant water bug, but never seen one. "Giant water bug" is really the name of the creature, which is an enormous, heavy-bodied brown beetle. It eats insects, tadpoles, fish, and frogs. Its grasping forelegs are mighty and hooked inward. It seizes a victim with these legs, hugs it tight, and paralyzes it with enzymes injected during a vicious bite. That one bite is the only bite it ever takes. Through the puncture shoot the poisons that dissolve the victim's muscles and bones and organs—all but the skin—and through it the giant water bug sucks out the victim's body, reduced to a juice. This event is quite common in warm fresh water. The frog I saw was being sucked by a giant water bug. I had been kneeling on the island grass; when the unrecognizable flap of frog skin settled on the creek bottom, swaying, I stood up and brushed the knees of my pants. I couldn't catch my breath.

Questions for Study and Discussion

1. Why do you suppose that Dillard could not catch her breath after the experience she describes?
2. Paragraph 1 contains sentences that are varied in both length and structure, including loose sentences as well as periodic sentences, long ones as well as short. Identify two loose sentences and two periodic sentences, and compare the effects each one has on the narrative.
3. Can you recognize a relationship between kinds of sentences and the content they contain? In other words, does Dillard use loose sentences for certain

kinds of information and periodic sentences for other kinds? Support your answer with examples from the selection.

4. The first sentence in paragraph 2 contains a semicolon. Would the sentence have a different sense if the two clauses were instead joined with a coordinating conjunction—for example, *and* or *so*? Would they be different if punctuated with a period? How?
5. A simile is a comparison introduced by *like* or *as*. For example, paragraph 2 contains the simile "formless as a pricked balloon." Identify two other similes in this selection, and explain what they contribute to the description.
6. Can you characterize the words Dillard uses to describe the water bug in paragraph 3? What does her choice of words indicate about her feeling about the bug? (Glossary: *Diction*)

Vocabulary

Refer to your dictionary to define the following words as they are used in this selection. Then use each word in a sentence of your own.

dire (1)	taut (2)
schematic (1)	appalled (2)
dumbstruck (2)	enzymes (3)

Suggested Writing Assignment

Without changing the meaning, rewrite the following paragraph using a variety of sentence structures to add interest and emphasis.

> The hunter crept through the leaves. The leaves had fallen. The leaves were dry. The hunter was tired. The hunter had a gun. The gun was new. The hunter saw a deer. The deer had antlers. A tree partly hid the antlers. The deer was beautiful. The hunter shot at the deer. The hunter missed. The shot frightened the deer. The deer bounded away.

Salvation

Langston Hughes

Born in Joplin, Missouri, Langston Hughes (1902–1967), an important figure in the Harlem Renaissance, wrote poetry, fiction, and plays, and contributed a column to the New York Post. *He is best known for* The Weary Blues *(1926) and other books of poetry that express his racial pride, his familiarity with black traditions, and his understanding of jazz rhythms. As you read the following selection from his autobiography* The Big Sea *(1940), notice how Hughes varies the lengths and types of sentences he uses for the sake of emphasis.*

I was saved from sin when I was going on thirteen. But not really saved. It happened like this. There was a big revival at my Auntie Reed's church. Every night for weeks there had been much preaching, singing, praying, and shouting, and some very hardened sinners had been brought to Christ, and the membership of the church had grown by leaps and bounds. Then just before the revival ended, they held a special meeting for children, "to bring the young lambs to the fold." My aunt spoke of it for days ahead. That night I was escorted to the front row and placed on the mourners' bench with all the other young sinners, who had not yet been brought to Jesus.

My aunt told me that when you were saved you saw a light, and something happened to you inside! And Jesus came into your life! And God was with you from then on! She said you could see and hear and feel Jesus in your soul. I believed her. I have heard a great many old people say the same thing and it seemed to me they ought to know. So I sat there calmly in the hot, crowded church, waiting for Jesus to come to me.

The preacher preached a wonderful rhythmical sermon,

all moans and shouts and lonely cries and dire pictures of hell, and then he sang a song about the ninety and nine safe in the fold, but one little lamb was left out in the cold. Then he said: "Won't you come? Won't you come to Jesus? Young lambs, won't you come?" And he held out his arms to all us young sinners there on the mourners' bench. And the little girls cried. And some of them jumped up and went to Jesus right away. But most of us just sat there.

4 A great many old people came and knelt around us and prayed, old women with jet-black faces and braided hair, old men with work-gnarled hands. And the church sang a song about the lower lights are burning, some poor sinners to be saved. And the whole building rocked with prayer and song.

5 Still I kept waiting to *see* Jesus.

6 Finally all the young people had gone to the altar and were saved, but one boy and me. He was a rounder's son named Westley. Westley and I were surrounded by sisters and deacons praying. It was very hot in the church, and getting late now. Finally Westley said to me in a whisper: "God damn! I'm tired o' sitting here. Let's get up and be saved." So he got up and was saved.

7 Then I was left all alone on the mourner's bench. My aunt came and knelt at my knees and cried, while prayers and songs swirled all around me in the little church. The whole congregation prayed for me alone, in a mighty wail of moans and voices. And I kept waiting serenely for Jesus, waiting, waiting—but he didn't come. I wanted to see him, but nothing happened to me. Nothing! I wanted something to happen to me, but nothing happened.

8 I heard the songs and the minister saying: "Why don't you come? My dear child, why don't you come to Jesus? Jesus is waiting for you. He wants you. Why don't you come? Sister Reed, what is this child's name?"

9 "Langston," my aunt sobbed.

10 "Langston, why don't you come? Why don't you come and be saved? Oh, Lamb of God! Why don't you come?"

11 Now it was really getting late. I began to be ashamed of myself, holding everything up so long. I began to wonder what God thought about Westley, who certainly hadn't seen Jesus either, but who was now sitting proudly on the plat-

form, swinging his knickerbockered legs and grinning down at me, surrounded by deacons and old women on their knees praying. God had not struck Westley dead for taking his name in vain or for lying in the temple. So I decided that maybe to save further trouble, I'd better lie, too, and say that Jesus had come, and get up and be saved.

So I got up.

Suddenly the whole room broke into a sea of shouting, as they saw me rise. Waves of rejoicing swept the place. Women leaped in the air. My aunt threw her arms around me. The minister took me by the hand and led me to the platform.

When things quieted down, in a hushed silence, punctuated by a few ecstatic "Amens," all the new young lambs were blessed in the name of God. Then joyous singing filled the room.

That night, for the last time in my life but one—for I was a big boy twelve years old—I cried. I cried, in bed alone, and couldn't stop. I buried my head under the quilts, but my aunt heard me. She woke up and told my uncle I was crying because the Holy Ghost had come into my life, and because I had seen Jesus. But I was really crying because I couldn't bear to tell her that I had lied, that I had deceived everybody in the church, that I hadn't seen Jesus, and that now I didn't believe there was a Jesus any more, since he didn't come to help me.

Questions for Study and Discussion

1. Why does young Langston Hughes expect to be saved at the revival meeting? Once the children are in church, what appeals are made to them to encourage them to seek salvation?
2. What would be gained or lost if the essay began with the first two sentences combined as follows: "I was saved from sin when I was going on thirteen, but I was not really saved"?

3. Identify the coordinating conjunctions in paragraph 3. Rewrite the paragraph without them. Compare your paragraph with the original, and explain what Hughes gains by using coordinating conjunctions. (Glossary: *Coordination*)
4. Identify the subordinating conjunctions in paragraph 15. What is it about the ideas in this last paragraph that makes it necessary for him to use these subordinating conjunctions?
5. How do the short one-sentence paragraphs aid Hughes in telling his story?
6. How does Hughes's choice of words, or diction, help to establish a realistic atmosphere for a religious revival meeting?

Vocabulary

Refer to your dictionary to define the following words as they are used in this selection. Then use each word in a sentence of your own.

dire (3)
gnarled (4)
vain (11)
punctuated (14)
ecstatic (14)

Suggested Writing Assignment

Reread the introduction to this chapter. Then review one of the essays that you have written, paying particular attention to sentence structure. Recast sentences as necessary in order to make your writing more interesting and effective.

II

THE LANGUAGE OF THE ESSAY

7

Diction

Diction refers to a writer's choice and use of words. Good diction is precise and appropriate—the words mean exactly what the writer intends, and the words are well suited to the writer's subject, purpose, and intended audience.

For careful writers it is not enough merely to come close to saying what they want to say; they select words that convey their exact meaning. Perhaps Mark Twain put this best when he said, "The difference between the right word and the almost right word is the difference between lightning and the lightning bug." Inaccurate and imprecise diction not only fails to express the writer's intended meaning but also may cause confusion and misunderstanding for the reader.

In order to use words precisely, you need not have a large vocabulary, but you must know the correct meanings of the words you use. In order to use words effectively, you must understand the denotations and connotations of words as well as the importance of balancing abstract words with concrete words and general words with specific words. In addition, you should avoid clichés, expressions that are trite and worn out, and use jargon only when appropriate for your audience. Finally, you should become familiar with the various levels of diction from formal to informal and know how to use them appropriately.

Connotation and Denotation

Both connotation and denotation refer to the meanings of words. Denotation is the dictionary meaning of a word, the literal meaning. Connotative meanings are the associations or emotional overtones that words have acquired gradually. For example, the word *home* denotes a place where someone lives, but it connotes warmth, security, family, comfort, affection, and other more private thoughts and images. The word *residence* also denotes a place where someone lives, but it connotations are colder and more formal.

Many words in English have synonyms, words with very similar denotations: for example, *mob, crowd, multitude,* and *bunch.* Deciding which to use depends largely on the connotations that each synonym has and the context in which the word is to be used. For example, you might say, "There was a crowd at the lecture," but not "There was a mob at the lecture." Good writers are sensitive to both the denotations and the connotations of words.

Abstract and Concrete Words

Abstract words name ideas, conditions, emotions—things nobody can touch, see, or hear. Some abstract words are *love, wisdom, cowardice, beauty, fear,* and *liberty.* People often disagree about abstract things. You may find a forest beautiful, while someone else might find it frightening, and neither of you would be wrong. Beauty and fear are abstract ideas; they exist in your mind, not in the forest along with the trees and the owls. Concrete words refer to things we can touch, see, hear, smell, and taste, such as *sandpaper, soda, birch trees, smog, cow, sailboat, rocking chair,* and *pancake.* If you disagree with someone on a concrete issue—say, you claim that the forest is mostly birch trees, while the other person says it is mostly pine—only one of you can be right, and both of you can be wrong; what kinds of trees grow in the forest is a concrete fact, not an abstract idea.

Good writing balances ideas and facts, and it also balances abstract and concrete diction. If the writing is too abstract, with too few concrete facts and details, it will be unconvincing and tiresome. If the writing is too concrete, devoid of ideas and emotions, it can seem pointless and dry.

General and Specific Words

General and *specific* do not necessarily refer to opposites. The same word can often be either general or specific, depending on the context: *Dessert* is more specific than *food,* but more general than *chocolate cream pie.* Being very specific is like being concrete: *chocolate cream pie* is something you can see and taste. Being general, on the other hand, is like being abstract. *Food, dessert,* and even *pie* are general classes of things that bring no particular taste or image to mind.

Good writing moves back and forth from the general to the specific. Without specific words, generalities can be unconvincing and even confusing: the writer's idea of "good food" may be very different from the reader's. But writing that does not relate specifics to each other by generalization often lacks focus and direction.

Clichés

Some words, phrases, and expressions have become trite through overuse. Let's assume your roommate has just returned from an evening out. You ask her "How was the concert?" She responds, "The concert was okay, but they had us *packed in* there *like sardines.* How was your evening?" And you reply, "Well, I finished my term paper, but the noise here is enough to *drive me crazy.* The dorm is a real *zoo.*" At one time the italicized expressions were vivid and colorful, but through constant use they have grown stale and ineffective. The experienced writer always tries to avoid such clichés as: *believe it or not, doomed to failure, hit the spot, let's face it, sneaking suspicion, step in the right direction,* and *went to great lengths.*

Jargon

Jargon, or technical language, is the special vocabulary of a trade or profession. Writers who use jargon do so with an awareness of their audience. If their audience is a group of coworkers or professionals, jargon may be used freely. If the audience is a more general one, jargon should be used sparingly and carefully so that readers can understand it. Jargon becomes inappropriate when it is overused, used out of context, or used pretentiously. For example, computer terms such as *input, output,* and *feedback* are sometimes used in place of *contribution, result,* and *response* in other fields, especially in business. If you think about it, the terms suggest that people are machines, receiving and processing information according to a program imposed by someone else.

Formal and Informal Diction

Diction is appropriate when it suits the occasion for which it is intended. If the situation is informal—a friendly letter, for example—the writing may be colloquial; that is, its words may be chosen to suggest the way people talk with each other. If, on the other hand, the situation is formal—a term paper or a research report, for example—then the words should reflect this formality. Informal writing tends to be characterized by slang, contractions, references to the reader, and concrete nouns. Formal writing tends to be impersonal, abstract, and free of contractions and references to the reader. Formal writing and informal writing are, of course, the extremes. Most writing falls between these two extremes and is a blend of those formal and informal elements that best fit the context.

THE GETTYSBURG ADDRESS

Abraham Lincoln

With the possible exception of "The Declaration of Independence," perhaps no document of American history is as famous as "The Gettysburg Address." Abraham Lincoln (1809–1865), one of the most beloved of all presidents, delivered the address on the Gettysburg battlefield on November 19, 1863. Although the address is only three paragraphs long, its message is powerfully stated. Lincoln's profound sentiments and careful diction make the address a nearly flawless model of formal English prose.

Four score and seven years ago our fathers brought forth on this continent, a new nation, conceived in Liberty, and dedicated to the proposition that all men are created equal. 1

Now we are engaged in a great civil war, testing whether that nation, or any nation so conceived and so dedicated, can long endure. We are met on a great battle-field of that war. We have come to dedicate a portion of that field, as a final resting place for those who here gave their lives that that nation might live. It is altogether fitting and proper that we should do this. 2

But, in a larger sense, we can not dedicate—we can not consecrate—we can not hallow—this ground. The brave men, living and dead, who struggled here, have consecrated it, far above our poor power to add or detract. The world will little note, nor long remember what we say here, but it can never forget what they did here. It is for us the living, rather, to be dedicated here to the unfinished work which they who fought here have thus far so nobly advanced. It is rather for us to be here dedicated to the great task remaining before us—that from these honored dead we take increased devotion to that cause for which they gave the last 3 full measure of devotion—that we here highly resolve that these dead shall not have died in vain—that this nation, under God, shall have a new birth of freedom—and that government of the people, by the people, for the people, shall not perish from the earth.

Questions for Study and Discussion

1. To what Civil War issue does Lincoln's opening sentence refer?
2. Lincoln's diction in the opening paragraph of "The Gettysburg Address" is calculated to achieve a certain effect on listeners and readers. Discuss the nature of this effect by comparing the opening paragraph to the following one: "Eighty-seven years ago our ancestors formed a new nation based on liberty and devoted to the notion that all men are created equal."
3. In an early draft of the address, the last sentence in paragraph 2 reads, "This we may, in all propriety, do." Why do you suppose Lincoln rewrote this sentence?
4. In the first sentence of paragraph 3, Lincoln uses the words *dedicate, consecrate,* and *hallow.* Do these words have the same denotative meaning? Why do you think Lincoln placed them in this particular order?
5. The tone of "The Gettysburg Address" can be described as reverential. Cite specific examples of Lincoln's diction that help to create this tone. (Glossary: *Tone*)

Vocabulary

Refer to your dictionary to define the following words as they are used in this selection. Then use each word in a sentence of your own.

proposition (1)
detract (3)
resolve (3)
vain (3)

Suggested Writing Assignment

Write two paragraphs in which you describe the same incident, person, scene, or thing. In the first paragraph, use formal language and in the second, informal language. Keep the factual content of the two paragraphs constant; vary only the language.

The Flight of the Eagles

N. Scott Momaday

N. Scott Momaday, a professor of English at Stanford University, is a Kiowa Indian. He has based much of his writing on his Indian ancestry, particularly on his childhood experiences with his Kiowa grandmother. In 1969 he won the Pulitzer Prize for his novel House Made of Dawn *(1968). His other works include* The Way to Rainy Mountain *(1969),* Angle of Geese and Other Poems *(1974), and* The Gourd Dancer *(1976). In the following selection, taken from* House Made of Dawn, *Momaday closely observes the mating flight of a pair of golden eagles. Notice how his sensitive choice of verbs enables him to capture the beautiful and graceful movements of these birds.*

They were golden eagles, a male and a female, in their mating flight. They were cavorting, spinning and spiraling on the cold, clear columns of air, and they were beautiful. They swooped and hovered, leaning on the air, and swung close together, feinting and screaming with delight. The female was full-grown, and the span of her broad wings was greater than any man's height. There was a fine flourish to her motion; she was deceptively, incredibly fast, and her pivots and wheels were wide and full-blown. But her great weight was streamlined and perfectly controlled. She carried a rattlesnake; it hung shining from her feet, limp and curving out in the trail of her flight. Suddenly her wings and tail fanned, catching full on the wind, and for an instant she was still, widespread and spectral in the blue, while her mate flared past and away, turning around in the distance to look for her. Then she began to beat upward at an angle from the rim until she was small in the sky, and she let go of the snake. It fell slowly, writhing and rolling, floating out like a bit of silver thread against the wide backdrop of the land. She held still above, buoyed up on the cold current, her crop and hackles gleaming like copper in the sun. The male swerved and sailed. He was younger than she and a little more than half as large. He was quicker, tighter in his moves. He let the carrion drift by; then suddenly he gathered himself and stooped, sliding down in a blur of motion to the strike. He hit the snake in the head, with not the slightest deflection of his course or speed, cracking its long body like a whip. Then he rolled and swung upward in a great pendulum arc, riding out his momentum. At the top of his glide he let go of the snake in turn, but the female did not go for it. Instead she soared out over the plain, nearly out of sight, like a mote receding into the haze of the far mountain. The male followed.

Questions for Study and Discussion

1. What are the differences between the two eagles as Momaday describes them?
2. In describing the mating flight of the golden eagles, Momaday has tried to capture their actions accurately. Identify the strong verbs that he uses, and discuss how these verbs enhance his description. (Glossary: *Verbs*)
3. Comment on the denotative and connotative meanings of the italicized words and phrases in the following excerpts:
   a. on the *cold, clear* columns of air
   b. feinting and screaming with *delight*
   c. a *fine flourish* to her motion
   d. her *pivots* and *wheels* were wide and full-blown
   e. her *crop* and *hackles* gleaming
4. Identify several examples of Momaday's use of concrete and specific diction. What effect does this diction have on you?

5. Identify the figures of speech that Momaday uses in this selection and tell how you think each one functions in the essay. (Glossary: *Figures of Speech*)

Vocabulary

Refer to your dictionary to define the following words as they are used in this selection. Then use each word in a sentence of your own.

cavorting
feinting
spectral

Suggested Writing Assignment

Select one of the following activities as the subject for a brief descriptive essay. Be sure to use strong verbs, as Momaday has done, in order to describe the action accurately and vividly.

the movements of a dancer
the actions of a kite
the antics of a pet
a traffic jam
a violent storm

ON BEING 17, BRIGHT, AND UNABLE TO READ

David Raymond

When the following article appeared in The New York Times *in 1976, David Raymond was a high school student in Connecticut. In his essay he poignantly discusses his great difficulty in reading because of dyslexia and the many problems he experienced in school as a result. As you read, pay attention to the naturalness of the author's diction.*

One day a substitute teacher picked me to read aloud from the textbook. When I told her "No, thank you," she came unhinged. She thought I was acting smart, and told me so. I kept calm, and that got her madder and madder. We must have spent 10 minutes trying to solve the problem, and finally she got so red in the face I thought she'd blow up. She told me she'd see me after class. 1

Maybe someone like me was a new thing for that teacher. But she wasn't new to me. I've been through scenes like that all my life. You see, even though I'm 17 and a junior in high school, I can't read because I have dyslexia. I'm told I read "at a fourth-grade level," but from where I sit, that's not reading. You can't know what that means unless you've been there. It's not easy to tell how it feels when you can't read your homework assignments or the newspaper or a menu in a restaurant or even notes from your own friends. 2

My family began to suspect I was having problems almost from the first day I started school. My father says my early years in school were the worst years of his life. They weren't so good for me, either. As I look back on it now, I can't find the words to express how bad it really was. I wanted to die. I'd come home from school screaming, "I'm dumb. I'm dumb—I wish I were dead!" 3

I guess I couldn't read anything at all then—not even my own name—and they tell me I didn't talk as good as other kids. But what I remember about those days is that I couldn't throw a ball where it was supposed to go, I couldn't learn to swim, and I wouldn't learn to ride a bike, because no matter what anyone told me, I knew I'd fail.

Sometimes my teachers would try to be encouraging. When I couldn't read the words on the board they'd say, "Come on, David, you know that word." Only I didn't. And it was embarrassing. I just felt dumb. And dumb was how the kids treated me. They'd make fun of me every chance they got, asking me to spell "cat" or something like that. Even if I knew how to spell it, I wouldn't; they'd only give me another word. Anyway, it was awful, because more than anything I wanted friends. On my birthday when I blew out the candles I didn't wish I could learn to read; what I wished for was that the kids would like me.

With the bad reports coming from school, and with me moaning about wanting to die and how everybody hated me, my parents began looking for help. That's when the testing started. The school tested me, the child-guidance center tested me, private psychiatrists tested me. Everybody knew something was wrong—especially me.

It didn't help much when they stuck a fancy name onto it. I couldn't pronounce it then—I was only in second grade—and I was ashamed to talk about it. Now it rolls off my tongue, because I've been living with it for a lot of years—dyslexia.

All through elementary school it wasn't easy. I was always having to do things that were "different," things the other kids didn't have to do. I had to go to a child psychiatrist, for instance.

One summer my family forced me to go to a camp for children with reading problems. I hated the idea, but the camp turned out pretty good, and I had a good time. I met a lot of kids who couldn't read and somehow that helped. The director of the camp said I had a higher I.Q. than 90 percent of the population. I didn't believe him.

About the worst thing I had to do in fifth and sixth grade was go to a special education class in another school in our town. A bus picked me up, and I didn't like that at all. The bus also picked up emotionally disturbed kids and retarded kids. It was like going to a school for the retarded. I always worried that someone I knew would see me on that bus. It was a relief to go to the regular junior high school.

11 Life began to change a little for me then, because I began to feel better about myself. I found the teachers cared; they had meetings about me and I worked harder for them for a while. I began to work on the potter's wheel, making vases and pots that the teachers said were pretty good. Also, I got a letter for being on the track team. I could always run pretty fast.

12 At high school the teachers are good and everyone is trying to help me. I've gotten honors some marking periods and I've won a letter on the cross-country team. Next quarter I think the school might hold a show of my pottery. I've got some friends. But there are still some embarrassing times. For instance, every time there is writing in the class, I get up and go to the special education room. Kids ask me where I go all the time. Sometimes I say, "to Mars."

13 Homework is a real problem. During free periods in school I go into the special ed room and staff members read assignments to me. When I get home my mother reads to me. Sometimes she reads an assignment into a tape recorder, and then I go into my room and listen to it. If we have a novel or something like that to read, she reads it out loud to me. Then I sit down with her and we do the assignment. She'll write, while I talk my answers to her. Lately I've taken to dictating into a tape recorder, and then someone—my father, a private tutor or my mother—types up what I've dictated. Whatever homework I do takes someone else's time, too. That makes me feel bad.

14 We had a big meeting in school the other day—eight of us, four from the guidance department, my private tutor, my parents and me. The subject was me. I said I wanted to go to college, and they told me about colleges that have facilities and staff to handle people like me. That's nice to hear.

15 As for what happens after college, I don't know and I'm worried about that. How can I make a living if I can't read? Who will hire me? How will I fill out the application form?

The only thing that gives me any courage is the fact that I've learned about well-known people who couldn't read or had other problems and still made it. Like Albert Einstein, who didn't talk until he was 4 and flunked math. Like Leonardo da Vinci, who everyone seems to think had dyslexia.

I've told this story because maybe some teacher will read it and go easy on a kid in the classroom who has what I've got. Or, maybe some parent will stop nagging his kid, and stop calling him lazy. Maybe he's not lazy or dumb. Maybe he just can't read and doesn't know what's wrong. Maybe he's scared, like I was.

Questions for Study and Discussion

1. What does Raymond say his purpose is in telling his story?
2. Would you characterize the diction in this selection as formal or informal? General or specific? Concrete or abstract? Is this diction appropriate considering Raymond's topic?
3. Raymond uses many colloquial and idiomatic expressions, such as "she got so red in the face I thought she'd blow up" and "she came unhinged." Identify other examples of such diction and tell how they affect the essay.
4. In the context of the essay, comment on the appropriateness of each of the following possible choices of diction. Which word is better in each case? Why?
   a. *selected* for *picked* (1)
   b. *experience* for *thing* (2)
   c. *speak as well* for *talk as good* (4)
   d. *negative* for *bad* (6)
   e. *important* for *big* (14)
   f. *failed* for *flunked* (15)
   g. *frightened* for *scared* (16)

Vocabulary

dyslexia (2)

Suggested Writing Assignment

Imagine that you are away at school. Recently you were caught in a radar speed trap—you were going 70 miles per hour in a 55-mile-per-hour zone—and have just lost your license; you will not be able to go home this coming weekend, as you had planned. Write two letters in which you explain why you will not be able to go home, one to your parents and the other to your best friend. Your audience is different in each case, so be sure to choose your diction accordingly.

8

TONE

Tone is the attitude a writer takes toward the subject and the audience. The tone may be friendly or hostile, serious or humorous, intimate or distant, enthusiastic or skeptical.

As you read the following paragraphs, notice how each writer has created a different tone and how that tone is supported by the diction—the writer's particular choice and use of words.

Nostalgic

My generation is special because of what we missed rather than what we got, because in a certain sense we are the first and the last. The first to take technology for granted. (What was a space shot to us, except an hour cut from Social Studies to gather before a TV in the gym as Cape Canaveral counted down?) The first to grow up with TV. My sister was 8 when we got our set, so to her it seemed magic and always somewhat foreign. She had known books already and would never really replace them. But for me, the TV set was, like the kitchen sink and the telephone, a fact of life.

Joyce Maynard, "An 18-Year-Old Looks Back on Life"

Angry

Cans. Beer cans. Glinting on the verges of a million miles of roadways, lying in scrub, grass, dirt, leaves, sand, mud, but never hidden. Piels, Rheingold, Ballantine, Schaefer, Schlitz, shining in the sun or picked by moon or the beams of headlights at night; washed by rain or flattened by wheels, but never dulled, never buried, never destroyed. Here is the mark of savages, the testament of wasters, the stain of prosperity.

Marya Mannes, "Wasteland"

Humorous

In perpetrating a revolution, there are two requirements: someone or something to revolt against and someone to actually show up and do the revolting. Dress is usually casual and both parties may be flexible about time and place but if either faction fails to attend the whole enterprise is likely to come off badly. In the Chinese Revolution of 1650 neither party showed up and the deposit on the hall was forfeited.

Woody Allen,
"A Brief, Yet Helpful Guide to Civil Disobedience"

Resigned

I make my living humping cargo for Seaboard World Airlines, one of the big international airlines at Kennedy Airport. They handle strictly all cargo. I was once told that one of the Rockefellers is the major stockholder for the airline, but I don't really think about that too much. I don't get paid to think. The big thing is to beat that race with the time clock every morning of your life so the airline will be happy. The worst thing a man could ever do is to make suggestions about building a better airline. They pay people $40,000 a year to come up with better ideas. It doesn't matter that these ideas never work; it's just that they get nervous when a guy from South Brooklyn or Ozone Park acts like he has a brain.

Patrick Fenton, "Confessions of a Working Stiff"

Ironic

Once upon a time there was a small, beautiful, green and graceful country called Vietnam. It needed to be saved. (In later years no one could remember exactly what it needed to be saved from, but that is another story.) For many years Vietnam was in the process of being saved by France, but the French eventually tired of their labors and left. Then America took on the job. America was well equipped for country-saving. It was the richest and most powerful nation on earth. It had, for example, nuclear explosives on hand and ready to use equal to six tons of TNT for every man, woman, and child in the world. It had huge and very efficient factories, brilliant and dedicated scientists, and most (but not everybody) would agree, it had good intentions. Sadly, America had one fatal flaw—its inhabitants were in love with technology and thought it could do no wrong. A visitor to America during the time of this story would probably have guessed its outcome after seeing how its inhabitants were treating their own country. The air was mostly foul, the water putrid, and most of the land was either covered with concrete or garbage. But Americans were never much on introspection, and they didn't foresee the result of their loving embrace on the small country. They set out to save Vietnam with the same enthusiasm and determination their forefathers had displayed in conquering the frontier.

The Sierra Club, "A Fable for Our Times"

THE LANGUAGE OF THE EYES

Flora Davis

A free-lance writer, Flora Davis has held various positions in the magazine publishing field—advertising copywriter, travel editor, fashion editor, and feature writer. Her book Inside Intuition: What We Know about Nonverbal Communication *was published in 1973. Be aware of Davis' tone as you read the following selection, in which the author considers eye behavior as an element of communication.*

One of the most potent elements in body language is eye behavior. You shift your eyes, meet another person's gaze or fail to meet it—and produce an effect out of all proportion to the trifling muscular effort you've made. 1

When two Americans look searchingly into each other's eyes, emotions are heightened and the relationship tipped toward greater intimacy. However, Americans are careful about how and when they meet another's eyes. In our normal conversation, each eye contact lasts only about a second before one or both individuals look away. 2

Because the longer meeting of the eyes is rare, it is weighted with significance when it happens and can generate a special kind of human-to-human awareness. A girl who has taken part in civil rights demonstrations reported that she was advised, if a policeman confronted her, to look straight into his eyes. 3

"Make him *see* you as another human being and he's more likely to treat you as one," she was told. 4

Most of the time, the American interprets a lingering look as a sign of sexual attraction and scrupulously avoids this minor intimacy, except in appropriate circumstances. 5

"That man makes me so uncomfortable," a young woman 6

complained. "Half the time when I glance at him he's already looking at me—and he keeps right on looking."

By simply using his eyes, a man can make a woman aware of him sexually, comfortably or uncomfortably.

Americans abroad sometimes find local eye behavior hard to interpret.

"My first day in Tel Aviv was disturbing," one man recalled. "People not only stared right at me on the street, they actually looked me up and down. I kept wondering if I was uncombed or unzipped or if I just looked too American. Finally, a friend explained that Israelis think nothing of staring at others on the street."

Proper street behavior in the United States requires a nice balance of attention and inattention. You are supposed to look at a passerby just enough to show that you're aware of his presence. If you look too little, you appear haughty or furtive, too much and you're inquisitive. Usually what happens is that people eye each other until they are about eight feet apart, at which point both cast down their eyes. Sociologist Erving Goffman describes this as "a kind of dimming of lights."

Much of eye behavior is so subtle that we react to it only on the intuitive level. The next time you have a conversation with someone who makes you feel liked, notice what he does with his eyes. Chances are he looks at you more often than is usual with glances a little longer than the normal. You interpret this as a sign—a polite one—that he is interested in you as a person rather than just in the topic of conversation. Probably you also feel that he is both self-confident and sincere.

All this has been demonstrated in elaborate experiments. Subjects sit and talk in the psychologist's laboratory, innocent of the fact that their eye behavior is being observed from behind a one-way vision screen. In one fairly typical experiment, subjects were induced to cheat while performing a task, then were interviewed and observed. It was found that those who had cheated met the interviewer's eyes less often than was normal, an indication that "shifty eyes"—to use the mystery writers' stock phrase—*can* actually be a tip-off to an attempt to deceive or to feelings of guilt.

13 In parts of the Far East it is impolite to look at the other person at all during conversation. In England the polite listener fixes the speaker with an attentive stare and blinks his eyes occasionally as a sign of interest. That eye-blink says nothing to Americans, who expect the listener to nod or to murmur something—such as "mnhmn."

14 Let's examine a typical American conversation. Joan and Sandra meet on the sidewalk. Preliminary greetings over with, Joan begins to talk. She starts by looking right away from Sandra. As she hits her conversational stride, she glances back at her friend from time to time at the end of a phrase or a sentence. She does not look at her during hesitations or pauses but only at natural breaks in the flow of her talk. At the end of what she wants to say, she gives Sandra a rather longer glance. Experiments indicate that if she fails to do this, Sandra, not recognizing that it is her turn to talk, will hesitate or will say nothing at all.

15 When Sandra takes up the conversation, Joan, listening, sends her longer glances than she did when she herself had the floor. When their eyes meet, Joan usually makes some sign that she is listening.

16 It's not hard to see the logic behind this eye behavior. Joan looks away at the start of her statement and during hesitations to avoid being distracted while she organizes her thoughts. She glances at Sandra from time to time for feedback: to make sure she is listening, to see how she is reacting or for permission to go on talking. And while Sandra is doing the talking, Joan glances often at her to show that she is paying attention—to show that she's polite. For Americans, then, eye behavior does duty as a kind of conversational traffic signal, to control how talking time is shared.

17 You have only to observe an actual conversation to see that this pattern is not a precisely predictable one. None of the "facts" of eye behavior are cut and dried, for there are variations between individuals. People use their eyes differently and spend different—and characteristic—amounts of time looking at others. But if you know what to look for, the basic American idiom is there.

Questions for Study and Discussion

1. According to Davis, in what ways is eye behavior an important part of body language?
2. What is Davis' purpose for writing this essay?
3. Davis' tone in this selection—her attitude toward her subject—might be described as objective or neutral. Why is this tone appropriate?
4. How does Davis achieve an objective tone? In answering, consider the essay's organization and diction, and note the author's use of examples to support her general statements.

Vocabulary

Refer to your dictionary to define the following words as they are used in this selection. Then use each word in a sentence of your own.

potent (1)
trifling (1)
scrupulously (5)
haughty (10)
furtive (10)
idiom (17)

Suggested Writing Assignment

Using an objective tone, write a short essay on one of the following topics.

smoking in public places
academic honesty
renting an apartment
financing a college education
equality in sports
your college or university's early years

HOW TO FOLD SOUP

Steve Martin

Before becoming a popular comedian in his own right, Steve Martin was a writer for such entertainers as the Smothers Brothers, Sonny and Cher, John Denver, and Glen Campbell. He has recorded several comedy albums and has written and starred in the movie The Jerk. *The following selection is taken from his first book* Cruel Shoes *(1980). As you read the essay, note the humorously matter-of-fact tone used to treat a rather absurd subject.*

We middle-class folks are now all pretty much aware that the lunchpail is strictly a boorish accoutrement. It's just about impossible to maintain an air of dignity when you're carting around a clumsy tin box with a bologna sandwich in it. Yet, it *is* certainly stylish to bring one's own lunch to work. Many people who sought the *chic* of a brought-from-home lunch weren't about to tote that bulky lunchpail, and the answer for most citizens was to hide the food on their body, then at lunchtime produce it from various pockets and hidden belts. This is a wonderful solution and can even give the most dreary office building a certain outdoorsy feel. 1

However, with all the ingenuity involved in hiding various delicacies on the body, this process automatically excludes certain foods. For example, a turkey sandwich is welcome, but the cumbersome cantaloupe is not (science has provided some relief, of course, like the pecan-sized watermelon ready to be popped into the mouth). One person lined a pocket with vinyl so he could carry around dip and munch all day, dipping the chips into his vest pocket and having them emerge fully doused with onion spread. Another acquaintance had a sport coat equipped with a banana loader, arranged so that by lowering his arm a banana would secret- 2 ly drop into his hand. This proved ideal for long meetings that continued through lunch, as the drop was made so discreetly that others would naturally think you had been eating a banana all along.

These "tricks" may seem too elaborate for the average unique person desiring to bring their lunch from home, yet still insisting on a fully-balanced meal. The answer is soup. Soup is a robust addition to any meal and just about everyone has a favorite. But the primary concern is "how can you carry soup on your body without appearing ridiculous?" When you ask yourself this question, you are ready for soup folding.

Soup Folding

First prepare the soup of your choice and pour it into a bowl. Then, take the bowl and quickly turn it upside down on a cookie tray. Lift the bowl ever so gently so that the soup retains the shape of the bowl. *Gently* is the key word here. Then, with a knife cut the soup down the middle into halves, then quarters, and *gently* reassemble the soup into a cube. Some of the soup will have run off onto the cookie tray. Lift this soup up by the corners and fold slowly into a cylindrical soup staff. Square off the cube by stuffing the cracks with this cylindrical soup staff. Place the little packet in your purse or inside coat pocket, and pack off to work. When that lunch bell chimes, impress your friends by forming the soup back into a bowl shape, and enjoy! Enjoy it until that day when the lunchpail comes back into vogue and we won't need soup folding or cornstalks up the leg.

Questions for Study and Discussion

1. Is this essay merely silly, or does Steve Martin have a serious point to make? What modern tendencies might Martin be ridiculing?
2. Although the subject of the essay is clearly outrageous, Martin's tone is flat and matter-of-fact. How does his diction help to establish this tone?

3. In the last paragraph, Martin uses *process analysis*: that is, he gives step-by-step directions for "folding" soup. How does the use of process analysis contribute to the essay's flat tone? (Glossary: *Process Analysis*)

Vocabulary

Refer to your dictionary to define the following words as they are used in this selection. Then use each word in a sentence of your own.

boorish (1)
accoutrement (1)
chic (1)
ingenuity (2)
delicacies (2)
robust (3)
staff (4)

Suggested Writing Assignment

Following Steve Martin's example, write a short humorous essay using a matter-of-fact tone to discuss an absurd subject.

Meet Me at the Rinse Cycle

Jane O'Reilly

Jane O'Reilly, a free-lance writer, was a contributing editor of New York *magazine from 1968 to 1976. Her articles have appeared in* Atlantic, House and Garden, Ms., *and* New Republic; *the following selection first appeared in* Ms. *As you read it, note the humorous, ironic tone with which the author observes the negative effect of technological advances on human relationships.*

In Colonial times the women washed everyone's clothes once a month, whether they needed washing or not.

Recently, a Mother of Six confided to a women's magazine that she did six or seven loads of wash a day. She also complained of feeling isolated. Remarkably, she did not seem to connect the two statements. To me, Mother of Six was an eloquent example of why privately owned washing machines must be abolished for the good of democracy.

I fully sympathize with those who feel this sacrifice is too great. All my life I have wanted a washing machine. Only recently has ideology become the reason I don't have one instead of the fact that in my apartment building the installation cost is twice the appliance cost. I love to browse through the washing products section of my local supermarket. I bring soap as a house gift when I am invited for weekends, and I beg to be allowed to do the family wash, reveling in the magic of dirty in—clean out. Wash and Dry and Delicate Cycles seem to me to be technology's highest achievement.

But washing machines have turned out to be another sad example of technological achievement being a mixed blessing. It is perfectly obvious that a woman who does six loads of wash a day has too many clothes or too large and lazy a family. She uses too much soap, water and electricity. What is not so obvious is that she is at home with about five hundred dollars' worth of inefficiently utilized machinery when she could be somewhere else being part of that desirable social concept—a community.

5 We should build Laundromats the way the Romans built public baths. There should be a central, preferably vaulted, hall full of washers and dryers and ironing boards. Other halls should be equipped as nurseries, gymnasiums, and pool halls. There should be bingo on Tuesday and visits by political candidates on Thursdays. Perhaps even fish fries on Saturdays. Urban visionaries constantly suggest turning old railroad stations and warehouses into boutique complexes. Why not Laundromats instead?

6 The Laundromats that we already have serve as effective community centers only in very poor rural or urban areas. They are very good places for journalists to go to test public opinion, but they are rarely comfortable and they are not very good places to plug into the world of ideas. In order to foster an intelligent and informed discussion of those issues crucial to a democratic society, all television should be banned in the new Laundromats and no one should be allowed to drop off their wash for someone else do to.

7 It would be hardest to do without television. Nations launder as they live. I discovered that bit of wisdom on a trip abroad. In Edinburgh, little old ladies called us one by one out of a waiting room as bleak as a county jail to take our turns at nice yellow secondhand American machines. There were no facilities for folding, apparently because Scots prefer to scurry modestly home with their wash unrevealed to prying eyes. Some scandal resulted from my willingness to display my clean knickers to the crowd.

8 In Parisian *lavi-secs* [laundromats], there was always at least one romantic couple oblivious to the secrets told by their dirty linen. The romantic mood was held in check by the extraordinary cost of washing it: six francs, [about $1.00] per small load and more francs for water hot enough. In Italy, the Laundromats seemed to be continuously on strike. In Athens, conveniently for my theory, the newspapers were reporting a decline in community spirit in small Greek towns since the laying on of running water.

I became completely persuaded that Americans were ready for a return to the town pump while I was going around the Black Sea on a Norwegian cruise ship, the *Royal Viking Sea*. The *Sea* is the most elegant and technologically advanced merchant ship in the world, but still the canny designers included a launderette for the passengers.

It was the most sociable place on the ship. American women encrusted with diamonds came to look and stayed to chat. Husbands were brought in to inspect the mysteries of European washing machines. People who had not thought about their laundry for years held cocktail parties while they ironed their ball gowns and put a few pairs of socks through a rinse. Women, deprived by the isolation of the suburbs and their own money, learned the joys of beating someone else to the dryer.

The day the ship visited Odessa, I asked the Intourist guide if we could see a public laundry. She expressed shock and surprise: "We do our *own* laundry in our *own* machines at home."

Communist Russia is probably not the best place to explain that we have tried the future and it doesn't work. Let them find out the hard way.

Questions for Study and Discussion

1. What point does O'Reilly make in this essay? (Glossary: *Thesis*)
2. Why does O'Reilly recount her experience about the *Royal Viking Sea* (9–10)? What does she gain by juxtaposing this example with the one in Odessa (11–12)?
3. O'Reilly's tone is humorously tongue in cheek. How does she create this tone? Find two passages in the essay that show her tone and be able to explain why they do.
4. How well suited is O'Reilly's tone to her thesis and purpose? Would any other tone be appropriate?

Vocabulary

Refer to your dictionary to define the following words as they are used in this selection. Then use each word in a sentence of your own.

confided (2)
eloquent (2)
browse (3)
boutique (5)
oblivious (8)

Suggested Writing Assignment

Write a letter to your school or local newspaper in which you express your displeasure with a recent occurrence or situation. Assume one of the following tones for your letter, making sure that it is appropriate for your particular subject, purpose, and audience.

understanding
forceful but rational
sarcastic
irate
objective

Nobel Prize Acceptance Speech

William Faulkner

William Faulkner (1897–1962), one of America's greatest writers, lived for most of his life in Oxford, Mississippi. He is best known for his novels Sartoris *(1929),* The Sound and the Fury *(1929),* As I Lay Dying *(1930),* Sanctuary *(1931),* Light in August *(1932), and* Absalom, Absalom! *(1936). In accepting the 1949 Nobel Prize for Literature, Faulkner made the following speech urging young writers to consider the power of words and to remember the durability of humankind.*

I feel that this award was not made to me as a man, but to my work—a life's work in the agony and sweat of the human spirit, not for glory and least of all for profit, but to create out of the materials of the human spirit something which did not exist before. So this award is only mine in trust. It will not be difficult to find a dedication for the money part of it commensurate with the purpose and significance of its origin. But I would like to do the same with the acclaim too, by using this moment as a pinnacle from which I might be listened to by the young men and women already dedicated to the same anguish and travail, among whom is already that one who will some day stand here where I am standing.

Our tragedy today is a general and universal physical fear so long sustained by now that we can even bear it. There are no longer problems of the spirit. There is only the question: When will I be blown up? Because of this, the young man or woman writing today has forgotten the problems of the human heart in conflict with itself which alone can make good writing because only that is worth writing about, worth the agony and the sweat.

He must learn them again. He must teach himself that the

basest of all things is to be afraid; and, teaching himself that, forget it forever, leaving no room in his workshop for anything but the old verities and truths of the heart, the old universal truths lacking which any story is ephemeral and doomed—love and honor and pity and pride and compassion and sacrifice. Until he does so, he labors under a curse. He writes not of love but of lust, of defeats in which nobody loses anything of value, of victories without hope and, worst of all, without pity or compassion. His griefs grieve on no universal bones, leaving no scars. He writes not of the heart but of the glands.

4 Until he relearns these things, he will write as though he stood among and watched the end of man. I decline to accept the end of man. It is easy enough to say that man is immortal simply because he will endure: that when the last ding-dong of doom has clanged and faded from the last worthless rock hanging tideless in the last red and dying evening, that even then there will still be one more sound: that of his puny inexhaustible voice, still talking. I refuse to accept this. I believe that man will not merely endure: he will prevail. He is immortal, not because he alone among creatures has an inexhaustible voice, but because he has a soul, a spirit capable of compassion and sacrifice and endurance. The poet's, the writer's, duty is to write about these things. It is his privilege to help man endure by lifting his heart, by reminding him of the courage and honor and hope and pride and compassion and pity and sacrifice which have been the glory of his past. The poet's voice need not merely be the record of man, it can be one of the props, the pillars to help him endure and prevail.

Questions for Study and Discussion

1. What advice does Faulkner offer young writers? How would you interpret his last sentence?
2. Besides accepting the Nobel Prize, what is Faulkner's purpose in this speech? (Glossary: *Purpose)*
3. Pointing to specific examples in the speech, describe

Faulkner's tone. Is it cynical? Ironic? Optimistic? Something else? How is his tone appropriate to his purpose?

4. Which particular words and phrases does Faulkner repeat in his speech? How does this repetition strengthen his argument? How does it contribute to the general tone?

Vocabulary

Refer to your dictionary to define the following words as they are used in this selection. Then use each word in a sentence of your own.

commensurate (1)
pinnacle (1)
travail (1)
verities (3)
ephemeral (3)
inexhaustible (4)

Suggested Writing Assignment

Following Faulkner's model, compose a short speech in which you state your view regarding an important contemporary issue. If you like, make a strong emotional appeal to your audience, but be careful not to lose sight of your objective.

9

FIGURATIVE LANGUAGE

Figurative language is language used in an imaginative rather than a literal sense. Although it is most often associated with poetry, figurative language is used widely in our daily speech and in our writing. Prose writers have long known that figurative language not only brings freshness and color to writing, but also helps to clarify ideas.

Two of the most commonly used figures of speech are the simile and the metaphor. A *simile* is an explicit comparison between two essentially different ideas or things that uses the words *like* or *as* to link them.

> Canada geese sweep across the hills and valleys like a formation of strategic bombers.
>
> Benjamin B. Bachman

> I walked toward her and hailed her as a visitor to the moon might salute a survivor of a previous expedition.
>
> John Updike

A *metaphor,* on the other hand, makes an implicit comparison between dissimilar ideas or things without using *like* or *as.*

> She was very old and small and she walked slowly in the dark pine shadows, moving a little from side to side in her steps, with the balanced heaviness and lightness of a pendulum in a grandfather clock.
>
> Eudora Welty

> Charm is the ultimate weapon, the supreme seduction, against which there are few defenses.
>
> Laurie Lee

In order to take full advantage of the richness of a particular comparison, writers sometimes use several sentences or even a whole paragraph to develop a metaphor. Such a comparison is called an *extended metaphor*.

> The point is that you have to strip down your writing before you can build it back up. You must know what the essential tools are and what job they were designed to do. If I may belabor the metaphor on carpentry, it is first necessary to be able to saw wood neatly and to drive nails. Later you can bevel the edges or add elegant finials, if that is your taste. But you can never forget that you are practicing a craft that is based on certain principles. If the nails are weak, your house will collapse. If your verbs are weak and your syntax is rickety, your sentences will fall apart.
>
> William Zinsser

Another frequently used figure of speech is *personification*. In personification the writer attributes human qualities to animals or inanimate objects.

> Blond October comes striding over the hills wearing a crimson shirt and faded green trousers.
>
> Hal Borland

> Indeed, haste can be the assassin of elegance.
>
> T. H. White

In the preceding examples, the writers have, through the use of figurative language, both livened up their prose and given emphasis to their ideas. Keep in mind that figurative language should never be used merely to "dress up" writing; above all, it should help you to develop your ideas and to clarify your meaning for the reader.

The Wilderness

David Perlman

After visiting the Dinosaur National Monument in Utah, newswriter David Perlman joined sportsmen, park advocates, and conservationists in the successful battle against the dam that the Bureau of Reclamation had proposed to construct near the juncture of the Green and Yampa rivers. That victory is seen by many as a milestone in the conservation movement. The following article first appeared in the San Francisco Chronicle *on June 29, 1954. As you read it, pay particular attention to Perlman's use of figurative language as he describes his trip down the Yampa and Green rivers.*

At Big Joe and Tepee Rapids on the Yampa river, and at Moonshine Draw and Sob Rapids on the Green, you hold your breath when the white water breaks. 1

From a few yards away you can see the water boiling and hear its roar as it plunges over hidden rocks, sending spray high and rushing into whirlpools alive with treachery. 2

You can look upward at a thousand feet of canyon wall rising sheer above you; you strain at the oars to keep your bouncing rubber boat headed straight into the seething current. 3

There's no way out of the rapids now—no way to go except straight through. So you hold your breath and make the plunge. 4

The boat bucks like a live animal. Waves break over your bow and the slick, sharp edges of giant boulders rear up like butcher knives. The boat shoots faster and faster, and suddenly the rapids are behind you. It's been a surging, exhilarating thrill; in a moment you breathe again and look ahead to the challenge of the next white water. 5

From Lily Park, in Colorado, to the lower reaches of Split Mountain Gorge, in Utah, is little more than 40 miles, and an airplane can fly over the placid, wooded parks in 10 minutes. But along the rivers that have gouged their way through mountain ranges over millions upon millions of years, the distance is nearer 80 miles, and it has just taken me six days to make the canyon trip by boat.

I accompanied a group from California's Sierra Club. There were college kids along, and elderly men and women, and children as young as 4½. I joined them because the two rivers they were going to see, the Yampa and the Green, are the crux of a great controversy now raging in Congress. These two ancient waterways join in the heart of the Dinosaur National Monument; their waters mingle and then flow southward into the Colorado.

The fight in Congress centers at the confluence of the Yampa and the Green. Here the Bureau of Reclamation is seeking authority to launch a vast water project for the upper Colorado River Basin with a mammoth dam 500 feet high, a dam that would impound the waters of the Yampa and the Green for hydro power and flood control, a dam that would change the living canyon bottoms into a hundred miles of silent reservoir.

Along the Yampa river, not far upstream from the proposed site for Echo Park Dam in Dinosaur National Monument, there is a deep and mysterious stretch of canyon that men call the Grand Overhang.

Its vast sandstone wall reaches upward and outward for hundreds of feet, blotting out even the sky directly overhead. You run your tiny river boat close under this immensity of sandstone, as I did a few days ago, and you find yourself in the most intimate contact with the timeless quality of earth.

It was 200 million years ago that this great overhang was sculptured in the living rock. But its story began far longer ago than that. It began in the dim, pre-Cambrian past when vast seas heaved over the land troughs of the American west.

For age upon countless age the silts and sediments of vanished rivers laid down their deposits in these seas. And the slow cycles of organic birth and death sent a gentle rain of living matter down through the water to cushion the sea bed and add still more immeasurable depths to the rising bottom.

13 Eventually this watery region became a great flat plain, ringed by volcanic mountains and threaded with sluggish rivers. Here, in the boggy fastness of the river borders, lived the dinosaurs of the Mesozoic era, cropping the succulent water plants and preying, at last, on each other.

14 Then the seas moved in again, burying all this early land life and burying, too, the river sediments. And after still more time the seas receded, new rivers coursed across the land, and there began a great revolution that lasted millions of years. It was a mountain-building epoch, and the land slowly became folded, seamed and uplifted as the earth's crust responded to deep, internal pressures.

15 The land rose ponderously, like the back of a brontosaurus heaving itself from a swamp. In a long line, running uniquely from east to west, the Uinta mountains of Colorado and Utah arched higher and higher. The southern flanks of those mountains soared in dizzy escarpments.

16 But oddly enough the rivers of that ancient time clung to their courses, despite the mountain-building revolution. With each upward thrust of the mountains, the rivers bit ever more deeply into the rising land, and etched the spectacular gorges that are now the heart and magnificence of what is called the Dinosaur National Monument.

17 Only a few days ago, at fabled Steamboat Rock, I watched the Green river flow down from the north, still carrying in its waters a heavy burden of silt as it continues to wash and expose the red quartzitic cliffs of the Uinta mountain formations that date back a billion years.

18 On the Yampa, our caravan of boats rowed beneath sheer canyons carved from Morgan sandstones, deep maroon and heavy with fossils, laid down in Pennsylvania times 230-odd million years ago. The rushing current swept us past other cliffs where the red Morgan rocks give way to the brilliant buff-yellow walls of Weber sandstones, a newer formation some 30 million years younger than the Morgan.

19 These are the canyon walls that would cease to exist with

the building of the Echo Park Dam, their panoply of geologic history drowned beneath the fluctuating levels of a reservoir.

Questions for Study and Discussion

1. What is Perlman's attitude toward the proposed Echo Park Dam in Dinosaur National Monument? Why does he attach so much importance to the Grand Overhang?
2. Perlman uses three similes in his essay. Identify them and explain what is being compared in each one.
3. Perlman uses several rhetorical strategies in developing his argument, including description, narration, comparison and contrast, and cause and effect. Locate passages in which each of these rhetorical devices is used. Then tell how each enhances Perlman's argument. (See the discussions under these headings in the Glossary if you are not sure exactly what they mean.)
4. What effect do the italicized words have in each of the following quotations from this selection? How do these words contribute to Perlman's argument? (Glossary: *Connotation/Denotation*)
   a. see the water *boiling* and hear its *roar* (2)
   b. whirlpools alive with *treachery* (2)
   c. the *seething* current (3)
   d. the boat *shoots* faster and faster (5)
   e. change the *living* canyon bottoms into a hundred miles of *silent* reservoir (8)
   f. *etched* the spectacular gorges (16)

Vocabulary

Refer to your dictionary to define the following words as they are used in this selection. Then use each word in a sentence of your own.

sheer (3)
exhilarating (5)
placid (6)
crux (7)
mingle (7)
impound (8)
succulent (13)
ponderously (15)
fluctuating (19)

Suggested Writing Assignment

Write an essay describing one of the places listed below or any other place of your choice. Use at least one simile and one metaphor to clarify and enliven your description.

a factory
a place of worship
a fast-food restaurant
your dormitory
your college library
your favorite place on campus
your hometown

THE INNER GAME OF PINBALL

J. Anthony Lukas

After graduating from Harvard, J. Anthony Lukas became a reporter for the Baltimore Sun *and later a member of the staff of* The New York Times. *In 1968 Lukas was awarded a Pulitzer Prize for local reporting. His articles have appeared in* Harper's, Esquire, New Republic, Reader's Digest, *and* Saturday Review. *In this selection from "The Inner Game of Pinball," first published in* Atlantic Monthly, *Lukas explains why he sees pinball as a metaphor for life.*

Each of us has a game through which he plays out life's conundrums, orders them in some intelligible fashion, and then begins to master them. . . . For me it is pinball. Pinball is a metaphor for life, pitting man's skill, nerve, persistence, and luck against the perverse machinery of human existence. The playfield is rich with rewards: targets that bring huge scores, bright lights, chiming bells, free balls, and extra games. But it is replete with perils, too: culs-de-sac, traps, gutters, and gobble holes down which the ball may disappear forever.

Each pull of the plunger launches the ball into a miniature universe of incalculable possibilities. As the steel sphere hurtles into the ellipse at the top of the playfield, it hangs for a moment in exquisite tension between triumph and disaster. Down one lane lies a hole worth thousands, down another a sickening lurch to oblivion. The ball trembles on the lip, seeming to lean first one way, then the other.

A player is not powerless to control the ball's wild flight, any more than man is powerless to control his own life. He may nudge the machine with hands, arms, or hips, jogging it just enough to change the angle of the ball's descent. And he is armed with "flippers" which can propel the ball back up the playfield, aiming at the targets with the richest payoffs.

But, just as man's boldest strokes and bravest ventures often boomerang, so an ill-timed flip can ricochet the ball straight down "death alley," and a too vigorous nudge will send the machine into "tilt." Winning pinball, like a rewarding life, requires delicate touch, fine calibrations, careful discrimination between boldness and folly.

Questions for Study and Discussion

1. What, in essence, is Lukas' argument?
2. In this extended metaphor Lukas compares life to the game of pinball. What are the specific points of the comparison?
3. Why do you suppose Lukas does not mention any of the dissimilarities between pinball and life?

Vocabulary

Refer to your dictionary to define the following words as they are used in this selection. Then use each word in a sentence of your own.

perverse (1)
replete (1)
hurtles (2)
lurch (2)
ricochet (3)

Suggested Writing Assignment

Describe a memorable experience you have had—one which was especially impressive and influential in your life. Use similes and metaphors to help you capture the essence of that experience. If you like, select one of the following subjects for your description.

an adventurous trip
a family reunion
meeting a famous person
a death in the family
a move to a new home

Notes on Punctuation

Lewis Thomas

Lewis Thomas has had a distinguished career as a physician, administrator, researcher, teacher, and writer. In 1971 he started writing a series of essays for The New England Journal of Medicine, *many of which were collected in* The Lives of a Cell: Notes of a Biology Watcher *(1973). "Notes on Punctuation" is taken from* The Medusa and the Snail, *a second collection of essays which appeared in 1979. In this selection Thomas discusses the meaning and practical value of various marks of punctuation and shows those punctuation marks at work. As you read the selection, note the figurative language Thomas uses to help clarify the meaning of punctuation.*

There are no precise rules about punctuation (Fowler lays out some general advice (as best he can under the complex circumstances of English prose (he points out, for example, that we possess only four stops (the comma, the semicolon, the colon and the period (the question mark and exclamation point are not, strictly speaking, stops; they are indicators of tone (oddly enough, the Greeks employed the semicolon for their question mark (it produces a strange sensation to read a Greek sentence which is a straightforward question: Why weepest thou; (instead of Why weepest thou? (and, of course, there are parentheses (which are surely a kind of punctuation making this whole matter much more complicated by having to count up the left-handed parentheses in order to be sure of closing with the right number (but if the parentheses were left out, with nothing to work with but the stops, we would have considerably more flexibility in the deploying of layers of meaning than if we tried to separate all the clauses by physical barriers (and in the latter case, while we might have more precision and exactitude for our meaning, we would lose the essential flavor of language, which is its wonderful ambiguity)))))))))))).

2 The commas are the most useful and usable of all the stops. It is highly important to put them in place as you go along. If you try to come back after doing a paragraph and stick them in the various spots that tempt you you will discover that they tend to swarm like minnows into all sorts of crevices whose existence you hadn't realized and before you know it the whole long sentence becomes immobilized and lashed up squirming in commas. Better to use them sparingly, and with affection, precisely when the need for each one arises, nicely, by itself.

3 I have grown fond of semicolons in recent years. The semicolon tells you that there is still some question about the preceding full sentence; something needs to be added; it reminds you sometimes of the Greek usage. It is almost always a greater pleasure to come across a semicolon than a period. The period tells you that is that; if you didn't get all the meaning you wanted or expected, anyway you got all the writer intended to parcel out and now you have to move along. But with a semicolon there you get a pleasant little feeling of expectancy; there is more to come; read on; it will get clearer.

4 Colons are a lot less attractive, for several reasons: firstly, they give you the feeling of being rather ordered around, or at least having your nose pointed in a direction you might not be inclined to take if left to yourself, and, secondly, you suspect you're in for one of those sentences that will be labeling the points to be made: firstly, secondly and so forth, with the implication that you haven't sense enough to keep track of a sequence of notions without having them numbered. Also, many writers use this system loosely and incompletely, starting out with number one and number two as though counting off on their fingers but then going on and on without the succession of labels you've been led to expect, leaving you floundering about searching for the ninethly or seventeenthly that ought to be there but isn't.

5 Exclamation points are the most irritating of all. Look! they say, look at what I just said! How amazing is my

thought! It is like being forced to watch someone else's small child jumping up and down crazily in the center of the living room shouting to attract attention. If a sentence really has something of importance to say, something quite remarkable, it doesn't need a mark to point it out. And if it is really, after all, a banal sentence needing more zing, the exclamation point simply emphasizes its banality!

Quotation marks should be used honestly and sparingly, when there is a genuine quotation at hand, and it is necessary to be very rigorous about the words enclosed by the marks. If something is to be quoted, the *exact* words must be used. If part of it must be left out because of space limitations, it is good manners to insert three dots to indicate the omission, but it is unethical to do this if it means connecting two thoughts which the original author did not intend to have tied together. Above all, quotation marks should not be used for ideas that you'd like to disown, things in the air so to speak. Nor should they be put in place around clichés; if you want to use a cliché you must take full responsibility for it yourself and not try to fob it off on anon., or on society. The most objectionable misuse of quotation marks, but one which illustrates the dangers of misuse in ordinary prose, is seen in advertising, especially in advertisements for small restaurants, for example "just around the corner," or "a good place to eat." No single, identifiable, citable person ever really said, for the record, "just around the corner," much less "a good place to eat," least likely of all for restaurants of the type that use this type of prose.

The dash is a handy device, informal and essentially playful, telling you that you're about to take off on a different tack but still in some way connected with the present course—only you have to remember that the dash is there, and either put a second dash at the end of the notion to let the reader know that he's back on course, or else end the sentence, as here, with a period.

The greatest danger in punctuation is for poetry. Here it is necessary to be as economical and parsimonious with commas and periods as with the words themselves, and any marks that seem to carry their own subtle meanings, like dashes and little rows of periods, even semicolons and question marks, should be left out altogether rather than inserted to clog up the thing with ambiguity. A single exclamation point in a poem, no matter what else the poem has to say, is enough to destroy the whole work.

The things I like best in T. S. Eliot's poetry, especially in the *Four Quartets*, are the semicolons. You cannot hear them, but they are there, laying out the connections between the images and the ideas. Sometimes you get a glimpse of a semicolon coming, a few lines farther on, and it is like climbing a steep path through woods and seeing a wooden bench just at a bend in the road ahead, a place where you can expect to sit for a moment, catching your breath. 9

Commas can't do this sort of thing; they can only tell you how the different parts of a complicated thought are to be fitted together, but you can't sit, not even take a breath, just because of a comma, 10

Questions for Study and Discussion

1. What point does Thomas make about punctuation in this essay?
2. Point out the four similes that Thomas uses in this selection. What is being compared in each? Why is each comparison appropriate?
3. In paragraph 5 Thomas personifies—attributes human qualities to—exclamation points. What other examples of personification can you find in the essay? Why is this figure of speech especially appropriate in this essay? How does it help Thomas to make his point?
4. Why do you suppose Thomas elected to use figurative language in an essay on punctuation?
5. While explaining the function of each mark of punctuation, Thomas writes in a manner that allows him to use that mark of punctuation. This is an example of illustration. When did you become aware of this strategy? Did it help you to better understand

and appreciate the uses of punctuation? If so, how? (Glossary: *Illustration*)

Vocabulary

Refer to your dictionary to define the following words as they are used in this selection. Then use each word in a sentence of your own.

deploying (1)
ambiguity (1)
parcel out (3)
floundering (4)
banal (5)

Suggested Writing Assignment

Write a short essay in which you discuss a favorite subject (for example, movies, politics, traveling, nature, sports, cooking). Make use of figurative language—similes, metaphors, personification—as you describe the precise nature of your feelings about that subject.

III

TYPES OF ESSAYS

10

ILLUSTRATION

Illustration is the use of examples to make ideas more concrete and to make generalizations more specific and detailed. Examples enable writers not just to tell but to show what they mean. For example, an essay about recently developed alternative sources of energy becomes clear and interesting with the use of some examples—say, solar energy or the heat from the earth's core. The more specific the example, the more effective it is. Along with general statements about solar energy, the writer might offer several examples of how the home building industry is installing solar collectors instead of conventional hot water systems, or building solar greenhouses to replace conventional central heating.

In an essay a writer uses examples to clarify or support the thesis; in a paragraph, to clarify or support the main idea. Sometimes a single striking example suffices; sometimes a whole series of related examples is necessary. The following paragraph presents a single extended example—an anecdote, or story—that illustrates the author's point about cultural differences:

> Whenever there is a great cultural distance between two people, there are bound to be problems arising from differences in behavior and expectations. An example is the American couple who consulted a psychiatrist about their marital problems. The husband was from New England and had been brought up by reserved parents who taught him to control his emotions and to respect the need for privacy. His wife was from an Italian family and had been brought up in close contact with all the members of her large family, who were extremely warm, volatile and demonstrative. When the husband came home after a hard day at the office, dragging his feet and longing for peace and quiet, his wife

> would rush to him and smother him. Clasping his hands, rubbing his brow, crooning over his weary head, she never left him alone. But when the wife was upset or anxious about her day, the husband's response was to withdraw completely and leave her alone. No comforting, no affectionate embrace, no attention—just solitude. The woman became convinced her husband didn't love her and, in desperation, she consulted a psychiatrist. Their problem wasn't basically psychological but cultural.
>
> Edward T. Hall

This single example is effective because it is *representative*—that is, essentially similar to other such problems he might have described and familiar to many readers. Hall tells the story with enough detail that readers can understand the couple's feelings and so better understand the point he is trying to make.

In contrast, Edwin Way Teale supports his topic sentence about country superstitions with eleven examples:

> In the folklore of the country, numerous superstitions relate to winter weather. Back-country farmers examine their corn husks—the thicker the husk, the colder the winter. They watch the acorn crop—the more acorns, the more severe the season. They observe where white-faced hornets place their paper nests—the higher they are, the deeper will be the snow. They examine the size and shape and color of the spleens of butchered hogs for clues to the severity of the season. They keep track of the blooming of dogwood in the spring—the more abundant the blooms, the more bitter the cold in January. When chipmunks carry their tails high and squirrels have heavier fur and mice come into country houses early in the fall, the superstitious gird themselves for a long, hard winter. Without any scientific basis, a wider-than-usual black band on a woolly-bear caterpillar is accepted as a sign that winter will arrive early and stay late. Even the way a cat sits beside the stove carries its message to the credulous. According to a belief once widely held in the Ozarks, a cat sitting with its tail to the fire indicates very cold weather is on the way.
>
> Edwin Way Teale

Teale uses numerous examples because he is writing about various superstitions. Also, putting all those strange beliefs side by side in a kind of catalogue makes the paragraph fun to read as well as informative.

Illustration is often found in effective writing; nearly every essay in this book contains one or more examples. Likewise this introduction has used examples to clarify its points about illustration.

That Astounding Creator—Nature

Jean George

Jean George is the author of many books, including My Side of the Mountain *(1967),* Julie of the Wolves *(1972), and* The American Walk Book *(1979). She is a roving reporter for* Reader's Digest *and a contributor to such magazines as* National Wildlife, Audubon, *and* National Geographic. *In the following selection she offers several fascinating and little known examples to illustrate her main points.*

A bird that eats feathers, a mammal that never drinks, a fish that grows a fishing line and worm on its head to catch other fish. Creatures in a nightmare? No, they are very much with us as co-inhabitants of this earth.

Nature has fashioned most animals to fit the many faces of the land—moose to marshes, squirrels to trees, camels to deserts, frogs to lily pads. Give nature an environment or situation and she will evolve a creature, adapting a toe here, an eye there, until the being fits the niche. As a result of this hammering and fitting, however, some really unbelievable creatures circle the sun with us.

One summer in Maine I saw a sleek mother horned grebe herding her three bobbing young to supper among the green pickerelweed. Suddenly I noticed through my binoculars that she was feeding her babies quantities of feathers from a deserted duck's nest. As she stuffed the dry feathers into the gaping mouths, she made two or three pokes to get each one down. Finally she worked a dozen or so down her own throat; then, sailing low on the water, she vanished contentedly among the plants.

I later learned that 60 percent of the grebe's diet is

feathers. When I asked why, a biologist from the U.S. Fish and Wildlife Service answered, "Because nature finds a use for everything. Feathers seem to act as a strainer to prevent fishbones from entering and damaging the intestines."

5 Australia has many strange beasts, one of the oddest of which is the koala. Perfectly adapted to one specific tree, the eucalyptus, this living teddy bear does not need anything else, not even a drink! The moisture in the leaves is just right for the koala, making it the only land animal that doesn't need water to supplement its food.

6 The creature with the fishing line on its head was created for the dark canyons of the sea. Here food is so scarce that the deep-sea angler fish which preys on smaller fish, grew a line, and an appendage on the end that wiggles like a worm. This catches the attention of the occasional passerby. A fish approaches the bait, and the toothy angler swirls up and swallows him.

7 The gigantic ocean bottom creates other problems. A male angler fish could swim for years without meeting a female of his own species. Nature's solution to this problem is for the female to carry a dwarfed husband tightly fused to her body. Marine biologists believe that this nuptial begins when the eggs first hatch and there are many fry of both sexes. A male then grabs hold of a female with his mouth and hangs on until he has literally become a part of her. His mouth becomes fused to her stomach, and for the rest of his life the male remains attached to his mate, marking the most amazing union on earth.

8 Sound has shaped the bodies of many beasts. Noise tapped away at the bullfrog until his ears became bigger than his eyes. Now he hears so well that at the slightest sound of danger he quickly plops to safety under a sunken leaf. The rabbit has long ears to hear the quiet "whoosh" of the owl's wings, while the grasshopper's ears are on the base of his abdomen, the lowest point of his body, where he can detect the tread of a crow's foot or the stealthy approach of a shrew.

9 Sometimes food will determine an animal's appearance. Earthworms have shaped the woodcock, a snipelike bird of the forest floor. This creature has a long narrow bill that

looks like a pencil and fits neatly into the burrows of the worms. But the bill has its disadvantages; with it buried deep in a worm hole the woodcock is vulnerable to attack from above. The counteract this danger the woodcock has eyes near the top of his head. This singular device permits him to scan the trees for danger even when his beak is buried. A successful arrangement for longevity—but it certainly creates an odd-looking creature.

The need to catch elusive prey has evolved some staggering biological tricks. The sea anemone, a flowerlike animal of the tidemark, is usually riveted to one spot; yet it feeds on darting fish. A diabolically clever trap was necessary to catch them, so the anemone developed tentacles with bombs in the end of each. When a fish forages into these tentacles the ends shoot a thin thread into the fish's body. The thread in turn explodes a paralyzing poison. The stunned fish is hauled in by the tentacles and shoved into the anemone's gullet.

Nature seems to have gone all out in creating preposterous gadgets for self-defense. The jacana, a bird of the American tropics, for instance, is endowed with spurs which unfold like a switchblade at the bend of the bird's wings and with which he can slash his enemies to shreds.

Lizards are professionals in the art of warding off attack. The two-headed skink, whose tail is shaped like his head, confuses his enemy. A hawk, upon attacking this fellow, anticipates that he will run in the direction of the lifted head and make allowance for the movement. However, the bird usually strikes nothing, for he is aiming at the tail. The real head took off the other way.

In order to travel in a hostile world, the Portuguese man-of-war first mastered the art of floating. To do this it evolved a purple bag and inflated it with gas from a special gland. As a crowning idea it also grew a sail! Launched, the man-of-war can blow away from enemies or approach food by putting its sail up and down. When severely threatened, it forces the gas out of the float and submerges.

There is hardly any environment, however hostile, that some creature has not mastered. Land is, of course, the nemesis of the fish. If they flop out on it they die. If their ponds dry up, they are helpless. Given this situation, it was almost certain that some fish would evolve a way to beat it; and so there is a lungfish. It is an air breather and must come to the surface every 20 minutes or so; otherwise it drowns. When the ponds of Africa dry up in the arid season, the lungfish wrap themselves in mud and wait it out, sometimes for years. When the rains finally return, they resume their water life.

15 Just as nature adds things on creatures that need them, so she occasionally takes things away from those that don't. The adult Mayfly, for example, has no mouth or stomach. Last year, by a northern New York lake, I found myself amid hundreds of thousands of these insects. I told the conservation officer whom I was with that I was glad they didn't bite. He replied that they have no mouths to bite with. "An adult Mayfly lives but one day," he explained, "and that day is devoted entirely to pleasure. They do nothing but dance and mate all their short life, and so they do not need a mouth."

16 With all this elaborate evolution, it is not surprising that some of nature's inventions got out of hand. Into this category falls the speedometer of reindeer. A tendon snaps back and forth over a bone in the reindeer's foot, noisily tapping out the speed of his gait. Useless. And so is the nose on the stomach of the scorpion and the featherlike tongue of the toucan, a bird of Africa.

17 But probably the most dumbfounding of nature's extraordinary creations is the horned toad of our Southwest. A herpetologist once invited me to observe one of these lizards right after it had molted. In a sand-filled glass cage I saw a large male. Beside him lay his old skin. The herpetologist began to annoy the beast with mock attacks, and the old man of the desert with his vulnerable new suit became frightened. Suddenly his eyeballs reddened. A final fast lunge from my friend at the beast and I froze in astonishment—a fine spray of blood shot from the lizard's eye, like fire from a dragon! The beast had struck back with a weapon so shocking that it terrifies even the fiercest enemy.

18 Later I walked home, pondering the bizarre methods for

survival with which evolution has endowed earth's creatures, sometimes comical, sometimes pathetic. I knew the biologists were right: If any adaptation is possible, nature has tried it.

Questions for Study and Discussion

1. What is Jean George's thesis, or main point, in this essay? Where is it stated?
2. What is the relationship of paragraphs 3–6 to paragraph 1?
3. What examples does the author use to support the topic sentence of paragraph 7? of paragraphs 10 and 14?
4. How are paragraphs 11–13 related? How has the author unified them? (Glossary: *Unity*)

Vocabulary

Refer to your dictionary to define the following words as they are used in this selection. Then use each word in a sentence of your own.

fashioned (2)	tentacles (10)
niche (2)	arid (14)
stealthy (8)	dumbfounding (17)
longevity (9)	pathetic (18)

Suggested Writing Assignment

Most paragraphs in this essay have a clear topic sentence and several supporting examples. Using these paragraphs as models, select one of the following topic sentences and develop it with examples of your own.

Violence is a common element in successful movies.

College students should/should not participate in community projects.

Patriotism means more than mom and apple pie.

Fraternities and sororities are/are not an important part of campus life.

Television is/is not educational.

ONE ENVIRONMENT, MANY WORLDS

Judith and Herbert Kohl

Herbert Kohl is a teacher and the author of The Open Classroom *(1970);* Thirty-Six Children *(1973);* Reading, How To *(1974); and* On Teaching *(1976). Also a teacher, Judith Kohl is a student of animal behavior and archaeology. In the following selection from their book* The View from the Oak *(1977), the Kohls give one extended example as an illustration of their belief that no two creatures view their environment in exactly the same way.*

Our dog Sandy is a golden retriever. He sits in front of our house all day waiting for someone to come by and throw him a stick. Chasing sticks or tennis balls and bringing them back is the major activity in his life. If you pick up a stick or ball to throw, he acts quite strangely. He looks at the way your body is facing and as soon as you throw something, he runs in the direction you seemed to throw it. He doesn't look at what you threw. His head is down and he charges, all ears. If your stick lands in a tree or on a roof, he acts puzzled and confused. He runs to the sound of the falling stick and sometimes gets so carried away that he will crash into a person or tree in the way as he dashes to the place he hears the stick fall. As he gets close, his nose takes over and smells the odor of your hand on the stick.

Once we performed an experiment to see how sensitive Sandy's nose really was. We were on a beach that was full of driftwood. There was one particular pile that must have had hundreds of sticks. We picked up one stick, walked away from the pile and then threw it back into the pile. It was impossible for us to tell with any certainty which stick we had originally chosen. So many of them looked alike to us that the best we could do was pick out seven sticks which resembled the one that had been thrown.

We tried the same thing with Sandy, only before throwing the stick we carved an X on it. Then we threw it, not once but a dozen times into the pile. Each time he brought back that stick. Once we pretended to throw the stick and he charged the driftwood pile without noticing that one of us still had the stick. He circled the pile over and over, dug out sticks, became agitated but wouldn't bring another stick. It wasn't the shape or the size or look of the stick that he used to pick it out from all the others. It was the smell we left on the stick. 3

It is hard to imagine, but for dogs every living creature has its own distinctive smell. Each person can be identified by the smell left on things. Each of us gives off a particular combination of chemicals. We can detect the smell of sweat, but even when we are not sweating, we are giving off smells that senses finer than ours can detect. 4

The noses of people have about five million cells that sense smell. Dogs' noses have anywhere from 125 to 300 million cells. Moreover, these cells are closer to the surface than are cells in our noses, and more active. It has been estimated that dogs such as Sandy have noses that are a million times more sensitive than ours. Clothes we haven't worn for weeks, places we've only touched lightly indicate our presence to dogs. Whenever Sandy is left alone in the house, on our return we find him surrounded by our sweaters, coats, handkerchiefs, shirts. He surrounds himself with our smell as if to convince himself that we still exist and will return. 5

His ears are also remarkable. He can hear sounds that humans can't and at distances which are astonishing. It is hard for us to know and understand that world. Most of us don't realize that no two people's hands smell the same. Our ears are not the tuned direction finders his are. It takes a major leap of the imagination to understand and feel the world the way he does, to construct a complicated way of dealing with reality using such finely tuned smell and hearing. Yet his world is no more or less real than ours. His world and ours fit together in some ways and overlap in places. We have the advantage of being able to imagine what his experience is like, though he probably doesn't think too 6 much about how we see the world. From observing and trying to experience things through his ears and nose we can learn about hidden worlds around us and understand behavior that otherwise might seem strange or silly.

The environment is the world that all living things share. It is what is—air, fire, wind, water, life, sometimes culture. The environment consists of all the things that act and are acted upon. Living creatures are born into the environment and are part of it too. Yet there is no creature who perceives all of what is and what happens. Sandy perceives things we can't, and we perceive and understand many things beyond his world. For a dog like Sandy a book isn't much different than a stick, whereas for us one stick is pretty much like every other stick. There is no one world experienced by all living creatures. Though we all live in the same environment, we make many worlds.

Questions for Study and Discussion

1. What point do the Kohls make in this essay, and where is it stated? (Glossary: *Thesis*)
2. What distinction do they make between the words *environment* and *world*?
3. Why do you suppose the authors use exemplification to make their point?
4. How does the Kohls' use of examples give unity to their essay? (Glossary: *Unity*)

Vocabulary

Refer to your dictionary to define the following words as they are used in this selection. Then use each word in a sentence of your own.

agitated (3)
perceive (7)

Suggested Writing Assignment

Using the Kohls' statement "Though we all live in the same environment, we make many worlds" as your topic sentence, write an essay supporting this thesis with examples from your own experience. For instance, how is your world different from that of your parents, teachers, friends, or roommates?

At War with the System

Enid Nemy

Born in Winnipeg, Canada, Enid Nemy has had an active career in journalism. She worked as a reporter and an editor for Canadian newspapers before joining The New York Times *in 1963. At the* Times *she writes "New Yorkers, Etc.," an award-winning column devoted to New York City's people and events. Notice the author's use of examples in the following account of a professor's single-handed war with the business world.*

Business beware!

Do NOT trifle with Prof. David Klein.

Professor Klein looks like a nice, upper middle-class type. Most of the time he is. Sometimes he's not. Nice, that is.

"I behave reasonably outrageously by current standards," he admits without a hint of hedging or shilly-shallying.

Professor Klein has no middle-class hang-ups. He doesn't care about his credit rating (although it's still impeccable); he doesn't give a hoot whether business organizations and their employees think he's cheap or crazy, or both, and he isn't a bit abashed about making a scene, as long as the scene is quiet and well-bred.

Professor Klein is at war with the system "and if more people did what I do, business practices might improve," he said.

A distinguished looking man with a serious mien, twinkling eyes and a Vandyke beard, Mr. Klein began his campaign three or four years ago "when things began to deteriorate."

Take, for instance, one of his early experiences—a mere skirmish, but enough to whet the appetite.

The professor arrived at the Queen Elizabeth Hotel in Montreal after a tiring air trip and was told that his confirmed reservation could not be honored. There wasn't a room available. Sorry.

10 "I will give you three minutes to find me a room," he told the clerk quietly but firmly. "After three minutes, I am going to undress in the lobby, put on my pajamas and go to sleep on one of the sofas."

11 He got a room. He also got a lot of cheers and pats on the back from scores of other men waiting for overbooked rooms.

12 "But," Professor Klein recalled, a little sadly, "none of them would go ahead and do the same thing. I think I made my point in a reasonable, courteous way, but I also took a no-nonsense approach."

13 More recently, Mr. Klein, who has a master's degree from Columbia University, and is a professor of social science and human development at Michigan State University, has had several run-ins with retail operations. As a result, he has evolved his own charge system. He bills the store for any time he spends clearing up errors they have made on his orders or his account.

14 The current Klein rate is $10 a letter, a reasonable fee, he points out, when one considers not only his time but such expenses as photocopying checks that have already been cashed. Telephone calls are billed at $2 each. The fee scale is pre-inflation and is open to adjustment.

15 "I simply deduct the amount from my monthly charge account bill," he explained. "I add the total amount of time spent on letters and telephone calls when I'm billed incorrectly, or if orders come incomplete, or if merchandise is unsatisfactory.

16 "The complaint system has always struck me as terribly one-sided," he continued. "The store has people to handle complaints, and these people not only get paid to handle them but the basic cost of the department is added to the merchandise. The customer is not only paying a higher cost for everything because of store errors, but he or she is also expected to spend time writing or telephoning to clear up something that should never have happened in the first place."

17 The last time Professor Klein was put in the position of

clearing up a complaint (one letter, three telephone calls) he deducted $15 from his bill at the end of the month. He knew what would happen, because he had had a similar reaction before.

A store representative telephoned, and the following conversation ensued:

Professor Klein: "Miss X, are you being paid by your employer to make this call?"

Miss X: "Well, yes."

Professor Klein: "Well, I'm not, so you will understand why I am not motivated to continue it. Goodbye."

Professor Klein figures that there are three courses of action the store might take, and as far as he is concerned, it doesn't matter which one they choose.

"If they want to sue me, fine," he said, cheerfully. "If they want to cancel my charge account, fine. And if they want to cancel my debt and give me back a zero balance, fine. They have a choice."

To date, the several stores that have encountered the Klein method of retaliation have, eventually, deducted his "fee" from the amount owed them.

"I do this as much as a matter of principle as a matter of making money," the professor said.

"A lot of middle-class people live in terror of being considered cheap," he said. "I don't worry about that. A lot of my solid middle-class friends say 'how do you dare do it . . . you'll ruin your credit rating.' They think that the least little cross-eyed look will ruin your credit rating. The fact is that a credit rating isn't as delicate as all that."

Professor Klein has several other antisystem, antiannoyance strategies. Among them are the following:

¶When buying an expensive item in a retail establishment that honors credit cards, he will hold up both his credit card and his checkbook and ask if the store will give him a three percent discount for cash. "They do," he said.

¶When unsolicited junk mail arrives, with a stamped reply card or envelope enclosed, he returns the card or envelope with his label stuck on it. The label reads: "This represents my effort to discourage unsolicited junk mail by increasing its cost to the sender." He had 1,000 labels printed for $1, but is somewhat discouraged because the volume of unsolicited mail continues unabated. "They can't read," he lamented.

¶He rarely pays cash for airline tickets because "if I put them on my credit card, it usually takes three or four months for the bill to arrive, and I can be earning interest on that money . . . no wonder Pan American is in trouble." 30

"One of the few nice things about being middle- or upper middle-class is that you have an enormous amount of clout," he said. "If people used it in the right way, they could make enormous changes in retailing, and in other practices." 31

Questions for Study and Discussion

1. What is Professor Klein's message to the American consumer?
2. Besides charging retailers for his services, what other "antisystem, antiannoyance strategies" does Klein suggest?
3. In paragraphs 9–12 Nemy recounts Klein's experiences at the Queen Elizabeth Hotel. What purpose does this example serve in the essay?
4. Consider the example presented in paragraphs 17–21. What is the relationship between this example and the material in paragraphs 13–16?

Vocabulary

Refer to your dictionary to define the following words as they are used in this selection. Then use each word in a sentence of your own.

hedging (4)	retaliation (24)
impeccable (5)	unsolicited (29)
ensued (18)	clout (31)

Suggested Writing Assignment

Using one of the following statements as your topic sentence, write an essay giving examples from personal experience or from reading to support your opinion.

Consumers have more power than they realize.

Most products do/do not measure up to the claims of their advertisements.

Religion is/is not alive and well.

Government works far better than its critics claim.

Being able to write well is more than a basic skill.

THIS IS PROGRESS?

Alan L. Otten

After graduating from the Columbia University School of Journalism, Alan Otten joined the staff of The Wall Street Journal, *where during the seventies he wrote the weekly column "Politics and People." In 1978 the* Journal *appointed Otten European Bureau Chief in London. In "This is Progress?" Otten provides an extensive array of examples to support his view that progress is not made without some unexpected side effects.*

A couple I know checked into one of the new Detroit hotels a few months ago and, in due course, left a 7 a.m. wake-up call. 1

Being an early riser, however, the husband was up long before 7, and decided he'd go down to breakfast and let his wife sleep late. He dialed the hotel switchboard, explained the situation, and said he'd like to cancel the wake-up call. 2

"Sorry, sir," the answer came, "but we can't do that. It's in the computer, and there's no way to get it out now." 3

Consider another story. A while back, a reporter phoned a congressional committee and asked to speak to the staff director. Unfortunately, he was told, the staff director wouldn't be in that morning; there'd been a power failure at his home. Well, the reporter persisted, that was certainly too bad, but just why did a power failure prevent him from coming to work? 4

"He can't get his car out of the garage," the secretary explained. "The garage doors are electrically controlled." 5

As these two anecdotes suggest, this is a column in praise of progress: those wonderful advances in science and technology that leave the world only slightly more snafued than before. 6

The balance sheet will eschew such common complaints 7

as the way the modern office grinds to a halt whenever the copying machine is out of order. Or the computerized magazine subscription lists that take only four times longer than formerly to effect changes of address and which start mailing renewal notices six months before the subscription expires and then continue at weekly intervals.

Or the form letters that provide The New Yorker with so many droll end-of-the-column items, like the letter that was sent to the "News Desk, Wall Street Journal," and led off, "Dear Mr. Desk . . . ." Or the new drugs, operations and health regimens that in due time are shown to be more dangerous than the illnesses.

Computers bulk centrally in many of the "this is progress?" stories. For instance, a friend recently went to make a deposit at her local bank in upstate New York. The deposit couldn't be accepted, she was informed, "because it's raining too hard." Seems that when the rain gets beyond a certain intensity, the wires transmitting the message from the branch banks to the computer at the main bank in Albany send jumbled signals—and so branch-bank operations have to be suspended temporarily.

Every newspaper person knows that each technological advance in the printing process somehow makes news deadlines earlier, rather than later as might logically be assumed. Computers, though, can foul things up in other ways, too. At a recent conference on press coverage of presidential campaigns, many participants suggested that the lengthy background stories prepared early in the campaign by the wire services or such special news services as those of The New York Times and Washington Post might be saved by subscribing papers and then used late in the campaign, when the public was more in the mood to pay attention.

"Are you kidding?" demanded a publisher present. "That stuff now all comes in computerized, and it's erased at the end of the day. We don't save any copy any more."

Computers aren't the only villains, to be sure. Everyone has observed bizarre scenes of a dozen people down on hands and knees searching the pavement or the grass or a tennis court for a lost contact lens. The other day, however, a colleague announced she was having trouble seeing out of one eye and was off to the optometrist's. About a half hour later, she was back, giggling. The night before, she had apparently put one contact lens on top of another in the case where she kept an extra lens, and had that morning unwittingly put two lenses in one eye.

13 During last winter's snow storms, the Amtrak Metroliners frequently had to be removed from service as snow clogged the motors so cleverly mounted underneath the new high-speed trains. (The cars are now beginning to be converted to a different motor-mounting scheme.) A number of high schools in this area have been built with windows that don't open; when the air conditioning fails on a hot spring or fall day, students are given the day off. Last fall, when the nation moved back to standard time, a young friend was appalled to find she was going to have to turn her time-and-date digital wristwatch ahead 30 days and 23 hours.

14 Still another acquaintance had his car battery go dead while his power windows were rolled down—and then the rains came and poured in while he was parked alongside the highway waiting for help.

15 Society's rush to credit cards has its convenient aspects—but also unpleasant ones. Just try to check into a hotel announcing that you prefer to pay cash rather than use a credit card. Scorn, suspicion, hostility, un-American, if not downright communistic.

16 Once upon a time, you could look up at the postmark on a letter and see exactly where and when it had been processed at the post office.

17 Now, not only does the postmark deny you some or all of this occasionally useful information, but it insists on selling you something instead: "National Guard Month—Gain Skills By Serving" or "Save Energy—Turn Off Lights."

18 And like most creations of American ingenuity, this, too, has been exported to less fortunate lands. A letter from Belgium the other day carried the exhortatory postmark: *"Prévenez l'Hypertension. Evitez le Sel."** In case your French wasn't up to it, there was a drawing of a salt shaker.

19 In all likelihood, corrective measures are being developed

*"Prevent high blood pressure. Avoid salt."

for many of the problems described above, and helpful correspondents will be writing in to tell me all about it. Yet I remain confident that new examples will come along to fill the gap. After all, that's progress.

Questions for Study and Discussion

1. The title of this essay is "This Is Progress?" What does the title relate about the main point of the essay? What is the main point? What does the question mark in the title indicate about the author's attitude toward his thesis?
2. In paragraphs 1–5 Otten tells the story of a couple in a Detroit hotel and the story of the staff director of a congressional committee who could not get his car out of the garage. Why do you think Otten opens with these anecdotes? Do you think they serve as a good opening? Can you think of any other way to begin this essay?
3. Otten provides many "this is progress?" examples. How does he organize these examples? How does he introduce his examples? How does he move from one example to another? (Glossary: *Organization* and *Transitions*)
4. How would you characterize Otten's tone in this essay? What in the essay leads you to your conclusion? (Glossary: *Tone*)

Vocabulary

Refer to your dictionary to define the following words as they are used in this selection. Then use each word in a sentence of your own.

anecdotes (6)
eschew (7)
droll (8)
regimens (8)
bizarre (12)
unwittingly (12)
appalled (13)

Suggested Writing Assignment

Do you agree or disagree with Otten's point of view in this essay? Write an essay explaining your position with examples from your own experience.

11

NARRATION

To *narrate* is to tell a story or to tell what happened. Whenever you relate an incident or use an anecdote to make a point, you use narration. In its broadest sense, narration is any account of an event or series of events. Although most often associated with fiction, narration is effective and useful in all kinds of writing.

Good narration has four essential features: a clear context, well-chosen details, a logical, often chronological organization, and an appropriate and consistent point of view. Consider, for example, the following paragraph from Willie Morris' "On a Commuter Train":

> One afternoon in late August, as the summer's sun streamed into the [railroad] car and made little jumping shadows on the windows, I sat gazing out at the tenement-dwellers, who were themselves looking out of their windows from the gray crumbling buildings along the tracks of upper Manhattan. As we crossed into the Bronx, the train unexpectedly slowed down for a few miles. Suddenly from out of my window I saw a large crowd near the tracks, held back by two policemen. Then, on the other side from my window, I saw a sight I would never be able to forget: a little boy almost severed in halves, lying at an incredible angle near the track. The ground was covered with blood, and the boy's eyes were opened wide, strained and disbelieving in his sudden oblivion. A policeman stood next to him, his arms folded, staring straight ahead at the windows of our train. In the orange glow of late afternoon the policemen, the crowd, the corpse of the boy were for a brief moment immobile, motionless, a small tableau to violence and death in the city. Behind me, in the next row of seats, there was a game of bridge. I heard one of the four men say as he looked out at the sight, "God, that's horrible." Another said, in a whisper, "Terrible,

> terrible." There was a momentary silence, punctuated only by the clicking of the wheels on the track. Then, after the pause, I heard the first man say: "Two hearts."
>
> Willie Morris

This paragraph contains all the elements of good narration. At the beginning Morris establishes a clear context for his narrative, telling when, where, and to whom the action happened. He has chosen details well, including enough detail so that we know what is happening but not so much that we become overwhelmed, confused, or bored. Morris organizes his narration logically, with a beginning that sets the scene, a middle that paints the picture, and an end that makes his point, all arranged chronologically. Finally, he tells the story from the first-person point of view: We experience the event directly through the writer's eyes and ears, as if we too had been on the scene of the action.

Morris could have told his story from the third-person point of view. In this point of view, the narrator is not a participant in the action, and does not use the pronoun *I*. In the following example, William Allen White narrates his daughter's fatal accident:

> The last hour of her life was typical of its happiness. She came home from a day's work at school, topped off by a hard grind with the copy on the High School Annual, and felt that a ride would refresh her. She climbed into her khakis, chattering to her mother about the work she was doing, and hurried to get her horse and be out on the dirt roads for the country air and the radiant green fields of the spring. As she rode through the town on an easy gallop she kept waving at passers-by. She knew everyone in town. For a decade the little figure with the long pig-tail and the red hair ribbon has been familiar on the streets of Emporia, and she got in the way of speaking to those who nodded at her. She passed the Kerrs, walking the horse, in front of the Normal Library, and waved at them; passed another friend a few hundred feet further on, and waved at her. The horse was walking and, as she turned into North Merchant street she took off her cowboy hat, and the horse swung into a lope. She passed the Tripletts and waved her

cowboy hat at them, still moving gaily north on Merchant street. A Gazette carrier passed—a High School boy friend—and she waved at him, but with her bridle hand: the horse veered quickly, plunged into the parking where the low-hanging limb faced her, and, while she still looked back waving, the blow came. But she did not fall from the horse; she slipped off, dazed a bit, staggered and fell in a faint. She never quite recovered consciousness.

William Allen White

Big White

Skip Rozin

Having worked as a newspaper reporter and sportswriter, Skip Rozin became a free-lance writer in 1971. His work has appeared in Harper's *and* Audubon *magazines, as well as in* The New York Times. *In 1979 Rozin published his first book,* One Step From Glory, *the story of athletes who never succeeded in professional sports. In "Big White," Rozin tells the story of his frustrating battle with a vending machine with a mind of its own. As you read the essay, pay particular attention to the sequence of events in Rozin's narrative.*

A strange calm settled over me as I stood before the large white vending machine and dropped a quarter into the appropriate slot. I listened as the coin clunked into register. Then I pressed the button marked "Hot Chocolate." From deep inside a paper cup slid down a chute, crackling into place on a small metal rack. Through an unseen tube poured coffee, black as night and smoking hot. 1

I even smiled as I moved to my customary place at the last table, sat down, and gazed across to the white machine, large and clean and defiant. Not since it had been moved in between the candy machine and the sandwich machine had I known peace. Every morning for two weeks I had selected a beverage, and each time the machine dispensed something different. When I pushed the button for hot chocolate, black coffee came out. When I pushed the button for tea with sugar, coffee with half and half came out. So the cup of coffee before me was no surprise. It was but one final test; my plan had already been laid. 2

Later in the day, after everyone else had left the building, I returned to the snack bar, a yellow legal pad in my hand and 3 a fistful of change in my pocket. I approached the machine and, taking each button in order, began feeding in quarters. After the first quarter I pressed the button labeled "Black Coffee." Tea with sugar came out, and I recorded that on the first line of my pad. I dropped in a second quarter and pressed the button for coffee with sugar. Plain tea came out, and I wrote that down.

I pressed all nine of the buttons, noting what came out. Then I placed each cup on the table behind me. When I had gone through them all, I repeated the process, and was delighted to find the machine dispensing the same drinks as before.

None was what I had ordered, but each error was consistent with my list.

I was thrilled. To celebrate, I decided to purchase a fresh cup of chocolate.

Dropping in two dimes and a nickel and consulting my pad, I pressed the "Coffee with Sugar and Half and Half" button. The machine clicked in response, and a little cup slid down the chute, bouncing as it hit bottom. But that was all. Nothing else happened. No hot chocolate poured into my cup. No black coffee came down. Nothing.

I was livid. I forced five nickels into the slot and punched the button for black coffee. A cup dropped into place, but nothing more. I put five more nickels in and pushed another button, and another cup dropped down—empty. I dug into my pocket for more change, but found only three dimes. I forced them in, and got back a stream of hot water and a nickel change. I went berserk.

"White devil!" I screamed as I slammed my fists against the machine's clean enamel finish. "You white devil!"

I beat on the buttons and rammed the coin-return rod down. I wanted the machine to know what pain was. I slapped at its metal sides and kicked its base with such force that I could almost hear the bone in my foot crack, then wheeled in agony on my good foot, and with one frantic swing, sent the entire table of coffee-, tea-, and chocolate-filled cups sailing.

That was last night. They have cleaned up the snack bar since then, and I have had my foot X-rayed and wrapped in that brown elastic they use for sprains. I am now sitting with my back to the row of vending machines. I know by the steadiness of my hand as I pour homemade hot chocolate from my thermos that no one can sense what I have been through—except, of course, the great white machine over against the wall.

Even now, behind me, in the space just below the coin slot, a tiny sign blinks off and on: 12

"Make Another Selection," it taunts. "Make Another Selection." 13

Questions for Study and Discussion

1. What do you think is the point of Rozin's essay? What makes the narrative more than a humorous story about a man and a difficult vending machine?
2. Like all good storytellers, Rozin, establishes a clear context in his narrative, indicating who, what, when, where, and why. What are the answers to these five questions, and where is this information provided?
3. Briefly describe the way Rozin organizes his narrative. Are the events presented in a strictly chronological order?
4. The last sentence in paragraph 2 acts as a transition for the rest of the essay. How does it serve to introduce the main part of the narrative?

Vocabulary

Refer to your dictionary to define the following words as they are used in this selection. Then use each word in a sentence of your own.

defiant (2)
livid (8)
berserk (8)
wheeled (10)

Suggested Writing Assignment

Most of us have had frustrating experiences with mechanical objects that seem to have perverse minds of their own. Write a brief narrative recounting one such experience—with a vending machine, television set, pay toilet, computer, pay telephone, typewriter, or any other such "big white." Be sure to establish a clear context for your narrative.

How I Designed an A-Bomb in My Junior Year at Princeton

John Aristotle Phillips and David Michaelis

During his junior year at Princeton University, John Aristotle Phillips developed the design for a workable atomic bomb as a physics term paper. He later collaborated with his classmate David Michaelis on Mushroom: The Story of the A-Bomb Kid *(1978), an account of the project. In the following selection, Phillips and Michaelis tell the suspenseful story of the three months leading up to the completion of Phillips' paper—one that is now a U.S. government classified document.*

1 The first semester of my junior year at Princeton University is a disaster, and my grades show it. D's and F's predominate, and a note from the dean puts me on academic probation. Flunk one more course, and I'm out.

2 Fortunately, as the new semester gets under way, my courses begin to interest me. Three hours a week, I attend one called Nuclear Weapons Strategy and Arms Control in which three professors lead 12 students through intense discussions of counterforce capabilities and doomsday scenarios. The leader is Hal Feiveson, renowned for his strong command of the subject matter. Assisting him are Marty Sherwin, an authority on cold-war diplomacy, and Freeman Dyson, an eminent physicist.

3 One morning, Dyson opens a discussion of the atomic bomb: "Let me describe what occurs when a 20-kiloton bomb is exploded, similar to the two dropped on Hiroshima and Nagasaki. First, the sky becomes illuminated by a brilliant white light. Temperatures are so high around the point of explosion that the atmosphere is actually made incandescent. To an observer standing six miles away the ball of fire appears brighter than a hundred suns.

"As the fireball begins to spread up and out into a mushroom-shaped cloud, temperatures spontaneously ignite all flammable materials for miles around. Wood-frame houses catch fire. Clothing bursts into flame, and people suffer intense third-degree flash burns over their exposed flesh. The very high temperatures also produce a shock wave and a variety of nuclear radiations capable of penetrating 20 inches of concrete. The shock wave levels everything in the vicinity of ground zero; hurricane-force winds then rush into the vacuum left by the expanding shock wave and sweep up the rubble of masonry, glass and steel, hurling it outward as lethal projectiles.

Silence falls over the room as the titanic proportions of the destruction begin to sink in.

"It takes only 15 pounds of plutonium to fabricate a crude atomic bomb," adds Hal Feiveson. "If breeder reactors come into widespread use, there will be sufficient plutonium shipped around the country each year to fashion thousands of bombs. Much of it could be vulnerable to theft or hijacking."

The class discusses a possible scenario. A 200-pound shipment disappears en route between a reprocessing facility and a nuclear reactor. State and local police discover only an empty truck and a dead driver. Two weeks later, a crude fission bomb is detonated in Wall Street. Of the half-million people who crowd the area during the regular business day, 100,000 are killed outright. A terrorist group claims responsibility and warns the President that if its extravagant political demands are not met, there will be another explosion within a week.

"That's impossible," a student objects. "Terrorists don't have the know-how to build a bomb."

"You have to be brilliant to design an A-bomb," says another. "Besides, terrorists don't have access to the knowledge."

Impossible? Or is it? The specter of terrorists incinerating an entire city with a homemade atomic bomb begins to haunt me. I turn to John McPhee's book *The Curve of Binding Energy*, in which former Los Alamos nuclear physicist Ted Taylor postulates that a terrorist group could easily steal plutonium or uranium from a nuclear reactor and then design a workable atomic bomb with information available to the general public. According to Taylor, all the ingredients—except plutonium—are legally available at hardware stores and chemical-supply houses.

11 Suddenly, an idea comes to mind. Suppose an average—or below-average in my case—physics student could design a workable atomic bomb on paper? That would prove Taylor's point dramatically and show the federal government that stronger safeguards have to be placed on the storage of plutonium. If I could design a bomb, almost any intelligent person could. But I would have to do it in less than three months to turn it in as my junior independent project. I decide to ask Freeman Dyson to be my adviser.

12 "You understand," says Dyson, "my government security clearance will preclude me from giving you any more information than that which can be found in physics libraries? And that the law of 'no comment' governing scientists who have clearance to atomic secrets stipulates that, if asked a question about the design of a bomb, I can answer neither yes nor no?"

13 "Yes, sir," I reply. "I understand."

14 "Okay, then. I'll give you a list of textbooks outlining the general principles—and I wish you luck."

15 I'm tremendously excited as I charge over to the physics office to record my project, and can barely write down:

John Aristotle Phillips
Dr. Freeman Dyson, Adviser
"How to Build Your Own
Atomic Bomb"

16 A few days later, Dyson hands me a short list of books on nuclear-reactor technology, general nuclear physics and current atomic theory. "That's all?" I ask incredulously, having expected a bit more direction.

17 At subsequent meetings Dyson explains only the basic principles of nuclear physics, and his responses to my calculations grow opaque. If I ask about a particular design or figure, he will glance over what I've done and change the

subject. At first, I think this is his way of telling me I am correct. To make sure, I hand him an incorrect figure. He reads it and changes the subject.

Over spring vacation, I go to Washington, D.C., to search for records of the Los Alamos Project that were declassified between 1954 and 1964. I discover a copy of the literature given to scientists who joined the project in the spring of 1943. This text, *The Los Alamos Primer*, carefully outlines all the details of atomic fissioning known to the world's most advanced scientists in the early '40s. A whole batch of copies costs me about $25. I gather them together and go over to the bureaucrat at the front desk. She looks at the titles, and then looks up at me.

"Oh, you want to build a bomb, too?" she asks matter-of-factly.

I can't believe it. Do people go in there for bomb-building information every day? When I show the documents to Dyson, he is visibly shaken. His reaction indicates to me that I actually stand a chance of coming up with a workable design.

The material necessary to explode my bomb is plutonium-239, a man-made, heavy isotope. Visualize an atomic bomb as a marble inside a grapefruit inside a basketball inside a beach ball. At the center of the bomb is the initiator, a marble-size piece of metal. Around the initiator is a grapefruit-size ball of plutonium-239. Wrapped around the plutonium is a three-inch reflector shield made of beryllium. High explosives are placed symmetrically around the beryllium shield. When these detonate, an imploding shock wave is set off, compressing the grapefruit-size ball of plutonium to the size of a plum. At this moment, the process of atoms fissioning—or splitting apart—begins.

There are many subtleties involved in the explosion of an atomic bomb. Most of them center on the actual detonation of the explosives surrounding the beryllium shield. The grouping of these explosives is one of the most highly classified aspects of the atomic bomb, and it poses the biggest problems for me as I begin to design my bomb.

My base of operations is a small room on the second floor

of Ivy, my eating club. The conference table in the center of the room is covered with books, calculators, design paper, notes. My sleeping bag is rolled out on the floor. As the next three weeks go by, I stop going to classes altogether and work day and night. The other members at Ivy begin referring to me as The Hobo because of my unshaven face and disheveled appearance. I develop a terrible case of bloodshot eyes. Sleep comes rarely.

24 I approach every problem from a terrorist's point of view. The bomb must be inexpensive to construct, simple in design, and small enough to sit unnoticed in the trunk of a car or an abandoned U-Haul trailer.

25 As the days and nights flow by, linked together by cups of coffee and bologna sandwiches, I scan government documents for gaps indicating an area of knowledge that is still classified. Essentially, I am putting together a huge jigsaw puzzle. The edge pieces are in place and various areas are getting filled in, but pieces are missing. Whenever the outline of one shows up, I grab my coffee Thermos and sit down to devise the solution that will fill the gap.

26 With only two weeks left, the puzzle is nearly complete, but two pieces are still missing: which explosives to use, and how to arrange them around the plutonium.

27 During the next week I read that a high-explosive blanket around the beryllium shield might work. But after spending an entire night calculating, I conclude that it is not enough to guarantee a successful implosion wave. Seven days before the design is due, I'm still deadlocked.

28 The alarm clock falls off the table and breaks. I take this as a sign to do something drastic, and I start all over at the beginning. Occasionally I find errors in my old calculations, and I correct them. I lose sense of time.

29 With less than 24 hours to go, I run through a series of new calculations, mathematically figuring the arrangement of the explosives around the plutonium. If my equations are correct, my bomb might be just as effective as the Hiroshima and Nagasaki bombs. But I can't be sure until I know the exact nature of the explosives I will use.

30 Next morning, with my paper due at 5 p.m., I call the Du Pont Company from a pay phone and ask for the head of the

chemical-explosives division, a man I'll call S. F. Graves. If he gives me even the smallest lead, I'll be able to figure the rest out by myself. Otherwise, I'm finished.

"Hello, Mr. Graves. My name is John Phillips. I'm a student at Princeton, doing work on a physics project. I'd like to get some advice, if that's possible."

"What can I do for you?"

"Well," I stammer, "I'm doing research on the shaping of explosive products that create a very high density in a spherically shaped metal. Can you suggest a Du Pont product that would fit in this category?"

"Of course," he says, in a helpful manner.

I don't think he suspects, but I decide to try a bluff: "One of my professors told me that a simple explosive blanket would work in the high-density situation."

"No, no. Explosive blankets went out with the Stone Age. We sell [he names the product] to do the job in similar density-problem situations to the one you're talking about."

When I hang up the phone, I let out a whoop. Mr. Graves has given me just the information I need. Now, if my calculations are correct with respect to the new information, all I have to do is complete my paper by five.

Five minutes to five, I race over to the physics building and bound up the stairs. Inside the office, everybody stops talking and stares at me. I haven't shaved in over a week.

"Is your razor broken, young man?" asks one of the department secretaries.

"I came to hand in my project," I explain. "I didn't have time to shave. Sorry."

A week later, I return to the physics department to pick up my project. One thought has persisted: If I didn't guess correctly about the implosion wave, or if I made a mistake somewhere in the graphs, I'll be finished at Princeton.

A secretary points to the papers. I flip through them, but don't find mine. I look carefully; my paper is not there.

Trying to remain calm, I ask her if all the papers have been graded.

"Yes, of course," she says.

Slowly I return to my room. The absence of my paper can only mean that I blew it.

In the middle of the week, I go back to the physics-department office, hoping to catch the chairman for a few minutes. The secretary looks up, then freezes. 46

"Aren't you John Phillips?" she asks. 47

"Yes," I reply. 48

"Aren't you the boy who designed the atomic bomb?" 49

"Yes, and my paper wasn't . . ." 50

She takes a deep breath. "The question has been raised by the department whether your paper should be classified by the U.S. government." 51

"What? Classified?" 52

She takes my limp hand, shaking it vigorously. "Congratulations," she says, all smiles. "You got one of the only A's in the department. Dr. Wigner wants to see you right away. He says it's a fine piece of work. And Dr. Dyson has been looking for you everywhere." 53

For a second I don't say anything. Then the madness of the situation hits me. A small air bubble of giddiness rises in my throat. Here I have put on paper the plan for a device capable of killing thousands of people, and all I was worrying about was flunking out. 54

Questions for Study and Discussion

1. Phillips tells how he first decided to try to design an atomic bomb and how he actually accomplished that task. Having read the essay, would you be able to build an atomic bomb? If not, what do you think is Phillips' purpose in telling his story?
2. In paragraphs 3 and 4 Professor Dyson describes what happens when an atomic bomb is detonated. Why does Dyson give this description to the class? Why do you suppose Phillips recounts Dyson's description for the reader?
3. Why does Phillips use the present tense throughout the narration? What would have been gained or lost had he told his story in the past tense?
4. Phillips' narrative spans the spring semester of his

junior year at Princeton. How does he keep the reader informed of the passage of time?

5. Identify two analogies that Phillips uses in the essay. Explain why each analogy is effective. (Glossary: *Analogy*)

Vocabulary

Refer to your dictionary to define the following words as they are used in this selection. Then use each word in a sentence of your own.

scenarios (2)	fabricate (6)
eminent (2)	stipulates (12)
lethal (4)	opaque (17)
spontaneously (4)	disheveled (23)

Suggested Writing Assignment

Write an essay in which you narrate an experience that occurred over an extended period of time—for example, applying for admission to college. Before you start to write, make a list of the essential events that you will include. Because your narrative may cover several months, be sure to indicate clearly the passage of time.

Shame

Dick Gregory

Dick Gregory, the well-known comedian, has long been active in the civil rights movement. During the 1960s Gregory was also an outspoken critic of America's involvement in Vietnam. In the following episode from his autobiography Nigger *(1964), he narrates the story of a childhood experience that taught him the meaning of shame. Through his use of authentic dialogue and vivid details, he dramatically re-creates this experience for his readers.*

I never learned hate at home, or shame. I had to go to school for that. I was about seven years old when I got my first big lesson. I was in love with a little girl named Helene Tucker, a light-complexioned little girl with pigtails and nice manners. She was always clean and she was smart in school. I think I went to school then mostly to look at her. I brushed my hair and even got me a little old handkerchief. It was a lady's handkerchief, but I didn't want Helene to see me wipe my nose on my hand. The pipes were frozen again, there was no water in the house, but I washed my socks and shirt every night. I'd get a pot, and go over to Mister Ben's grocery store, and stick my pot down into his soda machine. Scoop out some chopped ice. By evening the ice melted to water for washing. I got sick a lot that winter because the fire would go out at night before the clothes were dry. In the morning I'd put them on, wet or dry, because they were the only clothes I had. 1

Everybody's got a Helene Tucker, a symbol of everything you want. I loved her for her goodness, her cleanness, her popularity. She'd walk down my street and my brothers and sisters would yell, "Here comes Helene," and I'd rub my tennis sneakers on the back of my pants and wish my hair 2 wasn't so nappy and the white folks' shirt fit me better. I'd run out on the street. If I knew my place and didn't come too close, she'd wink at me and say hello. That was a good feeling. Sometimes I'd follow her all the way home, and shovel the snow off her walk and try to make friends with her Momma and her aunts. I'd drop money on her stoop late at night on my way back from shining shoes in the taverns. And she had a Daddy, and he had a good job. He was a paper hanger.

I guess I would have gotten over Helene by summertime, but something happened in that classroom that made her face hang in front of me for the next twenty-two years. When I played the drums in high school it was for Helene and when I broke track records in college it was for Helene and when I started standing behind microphones and heard applause I wished Helene could hear it, too. It wasn't until I was twenty-nine years old and married and making money that I finally got her out of my system. Helene was sitting in that classroom when I learned to be ashamed of myself.

It was on a Thursday. I was sitting in the back of the room, in a seat with a chalk circle drawn around it. The idiot's seat, the troublemaker's seat.

The teacher thought I was stupid. Couldn't spell, couldn't read, couldn't do arithmetic. Just stupid. Teachers were never interested in finding out that you couldn't concentrate because you were so hungry, because you hadn't had any breakfast. All you could think about was noontime, would it ever come? Maybe you could sneak into the cloakroom and steal a bite of some kid's lunch out of a coat pocket. A bite of something. Paste. You can't really make a meal of paste, or put it on bread for a sandwich, but sometimes I'd scoop a few spoonfuls out of the paste jar in the back of the room. Pregnant people get strange tastes. I was pregnant with poverty. Pregnant with dirt and pregnant with smells that made people turn away, pregnant with cold and pregnant with shoes that were never bought for me, pregnant with five other people in my bed and no Daddy in the next room, and pregnant with hunger. Paste doesn't taste too bad when you're hungry.

The teacher thought I was a troublemaker. All she saw

from the front of the room was a little black boy who squirmed in his idiot's seat and made noises and poked the kids around him. I guess she couldn't see a kid who made noises because he wanted someone to know he was there.

It was on a Thursday, the day before the Negro payday. The eagle always flew on Friday. The teacher was asking each student how much his father would give to the Community Chest. On Friday night, each kid would get the money from his father, and on Monday he would bring it to the school. I decided I was going to buy me a Daddy right then. I had money in my pocket from shining shoes and selling papers, and whatever Helene Tucker pledged for her Daddy I was going to top it. And I'd hand the money right in. I wasn't going to wait until Monday to buy me a Daddy. 7

I was shaking, scared to death. The teacher opened her book and started calling out names alphabetically. 8

"Helene Tucker?" 9

"My daddy said he'd give two dollars and fifty cents." 10

"That's very nice, Helene. Very, very nice indeed." 11

That made me feel pretty good. It wouldn't take too much to top that. I had almost three dollars in dimes and quarters in my pocket. I stuck my hand in my pocket and held onto the money, waiting for her to call my name. But the teacher closed her book after she called everybody else in the class. 12

I stood up and raised my hand. 13

"What is it now?" 14

"You forgot me." 15

She turned toward the blackboard. "I don't have time to be playing with you, Richard." 16

"My Daddy said he'd . . ." 17

"Sit down, Richard, you're disturbing the class." 18

"My Daddy said he'd give . . . fifteen dollars." 19

She turned around and looked mad. "We are collecting this money for you and your kind, Richard Gregory. If your Daddy can give fifteen dollars you have no business being on relief." 20

"I got it right now, I got it right now, my Daddy gave it to me to turn in today, my Daddy said . . ." 21

"And furthermore," she said, looking right at me, her 22

nostrils getting big and her lips getting thin and her eyes opening wide, "we know you don't have a Daddy."

Helene Tucker turned around, her eyes full of tears. She felt sorry for me. Then I couldn't see her too well because I was crying, too.

"Sit down, Richard."

And I always thought the teacher kind of liked me. She always picked me to wash the blackboard on Friday, after school. That was a big thrill, it made me feel important. If I didn't wash it, come Monday the school might not function right.

"Where are you going, Richard?"

I walked out of school that day, and for a long time I didn't go back very often. There was shame there.

Now there was shame everywhere. It seemed like the whole world had been inside that classroom, everyone had heard what the teacher had said, everyone had turned around and felt sorry for me. There was shame in going to the Worthy Boys Annual Christmas Dinner for you and your kind, because everybody knew what a worthy boy was. Why couldn't they just call it the Boys Annual Dinner; why'd they have to give it a name? There was shame in wearing the brown and orange and white plaid mackinaw the welfare gave to three thousand boys. Why'd it have to be the same for everybody so when you walked down the street the people could see you were on relief? It was a nice warm mackinaw and it had a hood, and my Momma beat me and called me a little rat when she found out I stuffed it in the bottom of a pail full of garbage way over on Cottage Street. There was shame in running over to Mister Ben's at the end of the day and asking for his rotten peaches, there was shame in asking Mrs. Simmons for a spoonful of sugar, there was shame in running out to meet the relief truck. I hated that truck, full of food for you and your kind. I ran into the house and hid when it came. And then I started to sneak through alleys, to take the long way home so the people going into White's Eat Shop wouldn't see me. Yeah, the whole world heard the teacher that day, we all know you don't have a Daddy.

Questions for Study and Discussion

1. What does Gregory mean by "shame"?
2. How do the first three paragraphs of the essay help to establish a context for the narrative that follows?
3. Why do you think Gregory narrates this episode in the first-person point of view? What would be gained or lost if he instead wrote it in the third-person point of view?
4. Specific details can enhance the reader's understanding and appreciation of a narrative. Gregory's description of Helene Tucker's manners or the plaid of his mackinaw, for example, makes his account vivid and interesting. Cite several other specific details he gives, and consider how the narrative would be different without them.
5. Consider the diction of this essay. What effect does Gregory's repetition of the word *shame* have on you? Why do you think Gregory uses simple vocabulary to narrate this particular experience? (Glossary: *Diction*)

Vocabulary

Refer to your dictionary to define the following words as they are used in this selection. Then use each word in a sentence of your own.

nappy (2)
mackinaw (28)

Suggested Writing Assignment

Using Dick Gregory's essay as a model, write an essay narrating an experience that made you especially afraid, angry, surprised, embarrassed, or proud. Include sufficient detail so that your readers will know exactly what happened.

The Gopher

John Steinbeck

Novelist John Steinbeck (1902–1968), winner of the 1962 Nobel Prize for Literature, is best known for The Grapes of Wrath *(1939), the chronicle of a family of Oklahoma farmers who migrate to California during the Great Depression. The following chapter from Steinbeck's novel* Cannery Row *(1945) tells the story of a gopher's struggle for survival. As you read the selection, pay particular attention to its narrative point of view.*

A well-grown gopher took up residence in a thicket of mallow weeds in the vacant lot on Cannery Row. It was a perfect place. The deep green luscious mallows towered up crisp and rich and as they matured their little cheeses hung down provocatively. The earth was perfect for a gopher hole too, black and soft and yet with a little clay in it so that it didn't crumble and the tunnels didn't cave in. The gopher was fat and sleek and he had always plenty of food in his cheek pouches. His little ears were clean and well set and his eyes were as black as old-fashioned pin heads and just about the same size. His digging hands were strong and the fur on his back was glossy brown and the fawn-colored fur on his chest was incredibly soft and rich. He had long curving yellow teeth and a little short tail. Altogether he was a beautiful gopher and in the prime of his life.

He came to the place over land and found it good and he began his burrow on a little eminence where he could look out among the mallow weeds and see the trucks go by on Cannery Row. He could watch the feet of Mack and the boys as they crossed the lot to the Palace Flophouse. As he dug down into the coal-black earth he found it even more perfect, for there were great rocks under the soil. When he made his great chamber for the storing of food it was under a rock so that it could never cave in no matter how hard it rained. It was a place where he could settle down and raise any number of families and the burrow could increase in all directions.

3 It was beautiful in the early morning when he first poked his head out of the burrow. The mallows filtered green light down on him and the first rays of the rising sun shone into his hole and warmed it so that he lay there content and very comfortable.

4 When he had dug his great chamber and his four emergency exits and his waterproof deluge room, the gopher began to store food. He cut down only the perfect mallow stems and trimmed them to the exact length he needed and he took them down the hole and stacked them neatly in his great chamber, and arranged them so they wouldn't ferment or get sour. He had found the perfect place to live. There were no gardens about so no one would think of setting a trap for him. Cats there were, many of them, but they were so bloated with fish heads and guts from the canneries that they had long ago given up hunting. The soil was sandy enough so that water never stood about or filled a hole for long. The gopher worked and worked until he had his great chamber crammed with food. Then he made little side chambers for the babies who would inhabit them. In a few years there might be thousands of his progeny spreading out from this original hearthstone.

5 But as time went on the gopher began to be a little impatient, for no female appeared. He sat in the entrance of his hole in the morning and made penetrating squeaks that are inaudible to the human ear but can be heard deep in the earth by other gophers. And still no female appeared. Finally in a sweat of impatience he went up across the track until he found another gopher hole. He squeaked provocatively in the entrance. He heard a rustling and smelled female and then out of the hole came an old battle-torn bull gopher who mauled and bit him so badly that he crept home and lay in his great chamber for three days recovering and he lost two toes from one front paw from that fight.

6 Again he waited and squeaked beside his beautiful burrow in the beautiful place but no female ever came and after a

while he had to move away. He had to move two blocks up the hill to a dahlia garden where they put out traps every night.

Questions for Study and Discussion

1. "The Gopher" is more than a simple narrative about an animal finding a home, and then being forced to move on; it is also the story of life's basic unchanging patterns. What do you think Steinbeck's point is in telling this story?
2. List six striking details that Steinbeck gives in his description of the gopher. What dominant impression of the gopher do these details create for you? (Glossary: *Dominant Impression*)
3. What is the point of view in this essay? Why do you suppose Steinbeck chose this point of view?
4. Steinbeck organizes his narrative chronologically and uses transitional expressions to unify the sequence of events. Make a list of the transitional words and phrases that occur in the narrative. (Glossary: *Transitions*)
5. What are the connotations of the italicized words and phrases in the following excerpts from this selection:
   a. *took up residence* in a thicket (1)
   b. *deep green luscious* mallows *towered up crisp and rich* (1)
   c. The mallows *filtered* green light down on him (3)
   d. thousands of his progeny spreading out from this original *hearthstone* (4)
   e. in a *sweat of impatience* (5)

   Try to substitute different words with the same meanings for these italicized words. Be prepared to discuss the importance of Steinbeck's diction in this essay.

Vocabulary

Refer to your dictionary to define the following words as they are used in this selection. Then use each word in a sentence of your own.

provocatively (1)
eminence (2)
deluge (4)
ferment (4)
bloated (4)

Suggested Writing Assignment

Accounts of natural events often rely on scientific data and are often narrated in the third person. Carefully observe some natural event (fire, hurricane, birth of an animal, bird migration, etc.) and note significant details and facts about that occurrence. Then narrate a third-person report of the event.

12

Description

To describe is to create a verbal picture. A person, a place, a thing—even an idea or a state of mind—can be made vividly concrete through description. Here, for example, is Thomas Mann's brief description of a delicatessen:

> It was a narrow room, with a rather high ceiling, and crowded from floor to ceiling with goodies. There were rows and rows of hams and sausages of all shapes and colors—white, yellow, red, and black; fat and lean and round and long—rows of canned preserves, cocoa and tea, bright translucent glass bottles of honey, marmalade, and jam; round bottles and slender bottles, filled with liqueurs and punch—all these things crowded every inch of the shelves from top to bottom.

Writing any description requires, first of all, that the writer gather many details about a subject, relying not only on what the eyes see but on the other sense impressions—touch, taste, smell, hearing—as well. From this catalogue of details the writer selects those which will most effectively create a *dominant impression*—the single quality, mood, or atmosphere that the writer wishes to emphasize. Consider, for example, the details that Mary McCarthy uses to evoke the dominant impression in the following passage from *Memories of a Catholic Girlhood:*

> Whenever we children came to stay at my grandmother's house, we were put to sleep in the sewing room, a bleak, shabby, utilitarian rectangle, more office than bedroom, more attic than office, that played to the hierarchy of chambers the role of poor relation. It was a room without pride: the old sewing machine, some cast-off chairs, a shadeless lamp, rolls of wrapping paper, piles of cardboard boxes that might someday come in handy, papers of pins, and remnants of a material united with the iron folding cots put out for our use and

> the bare floor boards to give an impression of intense and ruthless temporality. Thin white spreads, of the kind used in hospitals and charity institutions, and naked blinds at the windows reminded us of our orphaned condition and of the ephemeral character of our visit; there was nothing here to encourage us to consider this our home.

The dominant impression that McCarthy creates is one of clutter, bleakness, and shabbiness. There is nothing in the sewing room that suggests permanence or warmth.

Writers must also carefully plan the order in which to present their descriptive details. The pattern of organization must fit the subject of the description logically and naturally, and must also be easy to follow. For example, visual details can be arranged spatially—from left to right, top to bottom, near to far, or in any other logical order. Other patterns include smallest to largest, softest to loudest, least significant to most significant, most unusual to least unusual. McCarthy suggests a jumble of junk not only by her choice of details but by the apparently random order in which she presents them.

How much detail is enough? There is no fixed answer. A good description includes enough vivid details to create a dominant impression and to bring a scene to life, but not so many that readers are distracted, confused, or bored. In an essay that is purely descriptive, there is room for much detail. Usually, however, writers use description to create the setting for a story, to illustrate ideas, to help clarify a definition or a comparison, or to make the complexities of a process more understandable. Such descriptions should be kept short, and should include just enough detail to make them clear and helpful.

Subway Station

Gilbert Highet

Gilbert Highet (1906–1978) was born in Scotland and became a naturalized United States citizen in 1951. A prolific writer and translator, Highet was for many years a professor of classics at Columbia University. The following selection is taken from his book Talents and Geniuses *(1957). Notice the author's keen eye for detail as he describes the unseemly world of a subway station.*

Standing in a subway station, I began to appreciate the place—almost to enjoy it. First of all, I looked at the lighting: a row of meager electric bulbs, unscreened, yellow, and coated with filth, stretched toward the black mouth of the tunnel, as though it were a bolt hole in an abandoned coal mine. Then I lingered, with zest, on the walls and ceiling: lavatory tiles which had been white about fifty years ago, and were now encrusted with soot, coated with the remains of a dirty liquid which might be either atmospheric humidity mingled with smog or the result of a perfunctory attempt to clean them with cold water; and, above them, gloomy vaulting from which dingy paint was peeling off like scabs from an old wound, sick black paint leaving a leprous white undersurface. Beneath my feet, the floor was a nauseating dark brown with black stains upon it which might be stale oil or dry chewing gum or some worse defilement; it looked like the hallway of a condemned slum building. Then my eye traveled to the tracks, where two lines of glittering steel—the only positively clean objects in the whole place—ran out of darkness into darkness above an unspeakable mass of congealed oil, puddles of dubious liquid, and a mishmash of old cigarette packets, mutilated and filthy newspapers, and the débris that filtered down from the street above through a barred grating in the roof. As I looked up toward the sunlight, I could see more débris sifting slowly downward, and making an abominable pattern in the slanting beam of dirt-laden sunlight. I was going on to relish more features of this unique scene: such as the advertisement posters on the walls—here a text from the Bible, there a half-naked girl, here a woman wearing a hat consisting of a hen sitting on a nest full of eggs, and there a pair of girl's legs walking up the keys of a cash register—all scribbled over with unknown names and well-known obscenities in black crayon and red lipstick; but then my train came in at last, I boarded it, and began to read. The experience was over for the time.

Questions for Study and Discussion

1. What dominant impression of the subway station does Highet create in his description? (Glossary: *Dominant Impression*)
2. To present a clearly focused dominant impression, a writer must be selective in the use of details. Make a list of those details that help create Highet's dominant impression.
3. Highet uses a spatial organization in his essay. Trace the order in which he describes the various elements of the subway station. (Glossary: *Organization*)
4. What similes and metaphors can you find in Highet's description? How do they help to make the description vivid? (Glossary: *Figures of Speech*)

Vocabulary

Refer to your dictionary to define the following words as they are used in this selection. Then use each word in a sentence of your own.

meager	congealed
zest	dubious
defilement	unique

Suggested Writing Assignment

Write a short essay in which you describe one of the following places, or another place of your choice. Arrange the details of your description from top to bottom, left to right, near to far, or according to some other spatial organization.

an airport terminal
a pizza parlor
a locker room
a barbershop or beauty salon
a bookstore
a campus dining hall

The Sounds of the City

James Tuite

James Tuite has had a long career at The New York Times, *where he once served as sports editor. As a free-lance writer he has contributed to all of the major sports magazines and has written* Snowmobiles and Snowmobiling *(1973) and* How to Enjoy Sports on TV *(1976). The following selection is a model of how a place can be described by using a sense other than sight. Tuite describes New York City by its sounds, which for him comprise the very life of the city.*

New York is a city of sounds: muted sounds and shrill sounds; shattering sounds and soothing sounds; urgent sounds and aimless sounds. The cliff dwellers of Manhattan—who would be racked by the silence of the lonely woods—do not hear these sounds because they are constant and eternally urban. 1

The visitor to the city can hear them, though, just as some animals can hear a high-pitched whistle inaudible to humans. To the casual caller to Manhattan, lying restive and sleepless in a hotel twenty or thirty floors above the street, they tell a story as fascinating as life itself. And back of the sounds broods the silence. 2

Night in midtown is the noise of tinseled honky-tonk and violence. Thin strains of music, usually the firm beat of rock 'n' roll or the frenzied outbursts of the discotheque, rise from ground level. This is the cacophony, the discordance of youth, and it comes on strongest when nights are hot and young blood restless. 3

Somewhere in the canyons below there is shrill laughter or raucous shouting. A bottle shatters against concrete. The whine of a police siren slices through the night, moving ever 4 closer, until an eerie Doppler effect* brings it to a guttural halt.

There are few sounds so exciting in Manhattan as those of fire apparatus dashing through the night. At the outset there is the tentative hint of the first-due company bullying his way through midtown traffic. Now a fire whistle from the opposite direction affirms that trouble is, indeed, afoot. In seconds, other sirens converging from other streets help the skytop listener focus on the scene of excitement.

But he can only hear and not see, and imagination takes flight. Are the flames and smoke gushing from windows not far away? Are victims trapped there, crying out for help? Is it a conflagration, or only a trash-basket fire? Or, perhaps, it is merely a false alarm.

The questions go unanswered and the urgency of the moment dissolves. Now the mind and the ear detect the snarling, arrogant bickering of automobile horns. People in a hurry. Taxicabs blaring, insisting on their checkered priority.

Even the taxi horns dwindle down to a precocious few in the gray and pink moments of dawn. Suddenly there is another sound, a morning sound that taunts the memory for recognition. The growl of a predatory monster? No, just garbage trucks that have begun a day of scavenging.

Trash cans rattle outside restaurants. Metallic jaws on sanitation trucks gulp and masticate the residue of daily living, then digest it with a satisfied groan of gears. The sounds of the new day are businesslike. The growl of buses, so scattered and distant at night, becomes a demanding part of the traffic bedlam. An occasional jet or helicopter injects an exclamation point from an unexpected quarter. When the wind is right, the vibrant bellow of an ocean liner can be heard.

The sounds of the day are as jarring as the glare of a sun that outlines the canyons of midtown in drab relief. A pneumatic drill frays countless nerves with its rat-a-tat-tat, for dig they must to perpetuate the city's dizzy motion. After

*The drop in pitch that occurs as a source of sound quickly passes by a listener.

each screech of brakes there is a moment of suspension, of waiting for the thud or crash that never seems to follow.

The whistles of traffic policemen and hotel doormen chirp from all sides, like birds calling for their mates across a frenzied aviary. And all of these sounds are adult sounds, for childish laughter has no place in these canyons. 11

Night falls again, the cycle is complete, but there is no surcease from sound. For the beautiful dreamers, perhaps, the "sounds of the rude world heard in the day, lulled by the moonlight have all passed away," but this is not so in the city. 12

Too many New Yorkers accept the sounds about them as bland parts of everyday existence. They seldom stop to listen to the sounds, to think about them, to be appalled or enchanted by them. In the big city, sounds are life. 13

Questions for Study and Discussion

1. What is Tuite's purpose in describing the sounds of New York City?
2. How does Tuite organize his essay? Do you think that the organization is effective? (Glossary: *Organization*)
3. Tuite describes "raucous shouting" and the "screech of brakes." Make a list of the various other sounds that he describes in his essay. How do the varied adjectives and verbs Tuite uses to capture the essence of each sound enhance his description? (Glossary: *Diction*)
4. Locate several metaphors and similes in the essay. What picture of the city does each one give you? (Glossary: *Figures of Speech*)
5. What dominant impression of New York City does Tuite create in this essay? (Glossary: *Dominant Impression*)

Vocabulary

Refer to your dictionary to define the following words as they are used in this selection. Then use each word in a sentence of your own.

muted (1)	precocious (8)
inaudible (2)	taunts (8)
restive (2)	vibrant (9)
raucous (4)	perpetuate (10)
tentative (5)	

Suggested Writing Assignment

In a short composition describe a city or another place that you know well. Try to capture as many sights, sounds, and smells as you can to depict the place you describe. Your goal should be to create a single dominant impression of the place, as Tuite does in his essay.

My Friend, Albert Einstein

Banesh Hoffmann

A mathematician, Banesh Hoffmann has served on the faculties of the University of Rochester, the Institute for Advanced Study at Princeton University, and Queens College. Hoffmann is the author of The Strange Story of the Quantum *(1947) and* The Tyranny of Testing *(1962) and co-author with Albert Einstein of an article on the theory of relativity. In the following selection, Hoffmann describes the kind of man he found Einstein to be.*

He was one of the greatest scientists the world has ever known, yet if I had to convey the essence of Albert Einstein in a single word, I would choose *simplicity*. Perhaps an anecdote will help. Once, caught in a downpour, he took off his hat and held it under his coat. Asked why, he explained, with admirable logic, that the rain would damage the hat, but his hair would be none the worse for its wetting. This knack for going instinctively to the heart of a matter was the secret of his major scientific discoveries—this and his extraordinary feeling for beauty. 1

I first met Albert Einstein in 1935, at the famous Institute for Advanced Study in Princeton, N.J. He had been among the first to be invited to the Institute, and was offered *carte blanche* as to salary. To the director's dismay, Einstein asked for an impossible sum: it was far too *small*. The director had to plead with him to accept a larger salary. 2

I was in awe of Einstein, and hesitated before approaching him about some ideas I had been working on. When I finally knocked on his door, a gentle voice said, "Come"—with a rising inflection that made the single word both a welcome and a question. I entered his office and found him seated at a table, calculating and smoking his pipe. Dressed in ill-fitting 3 clothes, his hair characteristically awry, he smiled a warm welcome. His utter naturalness at once set me at ease.

As I began to explain my ideas, he asked me to write the equations on the blackboard so he could see how they developed. Then came the staggering—and altogether endearing—request: "Please go slowly. I do not understand things quickly." This from Einstein! He said it gently, and I laughed. From then on, all vestiges of fear were gone.

Einstein was born in 1879 in the German city of Ulm. He had been no infant prodigy; indeed, he was so late in learning to speak that his parents feared he was a dullard. In school, though his teachers saw no special talent in him, the signs were already there. He taught himself calculus, for example, and his teachers seemed a little afraid of him because he asked questions they could not answer. At the age of 16, he asked himself whether a light wave would seem stationary if one ran abreast of it. From that innocent question would arise, ten years later, his theory of relativity.

Einstein failed his entrance examinations at the Swiss Federal Polytechnic School, in Zurich, but was admitted a year later. There he went beyond his regular work to study the masterworks of physics on his own. Rejected when he applied for academic positions, he ultimately found work, in 1902, as a patent examiner in Berne, and there in 1905 his genius burst into fabulous flower.

Among the extraordinary things he produced in that memorable year were his theory of relativity, with its famous offshoot, $E=mc^2$ (energy equals mass times the speed of light squared), and his quantum theory of light. These two theories were not only revolutionary, but seemingly contradictory: the former was intimately linked to the theory that light consists of waves, while the latter said it consists somehow of particles. Yet this unknown young man boldly proposed both at once—and he was right in both cases, though how he could have been is far too complex a story to tell here.

Collaborating with Einstein was an unforgettable experience. In 1937, the Polish physicist Leopold Infeld and I asked if we could work with him. He was pleased with the proposal, since he had an idea about gravitation waiting to be worked out in detail. Thus we got to know not merely the man and the friend, but also the professional.

9 The intensity and depth of his concentration were fantastic. When battling a recalcitrant problem, he worried it as an animal worries its prey. Often, when we found ourselves up against a seemingly insuperable difficulty, he would stand up, put his pipe on the table, and say in his quaint English, "I will a little tink" (he could not pronounce "th"). Then he would pace up and down, twirling a lock of his long, graying hair around his forefinger.

10 A dreamy, faraway and yet inward look would come over his face. There was no appearance of concentration, no furrowing of the brow—only a placid inner communion. The minutes would pass, and then suddenly Einstein would stop pacing as his face relaxed into a gentle smile. He had found the solution to the problem. Sometimes it was so simple that Infeld and I could have kicked ourselves for not having thought of it. But the magic had been performed invisibly in the depths of Einstein's mind, by a process we could not fathom.

11 Although Einstein felt no need for religious ritual and belonged to no formal religious group, he was the most deeply religious man I have known. He once said to me, "Ideas come from God," and one could hear the capital "G" in the reverence with which he pronounced the word. On the marble fireplace in the mathematics building at Princeton University is carved, in the original German, what one might call his scientific credo: "God is subtle, but he is not malicious." By this Einstein meant that scientists could expect to find their task difficult, but not hopeless: the Universe was a Universe of law, and God was not confusing us with deliberate paradoxes and contradictions.

12 Einstein was an accomplished amateur musician. We used to play duets, he on the violin, I at the piano. One day he surprised me by saying Mozart was the greatest composer of all. Beethoven "created" his music, but the music of Mozart was of such purity and beauty one felt he had merely "found" it—that it had always existed as part of the inner beauty of the Universe, waiting to be revealed.

13 It was this very Mozartean simplicity that most charac-

terized Einstein's methods. His 1905 theory of relativity, for example, was built on just two simple assumptions. One is the so-called principle of relativity, which means, roughly speaking, that we cannot tell whether we are at rest or moving smoothly. The other assumption is that the speed of light is the same no matter what the speed of the object that produces it. You can see how reasonable this is if you think of agitating a stick in a lake to create waves. Whether you wiggle the stick from a stationary pier, or from a rushing speedboat, the waves, once generated, are on their own, and their speed has nothing to do with that of the stick.

Each of these assumptions, by itself, was so plausible as to seem primitively obvious. But together they were in such violent conflict that a lesser man would have dropped one or the other and fled in panic. Einstein daringly kept both—and by so doing he revolutionized physics. For he demonstrated they could, after all, exist peacefully side by side, provided we gave up cherished beliefs about the nature of time.

Science is like a house of cards, with concepts like time and space at the lowest level. Tampering with time brought most of the house tumbling down, and it was this that made Einstein's work so important—and controversial. At a conference in Princeton in honor of his 70th birthday, one of the speakers, a Nobel Prize-winner, tried to convey the magical quality of Einstein's achievement. Words failed him, and with a shrug of helplessness he pointed to his wristwatch, and said in tones of awed amazement, "It all came from this." His very ineloquence made this the most eloquent tribute I have heard to Einstein's genius.

We think of Einstein as one concerned only with the deepest aspects of science. But he saw scientific principles in everyday things to which most of us would give barely a second thought. He once asked me if I had ever wondered why a man's feet will sink into either dry or completely submerged sand, while sand that is merely damp provides a firm surface. When I could not answer, he offered a simple explanation.

It depends, he pointed out, on *surface tension*, the elastic-skin effect of a liquid surface. This is what holds a drop together, or causes two small raindrops on a windowpane to pull into one big drop the moment their surfaces touch.

When sand is damp, Einstein explained, there are tiny amounts of water between grains. The surface tensions of these tiny amounts of water pull all the grains together, and friction then makes them hard to budge. When the sand is dry, there is obviously no water between grains. If the sand is fully immersed, there is water between grains, but no water *surface* to pull them together. 18

This is not as important as relativity; yet there is no telling what seeming trifle will lead an Einstein to a major discovery. And the puzzle of the sand does give us an inkling of the power and elegance of his mind. 19

Einstein's work, performed quietly with pencil and paper, seemed remote from the turmoil of everyday life. But his ideas were so revolutionary they caused violent controversy and irrational anger. Indeed, in order to be able to award him a belated Nobel Prize, the selection committee had to avoid mentioning relativity, and pretend the prize was awarded primarily for his work on the quantum theory. 20

Political events upset the serenity of his life even more. When the Nazis came to power in Germany, his theories were officially declared false because they had been formulated by a Jew. His property was confiscated, and it is said a price was put on his head. 21

When scientists in the United States, fearful that the Nazis might develop an atomic bomb, sought to alert American authorities to the danger, they were scarcely heeded. In desperation, they drafted a letter which Einstein signed and sent directly to President Roosevelt. It was this act that led to the fateful decision to go all-out on the production of an atomic bomb—an endeavor in which Einstein took no active part. When he heard of the agony and destruction that his $E=mc^2$ had wrought, he was dismayed beyond measure, and from then on there was a look of ineffable sadness in his eyes. 22

There was something elusively whimsical about Einstein. It is illustrated by my favorite anecdote about him. In his first year in Princeton, on Christmas Eve, so the story goes, some children sang carols outside his house. Having finished, they knocked on his door and explained they were col- 23 lecting money to buy Christmas presents. Einstein listened, then said, "Wait a moment." He put on his scarf and overcoat, and took his violin from its case. Then, joining the children as they went from door to door, he accompanied their singing of "Silent Night" on his violin.

How shall I sum up what it meant to have known Einstein and his works? Like the Nobel Prize-winner who pointed helplessly at his watch, I can find no adequate words. It was akin to the revelation of great art that lets one see what was formerly hidden. And when, for example, I walk on the sand of a lonely beach, I am reminded of his ceaseless search for cosmic simplicity—and the scene takes on a deeper, sadder beauty.

Questions for Study and Discussion

1. Hoffmann feels that the word *simplicity* captures the essence of Albert Einstein. What character traits does Hoffmann describe in order to substantiate this impression of the man? (Glossary: *Dominant Impression*)
2. Make a list of the details of Einstein's physical features. From these details, can you tell what Einstein looked like?
3. Hoffmann uses a number of anecdotes to develop his description of Einstein. In what ways are such anecdotes preferable to mere statements regarding Einstein's character? Refer to several examples to illustrate your opinion.
4. Why do you suppose Hoffmann begins his essay where he does instead of the sentence "Einstein was born in 1879 in the German city of Ulm"? (Glossary: *Beginnings/Endings*)

Vocabulary

Refer to your dictionary to define the following words as they are used in this selection. Then use each word in a sentence of your own.

anecdote (1)
awry (3)
vestiges (4)
prodigy (5)
recalcitrant (9)
fathom (10)
credo (11)
trifle (19)
ineffable (22)

Suggested Writing Assignment

Write a descriptive essay on a person you know well, perhaps a friend or a relative. Before writing, be sure that you establish a purpose for your description. Remember that your reader will not know that person; therefore, try to show what makes your subject different from other people.

13

Process Analysis

When you give directions for getting to your house, tell how to make ice cream, or explain how a president is elected, you are using *process analysis*.

Process analysis usually arranges a series of events in order and relates them to one another, as narration and cause and effect do, but it has different emphases. Whereas narration tells mainly *what* happens and cause and effect focuses on *why* it happens, process analysis tries to explain—in detail—*how* it happens.

There are two types of process analysis: directional and informational. The *directional* type provides instructions on how to do something. These instructions can be as brief as the directions printed on a label for making instant coffee or as complex as the directions in a manual for building a home computer. The purpose of directional process analysis is simple: to give the reader directions to follow that lead to the desired results.

The *informational* type of process analysis, on the other hand, tells how something works, how something is made, or how something occurred. You would use informational process analysis if you wanted to explain how the human heart functions, how an atomic bomb works, how hailstones are formed, how you selected the college you are attending, or how the polio vaccine was developed. Rather than giving specific directions, informational process analysis explains and informs.

Clarity is crucial for successful process analysis. The most effective way to explain a process is to divide it into steps and to present those steps in a clear (usually chronological) sequence. Transitional words and phrases such as *first, next,* and *in conclusion* help to connect steps to one another. Naturally, you must be sure that no step is omitted or out of order. Also, you may sometimes have to explain *why* a certain step is necessary, especially if it is not obvious. With intricate, abstract, or particularly difficult steps, you might use analogy or comparison to clarify the steps for your reader.

How to Build a Fire in a Fireplace

Bernard Gladstone

Bernard Gladstone is a free-lance writer about do-it-yourself building and home maintenance. As home improvement editor of The New York Times *for over ten years, he has written useful articles about common household problems, new home products, and the use of new and old tools. In the following selection from his book* The New York Times Complete Manual of Home Repair *(1971), Gladstone gives directions for building a fire in a fireplace.*

Though "experts" differ as to the best technique to follow when building a fire, one generally accepted method consists of first laying a generous amount of crumpled newspaper on the hearth between the andirons. Kindling wood is then spread generously over this layer of newspaper and one of the thickest logs is placed across the back of the andirons. This should be as close to the back of the fireplace as possible, but not quite touching it. A second log is then placed an inch or so in front of this, and a few additional sticks of kindling are laid across these two. A third log is then placed on top to form a sort of pyramid with air space between all logs so that flames can lick freely up between them.

A mistake frequently made is in building the fire too far forward so that the rear wall of the fireplace does not get properly heated. A heated back wall helps increase the draft and tends to suck smoke and flames rearward with less chance of sparks or smoke spurting out into the room.

Another common mistake often made by the inexperienced fire-tender is to try to build a fire with only one or two logs, instead of using at least three. A single log is difficult to ignite properly, and even two logs do not provide an efficient bed with adequate fuel-burning capacity.

Use of too many logs, on the other hand, is also a common fault and can prove hazardous. Building too big a fire can create more smoke and draft than the chimney can safely handle, increasing the possibility of sparks or smoke being thrown out into the room. For best results, the homeowner should start with three medium-size logs as described above, then add additional logs as needed if the fire is to be kept burning. 4

Questions for Study and Discussion

1. What type of process analysis is used in this essay, directional or informational? Why is this type of process analysis especially appropriate to the author's purpose?
2. Make a list of the steps Gladstone describes for building a fire in a fireplace.
3. What is the purpose of paragraphs 2, 3, and 4 in this process analysis?
4. Identify the transitional words that Gladstone uses in paragraph 1 to indicate the sequence of steps involved in making a fire. (Glossary: *Transitions*)

Vocabulary

Refer to your dictionary to define the following words as they are used in this selection. Then use each word in a sentence of your own.

hearth (1)
andirons (1)
kindling (1)

Suggested Writing Assignment

Write a directional process analysis for one of the following operations:

how to paddle a canoe
how to study for an exam
how to determine miles per gallon for an automobile
how to make your favorite sandwich
how to hem a dress
how to make popcorn
how to get from where your writing class meets to where you normally have lunch
how to tie a necktie

How Dictionaries Are Made

S. I. Hayakawa

S. I. Hayakawa is one of this country's leading semanticists. In this excerpt from his Language in Thought and Action, *Hayakawa explains how a dictionary is made in order to dispel certain myths about dictionaries and their use.*

It is widely believed that every word has a correct meaning, that we learn these meanings principally from teachers and grammarians (except that most of the time we don't bother to, so that we ordinarily speak "sloppy English"), and that dictionaries and grammars are the supreme authority in matters of meaning and usage. Few people ask by what authority the writers of dictionaries and grammars say what they say. I once got into a dispute with an Englishwoman over the pronunciation of a word and offered to look it up in the dictionary. The Englishwoman said firmly, "What for? I am English. I was born and brought up in England. The way I speak *is* English." Such self-assurance about one's own language is not uncommon among the English. In the United States, however, anyone who is willing to quarrel with the dictionary is regarded as either eccentric or mad. 1

Let us see how dictionaries are made and how the editors arrive at definitions. What follows applies, incidentally, only to those dictionary offices where first-hand, original research goes on—not those in which editors simply copy existing dictionaries. The task of writing a dictionary begins with reading vast amounts of the literature of the period or subject that the dictionary is to cover. As the editors read, they copy on cards every interesting or rare word, every unusual or peculiar occurrence of a common word, a large number of common words in their ordinary uses, and also the sentences in which each of these words appear, thus: 2

pail
The dairy *pails* bring home increase of milk
Keats, *Endymion* I, 44–45

That is to say, the context of each word is collected, along with the word itself. For a really big job of dictionary-writing, such as the *Oxford English Dictionary* (usually bound in about twenty-five volumes), millions of such cards are collected, and the task of editing occupies decades. As the cards are collected, they are alphabetized and sorted. When the sorting is completed, there will be for each word anywhere from two or three to several hundred illustrative quotations, each on its card.

To define a word, then, the dictionary-editor places before him the stack of cards illustrating that word; each of the cards represents an actual use of the word by a writer of some literary or historical importance. He reads the cards carefully, discards some, rereads the rest, and divides up the stack according to what he thinks are the several senses of the word. Finally, he writes his definitions, following the hard-and-fast rule that each definition *must* be based on what the quotations in front of him reveal about the meaning of the word. The editor cannot be influenced by what *he* thinks a given word *ought* to mean. He must work according to the cards or not at all.

The writing of a dictionary, therefore, is not a task of setting up authoritative statements about the "true meanings" of words, but a task of *recording*, to the best of one's ability, what various words *have meant* to authors in the distant or immediate past. *The writer of a dictionary is a historian, not a lawgiver.* If, for example, we had been writing a dictionary in 1890, or even as late as 1919, we could have said that the word "broadcast" means "to scatter" (seed, for example), but we could not have decreed that from 1921 on, the most common meaning of the word should become "to disseminate audible messages, etc., by radio transmission." To regard the dictionary as an "authority," therefore, is to credit the dictionary-writer with gifts of prophecy which neither he nor anyone else possesses. In choosing our words when we speak or write, we can be *guided* by the historical record afforded us by the dictionary, but we cannot be *bound* by it, because new situations, new experiences, new inventions, new feelings are always compelling us to give new uses to old words. Looking under a "hood," we should ordinarily have found, five hundred years ago, a monk; today, we find a motorcar engine.

Questions for Study and Discussion

1. What is Hayakawa's thesis in this essay? Where is it stated? What is his purpose for writing this essay? (Glossary: *Thesis* and *Purpose*)
2. What type of process analysis is used in this essay? Would another type of process analysis be appropriate? Why, or why not?
3. In paragraphs 2–4 Hayakawa describes how dictionaries are made. Make a list of the steps involved in this process in their proper order.
4. Hayakawa uses examples to clarify points discussed in his essay. Cite the examples he shows in paragraphs 1, 2, and 5, and be prepared to discuss why he uses them.

Vocabulary

Refer to your dictionary to define the following words as they are used in this selection. Then use each word in a sentence of your own.

eccentric (1)
context (3)
authoritative (5)
disseminate (5)
prophecy (5)

Suggested Writing Assignment

Write an informational process analysis explaining how one of the following works:

a checking account
cell division
an automobile engine
the human eye
economic supply and demand
a microwave oven

How to Take a Job Interview

Kirby W. Stanat

A former personnel recruiter and placement officer at the University of Wisconsin-Milwaukee, Kirby W. Stanat has helped thousands of people get jobs. His book Job Hunting Secrets and Tactics *(1977) tells readers what they need to know in order to get the jobs they want. In this selection Stanat analyzes the campus interview, a process that hundreds of thousands of college students undergo each year as they seek to enter the job market.*

To succeed in campus job interviews, you have to know where that recruiter is coming from. The simple answer is that he is coming from corporate headquarters. 1

That may sound obvious, but it is a significant point that too many students do not consider. The recruiter is not a free spirit as he flies from Berkeley to New Haven, from Chapel Hill to Boulder. He's on an invisible leash to the office, and if he is worth his salary, he is mentally in corporate headquarters all the time he's on the road. 2

If you can fix that in your mind—that when you walk into that bare-walled cubicle in the placement center you are walking into a branch office of Sears, Bendix or General Motors—you can avoid a lot of little mistakes and maybe some big ones. 3

If, for example, you assume that because the interview is on campus the recruiter expects you to look and act like a student, you're in for a shock. A student is somebody who drinks beer, wears blue jeans and throws a Frisbee. No recruiter has jobs for student Frisbee whizzes. 4

A cool spring day in late March, Sam Davis, a good recruiter who has been on the college circuit for years, is on my campus talking to candidates. He comes out to the wait- 5 ing area to meet the student who signed up for an 11 o'clock interview. I'm standing in the doorway of my office taking in the scene.

Sam calls the candidate: "Sidney Student." There sits Sidney. He's at a 45 degree angle, his feet are in the aisle, and he's almost lying down. He's wearing well-polished brown shoes, a tasteful pair of brown pants, a light brown shirt, and a good looking tie. Unfortunately, he tops off this well-coordinated outfit with his Joe's Tavern Class A Softball Championship jacket, which has a big woven emblem over the heart.

If that isn't bad enough, in his left hand is a cigarette and in his right hand is a half-eaten apple.

When Sam calls his name, the kid is caught off guard. He ditches the cigarette in an ashtray, struggles to his feet, and transfers the apple from the right to the left hand. Apple juice is everywhere, so Sid wipes his hand on the seat of his pants and shakes hands with Sam.

Sam, who by now is close to having a stroke, gives me that what-do-I-have-here look and has the young man follow him into the interviewing room.

The situation deteriorates even further—into pure Laurel and Hardy. The kid is stuck with the half-eaten apple, doesn't know what to do with it, and obviously is suffering some discomfort. He carries the apple into the interviewing room with him and places it in the ashtray on the desk—right on top of Sam's freshly lit cigarette.

The interview lasts five minutes . . .

Let us move in for a closer look at how the campus recruiter operates.

Let's say you have a 10 o'clock appointment with the recruiter from the XYZ Corporation. The recruiter gets rid of the candidate in front of you at about 5 minutes to 10, jots down a few notes about what he is going to do with him or her, then picks up your résumé or data sheet (which you have submitted in advance) . . .

Although the recruiter is still in the interview room and you are still in the lobby, your interview is under way. You're on. The recruiter will look over your sheet pretty carefully before he goes out to call you. He develops a mental picture of you.

He thinks, "I'm going to enjoy talking with this kid," or "This one's going to be a turkey." The recruiter has already begun to make a screening decision about you. 15

His first impression of you, from reading the sheet, could come from your grade point. It could come from misspelled words. It could come from poor erasures or from the fact that necessary information is missing. By the time the recruiter has finished reading your sheet, you've already hit the plus or minus column. 16

Let's assume the recruiter got a fairly good impression from your sheet. 17

Now the recruiter goes out to the lobby to meet you. He almost shuffles along, and his mind is somewhere else. Then he calls your name, and at that instant he visibly clicks into gear. He just went to work. 18

As he calls your name he looks quickly around the room, waiting for somebody to move. If you are sitting on the middle of your back, with a book open and a cigarette going, and if you have to rebuild yourself to stand up, the interest will run right out of the recruiter's face. You, not the recruiter, made the appointment for 10 o'clock, and the recruiter expects to see a young professional come popping out of that chair like today is a good day and you're anxious to meet him. 19

At this point, the recruiter does something rude. He doesn't walk across the room to meet you halfway. He waits for you to come to him. Something very important is happening. He wants to see you move. He wants to get an impression about your posture, your stride, and your briskness. 20

If you slouch over him, sidewinderlike, he is not going to be impressed. He'll figure you would probably slouch your way through your workdays. He wants you to come at him with lots of good things going for you. If you watch the recruiter's eyes, you can see the inspection. He glances quickly at shoes, pants, coat, shirt; dress, blouse, hose—the whole works. 21

After introducing himself, the recruiter will probably say, 22

"Okay, please follow me," and he'll lead you into his interviewing room.

When you get to the room, you may find that the recruiter will open the door and gesture you in—with him blocking part of the doorway. There's enough room for you to get past him, but it's a near thing.

As you scrape past, he gives you a closeup inspection. He looks at your hair; if it's greasy, that will bother him. He looks at your collar; if it's dirty, that will bother him. He looks at your shoulders; if they're covered with dandruff, that will bother him. If you're a man, he looks at your chin. If you didn't get a close shave, that will irritate him. If you're a woman, he checks your makeup. If it's too heavy, he won't like it.

Then he smells you. An amazing number of people smell bad. Occasionally a recruiter meets a student who smells like a canal horse. That student can expect an interview of about four or five minutes.

Next the recruiter inspects the back side of you. He checks your hair (is it combed in front but not in back?), he checks your heels (are they run down?), your pants (are they baggy?), your slip (is it showing?), your stockings (do they have runs?).

Then he invites you to sit down.

At this point, I submit, the recruiter's decision on you is 75 to 80 percent made.

Think about it. The recruiter has read your résumé. He knows who you are and where you are from. He knows your marital status, your major and your grade point. And he knows what you have done with your summers. He has inspected you, exchanged greetings with you and smelled you. There is very little additional hard information that he must gather on you. From now on it's mostly body chemistry.

Many recruiters have argued strenuously with me that they don't make such hasty decisions. So I tried an experiment. I told several recruiters that I would hang around in the hall outside the interview room when they took candidates in.

I told them that as soon as they had definitely decided not

to recommend (to department managers in their companies) the candidate they were interviewing, they should snap their fingers loud enough for me to hear. It went like this.

First candidate: 38 seconds after the candidate sat down: Snap! 32

Second candidate: 1 minute, 42 seconds: Snap! 33

Third candidate: 45 seconds: Snap! 34

One recruiter was particularly adamant, insisting that he didn't rush to judgment on candidates. I asked him to participate in the snapping experiment. He went out in the lobby, picked up his first candidate of the day, and headed for an interview room. 35

As he passed me in the hall, he glared at me. And his fingers went "Snap!" 36

Questions for Study and Discussion

1. What are Stanat's purpose and thesis in telling the reader how the recruitment process works? (Glossary: *Purpose* and *Thesis*)
2. In paragraphs 12–29 Stanat explains how the campus recruiter works. Make a list of the steps in that process.
3. Identify the transitional devices that Stanat uses in paragraphs 12–29 to mark clearly the sequence of steps in the recruitment process. (Glossary: *Transitions*)
4. For what audience has Stanat written this essay? What in the essay leads you to this conclusion? (Glossary: *Audience*)
5. Stanat's tone—his attitude toward his subject and audience—in this essay is informal. What in his sentence structure and diction creates this informality? Cite examples. How might the tone be made more formal for a different audience?

Vocabulary

Refer to your dictionary to define the following words as they are used in this selection. Then use each word in a sentence of your own.

cubicle (3)
deteriorates (10)
résumé (13)
adamant (35)

Suggested Writing Assignment

Stanat analyzes the recruitment process from the standpoint of an experienced recruiter. Using the information that he provides, write a directional process analysis of the recruitment interview. You may find it helpful before starting to write to make a list of the specific directions you will include in your essay.

14

DEFINITION

To communicate precisely what you want to say, you will frequently need to *define* key words. Your reader needs to know just what you mean when you use unfamiliar words, such as *accouterment* or words that are open to various interpretations, such as *liberal* or words that, while generally familiar, are used in a particular sense. Failure to define important terms, or to define them accurately, confuses readers and hampers communication.

There are three basic ways to define a word; each is useful in its own way. The first method is to give a *synonym*, a word that has nearly the same meaning as the word you wish to define: *face* for *countenance*, *nervousness* for *anxiety*. No two words ever have *exactly* the same meaning, but you can, nevertheless, pair an unfamiliar word with a familiar one and thereby clarify your meaning.

Another way to define a word quickly, often within a single sentence, is to give a *formal definition*; that is, to place the term to be defined in a general class and then to distinguish it from other members of that class by describing its particular characteristics. For example:

WORD	CLASS	CHARACTERISTICS
A *watch*	is *a mechanical* device	*for telling time* and is usually *carried* or *worn*.
Semantics	is an *area of linguistics*	*concerned with the study of the meaning of words.*

The third method is known as *extended definition*. While some extended definitions require only a single paragraph, more often than not you will need several paragraphs or even an entire essay to define a new or difficult term or to rescue a controversial word from misconceptions and associations that may obscure its meaning.

One controversial term that illustrates the need for extended definition is *obscene*. What is obscene? Books that are banned in one school system are considered perfectly acceptable in another. Movies that are shown in one town cannot be shown in a neighboring town. Clearly, the meaning of *obscene* has been clouded by contrasting personal opinions as well as by conflicting social norms. Therefore, if you use the term *obscene* (and especially if you tackle the issue of obscenity itself), you must be careful to define clearly and thoroughly what you mean by that term—that is, you have to give an extended definition. There are a number of methods you might use to develop such a definition. You could define *obscene* by explaining what it does not mean. You could also make your meaning clear by narrating an experience, by comparing and contrasting it to related terms such as *pornographic* or *exotic*, by citing specific examples, or by classifying the various types of obscenity.

A JERK

Sidney J. Harris

Since 1944 Sidney J. Harris has written for the Chicago Daily News *the syndicated column "Strictly Personal," in which he has considered virtually every aspect of contemporary American life. In the following essay from his book* Last Things First *(1961), Harris defines the term* jerk *by differentiating it from other similar slang terms.*

I don't know whether history repeats itself, but biography certainly does. The other day, Michael came in and asked me what a "jerk" was—the same question Carolyn put to me a dozen years ago. 1

At that time, I fluffed her off with some inane answer, such as "A jerk isn't a very nice person," but both of us knew it was an unsatisfactory reply. When she went to bed, I began trying to work up a suitable definition. 2

It is a marvelously apt word, of course. Until it was coined, not more than 25 years ago, there was really no single word in English to describe the kind of person who is a jerk—"boob" and "simp" were too old hat, and besides they really didn't fit, for they could be lovable, and a jerk never is. 3

Thinking it over, I decided that a jerk is basically a person without insight. He is not necessarily a fool or a dope, because some extremely clever persons can be jerks. In fact, it has little to do with intelligence as we commonly think of it; it is, rather, a kind of subtle but persuasive aroma emanating from the inner part of the personality. 4

I know a college president who can be described only as a jerk. He is not an unintelligent man, nor unlearned, nor even unschooled in the social amenities. Yet he is a jerk *cum laude*, because of a fatal flaw in his nature—he is totally incapable of looking into the mirror of his soul and shuddering at what he sees there. 5

A jerk, then, is a man (or woman) who is utterly unable to see himself as he appears to others. He has no grace, he is tactless without meaning to be, he is a bore even to his best friends, he is an egotist without charm. All of us are egotists to some extent, but most of us—unlike the jerk—are perfectly and horribly aware of it when we make asses of ourselves. The jerk never knows.

Questions for Study and Discussion

1. What, according to Harris, is a jerk?
2. Jerks, boobs, simps, fools, and dopes are all in the same class. How does Harris differentiate a jerk from a boob or a simp on the one hand, and a fool or a dope on the other?
3. In paragraph 5 Harris presents the example of the college president. How does this example support his definition?

Vocabulary

Refer to your dictionary to define the following words as they are used in this selection. Then use each word in a sentence of your own.

inane (2)	emanating (4)
apt (3)	amenities (5)
coined (3)	tactless (6)

Suggested Writing Assignments

1. Write one or two paragraphs in which you give your own definition of *jerk* or another slang term of your choice.
2. Every generation develops its own slang, which generally enlivens the speech and writing of those who use it. Ironically, however, no generation can arrive at a consensus definition of even its most popu-

lar slang terms—for example, *nimrod, air-head, flag.* Select a slang term that you use frequently, and write an essay in which you define the term. Read your definition aloud in class. Do the other members of your class agree with your definition?

What Is Freedom?

Jerald M. Jellison and John H. Harvey

Jerald M. Jellison, professor of psychology at the University of Southern California, specializes in theories of human social behavior. John H. Harvey, professor of social psychology at Vanderbilt University, recently coedited a collection of studies in social behavior. In this selection from Psychology Today, *Jellison and Harvey use an illustrative story to help them define* freedom, *an important but elusive concept.*

The pipe under your kitchen sink springs a leak and you call in a plumber. A few days later you get a bill for $40. At the bottom is a note saying that if you don't pay within 30 days, there'll be a 10 percent service charge of $4. You feel trapped, with no desirable alternative. You pay $40 now or $44 later.

Now make two small changes in the script. The plumber sends you a bill for $44, but the note says that if you pay within 30 days you'll get a special $4 discount. Now you feel pretty good. You have two alternatives, one of which will save you $4.

In fact, your choices are the same in both cases—pay $40 now or $44 later—but your feelings about them are different. This illustrates a subject we've been studying for several years: What makes people feel free and why does feeling free make them happy? One factor we've studied is that individuals feel freer when they can choose between positive alternatives (delaying payment or saving $4) rather than between negative ones (paying immediately or paying $4 more).

Choosing between negative alternatives often seems like no choice at all. Take the case of a woman trying to decide whether to stay married to her inconsiderate, incompetent husband, or get a divorce. She doesn't want to stay with him, but she feels divorce is a sign of failure and will stigmatize her socially. Or think of the decision faced by many young men a few years ago, when they were forced to choose between leaving their country and family or being sent to Vietnam.

5 When we face decisions involving only alternatives we see as negatives, we feel so little freedom that we twist and turn searching for another choice with some positive characteristics.

6 Freedom is a popular word. Individuals talk about how they feel free with one person and not with another, or how their bosses encourage or discourage freedom on the job. We hear about civil wars and revolutions being fought for greater freedom, with both sides righteously making the claim. The feeling of freedom is so important that people say they're ready to die for it, and supposedly have.

7 Still, most people have trouble coming up with a precise definition of freedom. They give answers describing specific situations—"Freedom means doing what I want to do, not what the Government wants me to do," or "Freedom means not having my mother tell me when to come home from a party"—rather than a general definition covering many situations. The idea they seem to be expressing is that freedom is associated with making decisions, and that other people sometimes limit the number of alternatives from which they can select.

Questions for Study and Discussion

1. What general definition of *freedom* do Jellison and Harvey present? Where in the essay is that definition given?
2. When, according to Jellison and Harvey, do individuals feel free?
3. Explain how Jellison and Harvey use examples to develop their definition of *freedom*. (You may find it helpful to outline the essay paragraph by paragraph.)

4. Paragraph 5 is pivotal in this essay. Explain why it is so important. (It might be helpful to consider the essay without paragraph 5.)
5. The author's tone in this essay is informal, almost conversational. Cite examples of diction and sentence structure to show how they establish and maintain this tone. (Glossary: *Tone*)

Vocabulary

Refer to your dictionary to define the following words as they are used in this selection. Then use each word in a sentence of your own.

script (2)
incompetent (4)
stigmatize (4)
righteously (6)

Suggested Writing Assignment

Write a short essay in which you define one of the following abstract terms. Begin your essay with an illustrative example as Jellison and Harvey do in their essay.

charm	trust
friendship	commitment
hatred	religion
leadership	love

The Barrio

Robert Ramirez

Robert Ramirez has worked as a cameraman, reporter, anchorman, and producer for the news team at KGBT-TV in Edinburg, Texas. Presently, he works in the Latin American division of the Northern Trust Bank in Chicago. In the following essay, Ramirez discusses those distinctive characteristics that, when taken together, define the district called the barrio.

The train, its metal wheels squealing as they spin along the silvery tracks, rolls slower now. Through the gaps between the cars blinks a streetlamp, and this pulsing light on a barrio streetcorner beats slower, like a weary heartbeat, until the train shudders to a halt, the light goes out, and the barrio is deep asleep. 1

Throughout Aztlán (the Nahuatl term meaning "land to the north"), trains grumble along the edges of a sleeping people. From Lower California, through the blistering Southwest, down the Rio Grande to the muddy Gulf, the darkness and mystery of dreams engulf communities fenced off by railroads, canals, and expressways. Paradoxical communities, isolated from the rest of the town by concrete columned monuments of progress, and yet stranded in the past. They are surrounded by change. It eludes their reach, in their own backyards, and the people, unable and unwilling to see the future, or even touch the present, perpetuate the past. 2

Leaning from the expressway or jolting across the tracks, one enters a different physical world permeated by a different attitude. The physical dimensions are impressive. It is a large section of town which extends for fifteen blocks north and south along the tracks, and then advances eastward, thinning into nothingness beyond the city limits. With- 3 in the invisible (yet sensible) walls of the barrio, are many, many people living in too few houses. The homes, however, are much more numerous than on the outside.

Members of the barrio describe the entire area as their home. It is a home, but it is more than this. The barrio is a refuge from the harshness and the coldness of the Anglo world. It is a forced refuge. The leprous people are isolated from the rest of the community and contained in their section of town. The stoical pariahs of the barrio accept their fate, and from the angry seeds of rejection grow the flowers of closeness between outcasts, not the thorns of bitterness and the mad desire to flee. There is no want to escape, for the feeling of the barrio is known only to its inhabitants, and the material needs of life can also be found here.

The *tortillería* [tortilla factory] fires up its machinery three times a day, producing steaming, round, flat slices of barrio bread. In the winter, the warmth of the tortilla factory is a wool *sarape* [blanket] in the chilly morning hours, but in the summer, it unbearably toasts every noontime customer.

The *panadería* [bakery] sends its sweet messenger aroma down the dimly lit street, announcing the arrival of fresh, hot sugary *pan dulce* [sweet rolls].

The small corner grocery serves the meal-to-meal needs of customers, and the owner, a part of the neighborhood, willingly gives credit to people unable to pay cash for foodstuffs.

The barbershop is a living room with hydraulic chairs, radio, and television, where old friends meet and speak of life as their salted hair falls aimlessly about them.

The pool hall is a junior level country club where *'chucos,* [young men] strangers in their own land, get together to shoot pool and rap, while veterans, unaware of the cracking, popping balls on the green felt, complacently play dominoes beneath rudely hung *Playboy* foldouts.

The *cantina* [canteen or snackbar] is the night spot of the barrio. It is the country club and the den where the rites of puberty are enacted. Here the young become men. It is in the taverns that a young dude shows his *machismo* through the quantity of beer he can hold, the stories of *rucas* [women] he has had, and his willingness and ability to defend his image against hardened and scarred old lions.

11 No, there is no frantic wish to flee. It would be absurd to leave the familiar and nervously step into the strange and cold Anglo community when the needs of the Chicano can be met in the barrio.

12 The barrio is closeness. From the family living unit, familial relationships stretch out to immediate neighbors, down the block, around the corner, and to all parts of the barrio. The feeling of family, a rare and treasurable sentiment, pervades and accounts for the inability of the people to leave. The barrio is this attitude manifested on the countenances of the people, on the faces of their homes, and in the gaiety of their gardens.

13 The color-splashed homes arrest your eyes, arouse your curiosity, and make you wonder what life scenes are being played out in them. The flimsy, brightly colored, wood-frame houses ignore no neon-brilliant color. Houses trimmed in orange, chartreuse, lime-green, yellow, and mixtures of these and other hues beckon the beholder to reflect on the peculiarity of each home. Passing through this land is refreshing like Brubeck*, not narcoticizing like revolting rows of similar houses, which neither offend nor please.

14 In the evenings, the porches and front yards are occupied with men calmly talking over the noise of children playing baseball in the unpaved extension of the living room, while the women cook supper or gossip with female neighbors as they water the *jardines* [gardens]. The gardens mutely echo the expressive verses of the colorful houses. The denseness of multicolored plants and trees gives the house the appearance of an oasis or a tropical island hideaway, sheltered from the rest of the world.

15 Fences are common in the barrio, but they are fences and not the walls of the Anglo community. On the western side of town, the high wooden fences between houses are thick, impenetrable walls, built to keep the neighbors at bay. In the barrio, the fences may be rusty, wire contraptions or thick

---

*Dave Brubeck, pianist, composer, and conductor of "cool" modern jazz.

green shrubs. In either case you can see through them and feel no sense of intrusion when you cross them.

Many lower-income families of the barrio manage to maintain a comfortable standard of living through the communal action of family members who contribute their wages to the head of the family. Economic need creates interdependence and closeness. Small barefooted boys sell papers on cool, dark Sunday mornings, deny themselves pleasantries, and give their earnings to *mamá*. The older the child, the greater the responsibility to help the head of the household provide for the rest of the family.

There are those, too, who for a number of reasons have not achieved a relative sense of financial security. Perhaps it results from too many children too soon, but it is the homes of these people and their situation that numbs rather than charms. Their houses, aged and bent, oozing children, are fissures in the horn of plenty. Their wooden homes may have brick-pattern asbestos tile on the outer walls, but the tile is not convincing.

Unable to pay city taxes or incapable of influencing the city to live up to its duty to serve all the citizens, the poorer barrio families remain trapped in the nineteenth century and survive as best they can. The backyards have well-worn paths to the outhouses, which sit near the alley. Running water is considered a luxury in some parts of the barrio. Decent drainage is usually unknown, and when it rains, the water stands for days, an incubator of health hazards and an avoidable nuisance. Streets, costly to pave, remain rough, rocky trails. Tires do not last long, and the constant rattling and shaking grind away a car's life and spread dust through screen windows.

The houses and their *jardines*, the jollity of the people in an adverse world, the brightly feathered alarm clock pecking away at supper and cautiously eyeing the children playing nearby, produce a mystifying sensation at finding the noble savage alive in the twentieth century. It is easy to look at the positive qualities of life in the barrio, and look at them with a distantly envious feeling. One wishes to experience the feelings of the barrio and not the hardships. Remembering the illness, the hunger, the feeling of time running out on you, the walls, both real and imagined, reflecting on living in the past, one finds his envy becoming more elusive, until it has vanished altogether.

Back now beyond the tracks, the train creaks and groans, the cars jostle each other down the track, and as the light begins its pulsing, the barrio, with all its meanings, greets a new dawn with yawns and restless stretchings. 20

Questions for Study and Discussion

1. What is a barrio? How does it serve the needs of its inhabitants?
2. Ramirez relies heavily on description in his definition of the word *barrio*, describing the physical appearance of the barrio as well as the feelings that the inhabitants have for the barrio. Briefly summarize the important physical details and emotional associations he provides, and comment on their contribution to his definition.
3. In defining *barrio* Ramirez also uses the words *home, refuge, family, closeness,* and *neighborhood.* What connotations do these words have? Do they add a particular element to the definition? Are they essential to Ramirez's definition, or just helpful? (Glossary: *Connotation/Denotation*)
4. Identify three similes or metaphors that Ramirez uses in this essay. In what ways is each appropriate and effective? (Glossary: *Figures of Speech*)
5. Explain Ramirez's use of the imagery of walls and fences to develop his theme of cultural isolation. What might this imagery be symbolic of? (Glossary: *Symbol*)
6. For what audience is Ramirez writing? What evidence do you find in the essay to support your answer? (Glossary: *Audience*)

Vocabulary

Refer to your dictionary to define the following words as they are used in this selection. Then use each word in a sentence of your own.

paradoxical (2)	aroma (6)
eludes (2)	countenances (12)
permeated (3)	fissures (17)
stoical (4)	elusive (19)

Suggested Writing Assignment

Write a brief essay in which you draw upon personal experiences and observations in order to define one of the following concepts:

the subway
the beach
Christmas morning
an open-air or farmers' market
the airport lobby
your neighborhood

15

Division and Classification

To divide is to separate a class of things or ideas into categories, whereas to classify is to group separate things or ideas into those categories. The two processes can operate separately but often go together. Division and classification can be a useful organizational strategy in writing. Here, for example, is a passage about levers in which the writer first uses division to establish three categories of levers and then uses classification to group individual levers into those categories:

> Every lever has one fixed point called the "fulcrum" and is acted upon by two forces—the "effort" (exertion of hand muscles) and the "weight" (object's resistance). Levers work according to a simple formula: the effort (how hard you push or pull) multiplied by its distance from the fulcrum (effort arm) equals the weight multiplied by its distance from the fulcrum (weight arm). Thus two pounds of effort exerted at a distance of four feet from the fulcrum will raise eight pounds located one foot from the fulcrum.
>
> There are three types of levers, conventionally called "first kind," "second kind," and "third kind." Levers of the first kind have the fulcrum located between the effort and the weight. Examples are a pump handle, an oar, a crowbar, a weighing balance, a pair of scissors, and a pair of pliers. Levers of the second kind have the weight in the middle and magnify the effort. Examples are the handcar crank and doors. Levers of the third kind, such as a power shovel or a baseball batter's forearm, have the effort in the middle and always magnify the distance.

In writing, division and classification are affected directly by the writer's practical purpose. That purpose—what the writer wants to explain or prove—determines the class of things or ideas being divided and classified. For instance, a writer might divide television programs according to their audiences—adults, families, or children—and then classify individual programs into each of these categories in order to show how much emphasis the television stations place on reaching each audience. A different purpose would require different categories. A writer concerned about the prevalence of violence in television programming would first divide television programs into those which include fights and murders, and those which do not, and would then classify a large sample of programs into those categories. Other writers with different purposes might divide television programs differently—by the day and time of broadcast, for example, or by the number of women featured in prominent roles—and then classify individual programs accordingly.

The following guidelines can help you in using division and classification in your writing:

1. *Identify a clear purpose, and be sure that your principle of division is appropriate to that purpose.* To determine the makeup of a student body, for example, you might consider the following principles of division: college or program, major, class level, sex. It would not be helpful to divide students on the basis of their toothpaste unless you had a purpose and thus a reason for doing so.
2. *Divide your subject into categories that are mutually exclusive.* An item can belong to only one category. For example, it would be unsatisfactory to divide students as men, women, and athletes.
3. *Make your division and classification complete.* Your categories should account for all items in a subject class. In dividing students on the basis of geographic origin, for example, it would be inappropriate to consider only home states, for such a division would not account for foreign students. Then, for your classification to be complete, every student must be placed in one of the established categories.
4. *Be sure to state clearly the conclusion that your*

division and classification lead you to draw. For example, a study of the student body might lead to the conclusion that 45 percent of the male athletes with athletic scholarships come from west of the Mississippi.

Children's Insults

Peter Farb

From his undergraduate years at Vanderbilt University on, Peter Farb (1929–1980) had an intense interest in language and its role in human behavior. Farb was a consultant to the Smithsonian Institution, a curator of the Riverside Museum in New York City, and a visiting lecturer in English at Yale. In this essay, taken from Word Play: What Happens When People Talk *(1973), Farb classifies the names children use to insult one another.*

The insults spoken by adults are usually more subtle than the simple name-calling used by children, but children's insults make obvious some of the verbal strategies people carry into adult life. Most parents engage in wishful thinking when they regard name-calling as good-natured fun which their children will soon grow out of. Name-calling is not good-natured and children do not grow out of it; as adults they merely become more expert in its use. Nor is it true that "sticks and stones may break my bones, but names will never hurt me." Names can hurt very much because children seek out the victim's true weakness, then jab exactly where the skin is thinnest. Name-calling can have major impact on a child's feelings about his identity, and it can sometimes be devastating to his psychological development.

Almost all examples of name-calling by children fall into four categories:

1. Names based on physical peculiarities, such as deformities, use of eyeglasses, racial characteristics, and so forth. A child may be called *Flattop* because he was born with a misshapen skull—or, for obvious reasons, *Fat Lips, Gimpy, Four Eyes, Peanuts, Fatso, Kinky,* and so on.

2. Names based on a pun or parody of the child's own name. Children with last names like Fitts, McClure, and Farb usually find them converted to *Shits, Manure,* and *Fart.*
3. Names based on social relationships. Examples are *Baby* used by a sibling rival or *Chicken Shit* for someone whose courage is questioned by his social group.
4. Names based on mental traits—such as *Clunkhead, Dummy, Jerk,* and *Smartass.*

These four categories were listed in order of decreasing offensiveness to the victims. Children regard names based on physical peculiarities as the most cutting, whereas names based on mental traits are, surprisingly, not usually regarded as very offensive. Most children are very vulnerable to names that play upon the child's rightful name—no doubt because one's name is a precious possession, the mark of a unique identity and one's masculinity or femininity. Those American Indian tribes that had the custom of never revealing true names undoubtedly avoided considerable psychological damage.

Questions for Study and Discussion

1. What is Farb's contention in this selection? Where is it revealed? For what reason does he divide and classify children's insults?
2. Why does Farb feel that name-calling should not be dismissed lightly?
3. Farb states that children "regard names based on physical peculiarities as the most cutting." Why do suppose this might be true?
4. What principle of division does Farb use to establish his four categories of children's insults? What are the categories, and how does he order them? Be prepared to cite examples from the text.

5. List some insults that you remember from your own childhood or adolescence. Classify the insults according to Farb's system. Do any items on your list not fit into one of his categories? What new categories can you establish?

Vocabulary

Refer to your dictionary to define the following words as they are used in this selection. Then use each word in a sentence of your own.

subtle (1)	sibling (2)
peculiarities (2)	vulnerable (2)
deformities (2)	unique (2)

Suggested Writing Assignment

Consider the following classes of items and determine at least two principles of division that can be used for each class. Then write a paragraph or two in which you classify one of the groups of items according to a single principle of division. For example, in discussing crime one could use the seriousness of the crime or the type of crime as principles of division. If the seriousness of the crime were used, this might yield two categories: felonies, or major crimes; and misdemeanors, or minor crimes. If the type of crime were used, this would yield categories such as burglary, murder, assault, larceny, and embezzlement.

professional sports
social sciences
movies
roommates
cars
slang used by college students

The Ways of Meeting Oppression

Martin Luther King, Jr.

Martin Luther King, Jr. (1929–1968) was the leading spokesman for the rights of American blacks during the 1950s and 1960s before he was assassinated in 1968. He established the Southern Christian Leadership Conference, organized many civil rights demonstrations, and opposed the Viet Nam War and the draft. In 1964 he was awarded the Nobel Prize for Peace. In the following essay, taken from his book Stride Toward Freedom *(1958), King classifies the three ways oppressed people throughout history have reacted to their oppressors.*

Oppressed people deal with their oppression in three characteristic ways. One way is acquiescence: the oppressed resign themselves to their doom. They tacitly adjust themselves to oppression, and thereby become conditioned to it. In every movement toward freedom some of the oppressed prefer to remain oppressed. Almost 2800 years ago Moses set out to lead the children of Israel from the slavery of Egypt to the freedom of the promised land. He soon discovered that slaves do not always welcome their deliverers. They become accustomed to being slaves. They would rather bear those ills they have, as Shakespeare pointed out, than flee to others that they know not of. They prefer the "fleshpots of Egypt" to the ordeals of emancipation. 1

There is such a thing as the freedom of exhaustion. Some people are so worn down by the yoke of oppression that they give up. A few years ago in the slum areas of Atlanta, a Negro guitarist used to sing almost daily: "Ben down so long that down don't bother me." This is the type of negative freedom and resignation that often engulfs the life of the oppressed. 2

But this is not the way out. To accept passively an unjust system is to cooperate with that system; thereby the oppressed become as evil as the oppressor. Noncooperation with evil is as much a moral obligation as is cooperation with good. The oppressed must never allow the conscience of the oppressor to slumber. Religion reminds every man that he is his brother's keeper. To accept injustice or segregation passively is to say to the oppressor that his actions are morally right. It is a way of allowing his conscience to fall asleep. At this moment the oppressed fails to be his brother's keeper. So acquiescence—while often the easier way—is not the moral way. It is the way of the coward. The Negro cannot win the respect of his oppressor by acquiescing; he merely increases the oppressor's arrogance and contempt. Acquiescence is interpreted as proof of the Negro's inferiority. The Negro cannot win the respect of the white people of the South or the peoples of the world if he is willing to sell the future of his children for his personal and immediate comfort and safety.

A second way that oppressed people sometimes deal with oppression is to resort to physical violence and corroding hatred. Violence often brings about momentary results. Nations have frequently won their independence in battle. But in spite of temporary victories, violence never brings permanent peace. It solves no social problem; it merely creates new and more complicated ones.

Violence as a way of achieving racial justice is both impractical and immoral. It is impractical because it is a descending spiral ending in destruction for all. The old law of an eye for an eye leaves everybody blind. It is immoral because it seeks to humiliate the opponent rather than win his understanding; it seeks to annihilate rather than to convert. Violence is immoral because it thrives on hatred rather than love. It destroys community and makes brotherhood impossible. It leaves society in monologue rather than dialogue. Violence ends by defeating itself. It creates bitterness in the survivors and brutality in the destroyers. A voice echoes through time saying to every potential Peter, "Put up your sword."* History is cluttered with the wreckage of nations that failed to follow this command.

6 If the American Negro and other victims of oppression succumb to the temptation of using violence in the struggle for freedom, future generations will be the recipients of a desolate night of bitterness, and our chief legacy to them will be an endless reign of meaningless chaos. Violence is not the way.

7 The third way open to oppressed people in their quest for freedom is the way of nonviolent resistance. Like the synthesis in Hegelian philosophy, the principle of nonviolent resistance seeks to reconcile the truths of two opposites—the acquiescence and violence—while avoiding the extremes and immoralities of both. The nonviolent resister agrees with the person who acquiesces that one should not be physically aggressive toward his opponent; but he balances the equation by agreeing with the person of violence that evil must be resisted. He avoids the nonresistance of the former and the violent resistance of the latter. With nonviolent resistance, no individual or group need submit to any wrong, nor need anyone resort to violence in order to right a wrong.

8 It seems to me that this is the method that must guide the actions of the Negro in the present crisis in race relations. Through nonviolent resistance the Negro will be able to rise to the noble height of opposing the unjust system while loving the perpetrators of the system. The Negro must work passionately and unrelentingly for full stature as a citizen, but he must not use inferior methods to gain it. He must never come to terms with falsehood, malice, hate, or destruction.

9 Nonviolent resistance makes it possible for the Negro to remain in the South and struggle for his rights. The Negro's problem will not be solved by running away. He cannot listen to the glib suggestion of those who would urge him to migrate en masse to other sections of the country. By grasp-

*The apostle Peter had drawn his sword to defend Christ from arrest. The voice was Christ's, who surrendered himself for trial and crucifixion (John 18:11).

ing his great opportunity in the South he can make a lasting contribution to the moral strength of the nation and set a sublime example of courage for generations yet unborn.

By nonviolent resistance, the Negro can also enlist all men of good will in his struggle for equality. The problem is not a purely racial one, with Negroes set against whites. In the end, it is not a struggle between people at all, but a tension between justice and injustice. Nonviolent resistance is not aimed against oppressors but against oppression. Under its banner consciences, not racial groups, are enlisted.

Questions for Study and Discussion

1. What are the disadvantages that King sees in meeting oppression with acquiescence or with violence?
2. What is King's purpose in writing this essay? How does classifying the three types of resistance to oppression serve this purpose?
3. What principle of division does King use in this essay?
4. Why do you suppose that King discusses acquiescence, violence, and nonviolent resistance in that order? (Glossary: *Organization*)
5. King states that he favors nonviolent resistance over the other two ways of meeting oppression. Look closely at the words he uses to describe nonviolent resistance and those he uses to describe acquiescence and violence. How does his choice of words contribute to his argument? Show examples. (Glossary: *Connotation/Denotation*)

Vocabulary

Refer to your dictionary to define the following words as they are used in this selection. Then use each word in a sentence of your own.

acquiescence (1)
tacitly (1)
corroding (4)
annihilate (5)
desolate (6)
synthesis (7)
sublime (9)

Suggested Writing Assignment

Write an essay about a problem of some sort in which you use division and classification to discuss various possible solutions. You might discuss something personal such as the problems of giving up smoking or something that concerns everyone such as the difficulties of coping with limited supplies of oil and gasoline. Whatever your topic, use an appropriate principle of division to establish categories that suit the purpose of your discussion.

FRIENDS, GOOD FRIENDS —AND SUCH GOOD FRIENDS

Judith Viorst

Judith Viorst has written several volumes of light verse as well as many articles that have appeared in popular magazines. The following essay appeared in her regular column in Redbook. *In it she analyzes and classifies the various types of friends that a person can have. As you read the essay, assess its validity by trying to place your friends in Viorst's categories.*

Women are friends, I once would have said, when they totally love and support and trust each other, and bare to each other the secrets of their souls, and run—no questions asked—to help each other, and tell harsh truths to each other (no, you can't wear that dress unless you lose ten pounds first) when harsh truths must be told.

Women are friends, I once would have said, when they share the same affection for Ingmar Bergman, plus train rides, cats, warm rain, charades, Camus, and hate with equal ardor Newark and Brussels sprouts and Lawrence Welk and camping.

In other words, I once would have said that a friend is a friend all the way, but now I believe that's a narrow point of view. For the friendships I have and the friendships I see are conducted at many levels of intensity, serve many different functions, meet different needs and range from those as all-the-way as the friendship of the soul sisters mentioned above to that of the most nonchalant and casual playmates.

Consider these varieties of friendship:

1. Convenience friends. These are women with whom, if our paths weren't crossing all the time, we'd have no particular reason to be friends: a next-door neighbor, a woman

in our car pool, the mother of one of our children's closest friends or maybe some mommy with whom we serve juice and cookies each week at the Glenwood Co-op Nursery.

Convenience friends are convenient indeed. They'll lend us their cups and silverware for a party. They'll drive our kids to soccer when we're sick. They'll take us to pick up our car when we need a lift to the garage. They'll even take our cats when we go on vacation. As we will for them. 6

But we don't, with convenience friends, ever come too close or tell too much; we maintain our public face and emotional distance. "Which means," says Elaine, "that I'll talk about being overweight but not about being depressed. Which means I'll admit being mad but not blind with rage. Which means that I might say that we're pinched this month but never that I'm worried sick over money." 7

But which doesn't mean that there isn't sufficient value to be found in these friendships of mutual aid, in convenience friends. 8

2. Special-interest friends. These friendships aren't intimate, and they needn't involve kids or silverware or cats. Their value lies in some interest jointly shared. And so we may have an office friend or a yoga friend or a tennis friend or a friend from the Women's Democratic Club. 9

"I've got one woman friend," says Joyce, "who likes, as I do, to take psychology courses. Which makes it nice for me—and nice for her. It's fun to go with someone you know and it's fun to discuss what you've learned, driving back from the classes." And for the most part, she says, that's all they discuss. 10

"I'd say that what we're doing is *doing* together, not being together," Suzanne says of her Tuesday-doubles friends. "It's mainly a tennis relationship, but we play together well. And I guess we all need to have a couple of playmates." 11

I agree. 12

My playmate is a shopping friend, a woman of marvelous taste, a woman who knows exactly *where* to buy *what*, and furthermore is a woman who always knows beyond a doubt what one ought to be buying. I don't have the time to keep up with what's new in eyeshadow, hemlines and shoes and whether the smock look is in or finished already. But since 13 (oh, shame!) I care a lot about eyeshadow, hemlines and shoes, and since I don't *want* to wear smocks if the smock look is finished, I'm very glad to have a shopping friend.

3. Historical friends. We all have a friend who knew us when . . . maybe way back in Miss Meltzer's second grade, when our family lived in that three-room flat in Brooklyn, when our dad was out of work for seven months, when our brother Allie got in that fight where they had to call the police, when our sister married the endodontist from Yonkers and when, the morning after we lost our virginity, she was the first, the only, friend we told.

The years have gone by and we've gone separate ways and we've little in common now, but we're still an intimate part of each other's past. And so whenever we go to Detroit we always go to visit this friend of our girlhood. Who knows how we looked before our teeth were straightened. Who knows how we talked before our voice got un-Brooklyned. Who knows what we ate before we learned about artichokes. And who, by her presence, puts us in touch with an earlier part of ourself, a part of ourself it's important never to lose.

"What this friend means to me and what I mean to her," says Grace, "is having a sister without sibling rivalry. We know the texture of each other's lives. She remembers my grandmother's cabbage soup. I remember the way her uncle played the piano. There's simply no other friend who remembers those things."

4. Crossroads friends. Like historical friends, our crossroads friends are important for *what was*—for the friendship we shared at a crucial, now past, time of life. A time, perhaps, when we roomed in college together; or worked as eager young singles in the Big City together; or went together, as my friend Elizabeth and I did, through pregnancy, birth and that scary first year of new motherhood.

Crossroads friends forge powerful links, links strong enough to endure with not much more contact than once-a-year letters at Christmas. And out of respect for those crossroads years, for those dramas and dreams we once shared, we will always be friends.

5. Cross-generational friends. Historical friends and crossroads friends seem to maintain a special kind of intimacy—dormant but always ready to be revived—and though we may rarely meet, whenever we do connect, it's personal and intense. Another kind of intimacy exists in the friendships that form across generations in what one woman calls her daughter-mother and her mother-daughter relationships. 19

Evelyn's friend is her mother's age—"but I share so much more than I ever could with my mother"—a woman she talks to of music, of books and of life. "What I get from her is the benefit of her experience. What she gets—and enjoys—from me is a youthful perspective. It's a pleasure for both of us." 20

I have in my own life a precious friend, a woman of 65 who has lived very hard, who is wise, who listens well; who has been where I am and can help me understand it; and who represents not only an ultimate ideal mother to me but also the person I'd like to be when I grow up. 21

In our daughter role we tend to do more than our share of self-revelation; in our mother role we tend to receive what's revealed. It's another kind of pleasure—playing wise mother to a questing younger person. It's another very lovely kind of friendship. 22

6. Part-of-a-couple friends. Some of the women we call our friends we never see alone—we see them as part of a couple at couples' parties. And though we share interests in many things and respect each other's views, we aren't moved to deepen the relationship. Whatever the reason, a lack of time or—and this is more likely—a lack of chemistry, our friendship remains in the context of a group. But the fact that our feeling on seeing each other is always, "I'm *so* glad she's here" and the fact that we spend half the evening talking together says that this too, in its own way, counts as a friendship. 23

(Other part-of-a-couple friends are the friends that came with the marriage, and some of these are friends we could live without. But sometimes, alas, she married our husband's best friend; and sometimes, alas, she *is* our husband's best friend. And so we find ourself dealing with her, some- 24 what against our will, in a spirit of what I'll call *reluctant* friendship.)

7. Men who are friends. I wanted to write just of women friends, but the women I've talked to won't let me—they say I must mention man-woman friendships too. For these friendships can be just as close and as dear as those that we form with women. Listen to Lucy's description of one such friendship:

"We've found we have things to talk about that are different from what he talks about with my husband and different from what I talk about with his wife. So sometimes we call on the phone or meet for lunch. There are similar intellectual interests—we always pass on to each other the books that we love—but there's also something tender and caring too."

In a couple of crises, Lucy says, "he offered himself for talking and for helping. And when someone died in his family he wanted me there. The sexual, flirty part of our friendship is very small, but *some*—just enough to make it fun and different." She thinks—and I agree—that the sexual part, though small, is always *some*, is always there when a man and a woman are friends.

It's only in the past few years that I've made friends with men, in the sense of a friendship that's *mine*, not just part of two couples. And achieving with them the ease and the trust I've found with women friends has value indeed. Under the dryer at home last week, putting on mascara and rouge, I comfortably sat and talked with a fellow named Peter. Peter, I finally decided, could handle the shock of me minus mascara under the dryer. Because we care for each other. Because we're friends.

8. There are medium friends, and pretty good friends, and very good friends indeed, and these friendships are defined by their level of intimacy. And what we'll reveal at each of these levels of intimacy is calibrated with care. We might tell a medium friend, for example, that yesterday we had a fight with our husband. And we might tell a pretty good friend that this fight with our husband made us so mad that we slept on the couch. And we might tell a very good friend

that the reason we got so mad in that fight that we slept on the couch had something to do with that girl who works in his office. But it's only to our very best friends that we're willing to tell all, to tell what's going on with that girl in his office.

30 The best of friends, I still believe, totally love and support and trust each other, and bare to each other the secrets of their souls, and run—no questions asked—to help each other, and tell harsh truths to each other when they must be told.

31 But we needn't agree about everything (only 12-year-old girl friends agree about *everything*) to tolerate each other's point of view. To accept without judgment. To give and to take without ever keeping score. And to *be* there, as I am for them and as they are for me, to comfort our sorrows, to celebrate our joys.

Questions for Study and Discussion

1. What is Viorst's purpose in this essay? Why is division and classification an appropriate strategy for her to use?
2. Into what categories does Viorst divide her friends?
3. What principles of division does Viorst use to establish her categories of friends? Where does she state these principles?
4. Discuss the ways in which Viorst makes her categories distinct and memorable.
5. Viorst wrote this essay for *Redbook*, and so her audience was women between the ages of twenty-five and thirty-five. If she had been writing on the same topic for an audience of men of the same age, how might her categories have been different? How might her examples have been different? (Glossary: *Audience*)

Vocabulary

Refer to your dictionary to define the following words as they are used in this selection. Then use each word in a sentence of your own.

ardor (2)	forge (18)
nonchalant (3)	dormant (19)
sibling (16)	perspective (20)

Suggested Writing Assignment

Viorst's essay explores the various types of friends that one can have. Using her essay as a model, consider one of the following topics for an essay of classification.

movies	country music
college courses	newspapers
spectators	pets
lifestyles	grandparents

16

COMPARISON AND CONTRAST

A *comparison* points out the ways that two or more persons, places or things are alike. A *contrast* points out how they differ. The subjects of a comparison or contrast should be in the same class or general category; if they have nothing in common, there is no good reason for setting them side by side.

The function of any comparison or contrast is to clarify and explain. The writer's purpose may be simply to inform, or to make readers aware of similarities or differences that are interesting and significant in themselves. Or, the writer may explain something unfamiliar by comparing it with something very familiar, perhaps explaining squash by comparing it with tennis. Finally, the writer can point out the superiority of one thing by contrasting it with another—for example, showing that one product is the best by contrasting it with all its competitors.

As a writer, you have two main options for organizing a comparison or contrast: the subject-by-subject pattern or the point-by-point pattern. For a short essay comparing and contrasting the Atlanta Braves and the Los Angeles Dodgers, you would probably follow the *subject-by-subject* pattern of organization. By this pattern you first discuss the points you wish to make about one team, and then go on to discuss the corresponding points for the other team. An outline of your essay might look like this:

I. Atlanta Braves
   A. Pitching
   B. Fielding
   C. Hitting
II. Los Angeles Dodgers
   A. Pitching
   B. Fielding
   C. Hitting

The subject-by-subject pattern presents a unified discussion of each team by placing the emphasis on the teams and not on the three points of comparison. Since these points are relatively few, readers should easily remember what was said about the Braves' pitching when you later discuss the Dodgers' pitching and should be able to make the appropriate connections between them.

For a somewhat longer essay comparing and contrasting solar energy and wind energy, however, you should consider the *point-by-point* pattern of organization. With this pattern, your essay is organized according to the various points of comparison. Discussion alternates between solar and wind energy for each point of comparison. An outline of your essay might look like this:

I. Installation Expenses
   A. Solar
   B. Wind
II. Efficiency
   A. Solar
   B. Wind
III. Operating Costs
   A. Solar
   B. Wind
IV. Convenience
   A. Solar
   B. Wind
V. Maintenance
   A. Solar
   B. Wind
VI. Safety
   A. Solar
   B. Wind

The point-by-point pattern allows the writer to make immediate comparisons between solar and wind energy, thus enabling readers to consider each of the similarities and differences separately.

Each organizational pattern has its advantages. In general, the subject-by-subject pattern is useful in short essays where there are few points to be considered, whereas the point-by-point pattern is preferable in long essays where there are numerous points under consideration.

A good essay of comparison and contrast tells readers something significant that they do not already know. That is, it must do more than merely point out the obvious. As a rule, therefore, writers tend to draw contrasts between things that are usually perceived as being similar or comparisons between things usually perceived as different. In fact, comparison and contrast often go together. For example, an essay about Minneapolis and St. Paul might begin by showing how much they are alike, but end with a series of contrasts revealing how much they differ. Or, a consumer magazine might report the contrasting claims made by six car manufacturers, and then go on to demonstrate that the cars all actually do much the same thing in the same way.

Two Americas

J. William Fulbright

A former United States Senator from Arkansas, J. William Fulbright served as the chairman of the powerful Senate Foreign Relations Committee. His work on this committee gave him firsthand experience in developing American foreign policy and assessing world reaction to it. In "Two Americas," taken from his book The Arrogance of Power *(1966), Fulbright contrasts two prominent philosophies regarding American foreign policy and suggests that Americans should decide between the two.*

There are two Americas. One is the America of Lincoln and Adlai Stevenson; the other is the America of Teddy Roosevelt and the modern superpatriots. One is generous and humane, the other narrowly egotistical; one is self-critical, the other self-righteous; one is sensible, the other romantic; one is good-humored, the other solemn; one is inquiring, the other pontificating; one is moderate, the other filled with passionate intensity; one is judicious and the other arrogant in the use of great power.

We have tended in the years of our great power to puzzle the world by presenting to it now the one face of America, now the other, and sometimes both at once. Many people all over the world have come to regard America as being capable of magnanimity and farsightedness but no less capable of pettiness and spite. The result is an inability to anticipate American actions which in turn makes for apprehension and a lack of confidence in American aims.

The inconstancy of American foreign policy is not an accident but an expression of two distinct sides of the American character. Both are characterized by a kind of moralism, but one is the morality of decent instincts tempered by the knowledge of human imperfection and the other is the morality of absolute self-assurance fired by the crusading spirit. The one is exemplified by Lincoln, who found it strange, in the words of his second Inaugural Address, "that any man should dare to ask for a just God's assistance in wringing their bread from the sweat of other men's faces," but then added: "let us judge not, that we be not judged." The other is exemplified by Theodore Roosevelt, who in his December 6, 1904, Annual Message to Congress, without question or doubt as to his own and his country's capacity to judge right and wrong, proclaimed the duty of the United States to exercise an "internal police power" in the hemisphere on the ground that "Chronic wrongdoing, or an impotence which results in a general loosening of the ties of civilized society, may in America . . . ultimately require intervention by some civilized nation. . . ." Roosevelt of course never questioned that the "wrongdoing" would be done by our Latin neighbors and we of course were the "civilized nation" with the duty to set things right.

4 After twenty-five years of world power the United States must decide which of the two sides of its national character is to predominate—the humanism of Lincoln or the arrogance of those who would make America the world's policeman. One or the other will help shape the spirit of the age—unless of course we refuse to choose, in which case America may come to play a less important role in the world, leaving the great decisions to others.

5 The current tendency is toward a more strident and aggressive American foreign policy, which is to say, toward a policy closer to the spirit of Theodore Roosevelt than of Lincoln. We are still trying to build bridges to the communist countries and we are still, in a small way, helping the poorer nations to make a better life for their people; but we are also involved in a growing war against Asian communism, a war which began and might have ended as a civil war if American intervention had not turned it into a contest of ideologies, a war whose fallout is disrupting our internal life and complicating our relations with most of the world.

6 Our national vocabulary has changed with our policies. A few years ago we were talking of détente and building

bridges, of five-year plans in India and Pakistan, or agricultural cooperatives in the Dominican Republic, and land and tax reform all over Latin America. Today these subjects are still discussed in a half-hearted and desultory way but the focus of power and interest has shifted to the politics of war. Diplomacy has become largely image-making, and instead of emphasizing plans for social change, the policy-planners and political scientists are conjuring up "scenarios" of escalation and nuclear confrontation and "models" of insurgency and counterinsurgency.

The change in words and values is no less important than the change in policy, because words *are* deeds and style *is* substance insofar as they influence men's minds and behavior. What seems to be happening, as Archibald MacLeish has put it, is that "the feel of America in the world's mind" has begun to change and faith in "the idea of America" has been shaken for the world and, what is more important, for our own people. MacLeish is suggesting—and I think he is right—that much of the idealism and inspiration is disappearing from American policy, but he also points out that they are not yet gone and by no means are they irretrievable:

> . . . if you look closely and listen well, there is a human warmth, a human meaning which nothing has killed in almost twenty years and which nothing is likely to kill. . . . What has always held this country together is an idea—a dream if you will—a large and abstract thought of the sort the realistic and the sophisticated may reject but mankind can hold to.*

The foremost need of American foreign policy is a renewal of dedication to an "idea that mankind can hold to"—not a missionary idea full of pretensions about being the world's policemen but a Lincolnian idea expressing that powerful stand of decency and humanity which is the true source of America's greatness.

---

*Archibald MacLeish, Address to the Congress of International Publishers Association, May 31, 1965.

Questions for Study and Discussion

1. What is Fulbright's purpose in contrasting the two Americas, and where is that purpose stated?
2. Which of the two Americas does Ronald Reagan represent? What contemporary public figure would you say best represents the other America?
3. Does Fulbright use a subject-by-subject or a point-by-point pattern of organization to contrast the two Americas? Why do you suppose he uses the pattern that he does?
4. Why is Fulbright's use of parallel structure in paragraph 1 especially appropriate and effective in this essay? (Glossary: *Parallelism*)
5. In the context of Fulbright's essay, what purpose do paragraphs 7 and 8 serve?

Vocabulary

Refer to your dictionary to define the following words as they are used in this selection. Then use each word in a sentence of your own.

magnanimity (2)	scenarios (6)
apprehension (2)	escalation (6)
strident (5)	insurgency (6)
ideologies (5)	

Suggested Writing Assignment

Reread paragraph 1, in which Fulbright contrasts the two Americas. Notice how the paragraph is developed by the juxtaposition of the contrasting features of the two Americas. Select two items—people, products, events, institutions, places—and make a list of their contrasting features. Then write a paragraph modeled on Fulbright's paragraph using the entries on your list.

Bing and Elvis

Russell Baker

Russell Baker writes a syndicated column for The New York Times *for which he was awarded a Pulitzer Prize in 1979. In the following selection, which first appeared in the* Times *shortly after Bing Crosby's death in 1977, Baker compares and contrasts two of our most popular entertainers and in the process tells us something about the generations that produced them.*

The grieving for Elvis Presley and the commercial exploitation of his death were still not ended when we heard of Bing Crosby's death the other day. Here is a generational puzzle. Those of an age to mourn Elvis must marvel that their elders could really have cared about Bing, just as the Crosby generation a few weeks ago wondered what all the to-do was about when Elvis died.

Each man was a mass culture hero to his generation, but it tells us something of the difference between generations that each man's admirers would be hard-pressed to understand why the other could mean very much to his devotees.

There were similarities that ought to tell us something. Both came from obscurity to national recognition while quite young and became very rich. Both lacked formal music education and went on to movie careers despite lack of acting skills. Both developed distinctive musical styles which were originally scorned by critics and subsequently studied as pioneer developments in the art of popular song.

In short, each man's career followed the mythic rags-to-triumph pattern in which adversity is conquered, detractors are given their comeuppance and estates, fancy cars and world tours become the reward of perseverance. Traditionally this was supposed to be the history of the American business striver, but in our era of committee capitalism it occurs most often in the mass entertainment field, and so we look less and less to the board room for our heroes and more and more to the microphone.

5 Both Crosby and Presley were creations of the microphone. It made it possible for people with frail voices not only to be heard beyond the third row but also to caress millions. Crosby was among the first to understand that the microphone made it possible to sing to multitudes by singing to a single person in a small room.

6 Presley cuddled his microphone like a lover. With Crosby the microphone was usually concealed, but Presley brought it out on stage, detached it from its fitting, stroked it, pressed it to his mouth. It was a surrogate for his listener, and he made love to it unashamedly.

7 The difference between Presley and Crosby, however, reflected generational differences which spoke of changing values in American life. Crosby's music was soothing; Presley's was disturbing. It is too easy to be glib about this, to say that Crosby was singing to, first, Depression America and, then, to wartime America, and that his audience had all the disturbance they could handle in their daily lives without buying more at the record shop and movie theater.

8 Crosby's fans talk about how "relaxed" he was, how "natural," how "casual and easy going." By the time Presley began causing sensations, the entire country had become relaxed, casual and easy going, and its younger people seemed to be tired of it, for Elvis's act was anything but soothing and scarcely what a parent of that placid age would have called "natural" for a young man.

9 Elvis was unseemly, loud, gaudy, sexual—that gyrating pelvis!—in short, disturbing. He not only disturbed parents who thought music by Crosby was soothing but also reminded their young that they were full of the turmoil of youth and an appetite for excitement. At a time when the country had a population coming of age with no memory of troubled times, Presley spoke to a yearning for disturbance.

10 It probably helped that Elvis's music made Mom and Dad climb the wall. In any case, people who admired Elvis never

talk about how relaxed and easy going he made them feel. They are more likely to tell you he introduced them to something new and exciting.

To explain each man in terms of changes in economic and political life probably oversimplifies the matter. Something in the culture was also changing. Crosby's music, for example, paid great attention to the importance of lyrics. The "message" of the song was as essential to the audience as the tune. The words were usually inane and witless, but Crosby—like Sinatra a little later—made them vital. People remembered them, sang them. Words still had meaning.

Although many of Presley's songs were highly lyrical, in most it wasn't the words that moved audiences; it was the "sound." Rock 'n' roll, of which he was the great popularizer, was a "sound" event. Song stopped being song and turned into "sound," at least until the Beatles came along and solved the problem of making words sing to the new beat.

Thus a group like the Rolling Stones, whose lyrics are often elaborate, seems to the Crosby-tuned ear to be shouting only gibberish, a sort of accompanying background noise in a "sound" experience. The Crosby generation has trouble hearing rock because it makes the mistake of trying to understand the words. The Presley generation has trouble with Crosby because it finds the sound unstimulating and cannot be touched by the inanity of the words. The mutual deafness may be a measure of how far we have come from really troubled times and of how deeply we have come to mistrust the value of words.

Questions for Study and Discussion

1. What similarities between Crosby and Presley does Russell Baker see? What differences does he see? Why does he consider the similarities between these two singers before considering their differences?
2. What conclusion does Baker draw from his comparison and contrast of the two entertainers?

3. Does Baker use a point-by-point or a subject-by-subject pattern of organization in his essay? Why is the pattern that he uses particularly effective for the subject matter?
4. Though the tone in Baker's essay is serious and reflective, it remains basically informal. Identify specific words that help to establish this tone. (Glossary: *Tone*)

Vocabulary

Refer to your dictionary to define the following words as they are used in this selection. Then use each word in a sentence of your own.

mythic (4)	glib (7)
adversity (4)	placid (8)
surrogate (6)	inane (11)

Suggested Writing Assignment

Select one of the following topics for an essay of comparison and contrast. In selecting a topic you should consider (1) what your purpose will be, (2) whether you will emphasize similarities or differences, (3) what specific points you will discuss, and (4) what organizational pattern will best suit your purpose.

two cities
two friends
two restaurants
two actors or actresses
two popular music groups
two mountains

The Bright Child and the Dull Child

John Holt

*A former elementary and secondary school teacher, John Holt has also taught at Harvard and the University of California at Berkeley. Through his books—*How Children Fail *(1964),* What I Do on Monday *(1970),* How Children Learn *(1970), and* Escape from Childhood *(1976)—Holt has been recognized as a thoughtful critic of the philosophy and methods of American education. In the following selection Holt draws upon his many years of experience in the classroom, to sharply contrast the behavior patterns of the bright child with those of the dull child.*

Years of watching and comparing bright children and the not-bright, or less bright, have shown that they are very different kinds of people. The bright child is curious about life and reality, eager to get in touch with it, embrace it, unite himself with it. There is no wall, no barrier between him and life. The dull child is far less curious, far less interested in what goes on and what is real, more inclined to live in worlds of fantasy. The bright child likes to experiment, to try things out. He lives by the maxim that there is more than one way to skin a cat. If he can't do something one way, he'll try another. The dull child is usually afraid to try at all. It takes a good deal of urging to get him to try even once; if that try fails, he is through.

The bright child is patient. He can tolerate uncertainty and failure, and will keep trying until he gets an answer. When all his experiments fail, he can even admit to himself and others that for the time being he is not going to get an answer. This may annoy him, but he can wait. Very often, he does not want to be told how to do the problem or solve the puzzle he has struggled with, because he does not want to be cheated out of the chance to figure it out for himself in the future. Not so the dull child. He cannot stand uncertainty or failure. To him, an unanswered question is not a challenge or an opportunity, but a threat. If he can't find the answer quickly, it must be given to him, and quickly; and he must have answers for everything. Such are the children of whom a second-grade teacher once said, "But my children *like* to have questions for which there is only one answer." They did; and by a mysterious coincidence, so did she.

3 The bright child is willing to go ahead on the basis of incomplete understanding and information. He will take risks, sail uncharted seas, explore when the landscape is dim, the landmarks few, the light poor. To give only one example, he will often read books he does not understand in the hope that after a while enough understanding will emerge to make it worth while to go on. In this spirit some of my fifth graders tried to read *Moby Dick*. But the dull child will go ahead only when he thinks he knows exactly where he stands and exactly what is ahead of him. If he does not feel he knows exactly what an experience will be like, and if it will not be exactly like other experiences he already knows, he wants no part of it. For while the bright child feels that the universe is, on the whole, a sensible, reasonable, and trustworthy place, the dull child feels that it is senseless, unpredictable, and treacherous. He feels that he can never tell what may happen, particularly in a new situation, except that it will probably be bad.

Questions for Study and Discussion

1. List the main differences that Holt sees between the "bright child" and the "dull child."
2. Holt uses a point-by-point pattern of organization to discuss differences between the "bright child" and the "dull child." What would have been gained or lost with a subject-by-subject pattern of organization?

3. When using a point-by-point pattern of organization, the writer must take care to use transitions to guide the reader and ensure paragraph coherence. Cite examples of the various transitional devices Holt uses in paragraph 3. (Glossary: *Transitions*)

Vocabulary

Refer to your dictionary to define the following words as they are used in this selection. Then use each word in a sentence of your own.

inclined (1)
maxim (1)
treacherous (3)

Suggested Writing Assignment

Write a short essay in which you use a point-by-point pattern of organization to compare or contrast any one of the following:

Star Wars and *Gone With the Wind*
a sociology course and a psychology course
hot dogs and hamburgers
poker and bridge
Florida and California
the Yankees and the Red Sox

Fable for Tomorrow

Rachel Carson

Naturalist Rachel Carson (1907–1964) wrote The Sea Around Us *(1951),* Under the Sea Wind *(1952), and* The Edge of the Sea *(1955), sensitive investigations of marine life. But it was* Silent Spring *(1962), her study of herbicides and insecticides, that made Carson a controversial figure. Once denounced as an alarmist, she is now regarded as an early prophet of the ecology movement. In the following fable taken from* Silent Spring, *Carson uses contrast to show her readers the devastating effects of indiscriminate use of pesticides.*

There was once a town in the heart of America where all life seemed to live in harmony with its surroundings. The town lay in the midst of a checkerboard of prosperous farms, with fields of grain and hillsides of orchards where, in spring, white clouds of bloom drifted above the green fields. In autumn, oak and maple and birch set up a blaze of color that flamed and flickered across a backdrop of pines. Then foxes barked in the hills and deer silently crossed the fields, half hidden in the mists of the fall mornings. 1

Along the roads, laurel, viburnum and alder, great ferns and wildflowers delighted the traveler's eye through much of the year. Even in winter the roadsides were places of beauty, where countless birds came to feed on the berries and on the seed heads of the dried weeds rising above the snow. The countryside was, in fact, famous for the abundance and variety of its bird life, and when the flood of migrants was pouring through in spring and fall people traveled from great distances to observe them. Others came to fish the streams, which flowed clear and cold out of the 2 hills and contained shady pools where trout lay. So it had been from the days many years ago when the first settlers raised their houses, sank their wells, and built their barns.

Then a strange blight crept over the area and everything began to change. Some evil spell had settled on the community: mysterious maladies swept the flocks of chickens; the cattle and sheep sickened and died. Everywhere was a shadow of death. The farmers spoke of much illness among their families. In the town the doctors had become more and more puzzled by new kinds of sickness appearing among their patients. There had been several sudden and unexplained deaths, not only among adults but even among children, who would be stricken suddenly while at play and die within a few hours.

There was a strange stillness. The birds, for example—where had they gone? Many people spoke of them, puzzled and disturbed. The feeding stations in the backyards were deserted. The few birds seen anywhere were moribund; they trembled violently and could not fly. It was a spring without voices. On the mornings that had once throbbed with the dawn chorus of robins, catbirds, doves, jays, wrens, and scores of other bird voices there was now no sound; only silence lay over the fields and woods and marsh.

On the farms the hens brooded, but no chicks hatched. The farmers complained that they were unable to raise any pigs—the litters were small and the young survived only a few days. The apple trees were coming into bloom but no bees droned among the blossoms, so there was no pollination and there would be no fruit.

The roadsides, once so attractive, were now lined with browned and withered vegetation as though swept by fire. These, too, were silent, deserted by all living things. Even the streams were now lifeless. Anglers no longer visited them, for all the fish had died.

In the gutters under the eaves and between the shingles of the roofs, a white granular powder still showed a few patches; some weeks before it had fallen like snow upon the roofs and the lawns, the fields and streams.

No witchcraft, no enemy action had silenced the rebirth of

new life in this stricken world. The people had done it themselves.

9 This town does not actually exist, but it might easily have a thousand counterparts in America or elsewhere in the world. I know of no community that has experienced all the misfortunes I describe. Yet every one of these disasters has actually happened somewhere, and many real communities have already suffered a substantial number of them. A grim specter has crept upon us almost unnoticed, and this imagined tragedy may easily become a stark reality we all shall know.

Questions for Study and Discussion

1. A fable is a short narrative that makes an edifying or cautionary point. What is the point of Carson's fable?
2. How do comparison and contrast help Carson make her point?
3. Does Carson use a point-by-point or a subject-by-subject method of organization in this selection? How is the pattern of organization Carson uses appropriate for her purpose? Be prepared to cite examples from the text.

Vocabulary

Refer to your dictionary to define the following words as they are used in this selection. Then use each word in a sentence of your own.

migrants (2)
blight (3)
maladies (3)
moribund (4)
specter (9)

Suggested Writing Assignment

Using one of the following "before and after" situations, write a short essay of comparison and/or contrast.

before and after a diet
before and after urban renewal
before and after Christmas
before and after beginning college
before and after a final exam

17

Cause and Effect

Every time you try to answer a question that asks *why*, you engage in the process of *causal analysis*—you attempt to determine a *cause* or series of causes for a particular *effect*. When you try to answer a question that asks *what if*, you attempt to determine what effect will result from a particular cause. You will have frequent opportunity to use cause and effect analysis in the writing that you will do in college. For example, in history you might be asked to determine the causes of the Seven-Day War between Egypt and Israel; in political science you might be asked to determine the reasons why Ronald Reagan won the 1980 Presidential election; and, in sociology you might be asked to predict the effect that changes in Social Security legislation would have on senior citizens.

Determining causes and effects is usually thought-provoking and quite complex. One reason for this is that there are two types of causes: *immediate causes*, which are readily apparent because they are closest to the effect, and *ultimate causes*, which, being somewhat removed, are not so apparent and perhaps even hidden. Furthermore, ultimate causes may bring about effects which themselves become immediate causes, thus creating a *causal chain*. For example, consider the following causal chain: Sally, a computer salesperson, prepared extensively for a meeting with an important client (ultimate cause), impressed the client (immediate cause), and made a very large sale (effect). The chain did not stop there: The large sale caused her to be promoted by her employer (effect).

A second reason why causal analysis can be so complex is that an effect may have any number of possible or actual causes, and a cause may have any number of possible or actual effects. An upset stomach may be caused by eating spoiled food, but it may also be caused by overeating, flu, allergy, nervousness, pregnancy, or any combination of factors. Similarly, the high cost of electricity may have multiple effects: higher profits for utility companies, fewer sales of electrical appliances, higher prices for other products, and the development of alternative sources of energy.

Sound reasoning and logic, while present in all good writing, are central to any causal analysis. Writers of believable causal analysis examine their material objectively and develop their essays carefully. They are convinced by their own examination of the material, but are not afraid to admit other possible causes and effects. Above all, they do not let their own prejudices interfere with the logic of their analyses and presentations.

Because people are eager to link causes and effects, they sometimes commit an error in logic known as the "after this, therefore because of this" fallacy (in Latin, *post hoc, ergo propter hoc*). This fallacy leads people to believe that because one event occurred after another event the first event somehow caused the second; that is, they sometimes make causal connections that are not proven. For example, if students began to perform better after a free breakfast program was instituted at their school, one could not assume that the improvement was caused by the breakfast program. There could of course be any number of other causes for this effect, and a responsible writer on the subject would analyze and consider them all before suggesting the cause.

Never Get Sick in July

Marilyn Machlowitz

Marilyn Machlowitz earned her doctorate in psychology at Yale and is now a management psychologist. She contributes a regular column to Working Woman *magazine, has written* Workaholics *(1980), and is at work on a new book dealing with the consequences of succeeding at an early age. Notice in the following selection how Machlowitz analyzes the various reasons why it is a bad idea to get sick in July.*

One Harvard medical school professor warns his students to stay home—as he does—on the Fourth of July. He fears he will become one of the holiday's highway casualties and wind up in an emergency room with an inexperienced intern "practicing" medicine on *him*. 1

Just the mention of July makes medical students, nurses, interns, residents, and "real doctors" roll their eyes. While hospital administrators maintain that nothing is amiss that month, members of the medical profession know what happens when the house staff turns over and the interns take over each July 1. 2

This July 1, more than 13,000 new doctors will invade over 600 hospitals across the country. Within minutes they will be overwhelmed: last July 1, less than a month after finishing medical school, Dr. John Baumann, then twenty-five, walked into Washington, D.C.'s, Walter Reed Army Medical Center, where he was immediately faced with caring for "eighteen of the sickest people I had ever seen." 3

Pity the patient who serves as guinea pig at ten A.M.—or three A.M.—that first day. Indeed, according to Dr. Russell K. Laros, Jr., professor and vice-chairman of obstetrics, gynecology, and reproductive sciences at the University of California, San Francisco, "There is no question that pa- 4 tients throughout the country are mismanaged during July. Without the most meticulous supervision," he adds, "serious errors can be made."

And they are. Internship provides the first chance to practice one's illegible scrawl on prescription blanks, a golden opportunity to make lots of mistakes. Interns—who are still known to most people by that name, even though they are now officially called first-year residents—have ordered the wrong drug in the wrong dosage to be administered the wrong way at the wrong times to the wrong patient. While minor mistakes are most common, serious errors are the sources of hospital horror stories. One intern prescribed an anti-depressant without knowing that it would inactivate the patient's previously prescribed antihypertensive medication.* The patient then experienced a rapid increase in blood pressure and suffered a stroke.

When interns do not know what to do, when they cannot covertly consult *The Washington Manual* (a handbook of medical therapeutics), they can always order tests. The first time one intern attempted to perform a pleural biopsy—a fairly difficult procedure—he punctured the patient's lung. When an acquaintance of mine entered an emergency room one Friday night in July with what was only an advanced case of the flu, she wound up having a spinal tap. While negative findings are often necessary to rule out alternative diagnoses, some of the tests are really unwarranted. Interns admit that the results are required only so they can cover themselves in case a resident or attending physician decides to give them the third degree.

Interns' hours only increase their inadequacy. Dr. Jay Dobkin, president of the Physicians National Housestaff Association, a Washington-based organization representing 12,000 interns and residents, says that "working conditions . . . directly impact and influence the quality of patient care. After thirty-six hours 'on,' most interns find their abilities compromised." Indeed, their schedules (they average 110 hours a week) and their salaries (last year, they averaged

---

*A depressant medicine used to lower high blood pressure.

$13,145) make interns the chief source of cheap labor. No other hospital personnel will do as much "scut" work—drawing blood, for instance—or dirty work, such as manually disimpacting severely constipated patients.

8 Even private patients fall prey to interns, because many physicians prefer being affiliated with hospitals that have interns to perform these routine duties around the clock. One way to reduce the likelihood of falling into the hands of an intern is to rely upon a physician in group practice whose partners can provide substitute coverage. Then, too, it probably pays to select a physician who has hospital privileges at the best teaching institution in town. There, at least, you are unlikely to encounter any interns who slept through school, as some medical students admit they do: only the most able students survive the computer-matching process to win the prestigious positions at university hospitals.

9 It may be reassuring to remember that while veteran nurses joke about scheduling their vacations to start July 1, they monitor interns most carefully and manage to catch many mistakes. Residents bear much more responsibility for supervision and surveillance, and Dr. Lawrence Boxt, president of the 5,000-member, Manhattan-based Committee of Interns and Residents and a resident himself, emphasizes that residents are especially vigilant during July. One of the interns he represents agreed: "You're watched like a hawk. You have so much support and backup. They're not going to let you kill anybody." So no one who requires emergency medical attention should hesitate to be hospitalized in July.

10 I asked Dr. Boxt whether he also had any advice for someone about to enter a hospital for elective surgery.

11 "Yes," he said. "Stay away."

Questions for Study and Discussion

1. What, according to Machlowitz, are the immediate causes of the problems many hospitals experience during the month of July?

2. What does she say are the causes of intern inadequacy? How does she substantiate the cause and effect relationship?
3. What suggestions does Machlowitz give for minimizing patient risk during the month of July?
4. How would you interpret Dr. Boxt's answer to the final question Machlowitz asks him?

Vocabulary

Refer to your dictionary to define the following words as they are used in this selection. Then use each word in a sentence of your own.

meticulous (4)
diagnoses (6)
unwarranted (6)
compromised (7)
affiliated (8)
prestigious (8)
vigilant (9)

Suggested Writing Assignment

There is often more than one cause for an event. Make a list of at least six possible causes for one of the following:

a quarrel with a friend
an upset victory in a football game
a well-done exam
a broken leg
a change of major

Examine your list, and identify the causes which seem most probable. Which of these are immediate causes and which are ultimate causes? Using this material, write a short cause and effect essay.

The Collapse of Public Schools

John C. Sawhill

Beginning his career in a New York brokerage firm, John C. Sawhill worked as a management consultant and later became deputy director of the Federal Energy Administration. From 1975 to 1979 he served as the president of New York University. In 1979 Sawhill returned to government service, joining the Carter Administration in the Department of Energy. In the following selection Sawhill looks at a number of causes for the failure of public schools to provide good education. He concludes with some suggestions for change.

For more than two decades, America's public schools have been expected to cure society's discontents. In the mid-Fifties, we demanded that our schools create a harmony among races that existed nowhere else in American life. In the mid-Sixties, when our young were engaged in a rebellion that seemed to threaten virtually every ideal we embraced as a nation, we insisted that the schools restore social order and preserve the status quo. In the mid-Seventies, we instructed our schools to go one step further—to look first to the wants of the individual, to nurture a child's discovery of self, while at the same time distracting him from his attempts to reduce his school to rubble. 1

Clearly, this prolonged and ill-advised effort to make the educational system the principal tool for social change has contributed to such problems as the sharply increased incidence of functional illiteracy. 2

To rehabilitate our schools, we must look to the hard realities of *why* our system of public education is not working and learn from them. 3

As we examine the performance of our schools, six basic truths—most of them a result of our mixing altruism and education—emerge time and again. 4

1. *Schools are asked to do too much.* Racial, economic, and sexual inequalities; poor parenting; malnutrition; crime; and a lengthy list of other social disorders unquestionably affect an individual's capacity to participate in society. But while education can enhance the student's ability to cope with, and to change, the conditions of life around him, it cannot, in and of itself, make them better. In thrusting the schools to the forefront of social change, we have diverted their energies from their basic purpose—education.

The issue of acculturation of ethnic minorities provides a case in point. Greater emphasis has been placed on bilingual education in the public schools as the number and variety of ethnic minorities have grown in the nation. We are insisting both that the schools improve the way they teach English, so that language is removed as a barrier to learning, and that they increase the number of courses taught in students' native tongues, so that the pace of learning begun in their homelands continues uninterrupted. The conflict that such demands create can be seen in Chicago, where, as a condition of $90 million in aid, the federal government exacted a pledge that the public schools offer bilingual courses in 20 languages, from Arabic to Vietnamese.

While we do not yet know what effect the study of major courses in a native tongue has on a child's ability to learn English, we may be allowed the suspicion that it will prove as counter-productive as it sounds. In addition, the burden these extra courses place on the schools is obvious.

Once we stop asking the schools to do too much, they can get on with solving the more acute problem of performing their basic task—that of education—more effectively.

2. *Students cannot learn what they are not taught.* Current dismay over public education centers on the fact that substantial numbers of our children cannot perform even the most basic functions of reading, writing, and mathematics. Such poor performance is understandable, however, when we recognize that proficiency in basic skills no longer is required of public school students.

"Minimum competency" is the result of the schools' misguided efforts to serve two masters at the same time. On one hand, they are trying to respond to the public demand for sound, basic education by requiring a specific level of achievement in certain subjects. On the other hand, in their attempt to correct social inequities, schools are often setting standards so low as to be meaningless and even detrimental.

11 Although the concept of minimum competency is not inherently bad, it does require careful implementation. The depth to which public education can sink under the weight of problematic minimum-competency levels was demonstrated in New York this past spring when educators and others engaged in a spirited debate over the question of whether freshman reading standards are too *high* for graduating seniors. What began as a tool for ensuring performance has become an excuse for failure. This situation must be corrected.

12 Electives are sometimes used by schools as another means of preventing students from failing when they cannot educate them. Nationally, we can see a trend that moves even further away from requiring certain basics and toward instituting yet more electives—courses that range from studies amplifying basic skills to programs that can only be described as the marginalia of pop culture.

13 In Massachusetts, state educators compared a survey of elective courses developed between 1971 and 1976 with an analysis of Scholastic Achievement Test scores for students in 43 high schools. In this five-year period there was a 50 percent increase in English electives alone. The educators found that students with more electives showed greater than average declines in SAT scores.

14 Similarly, in New York, where the documented trend has been away from academic basics in recent years, two-thirds of the graduates of city high schools required additional precollege study upon entering the City University.

15 In contrast, a survey of 34 high schools in which students have maintained or improved their SAT scores revealed that these schools encourage enrollment in advanced academic courses and allow electives to be taken only in addition to required classes rather than as a substitute for them.

16 Thus we must temper our dismay at our children's inability to read, write, and solve simple mathematical problems with the recognition that little goes on in the classroom to provide them with the skills to do better.

17 3. *We do not know what makes for an effective learning*

experience. With the possible exception of one-to-one teaching, virtually all of our theories about factors that contribute to productive instruction have not held up. Even our most cherished socio-educational assumption—that racial and social integration contributes to learning (provided half of the class is white)—runs counter to the reality of public schools, where students are put in classes according to their abilities; ethnic minorities are thus effectively resegregated and educational inadequacies perpetuated.

As long as schools are diverted by social concerns from the experimentation essential to improving their performance, our students and teachers will continue to stumble through a succession of educational theories, reinventing the wheel daily out of necessity and, worse, becoming more entrenched in classroom practices that produce no positive results.

4. *What is good for the teacher is not always good for the pupil.* Increasingly in recent years, teachers have argued that higher salaries attract better teachers. Smaller classes, they have said, more time to prepare for class, and publicly financed teacher training improve the performance of those already in the profession. The result, our teachers tell us, is better education for our children. None of these assertions is supported by fact.

Teachers' salaries have risen steadily during the past 20 years. In the classroom, the ratio of one teacher for every 30 students in 1955 had dropped to one for every 20 by 1976. There has also been a substantial increase in the amount of time teachers spend outside the classroom in course preparation and professional training. Yet students are performing dismally on almost every test we have thus far devised to measure their academic competence.

As is the case with the learning experience itself, we must recognize finally that we do not know what makes a teacher effective.

5. *The way we finance public education is discriminatory and contributes to chaos in the schools.* Getting and spending the money to finance our public schools are among the most serious problems we face as a nation today.

Taxation of private property in itself has become an explosive issue. Reliance on property taxes discriminates against our cities and poorer suburban and rural areas. Property-poor localities must tax themselves at a higher rate to generate the same amount of tax dollars as their property-rich neighbors. Those who can afford to, move to areas where taxes are lower, and the money available for public education is thus further eroded in those localities where it is most needed.

Efforts have been made in the state courts and legislatures to equalize funding. While these efforts generally have resulted in increased aid to poorer districts, they have not addressed the major issue of linking public education to property taxes. 24

Meanwhile, increases in property taxes meet with growing resistance. The "taxpayers' revolt" is surprising only in that it did not surface sooner. Neither the very poor nor the very rich pay as much of the cost of education as the middle-class property owner. 25

The inequities of the property tax are also felt acutely by older property owners who enjoy only indirectly the benefits of public education. Many of those who must survive on fixed incomes have found that the value of their once-modest homes has tripled and even quadrupled in recent years. The result: steep increases in taxes that their incomes cannot grow to match. 26

While we have yet to see what long-term effects the taxpayers' revolt will have on public education, Cleveland provided us with a clue when voter rejection of a bond issue closed the schools twice in one year, left the city $130 million in debt, and pushed teachers' salaries months in arrears. 27

Getting the money to finance public education, however, is only half of the problem we face. Spending it wisely is equally important and sometimes even more perplexing. 28

Why is it, with increased teachers' salaries and per-pupil expenditures, that our students perform so poorly? Again, the answer can be found in our zeal to correct social disorders. Schools in localities with large low-income and minority populations must provide costly social services to their students, leaving even less money for actual education. 29

6. *Someone must be in charge*. Local, state, and federal government; community groups; unions; educational theo- 30

rists; parents; and even students have all taken a crack at running our schools, and the results are about the same. None has run them well. Schools and their employees' unions have developed intricate bureaucracies of their own, which spend more time explaining their failures than seeking solutions to the problems they face.

The responsibility for making decisions, controlling resources, and planning and implementing programs has been taken away from principals and teachers and dispersed throughout the educational bureaucracy, from the local school system all the way to the federal government.

We cannot expect our schools to function well when those most directly involved lack the authority to manage them effectively.

Acceptance of these six realities will not provide all the answers to the problems our schools face today. But they do suggest directions we might pursue:

We must recognize that schools exist to educate, and that the task is monumental enough without the attempt to right the social wrongs that have originated elsewhere.

We must recognize that—if the function of education is to enable us to become the most that we can be—there is no such thing as a minimum acceptable standard.

We must insist that time and money be used to strengthen basic academic curricula.

We must scrutinize our beliefs about what makes for an effective learning experience and discard those that have proved ineffective and wasteful; further, we cannot rely on teachers and educational theorists alone in making such decisions.

We must revolutionize the way in which schools are financed and establish firm priorities for spending.

And finally, we must return the management of our schools to those most directly involved in the delivery of educational services to the public.

Our schools provide a key to the future of society. We must take control of them, watch over them, and nurture them if they are to be set right again. To do less is to invite disaster upon ourselves, our children, and our nation.

Questions for Study and Discussion

1. What is the author's purpose? Why does cause and effect analysis suit his purpose?
2. What, according to Sawhill, is the cause for the failure of our public schools?
3. What are the six basic truths that Sawhill says "emerge time and again" when we examine why our schools do not work?
4. What is the relationship between the six truths that Sawhill discusses and the suggestions he makes at the end of the essay for improving the performance of our schools?
5. What effect has increased teachers' salaries and per-pupil expenditures had on academic performance? Has Sawhill presented sufficient evidence to substantiate his claims?

Vocabulary

Refer to your dictionary to define the following words as they are used in this selection. Then use each word in a sentence of your own.

virtually (1)	proficiency (9)
status quo (1)	detrimental (10)
enhance (5)	inherently (11)
acculturation (6)	scrutinize (37)

Suggested Writing Assignment

Write an essay in which you analyze the most significant reasons why you went to college. You may wish to discuss such matters as your high school experience, people and events that influenced your decision, and your goals in college as well as in later life.

When Television Is a School for Criminals

Grant Hendricks

Grant Hendricks is serving a life sentence in Michigan's Marquette maximum-security prison. When he submitted the following article to TV Guide *for publication, the editors found the results of his research so surprising that they verified the facts for themselves before publishing the article. Hendricks contends that penitentiary inmates watch television not only to pass the time but also to learn new techniques for committing yet more crimes—that television may, in fact, be a school for criminals.*

For years, psychologists and sociologists have tried to find some connection between crime and violence on television and crime and violence in American society. To date, no one has been able to prove—or disprove—that link. But perhaps the scientists, with their academic approaches, have been unable to mine the mother lode of information on violence, crime and television available in our prison systems.

I'm not about to dismiss the scientists' findings, but as a prisoner serving a life sentence in Michigan's Marquette maximum-security prison, I believe I can add a new dimension to the subject. Cons speak much more openly to one of their own than to outsiders. And because of this, I spent three weeks last summer conducting an informal survey of 208 of the 688 inmates here at Marquette, asking them what they felt about the correlation between the crime and violence they see on television and the crime and violence they have practiced as a way of life.

Making this survey, I talked to my fellow prisoners in the mess hall, in the prison yard, in the factory and in my cell block. I asked them, on a confidential basis, whether or not their criminal activities have ever been influenced by what they see on TV. A surprising 9 out of 10 told me that they have actually learned new tricks and improved their criminal expertise by watching crime programs. Four out of 10 said that they have attempted specific crimes they saw on television crime dramas, although they also admit that only about one-third of these attempts were successful.

Perhaps even more surprising is the fact that here at Marquette, where 459 of us have television sets in our individual cells, hooked up to a cable system, many cons sit and take notes while watching *Baretta, Kojak, Police Woman, Switch* and other TV crime shows. As one of my buddies said recently: "It's like you have a lot of intelligent, creative minds—all those Hollywood writers—working for *you*. They keep coming up with new ideas. They'll lay it all out for you, too: show you the type of evidence the cops look for—how they track you, and so on." 4

What kinds of lessons have been learned by TV-watching criminals? Here are some examples. 5

One of my prison-yard mates told me he "successfully" pulled off several burglaries, all patterned on a caper from *Police Woman*. 6

Another robbed a sporting-goods store by following the *modus operandi** he saw on an *Adam-12* episode. 7

By copying a *Paper Moon* scheme, one con man boasts he pulled off a successful bunco fraud—for which he has never been caught (he's currently serving time for another crime). 8

Of course, television doesn't guarantee that the crime you pull off will be successful. One inmate told me he attempted to rip off a dope house, modeling his plan on a *Baretta* script. But the heroin dealers he tried to rob called the cops and he was caught. Another prison-yard acquaintance mentioned that, using a *Starsky & Hutch* plot, he tried to rob a nightclub. But to his horror, the place was owned by underworld people. "I'm lucky to still be alive," he said. 9

On the question of violence, however, a much smaller number of Marquette inmates feel they were influenced by 10

*(Latin) *modus operandi*, or method of operation.

watching anything on television. Of the 59 men I interviewed who have committed rape, only 1 out of 20 said that he felt inspired or motivated to commit rape as a result of something he saw on television. Forty-seven of the 208 men I spoke to said that at one time or another they had killed another person. Of those, 31 are now serving life sentences for either first- or second-degree murder. Of these 31, only 2 said their crimes had been television-influenced. But of the 148 men who admitted to committing assault, about 1 out of 6 indicated that his crime had been inspired or motivated by something he saw on TV.

Still, one prisoner after another will tell you how he has been inspired, motivated and helped by television. And crime shows and TV-movies are not the only sources of information. CBS's *60 Minutes* provides choice viewing for Marquette's criminal population. One con told me: "They recently did a segment on *60 Minutes* on how easy it was to get phony IDs. Just like the hit man in 'Day of the Jackal,' but on *60 Minutes* it wasn't fiction—it was for real. After watching that show, you knew how to go out and score a whole new personality on paper—credit cards, driver's license, everything. It was fantastic."

Sometimes, watching television helps you learn to think on your feet. Like an old friend of mine named Shakey, who once escaped from the North Dakota State Penitentiary. While he hid in the basement of a private residence, they were putting up roadblocks all around the city of Bismarck. But Shakey was smart. He knew that there had to be some way for him to extricate himself from this mess. Then, all of a sudden it occurred to him: Shakey remembered a caper film he'd seen on television once, in which a fugitive had managed to breach several roadblocks by using an emergency vehicle.

With this basic plan in mind, he proceeded to the Bismarck City Hospital and, pretending to be hysterical, he stammered to the first white-coated attendant he met that his brother was lying trapped beneath an overturned farm tractor about 12 miles or so from town. He then climbed into the back of the ambulance, and with red lights blazing and siren screaming, the vehicle drove right through two roadblocks—and safely out of Bismarck.

Two days or so later, Shakey arrived back on the same ranch in Montana where he'd worked before his jail sentence. The foreman even gave him his job again. But Shakey was so proud of what he'd done that he made one big mistake: he boasted about his escape from the North Dakota state prison, and in the end he was turned over to the authorities, who sent him back to North Dakota—and prison. . . . 14

An 18-year-old inmate told me that while watching an old *Adam-12* show, he had learned exactly how to break open pay-phone coin boxes. He thought it seemed like a pretty good idea for picking up a couple of hundred dollars a day, so he gave it a try. To his surprise and consternation, the writers of *Adam-12* had failed to explain that Ma Bell has a silent alarm system built into her pay phones. If you start tampering with one, the operator can notify the police within seconds—even giving them the location of the phone being ripped off. He was arrested on his first attempt and received a one-year sentence. 15

Another prisoner told me that he had learned to hot-wire cars at the age of 14 by watching one of his favorite TV shows. A week later he stole his first car—his mother's. Five years later he was in Federal prison for transporting stolen vehicles across state lines. 16

This man, at the age of 34, has spent 15 years behind bars. According to him, "TV has taught me how to steal cars, how to break into establishments, how to go about robbing people, even how to roll a drunk. Once, after watching a *Hawaii Five-O*, I robbed a gas station. The show showed me how to do it. Nowadays [he's serving a term for attempted rape] I watch TV in my house [cell] from 4 P.M. until midnight. I just sit back and take notes. I see 'em doing it this way or that way, you know, and I tell myself that I'll do it the same way when I get out. You could probably pick any 10 guys in here and ask 'em and they'd tell you the same thing. Everybody's picking up on what's on the TV." . . . 17

One of my friends here in Marquette says that TV is just a reflection of what's happening "out there." According to him, "The only difference is that the people out there haven't been caught—and we have. But our reaction to things is basically the same. Like when they showed the movie 'Death Wish' here, the people reacted the same way they did on the 18 outside—they applauded Charles Bronson when he wasted all the criminals. The crooks applauded Bronson!"

Still, my research—informal though it is—shows that criminals look at television differently than straight people. Outside, TV is entertainment. Here, it helps the time go by. But it is also educational. As one con told me, television has been beneficial to his career in crime by teaching him all the things *not* to do. Another mentioned that he's learned a lot about how cops think and work by watching crime-drama shows. In the prison factory, one guy said that he's seen how various alarm systems operate by watching TV; and here in my cell block somebody said that because of television shows, he's been kept up-to-date on modern police procedures and equipment.

Another con told me: "In the last five to seven years we've learned that the criminal's worst enemy is the snitch. TV has built that up. On *Starsky & Hutch* they've even made a sympathetic character out of a snitch. So we react to that in here. Now the general feeling is that if you use a partner to commit a crime, you kill him afterwards so there's nobody to snitch on you."

For most of us cons in Marquette, it would be hard to do time without TV. It's a window on the world for us. We see the news shows, we watch sports and some of us take great pains to keep tuned into the crime shows. When I asked one con if he felt that watching TV crime shows in prison would be beneficial to his career, he just smiled and said, "Hey, I sit and take notes—do my homework, you know? No way would I sit in my cell and waste my time watching comedies for five hours—no way!"

Questions for Study and Discussion

1, What is Hendricks' purpose in this essay? Where does he state his purpose?
2. What particular cause and effect relationship does the author set out to establish in the essay? Does the essay seem sound and logical? Why or why not?

3. For what purpose does Hendricks use examples in this essay?
4. What does Hendricks gain by quoting his fellow inmates rather than paraphrasing them?
5. How objective is Hendricks in this essay? Is he a disinterested observer?

Vocabulary

Refer to your dictionary to define the following words as they are used in this selection. Then use each word in a sentence of your own.

correlation (2)
extricate (12)
hysterical (13)
consternation (15)

Suggested Writing Assignment

Write an essay in which you discuss the effects of television on you or on American society. You may wish to focus on the specific influences of one of the following aspects of television:

advertising
sports broadcasts
cultural programming
talk shows
national or international news
children's programming
educational television
situation comedies

WHO'S AFRAID OF MATH, AND WHY?

Sheila Tobias

Sheila Tobias served as Associate Provost of Wesleyan University, where she became interested in the reasons why certain students, notably women, choose not to pursue careers in math or math-related fields. On the basis of her research, Tobias, a "mathematics avoider" herself, founded the Math Clinic at Wesleyan. She is the author of Overcoming Math Anxiety *(1978), from which this essay is taken. As you read the essay, notice how Tobias systematically analyzes the possible causes of "math anxiety."*

The first thing people remember about failing at math is that it felt like sudden death. Whether the incident occurred while learning "word problems" in sixth grade, coping with equations in high school, or first confronting calculus and statistics in college, failure came suddenly and in a very frightening way. An idea or a new operation was not just difficult, it was impossible! And, instead of asking questions or taking the lesson slowly, most people remember having had the feeling that they would never go any further in mathematics. If we assume that the curriculum was reasonable, and that the new idea was but the next in a series of learnable concepts, the feeling of utter defeat was simply not rational; yet "math anxious" college students and adults have revealed that no matter how much the teacher reassured them, they could not overcome that feeling.

A common myth about the nature of mathematical ability holds that one either has or does not have a mathematical mind. Mathematical imagination and an intuitive grasp of mathematical principles may well be needed to do advanced research, but why should people who can do college-level work in other subjects not be able to do college-level math as well? Rates of learning may vary. Competency under time pressure may differ. Certainly low self-esteem will get in the way. But where is the evidence that a student needs a "mathematical mind" in order to succeed at learning math?

3 Consider the effects of this mythology. Since only a few people are supposed to have this mathematical mind, part of what makes us so passive in the face of our difficulties in learning mathematics is that we suspect all the while we may not be one of "them," and we spend our time waiting to find out when our nonmathematical minds will be exposed. Since our limit will eventually be reached, we see no point in being methodical or in attending to detail. We are grateful when we survive fractions, word problems, or geometry. If that certain moment of failure hasn't struck yet, it is only temporarily postponed.

4 Parents, especially parents of girls, often expect their children to be nonmathematical. Parents are either poor at math and had their own sudden-death experiences, or, if math came easily for them, they do not know how it feels to be slow. In either case, they unwittingly foster the idea that a mathematical mind is something one either has or does not have.

Mathematics and Sex

5 Although fear of math is not a purely female phenomenon, girls tend to drop out of math sooner than boys, and adult women experience an aversion to math and math-related activities that is akin to anxiety. A 1972 survey of the amount of high school mathematics taken by incoming freshmen at Berkeley revealed that while 57 percent of the boys had taken four years of high school math, only 8 percent of the girls had had the same amount of preparation. Without four years of high school math, students at Berkeley, and at most other colleges and universities, are ineligible for the calculus sequence, unlikely to attempt chemistry or physics, and inadequately prepared for statistics and economics.

6 Unable to elect these entry-level courses, the remaining 92 percent of the girls will be limited, presumably, to the career

choices that are considered feminine: the humanities, guidance and counseling, elementary school teaching, foreign languages, and the fine arts.

Boys and girls may be born alike with respect to math, but certain sex differences in performance emerge early according to several respected studies, and these differences remain through adulthood. They are:

1. Girls compute better than boys (elementary school and on).
2. Boys solve word problems better than girls (from age thirteen on).
3. Boys take more math than girls (from age sixteen on).
4. Girls learn to hate math sooner and possibly for different reasons.

Why the differences in performance? One reason is the amount of math learned and used at play. Another may be the difference in male-female maturation. If girls do better than boys at all elementary school tasks, then they may compute better for no other reason than that arithmetic is part of the elementary school curriculum. As boys and girls grow older, girls become, under pressure, academically less competitive. Thus, the falling off of girls' math performance between ages ten and fifteen may be because:

1. Math gets harder in each successive year and requires more work and commitment.
2. Both boys and girls are pressured, beginning at age ten, not to excel in areas designated by society to be outside their sex-role domains.
3. Thus girls have a good excuse to avoid the painful struggle with math; boys don't.

Such a model may explain girls' lower achievement in math overall, but why should girls even younger than ten have difficulty in problem-solving? In her review of the research on sex differences, psychologist Eleanor Maccoby noted that girls are generally more conforming, more suggestible, and more dependent upon the opinion of others than boys (all learned, not innate, behaviors). Being so, they may not be as willing to take risks or to think for themselves, two behaviors that are necessary in solving problems. Indeed, in one test of third-graders, girls were found to be not nearly as willing to estimate, to make judgments about "possible right answers," or to work with systems they had never seen before. Their very success at doing what is expected of them up to that time seems to get in the way of their doing something new.

10 If readiness to do word problems, to take one example, is as much a function of readiness to take risks as it is of "reasoning ability," then mathematics performance certainly requires more than memory, computation, and reasoning. The differences in math performance between boys and girls—no matter how consistently those differences show up—cannot be attributed simply to differences in innate ability.

11 Still, if one were to ask the victims themselves, they would probably disagree: they would say their problems with math have to do with the way they are "wired." They feel they are somehow missing something—one ability or several—that other people have. Although women want to believe they are not mentally inferior to men, many fear that, where math is concerned, they really are. Thus, we have to consider seriously whether mathematical ability has a biological basis, not only because a number of researchers believe this to be so, but because a number of victims agree with them.

The Arguments from Biology

12 The search for some biological basis for math ability or disability is fraught with logical and experimental difficulties. Since not all math under-achievers are women, and not all women are mathematics-avoidant, poor performance in math is unlikely to be due to some genetic or hormonal difference between the sexes. Moreover, no amount of research so far has unearthed a "mathematical competency" in some tangible, measurable substance in the body. Since "masculinity" cannot be injected into women to test whether or not it improves their mathematics, the theories that attribute such ability to genes or hormones must depend for their proof on circumstantial evidence. So long as about 7 percent of the Ph.D.'s in mathematics are earned by women, we have to conclude either that these women have

genes, hormones, and brain organization different from those of the rest of us, or that certain positive experiences in their lives have largely undone the negative fact that they are female, or both.

Genetically, the only difference between males and females (albeit a significant and pervasive one) is the presence of two chromosomes designated X in every female cell. Normal males exhibit an X-Y combination. Because some kinds of mental retardation are associated with sex-chromosomal anomalies, a number of researchers have sought a converse linkage between specific abilities and the presence or absence of the second X. But the linkage between genetics and mathematics is not supported by conclusive evidence.

Since intensified hormonal activity commences at adolescence, a time during which girls seem to lose interest in mathematics, much more has been made of the unequal amounts in females and males of the sex-linked hormones androgen and estrogen. Biological researchers have linked estrogen—the female hormone—with "simple repetitive tasks," and androgen—the male hormone—with "complex restructuring tasks." The assumption here is not only that such specific talents are biologically based (probably undemonstrable) but also that one cannot be good at *both* repetitive and restructuring kinds of assignments.

Sex Roles and Mathematics Competence

The fact that many girls tend to lose interest in math at the age they reach puberty (junior high school) suggests that puberty might in some sense cause girls to fall behind in math. Several explanations come to mind: the influence of hormones, more intensified sex-role socialization, or some extracurricular learning experience exclusive to boys of that age.

One group of seventh-graders in a private school in New England gave a clue as to what children themselves think about all of this. When asked why girls do as well as boys in math until the sixth grade, while sixth-grade boys do better from that point on, the girls responded: "Oh, that's easy. After sixth grade, we have to do real math." The answer to why "real math" should be considered to be "for boys" and not "for girls" can be found not in the realm of biology but only in the realm of ideology of sex differences.

17 Parents, peers, and teachers forgive a girl when she does badly in math at school, encouraging her to do well in other subjects instead. " 'There, there.' my mother used to say when I failed at math," one woman says. "But I got a talking-to when I did badly in French." Lynn Fox, who directs a program for mathematically gifted junior high boys and girls on the campus of Johns Hopkins University, has trouble recruiting girls and keeping them in her program. Some parents prevent their daughters from participating altogether for fear that excellence in math will make them too different. The girls themselves are often reluctant to continue with mathematics, Fox reports, because they fear social ostracism.

18 Where do these associations come from?

19 The association of masculinity with mathematics sometimes extends from the discipline to those who practice it. Students, asked on a questionnaire what characteristics they associate with a mathematician (as contrasted with a "writer"), selected terms such as rational, cautious, wise, and responsible. The writer, on the other hand, in addition to being seen as individualistic and independent, was also described as warm, interested in people, and altogether more compatible with a feminine ideal.

20 As a result of this psychological conditioning, a young woman may consider math and math-related fields to be inimical to femininity. In an interesting study of West German teenagers, Erika Schildkamp-Kuendiger found that girls who identified themselves with the feminine ideal underachieved in mathematics, that is, did less well than would have been expected of them based on general intelligence and performance in other subjects.

Street Mathematics: Things, Motion, Scores

21 Not all the skills that are necessary for learning mathematics are learned in school. Measuring, computing, and manipulating objects that have dimensions and dynamic

properties of their own are part of the everyday life of children. Children who miss out on these experiences may not be well primed for math in school.

Feminists have complained for a long time that playing with dolls is one way of convincing impressionable little girls that they may only be mothers or housewives—or, as in the case of the Barbie doll, "pinup girls"—when they grow up. But doll-playing may have even more serious consequences for little girls than that. Do girls find out about gravity and distance and shapes and sizes playing with dolls? Probably not.

A curious boy, if his parents are tolerant, will have taken apart a number of household and play objects by the time he is ten, and, if his parents are lucky, he may even have put them back together again. In all of this he is learning things that will be useful in physics and math. Taking parts out that have to go back in requires some examination of form. Building something that stays up or at least stays put for some time involves working with structure.

Sports is another source of math-related concepts for children which tends to favor boys. Getting to first base on a not very well hit grounder is a lesson in time, speed, and distance. Intercepting a football thrown through the air requires some rapid intuitive eye calculations based on the ball's direction, speed, and trajectory. Since physics is partly concerned with velocities, trajectories, and collisions of objects, much of the math taught to prepare a student for physics deals with relationships and formulas that can be used to express motion and acceleration.

What, then, can we conclude about mathematics and sex? If math anxiety is in part the result of math avoidance, why not require girls to take as much math as they can possibly master? If being the only girl in "trig" is the reason so many women drop math at the end of high school, why not provide psychological counseling and support for those young women who wish to go on? Since ability in mathematics is considered by many to be unfeminine, perhaps fear of success, more than any bodily or mental dysfunction, may interfere with girls' ability to learn math.

Questions for Study and Discussion

1. Tobias states that girls suffer more than boys from math anxiety. What does she say causes girls to be more fearful than boys?
2. What evidence does Tobias use to establish the main cause and effect relationship in this essay? Is her evidence sufficient? If not, what else might she have added? (Glossary: *Evidence*)
3. Why does Tobias downplay sex differences as a cause for differences in mathematical performance?
4. Tobias states, "A common myth about the nature of mathematical ability holds that one either has or does not have a mathematical mind." What does she think are the effects of this myth?
5. What is the cause and effect relationship discussed in paragraphs 15–20? What function does paragraph 18 serve in the development of that relationship?

Vocabulary

Refer to your dictionary to define the following words as they are used in this selection. Then use each word in a sentence of your own.

curriculum (1)
myth (2)
intuitive (2)
unwittingly (4)
aversion (5)
innate (9)
commences (14)
compatible (19)
inimical (20)

Suggested Writing Assignment

How do you feel about mathematics? Write a short essay discussing the reasons for your attitude. What *caused* you to feel the way that you do?

18

ARGUMENT

Argumentation is the attempt to persuade a reader to accept your point of view, to make a decision, or to pursue a particular course of action. Because the writer of an argument is often interested in explaining a subject, as well as in advocating a particular view, argumentation frequently adopts other rhetorical strategies. Nevertheless, it is the attempt to convince, not to explain, that is most important in an argumentative essay.

There are two basic types of argumentation: logical and persuasive. In *logical argumentation* the writer appeals to the reader's rational or intellectual faculties to convince him of the truth of a particular statement or belief. In *persuasive argumentation,* on the other hand, the writer appeals to the reader's emotions and opinions to move the reader to action. These two types of argumentation are seldom found in their pure forms, and the degree to which one or the other is emphasized in written work depends on the writer's subject, specific purpose, and intended audience. Although you may occasionally need or want to appeal to your readers' emotions, most often in your college work you will need to rely only on the fundamental techniques of logical argumentation.

There are two types of reasoning common to essays of argumentation: induction and deduction. *Inductive reasoning,* the more common type, moves from a set of specific examples to a general statement. In doing so, the writer makes what is known as an *inductive leap* from the evidence to the generalization. For example, after examining enrollment statistics, we can conclude that students do not like to take courses offered early in the morning or late in the afternoon. *Deductive reasoning,* on the other hand, moves from a general statement to a specific conclusion. It works on the model of the *syllogism,* a simple three-part argument that consists of a major premise, a minor premise, and a conclusion, as in the following example:

a. All women are mortal. (major premise)
b. Judy is a woman. (minor premise)
c. Judy is mortal. (conclusion)

A well-constructed argument avoids *logical fallacies*, flaws in the reasoning that will render the argument invalid. Following are some of the most common logical fallacies:

1. *Oversimplification*. The tendency to provide simple solutions to complex problems. "The reason we have inflation today is that OPEC has unreasonably raised the price of oil."
2. *Hasty Generalization*. A generalization that is based on too little evidence or on evidence that is not representative. "It was the best movie I saw this year, and so it should get an Academy Award."
3. *Post hoc, ergo propter hoc* ("After this, therefore because of this"). Confusing chance or coincidence with causation. Because one event comes after another one, it does not necessarily mean that the first event caused the second. "Ever since I went to the hockey game I've had a cold."
4. *Begging the question*. Assuming in a premise that which needs to be proven. "Conservation is the only means of meeting the energy crisis, therefore, we should seek out methods to conserve energy."
5. *False analogy*. Making a misleading analogy between logically unconnected ideas. "Of course he'll make a fine coach. He was an all-star basketball player."
6. *Either/or thinking*. The tendency to see an issue as having only two sides. "Used car salesmen are either honest or crooked."
7. *Non sequitur* ("It does not follow"). An inference or conclusion that does not follow from established premises or evidence. "She is a sincere speaker; she must know what she is talking about."

As you write your argumentative essays, you should keep the following advice in mind. Somewhere near the beginning of your essay, you should identify the issue to be discussed, explain why you think it is important, and point out what interest you and your readers share in the issue. Then, in the body of your essay, you should organize the various points of your argument. You may move from your least important point to your most important point, from the most familiar to the least familiar, from the easiest to accept or comprehend to the most difficult. For each point in your argument, you should provide sufficient appropriate supporting evidence—facts and statistics, illustrative examples and narratives, quotations from authorities. In addition, you should acknowledge the strongest opposing arguments and explain why you believe your position is more valid.

Be sure that you neither overstate nor understate your position. It is always wise to let the evidence convince your reader. Overstatement not only annoys readers but, more important, raises serious doubts about your own confidence in the power of your facts and reasoning. At the same time, no writer persuades by excessively understating or qualifying information with words and phrases such as *perhaps, maybe, I think, sometimes, most often, nearly always,* or *in my opinion*. The result sounds not rational and sensible but indecisive and fuzzy.

Darkness at Noon

Harold Krents

Harold Krents prepared for a career as a lawyer at Harvard and at Oxford and currently practices law in Washington, D.C. He is also the author of To Race the Wind *(1972). Blind from birth, Krents has long been interested in the plight of the handicapped. In "Darkness at Noon," he calls on his experiences as a blind person to persuade his readers that handicapped people should not be regarded as totally disabled people.*

Blind from birth, I have never had the opportunity to see myself and have been completely dependent on the image I create in the eye of the observer. To date it has not been narcissistic. 1

There are those who assume that since I can't see, I obviously also cannot hear. Very often people will converse with me at the top of their lungs, enunciating each word very carefully. Conversely, people will also often whisper, assuming that since my eyes don't work, my ears don't either. 2

For example, when I go to the airport and ask the ticket agent for assistance to the plane, he or she will invariably pick up the phone, call a ground hostess and whisper: "Hi, Jane, we've got a 76 here." I have concluded that the word "blind" is not used for one of two reasons: Either they fear that if the dread word is spoken, the ticket agent's retina will immediately detach or they are reluctant to inform me of my condition of which I may not have been previously aware. 3

On the other hand, others know that of course I can hear, but believe that I can't talk. Often, therefore, when my wife and I go out to dinner, a waiter or waitress will ask Kit if "*he* would like a drink" to which I respond that "indeed *he* would." 4

This point was graphically driven home to me while we were in England. I had been given a year's leave of absence from my Washington law firm to study for a diploma in law degree at Oxford University. During the year I became ill and was hospitalized. Immediately after admission, I was wheeled down to the X-ray room. Just at the door sat an elderly woman—elderly I would judge from the sound of her voice. "What is his name?" the woman asked the orderly who had been wheeling me.

"What's your name?" the orderly repeated to me.

"Harold Krents," I replied.

"Harold Krents," he repeated.

"When was he born?"

"When were you born?"

"November 5, 1944," I responded.

"November 5, 1944," the orderly intoned.

This procedure continued for approximately five minutes at which point even my saint-like disposition deserted me. "Look," I finally blurted out, "this is absolutely ridiculous. Okay, granted I can't see, but it's got to have become pretty clear to both of you that I don't need an interpreter."

"He says he doesn't need an interpreter," the orderly reported to the woman.

The toughest misconception of all is the view that because I can't see, I can't work. I was turned down by over forty law firms because of my blindness, even though my qualifications included a cum laude degree from Harvard College and a good ranking in my Harvard Law School class.

The attempt to find employment, the continuous frustration of being told that it was impossible for a blind person to practice law, the rejection letters, not based on my lack of ability but rather on my disability, will always remain one of the most disillusioning experiences of my life.

Fortunately, this view of limitation and exclusion is beginning to change. On April 16, the Department of Labor issued regulations that mandate equal-employment opportunities for the handicapped. By and large, the business community's response to offering employment to the disabled has been enthusiastic.

I therefore look forward to the day, with the expectation that it is certain to come, when employers will view their handicapped workers as a little child did me years ago when my family still lived in Scarsdale. 18

I was playing basketball with my father in our backyard according to procedures we had developed. My father would stand beneath the hoop, shout, and I would shoot over his head at the basket attached to our garage. Our next-door neighbor, aged five, wandered over into our yard with a playmate. "He's blind," our neighbor whispered to her friend in a voice that could be heard distinctly by Dad and me. Dad shot and missed; I did the same. Dad hit the rim: I missed entirely: Dad shot and missed the garage entirely. "Which one is blind?" whispered back the little friend. 19

I would hope that in the near future when a plant manager is touring the factory with the foreman and comes upon a handicapped and nonhandicapped person working together, his comment after watching them work will be, "Which one is disabled?" 20

Questions for Study and Discussion

1. What is Krents's point in this essay? How does he try to persuade us to his belief?
2. Does Krents use induction or deduction?
3. Krents discusses three misconceptions regarding the handicapped and provides an example of each. How persuasive do you find each of these examples? Why do you suppose Krents presents the misconceptions in the order that he does? (Glossary: *Organization*)
4. Identify several passages in which Krents uses irony to make a point. Why do you suppose Krents uses irony instead of direct statement to enhance his argument? (Glossary: *Irony*)
5. Krents concludes his essay with an anecdote. How does this anecdote serve the author's argument? How does it function in the context of his essay?

Vocabulary

Refer to your dictionary to define the following words as they are used in this selection. Then use each word in a sentence of your own.

narcissistic (1)	disposition (13)
enunciating (2)	disillusioning (16)
conversely (2)	mandate (17)

Suggested Writing Assignment

Harold Krents tells of three experiences he had as a blind person in order to persuade us to share his opinion about the way handicapped people should be treated. Using your own personal experiences, tell a story or narrate a series of events in order to persuade readers to accept your point of view on a particular topic. For example, you might wish to convince readers that sports have become too competitive, that self-discipline is valuable, or that honesty should be encouraged and rewarded.

The Egalitarian Error

Margaret Mead and Rhoda Metraux

Margaret Mead (1901–1978) was a noted educator, anthropologist, and author. Educated at Barnard College and Columbia University, she was for many years a professor of anthropology at Columbia. She spent much of her life studying foreign societies and became an expert in such fields as family structure, mental health, drugs, environmental problems, and women's roles in society. Her best-known books include Coming of Age in Samoa *(1928),* Male and Female *(1949),* The Study of Culture at a Distance *(1953), and* Childhood in Contemporary Cultures *(1955). Rhoda Metraux, also an anthropologist, was educated at Vassar, Yale, and Columbia. A contributor to anthropological journals, Metraux collaborated with Mead on* A Way of Seeing *(1970), from which the following selection was taken. As you read, notice the way the authors use examples to persuade readers to their interpretation of the basic democratic belief that all people are created equal.*

Almost all Americans want to be democratic, but many Americans are confused about what, exactly, democracy means. How do you know when someone is acting in a democratic—or an undemocratic—way? Recently several groups have spoken out with particular bitterness against the kind of democracy that means equal opportunity for all, regardless of race or national origin. They act as if all human beings did not belong to one species, as if some races of mankind were inferior to others in their capacity to learn what members of other races know and have invented. Other extremists attack religious groups—Jews or Catholics—or deny the right of an individual to be an agnostic. One reason that these extremists, who explicitly do not want to be democratic, can get a hearing even though their views run counter to the Constitution and our traditional values is that the people who *do* want to be democratic are frequently so muddled.

For many Americans, democratic behavior necessitates an outright denial of any significant differences among human beings. In their eyes it is undemocratic for anyone to refer, in the presence of any other person, to differences in skin color, manners or religious beliefs. Whatever one's private thoughts may be, it is necessary always to act as if everyone were exactly alike.

Behavior of this kind developed partly as a reaction to those who discriminated against or actively abused members of other groups. But it is artificial, often hypocritical behavior, nonetheless, and it dulls and flattens human relationships. If two people can't talk easily and comfortably but must forever guard against some slip of the tongue, some admission of what is in both persons' minds, they are likely to talk as little as possible. This embarrassment about differences reaches a final absurdity when a Methodist feels that he cannot take a guest on a tour of his garden because he might have to identify a wild plant with a blue flower, called the wandering Jew, or when a white lecturer feels he ought not to mention the name of Conrad's beautiful story *The Nigger of the "Narcissus."* But it is no less absurd when well-meaning people, speaking of the physically handicapped, tell prospective employers: "They don't want special consideration. Ask as much of them as you do of everyone else, and fire them if they don't give satisfaction!"

Another version of false democracy is the need to deny the existence of personal advantages. Inherited wealth, famous parents, a first-class mind, a rare voice, a beautiful face, an exceptional physical skill—any advantage has to be minimized or denied. Continually watched and measured, the man or woman who is rich or talented or well educated is likely to be called "undemocratic" whenever he does anything out of the ordinary—more or less of something than others do. If he wants acceptance, the person with a "superior" attribute, like the person with an "inferior" attribute, often feels obliged to take on a protective disguise, to act as if he were just like everybody else. One denies difference; the other minimizes it. And both believe, as they conform to these false standards, that they act in the name of democracy.

5 For many Americans, a related source of confusion is success. As a people we Americans greatly prize success. And in our eyes success all too often means simply outdoing other people by virtue of achievement judged by some single scale—income or honors or headlines or trophies—and coming out at "the top." Only one person, as we see it, can be the best—can get the highest grades, be voted the most attractive girl or the boy most likely to succeed. Though we often rejoice in the success of people far removed from ourselves—in another profession, another community, or endowed with a talent that we do not covet—we tend to regard the success of people close at hand, within our own small group, as a threat. We fail to realize that there are many kinds of success, including the kind of success that lies within a person. We do not realize, for example, that there could be in the same class one hundred boys and girls—each of them a "success" in a different kind of way. Individuality is again lost in a refusal to recognize and cherish the differences among people.

6 The attitude that measures success by a single yardstick and isolates the *one* winner and the kind of "democracy" that denies or minimizes differences among people are both deeply destructive. Imagine for a moment a family with two sons, one of whom is brilliant, attractive and athletic while the other is dull, unattractive and clumsy. Both boys attend the same high school. In the interest of the slower boy, the parents would want the school to set equally low standards for everyone. Lessons should be easy; no one should be forced to study dead languages* or advanced mathematics

*Languages no longer spoken, such as classical Greek and Latin.

in order to graduate. Athletics should be noncompetitive; every boy should have a chance to enjoy playing games. Everyone should be invited to all the parties. As for special attention to gifted children, this is not fair to the other children. An all-round education should be geared to the average, normal child.

But in the interest of the other boy, these same parents would have quite opposite goals. After all, we need highly trained people; the school should do the most it can for its best students. Funds should be made available for advanced classes and special teachers, for the best possible coach, the best athletic equipment. Young people should be allowed to choose friends on their own level. The aim of education should be to produce topflight students.

This is an extreme example, but it illustrates the completely incompatible aims that can arise in this kind of "democracy." Must our country shut its eyes to the needs of either its gifted or its less gifted sons? It would be a good deal more sensible to admit, as some schools do today, that children differ widely from one another, that all successes cannot be ranged on one single scale, that there is room in a real democracy to help each child find his own level and develop to his fullest potential.

Moving now to a wider scene, before World War I Americans thought of themselves as occupying a unique place in the world—and there was no question in most minds that this country was a "success." True, Europeans might look down on us for our lack of culture, but with a few notable, local exceptions, we simply refused to compete on European terms. There was no country in the world remotely like the one we were building. But since World War II we have felt the impact of a country whose size and strength and emphasis on national achievement more closely parallel our own. Today we are ahead of Russia, or Russia is ahead of us. Nothing else matters. Instead of valuing and developing the extraordinary assets and potential of our country for their own sake, we are involved in a simple set of competitions for wealth and power and dominance.

These are expensive and dangerous attitudes. When democracy ceases to be a cherished way of life and becomes instead the name of one team, we are using the word democracy to describe behavior that places us and all other men in jeopardy.

11 Individually, nationally and, today, internationally, the misreading of the phrase "all men are created equal" exacts a heavy price. The attitudes that follow from our misconceptions may be compatible with life in a country where land and rank and prestige are severely limited and the roads to success are few. But they are inappropriate in a land as rich, as open, as filled with opportunities as our own. They are the price we pay for being *less* democratic than we claim to be.

12 "All men are created equal" does not mean that all men are the same. What it does mean is that each should be accorded full respect and full rights as a unique human being—full respect for his humanity *and* for his differences from other people.

Questions for Study and Discussion

1. What is the authors' point in this essay? How do they attempt to persuade us to accept their belief? Cite examples from the essay.
2. Do the authors use induction or deduction?
3. What, specifically, do the authors mean when they say that "the people who *do* want to be democratic are frequently so muddled"? Do they convince you that this statement is true? If so, how do they convince you?
4. Why do the authors regard their anecdote about the two sons in paragraphs 6 and 7 as "an extreme example"? In terms of their argument, what seems to be their purpose in using this anecdote? What effect does the anecdote have on you?
5. What does the title mean? Why is it an appropriate title for this essay?

Vocabulary

Refer to your dictionary to define the following words as they are used in this selection. Then use each word in a sentence of your own.

egalitarian (title)
agnostic (1)
hypocritical (3)
covet (5)
incompatible (8)
exacts (11)
accorded (12)

Suggested Writing Assignment

Select one of the following statements from the essay as your thesis statement, and write a persuasive essay in which you defend it.

> "An all-around education should be geared to the average, normal child."
>
> "The aim of education should be to produce topflight students."

Pain Is Not the Ultimate Enemy

Norman Cousins

After attending Columbia University, Norman Cousins began a long, industrious career as an educator, journalist, and writer. He is perhaps best known as the editor of Saturday Review, *a position he held for thirty-eight years. He has written many books, most recently* Anatomy of An Illness as Perceived by the Patient: Reflections on Healing and Regeneration *(1979), a widely read account of how he coped with a nearly fatal illness. In the following essay, Cousins tells about the nature of pain and explains how painkillers work; he attempts to persuade us that we should not seek to deaden pain but to relieve its causes.*

Americans are probably the most pain-conscious people on the face of the earth. For years we have had it drummed into us—in print, on radio, over television, in everyday conversation—that any hint of pain is to be banished as though it were the ultimate evil. As a result, we are becoming a nation of pill-grabbers and hypochondriacs, escalating the slightest ache into a searing ordeal. 1

We know very little about pain and what we don't know makes it hurt all the more. Indeed, no form of illiteracy in the United States is so widespread or costly as ignorance about pain—what it is, what causes it, how to deal with it without panic. Almost everyone can rattle off the names of at least a dozen drugs that can deaden pain from every conceivable cause—all the way from headaches to hemorrhoids. There is far less knowledge about the fact that about 90 percent of pain is self-limiting, that it is not always an indication of poor health, and that, most frequently, it is the result of tension, stress, worry, idleness, boredom, frustration, 2 suppressed rage, insufficient sleep, overeating, poorly balanced diet, smoking, excessive drinking, inadequate exercise, stale air, or any of the other abuses encountered by the human body in modern society.

The most ignored fact of all about pain is that the best way to eliminate it is to eliminate the abuse. Instead, many people reach almost instinctively for the painkillers—aspirins, barbiturates, codeines, tranquilizers, sleeping pills, and dozens of other analgesics or desensitizing drugs.

Most doctors are profoundly troubled over the extent to which the medical profession today is taking on the trappings of a pain-killing industry. Their offices are overloaded with people who are morbidly but mistakenly convinced that something dreadful is about to happen to them. It is all too evident that the campaign to get people to run to a doctor at the first sign of pain has boomeranged. Physicians find it difficult to give adequate attention to patients genuinely in need of expert diagnosis and treatment because their time is soaked up by people who have nothing wrong with them except a temporary indisposition or a psychogenic ache.

Patients tend to feel indignant and insulted if the physican tells them he can find no organic cause for the pain. They tend to interpret the term "psychogenic" to mean that they are complaining of nonexistent symptoms. They need to be educated about the fact that many forms of pain have no underlying physical cause but are the result, as mentioned earlier, of tension, stress, or hostile factors in the general environment. Sometimes a pain may be a manifestation of "conversion hysteria," . . . the name given by Jean Charcot to physical symptoms that have their origins in emotional disturbances.

Obviously, it is folly for an individual to ignore symptoms that could be a warning of a potentially serious illness. Some people are so terrified of getting bad news from a doctor that they allow their malaise to worsen, sometimes past the point of no return. Total neglect is not the answer to hypochondria. The only answer has to be increased education about the way the human body works, so that more people will be able to steer an intelligent course between promiscuous pill-popping and irresponsible disregard of genuine symptoms.

7 Of all forms of pain, none is more important for the individual to understand than the "threshold" variety. Almost everyone has a telltale ache that is triggered whenever tension or fatigue reaches a certain point. It can take the form of a migraine-type headache or a squeezing pain deep in the abdomen or cramps or a pain in the lower back or even pain in the joints. The individual who has learned how to make the correlation between such threshold pains and their cause doesn't panic when they occur; he or she does something about relieving the stress and tension. Then, if the pain persists despite the absence of apparent cause, the individual will telephone the doctor.

8 If ignorance about the nature of pain is widespread, ignorance about the way pain-killing drugs work is even more so. What is not generally understood is that many of the vaunted pain-killing drugs conceal the pain without correcting the underlying condition. They deaden the mechanism in the body that alerts the brain to the fact that something may be wrong. The body can pay a high price for suppression of pain without regard to its basic cause.

9 Professional athletes are sometimes severely disadvantaged by trainers whose job it is to keep them in action. The more famous the athlete, the greater the risk that he or she may be subjected to extreme medical measures when injury strikes. The star baseball pitcher whose arm is sore because of a torn muscle or tissue damage may need sustained rest more than anything else. But his team is battling for a place in the World Series; so the trainer or team doctor, called upon to work his magic, reaches for a strong dose of butazolidine or other powerful pain suppressants. Presto, the pain disappears! The pitcher takes his place on the mound and does superbly. That could be the last game, however, in which he is able to throw a ball with full strength. The drugs didn't repair the torn muscle or cause the damaged tissue to heal. What they did was to mask the pain, enabling the pitcher to throw hard, further damaging the torn muscle. Little wonder that so many star athletes are cut down in their

prime, more the victims of overzealous treatment of their injuries than of the injuries themselves.

The king of all painkillers, of course, is aspirin. The U.S. Food and Drug Administration permits aspirin to be sold without prescription, but the drug, contrary to popular belief, can be dangerous and, in sustained doses, potentially lethal. Aspirin is self-administered by more people than any other drug in the world. Some people are aspirin-poppers, taking ten or more a day. What they don't know is that the smallest dose can cause internal bleeding. Even more serious perhaps is the fact that aspirin is antagonistic to collagen, which has a key role in the formation of connective tissue. Since many forms of arthritis involve disintegration of the connective tissue, the steady use of aspirin can actually intensify the underlying arthritic condition. . . .

Aspirin is not the only pain-killing drug, of course, that is known to have dangerous side effects. Dr. Daphne A. Roe, of Cornell University, at a medical meeting in New York City in 1974, presented startling evidence of a wide range of hazards associated with sedatives and other pain suppressants. Some of these drugs seriously interfere with the ability of the body to metabolize food properly, producing malnutrition. In some instances, there is also the danger of bone-marrow depression, interfering with the ability of the body to replenish its blood supply.

Pain-killing drugs are among the greatest advances in the history of medicine. Properly used, they can be a boon in alleviating suffering and in treating disease. But their indiscriminate and promiscuous use is making psychological cripples and chronic ailers out of millions of people. The unremitting barrage of advertising for pain-killing drugs, especially over television, has set the stage for a mass anxiety neurosis. Almost from the moment children are old enough to sit up-right in front of a television screen, they are being indoctrinated into the hypochondriac's clamorous and morbid world. Little wonder so many people fear pain more than death itself.

It might be a good idea if concerned physicans and educators could get together to make knowledge about pain an important part of the regular school curriculum. As for the populace at large, perhaps some of the same techniques used by public-service agencies to make people cancer-conscious can be used to counteract the growing terror of pain and illness in general. People ought to know that nothing is more remarkable about the human body than its recuperative drive, given a modicum of respect. If our broadcasting stations cannot provide equal time for responses to the pain-killing advertisements, they might at least set aside a few minutes each day for common-sense remarks on the subject of pain. As for the Food and Drug Administration, it might be interesting to know why an agency that has so energetically warned the American people against taking vitamins without prescriptions is doing so little to control over-the-counter sales each year of billions of pain-killing pills, some of which can do more harm than the pain they are supposed to suppress.

Questions for Study and Discussion

1. What is Cousins' purpose in this essay? What does he want us to believe? What does he want us to do?
2. If "pain is not the ultimate enemy," what, according to Cousins, is?
3. What does the example of the star baseball pitcher contribute to the persuasiveness of the essay?
4. What in Cousins' tone—his attitude toward his subject and audience—particularly contributes to the persuasiveness of the essay? Cite examples from the selection.
5. One strategy Cousins uses to develop his argument is causal analysis. Identify the passages in which he uses causal analysis. How exactly does it serve his argument? (Glossary: *Cause and Effect*)
6. For what audience do you suppose Cousins wrote this essay? In your opinion, would most readers be convinced by what Cousins says about pain? Are you convinced? Why, or why not?

Vocabulary

Refer to your dictionary to define the following words as they are used in this selection. Then use each word in a sentence of your own.

hypochondriacs (1)
searing (1)
promiscuous (6)
overzealous (9)
lethal (10)
antagonistic (10)
neurosis (12)

Suggested Writing Assignment

Write a persuasive essay in which you support or refute the following proposition: Television advertising is in large part responsible for Americans' belief that pain is the ultimate enemy.

CONFESSIONS OF A FEMALE CHAUVINIST SOW

Anne Roiphe

Anne Roiphe is best known as a novelist; her novels include Digging Out *(1967),* Up the Sandbox! *(1970),* Long Division *(1972), and* Torch Song *(1977). Each of these books deals with some aspect of a woman's search for identity. In "Confessions of a Female Chauvinist Sow," which first appeared in* New York *magazine, Roiphe examines the male stereotypes that women have created and attempts to persuade readers that women are not superior to but only equal to men. As you read the essay, notice the way Roiphe uses examples to argue inductively.*

I once married a man I thought was totally unlike my father and I imagined a whole new world of freedom emerging. Five years later it was clear even to me—floating face down in a wash of despair—that I had simply chosen a replica of my handsome daddy-true. The updated version spoke English like an angel but—good God!—underneath he was my father exactly: wonderful, but not the right man for me. 1

Most people I know have at one time or another been fouled up by their childhood experiences. Patterns tend to sink into the unconscious only to reappear, disguised, unseen, like marionette strings, pulling us this way or that. Whatever ails people—keeps them up at night, tossing and turning—also ails movements no matter how historically huge or politically important. The women's movement cannot remake consciousness, or reshape the future, without acknowledging and shedding all the unnecessary and ugly baggage of the past. It's easy enough now to see where men 2 have kept us out of clubs, baseball games, graduate schools; it's easy enough to recognize the hidden directions that limit Sis to cake-baking and Junior to bridge-building; it's now possible for even Miss America herself to identify what *they* have done to us, and, of course, *they* have and *they* did and *they* are. . . . But along the way we also developed our own hidden prejudices, class assumptions and an anti-male humor and collection of expectations that gave us, like all oppressed groups, a secret sense of superiority (co-existing with a poor self-image—it's not news that people can believe two contradictory things at once).

Listen to any group that suffers materially and socially. They have a lexicon with which they tease the enemy: ofay, goy, honky, gringo. "Poor pale devils," said Malcolm X loud enough for us to hear, although blacks had joked about that to each other for years. Behind some of the women's liberation thinking lurk the rumors, the prejudices, the defense systems of generations of oppressed women whispering in the kitchen together, presenting one face to their menfolk and another to their card clubs, their mothers and sisters. All this is natural enough but potentially dangerous in a revolutionary situation in which you hope to create a future that does not mirror the past. The hidden anti-male feelings, a result of the old system, will foul us up if they are allowed to persist.

During my teen years I never left the house on my Saturday night dates without my mother slipping me a few extra dollars—mad money, it was called. I'll explain what it was for the benefit of the new generation in which people just sleep with each other: the fellow was supposed to bring me home, lead me safely through the asphalt jungle, protect me from slithering snakes, rapists and the like. But my mother and I knew young men were apt to drink too much, to slosh down so many rye-and-gingers that some hero might well lead me in front of an oncoming bus, smash his daddy's car into Tiffany's window or, less gallantly, throw up on my new dress. Mad money was for getting home on your own, no matter what form of insanity your date happened to evidence. Mad money was also a wallflower's rope ladder; if the guy you came with suddenly fancied someone else, well, you didn't have to stay there and suffer, you could go home. Boys were fickle and likely to be unkind; my mother and I knew that, as surely as we knew they tried to make you do things in the dark they wouldn't respect you for afterwards, and in fact would spread the word and spoil your rep. Boys liked to be flattered; if you made them feel important they would eat out of your hand. So talk to them about their interests, don't alarm them with displays of intelligence—we all knew that, we groups of girls talking into the wee hours of the night in a kind of easy companionship we thought impossible with boys. Boys were prone to have a good time, get you pregnant, and then pretend they didn't know your name when you came knocking on their door for finances or comfort. In short, we believed boys were less moral than we were. They appeared to be hypocritical, self-seeking, exploitative, untrustworthy and very likely to be showing off their precious masculinity. I never had a girl friend I thought would be unkind or embarrass me in public. I never expected a girl to lie to me about her marks or sports skill or how good she was in bed. Altogether—without anyone's directly coming out and saying so—I gathered that men were sexy, powerful, very interesting, but not very nice, not very moral, humane and tender, like us. Girls played fairly while men, unfortunately, reserved their honor for the battlefield.

5 Why are there laws insisting on alimony and child support? Well, everyone knows that men don't have an instinct to protect their young and, given half a chance, with the moon in the right phase, they will run off and disappear. Everyone assumes a mother will not let her child starve, yet it is necessary to legislate that a father must not do so. We are taught to accept the idea that men are less than decent; their charms may be manifold but their characters are riddled with faults. To this day I never blink if I hear that a man has gone to find his fortune in South America, having left his pregnant wife, his blind mother and taken the family car. I still gasp in horror when I hear of a woman leaving her asthmatic infant for a rock group in Taos because I can't seem to avoid the assumption that men are naturally heels and women the ordained carriers of what little is moral in our dubious civilization.

My mother never gave me mad money thinking I would ditch a fellow for some other guy or that I would pass out drunk on the floor. She knew I would be considerate of my companion because, after all, I was more mature than the boys that gathered about. Why was I more mature? Women just are people-oriented; they learn to be empathetic at an early age. Most English students (students interested in humanity, not artifacts) are women. Men and boys—so the myth goes—conceal their feelings and lose interest in anybody else's. Everyone knows that even little boys can tell the difference between one kind of a car and another—proof that their souls are mechanical, their attention directed to the nonhuman.

I remember shivering in the cold vestibule of a famous men's athletic club. Women and girls are not permitted inside the club's door. What are they doing in there, I asked? They're naked, said my mother, they're sweating, jumping up and down a lot, telling each other dirty jokes and bragging about their stock market exploits. Why can't we go in? I asked. Well, my mother told me, they're afraid we'd laugh at them.

The prejudices of childhood are hard to outgrow. I confess that every time my business takes me past that club, I shudder. Images of large bellies resting on massage tables and flaccid penises rising and falling with the Dow Jones average flash through my head. There it is, chauvinism waving its cancerous tentacles from the depths of my psyche.

Minorities automatically feel superior to the oppressor because, after all, they are not hurting anybody. In fact, they feel morally better. The old canard that women need love, men need sex—believed for too long by both sexes—attributes moral and spiritual superiority to women and makes of men beasts whose urges send them prowling into the night. This false division of good and bad, placing deforming pressures on everyone, doesn't have to contaminate the future. We know that the assumptions we make about each other become a part of the cultural air we breathe and, in fact, become social truths. Women who want equality must be prepared to give it and to believe in it, and in order to do that it is not enough to state that you are as good as any man, but also it must be stated that he is as good as you and both will be humans together. If we want men to share in the care of the family in a new way, we must assume them as capable of consistent loving tenderness as we.

10 I rummage about and find in my thinking all kinds of anti-male prejudices. Some are just jokes and others I will have a hard time abandoning. First, I share an emotional conviction with many sisters that women given power would not create wars. Intellectually I know that's ridiculous; great queens have waged war before; the likes of Lurleen Wallace, Pat Nixon and Mrs. General Lavelle can be depended upon in the future to guiltlessly condemn to death other people's children in the name of some ideal of their own. Little girls, of course, don't take toy guns out of their hip pockets and say "Pow, pow" to all their neighbors and friends like the average well-adjusted little boy. However, if we gave little girls the six-shooters, we would soon have double the pretend body count.

11 Aggression is not, as I secretly think, a male-sex-linked characteristic: brutality is masculine only by virtue of opportunity. True, there are 1,000 Jack the Rippers for every Lizzie Borden, but that surely is the result of social forms. Women as a group are indeed more masochistic than men. The practical result of this division is that women seem nicer and kinder, but when the world changes, women will have a fuller opportunity to be just as rotten as men and there will be fewer claims of female moral superiority.

12 Now that I am entering early middle age, I hear many women complaining of husbands and ex-husbands who are attracted to younger females. This strikes the older woman as unfair, of course. But I remember a time when I thought all boys around my age and grade were creeps and bores. I wanted to go out with an older man: a senior or, miraculously, a college man. I had a certain contempt for my coevals, not realizing that the freshman in college I thought so desirable, was some older girl's creep. Some women never lose that contempt for men of their own age. That isn't fair either and may be one reason why some sensible men of middle years find solace in young women.

13 I remember coming home from school one day to find my mother's card game dissolved in hysterical laughter. The cards were floating in black rivers of running mascara.

What was so funny? A woman named Helen was lying on a couch pretending to be her husband with a cold. She was issuing demands for orange juice, aspirin, suggesting a call to a specialist, complaining of neglect, of fate's cruel finger, of heat, of cold, of sharp pains on the bridge of the nose that might indicate brain involvement. What was so funny? The ladies explained to me that all men behave just like that with colds, they are reduced to temper tantrums by simple nasal congestion, men cannot stand any little physical discomfort—on and on the laughter went.

The point of this vignette is the nature of the laughter—us laughing at them, us feeling superior to them, us ridiculing them behind their backs. If they were doing it to us we'd call it male chauvinist pigness; if we do it to them, it is inescapably female chauvinist sowness and, whatever its roots, it leads to the same isolation. Boys are messy, boys are mean, boys are rough, boys are stupid and have sloppy handwriting. A cacophony of childhood memories rushes through my head, balanced, of course, by all the well-documented feelings of inferiority and envy. But the important thing, the hard thing, is to wipe the slate clean, to start again without the meanness of the past. That's why it's so important that the women's movement not become anti-male and allow its most prejudiced spokesmen total leadership. The much-chewed-over abortion issue illustrates this. The women's-liberation position, insisting on a woman's right to determine her own body's destiny, leads in fanatical extreme to a kind of emotional immaculate conception in which the father is not judged even half-responsible—he has no rights, and no consideration is to be given to his concern for either the woman or the fetus.

Woman, who once was abandoned and disgraced by an unwanted pregnancy, has recently arrived at a new pride of ownership or disposal. She has traveled in a straight line that still excludes her sexual partner from an equal share in the wanted or unwanted pregnancy. A better style of life may develop from an assumption that men are as human as we. Why not ask the child's father if he would like to bring up the child? Why not share decisions, when possible, with the male? If we cut them out, assuming an old-style indifference on their part, we perpetrate the ugly divisiveness that has characterized relations between the sexes so far.

Hard as it is for many of us to believe, women are not really superior to men in intelligence or humanity—they are only equal. 16

Questions for Study and Discussion

1. What does Roiphe argue for in this essay? What does she argue against?
2. Roiphe uses induction in her essay. Where does she make the inductive leap from her evidence to her conclusion?
3. For what audience is Roiphe writing? What assumptions about that audience does she make?
4. Identify passages in which Roiphe uses comparison and contrast. In what ways does this strategy contribute to the persuasiveness of the essay? (Glossary: *Comparison and Contrast*)
5. Roiphe's tone is informal and subjective in this essay. Does this tone enhance the persuasiveness of her essay? If so, why? (Glossary: *Tone*)
6. Are you persuaded by Roiphe's argument? Why, or why not?
7. Why is Roiphe's title appropriate for the essay?

Vocabulary

Refer to your dictionary to define the following words as they are used in this selection. Then use each word in a sentence of your own.

replica (1)
prone (4)
manifold (5)
dubious (5)
empathetic (6)
vestibule (7)
vignette (14)

Suggested Writing Assignment

Write a persuasive essay in which you attempt to convince students that campus life is not balanced, that there is an over-emphasis on one activity or another. In considering the situation on your campus, think in terms of the following aspects of student life:

partying
exams
fraternities and sororities
student government
sports
career training
drinking
grades

I Wish They'd Do It Right

Jane Doe

The following essay appeared in The New York Times *on September 23, 1977. "Jane Doe" is a pseudonym; the author wished to remain anonymous. In the article, the author argues against her son's wish not to marry the woman he lives with. As you read, notice her reasons for defending marriage and how she anticipates and refutes opposing arguments.*

My son and his wife are not married. They have lived together for seven years without benefit of license. Though occasionally marriage has been a subject of conjecture, it did not seem important until the day they announced, jubilantly, that they were going to have a child. It was happy news. I was ready and eager to become a grandmother. Now, I thought, they will take the final step and make their relationship legal. 1

I was appraised of the Lamaze method of natural childbirth. I was prepared by Leboyer for birth without violence. I admired the expectant mother's discipline. She ate only organic foods, abstained from alcohol, avoided insecticides, smog and trauma. Every precaution was taken to insure the arrival of a healthy, happy infant. No royal birth had been prepared for more auspiciously. All that was lacking was legitimacy. 2

Finally, when my grandson was two weeks old, I dared to question their intentions. 3

"We don't believe in marriage," was all that was volunteered. 4

"Not even for your son's sake?" I asked. "Maybe he will." 5

Their eyes were impenetrable, their faces stiffened to masks. "You wouldn't understand," I was told. 6

And I don't. Surely they cannot believe they are pioneering, making revolutionary changes in society. That frontier 7 has long been tamed. Today marriage offers all the options. Books and talk shows have surfeited us with the freedom offered in open marriage. Lawyers, psychologists and marriage counselors are growing rich executing marriage contracts. And divorce, should it come to that, is in most states easy and inexpensive.

On the other hand, living together out of wedlock can be economically impractical as well as socially awkward. How do I present her—as my son's roommate? his spouse? his spice, as one facetious friend suggested? Even my son flounders in these waters. Recently, I heard him refer to her as his girl friend. I cannot believe that that description will be endearing to their son when he is able to understand.

I have resolved that problem for myself, bypassing their omission, introducing her as she is, as my daughter-in-law. But my son, in militant support of his ideology, refutes any assumption, however casual, that they have taken vows.

There are economic benefits which they are denying themselves. When they applied for housing in the married-students dormitory of the university where he is seeking his doctorate, they were asked for their marriage certificate. Not having one, they were forced to find other, more expensive quarters off campus. Her medical insurance, provided by the company where she was employed, was denied him. He is not her husband. There have been and will be other inconveniences they have elected to endure.

Their son will not enjoy the luxury of choice about the inconveniences and scurrility to which he will be subject from those of his peers and elders who dislike and fear society's nonconformists.

And if in the future, his parents should decide to separate, will he not suffer greater damage than the child of divorce, who may find comfort in the knowledge that his parents once believed they could live happily ever after, and committed themselves to that idea? The child of unwed parents has no sanctuary. His mother and father have assiduously avoided a pledge of permanency, leaving him drifting and insecure.

I know my son is motivated by idealism and honesty in his reluctance to concede to what he considers mere ceremony.

But is he wise enough to know that no one individual can fight all of society's foibles and frauds. Why does he persist in this, a battle already lost? Because though he rejects marriage, California, his residence, has declared that while couples living together in imitation of marriage are no longer under the jurisdiction of the family court, their relationship is viewed by the state as an implicit contract somewhat like a business agreement. This position was mandated when equal property rights were granted a woman who had been abandoned by the man she had lived with for a number of years.

14 Finally, the couple's adamancy has been depriving to all the rest of the family. There has been no celebration of wedding or anniversaries. There has been concealment from certain family elders who could not cope with the situation. Its irregularity has put constraint on the grandparents, who are stifled by one another's possible embarrassment or hurt.

15 I hope that one day very soon my son and his wife will acknowledge their cohabitation with a license. The rest of us will not love them any more for it. We love and support them as much as possible now. But it will be easier and happier for us knowing that our grandson will be spared the continued explanation and harassment, the doubts and anxieties of being a child of unmarried parents.

Questions for Study and Discussion

1. The author states that "living together out of wedlock can be economically impractical as well as socially awkward." How does she support this assertion? (Glossary: *Evidence*)
2. The author is concerned about the future welfare of her grandchild. What exactly does she fear? What does the discussion of her grandchild add to the persuasiveness of her argument?
3. How does she use the California law regarding couples living together to further her argument?

4. The author anticipates arguments her son and girlfriend might make in defending their position. What are these arguments, and where are they mentioned? Has she overlooked or avoided any?
5. What kind of argument is this, inductive or deductive? Is this kind of reasoning particularly appropriate to her argument? Why, or why not?
6. Doe's tone is objective and reasonable in this essay. What in her diction helps to establish this tone? Why does her tone serve her argument so well? (Glossary: *Tone* and *Diction*)

Vocabulary

Refer to your dictionary to define the following words as they are used in this selection. Then use each word in a sentence of your own.

conjecture (1)	refutes (9)
impenetrable (6)	implicit (13)
facetious (8)	adamancy (14)

Suggested Writing Assignment

Reread paragraph 14 of the essay. To what extent do a couple, married or unmarried, have responsibilities to their respective families? Write an essay in which you argue your position.

The Declaration of Independence

Thomas Jefferson

President, governor, statesman, lawyer, architect, philosopher, and writer, Thomas Jefferson (1743–1826) was a seminal figure in the early history of our country. In 1776 Jefferson drafted the Declaration of Independence. Although it was revised by Benjamin Franklin and other colleagues at the Continental Congress, the document retains in its sound logic and forceful, direct style the unmistakable qualities of Jefferson's prose. In 1809, after two terms as president, Jefferson retired to Monticello, a home he had designed and helped build. Ten years later he founded the University of Virginia. Jefferson died at Monticello on July 4, 1826, the fiftieth anniversary of the signing of the Declaration of Independence.

When in the course of human events, it becomes necessary for one people to dissolve the political bands which have connected them with another, and to assume among the Powers of the earth, the separate and equal station to which the Laws of Nature and of Nature's God entitle them, a decent respect to the opinions of mankind requires that they should declare the causes which impel them to the separation. 1

We hold these truths to be self-evident, that all men are created equal, that they are endowed by their Creator with certain unalienable Rights, that among these are Life, Liberty and the pursuit of Happiness. That to secure these rights, Governments are instituted among Men deriving their just powers from the consent of the governed. That whenever 2 any Form of Government becomes destructive of these ends, it is the Right of the People to alter or to abolish it, and to institute new Government, laying its foundation on such principles and organizing its powers in such form, as to them shall seem most likely to effect their Safety and Happiness. Prudence, indeed, will dictate that Governments long established should not be changed for light and transient causes; and accordingly all experience hath shown, that mankind are more disposed to suffer, while evils are sufferable, than to right themselves by abolishing the forms to which they are accustomed. But when a long train of abuses and usurpations pursuing invariably the same Object evinces a design to reduce them under absolute Despotism, it is their right, it is their duty, to throw off such government, and to provide new Guards for their future security. Such has been the patient sufferance of these Colonies; and such is now the necessity which constrains them to alter their former Systems of Government. The history of the present King of Great Britain is a history of repeated injuries and usurpations, all having in direct object the establishment of an absolute Tyranny over these States. To prove this, let Facts be submitted to a candid world.

He has refused his Assent to Laws, the most wholesome and necessary for the public good. 3

He has forbidden his Governors to pass Laws of immediate and pressing importance, unless suspended in their operation till his Assent should be obtained; and when so suspended, he has utterly neglected to attend to them. 4

He has refused to pass other Laws for the accommodation of large districts of people, unless those people would relinquish the right of Representation in the Legislature, a right inestimable to them and formidable to tyrants only. 5

He has called together legislative bodies at places unusual, uncomfortable, and distant from the depository of their Public Records, for the sole purpose of fatiguing them into compliance with his measures. 6

He has dissolved Representative Houses repeatedly, for opposing with manly firmness his invasions on the rights of the people. 7

He has refused for a long time, after such dissolutions, to cause others to be elected; whereby the Legislative Powers, incapable of Annihilation, have returned to the People at large for their exercise; the State remaining in the mean time exposed to all the dangers of invasion from without, and convulsions within. 8

He has endeavoured to prevent the population of these States; for that purpose obstructing the Laws of Naturalization of Foreigners; refusing to pass others to encourage their migration hither, and raising the conditions of new Appropriations of Lands. 9

He has obstructed the Administration of Justice, by refusing his Assent to Laws for establishing Judiciary Powers. 10

He has made Judges dependent on his Will alone, for the tenure of their offices, and the amount and payment of their salaries. 11

He has erected a multitude of New Offices, and sent hither swarms of Officers to harass our People, and eat out their substance. 12

He has kept among us, in time of peace, Standing Armies without the Consent of our Legislature. 13

He has affected to render the Military independent of and superior to the Civil Power. 14

He has combined with others to subject us to jurisdictions foreign to our constitution, and unacknowledged by our laws; giving his Assent to their acts of pretended Legislation: 15

For quartering large bodies of armed troops among us: 16

For protecting them, by a mock Trial, from Punishment for any Murders which they should commit on the Inhabitants of these States: 17

For cutting off our Trade with all parts of the world: 18

For imposing Taxes on us without our Consent: 19

For depriving us in many cases, of the benefits of Trial by Jury: 20

For transporting us beyond Seas to be tried for pretended offenses: 21

For abolishing the free System of English Laws in a Neighbouring Province, establishing therein an Arbitrary government, and enlarging its boundaries so as to render it at once 22 an example and fit instrument for introducing the same absolute rule into these Colonies:

For taking away our Charters, abolishing our most valuable Laws, and altering fundamentally the Forms of our Governments:

For suspending our own Legislatures, and declaring themselves invested with Power to legislate for us in all cases whatsoever.

He has abdicated Government here, by declaring us out of his Protection and waging War against us.

He has plundered our seas, ravaged our Coasts, burnt our towns and destroyed the Lives of our people.

He is at this time transporting large Armies of foreign Mercenaries to compleat works of death, desolation and tyranny, already begun with circumstances of Cruelty & perfidy scarcely paralleled in the most barbarous ages, and totally unworthy the Head of a civilized nation.

He has constrained our fellow Citizens taken Captive on the high Seas to bear Arms against their Country, to become the executioners of their friends and Brethren, or to fall themselves by their Hands.

He has excited domestic insurrections amongst us, and has endeavoured to bring on the inhabitants of our frontiers, the merciless Indian Savages, whose known rule of warfare, is an undistinguished destruction of all ages, sexes and conditions.

In every stage of these Oppressions We Have Petitioned for Redress in the most humble terms: Our repeated petitions have been answered only by repeated injury. A Prince, whose character is thus marked by every act which may define a Tyrant, is unfit to be the ruler of a free People.

Nor have We been wanting in attention to our British brethren. We have warned them from time to time of attempts by their legislature to extend an unwarrantable jurisdiction over us. We have reminded them of the circumstances of our emigration and settlement here. We have appealed to their native justice and magnanimity and we have conjured them by the ties of our common kindred to disavow these usurpations, which would inevitably interrupt our connections and correspondence. They too have been deaf to the voice of justice and of consanguinity. We must, therefore acquiesce in the necessity, which denounces our Separation, and hold them, as we hold the rest of mankind, Enemies in War, in Peace Friends.

32 We, therefore, the Representatives of the United States of America, in General Congress, Assembled, appealing to the Supreme Judge of the world for the rectitude of our intentions, do, in the Name, and by Authority of the good People of these Colonies, solemnly publish and declare, That these United Colonies are, and of Right ought to be Free and Independent States; that they are Absolved from all Allegiance to the British Crown, and that all political connection between them and the State of Great Britain, is and ought to be totally dissolved; and that as Free and Independent States, they have full power to levy War, conclude Peace, contract Alliances, establish Commerce, and to do all other Acts and Things which Independent States may of right do. And for the support of this Declaration, with a firm reliance on the protection of Divine Providence, we mutually pledge to each other our lives, our Fortunes and our sacred Honor.

Questions for Study and Discussion

1. In paragraph 2, Jefferson presents certain "self-evident" truths. What are these truths, and how are they related to his argument? Do you consider them self-evident?
2. The Declaration of Independence is a deductive argument; it can, therefore, be presented in the form of a syllogism. What are the major premise, the minor premise, and the conclusion of Jefferson's argument? (Glossary: *Syllogism*)
3. The list of charges against the king is given as evidence in support of Jefferson's minor premise. Does he offer any evidence in support of his major premise? (Glossary: *Evidence*)

4. How, specifically, does Jefferson refute the possible charge that the colonists had not tried to solve their problems by less drastic means?
5. Where in the Declaration does Jefferson use parallel structure? What does he achieve by using it? (Glossary: *Parallelism*)
6. While the basic structure of the Declaration reflects sound deductive reasoning, Jefferson's language, particularly when he lists the charges against the king, tends to be emotional. Identify as many examples of this emotional language as you can, and discuss possible reasons why Jefferson uses this kind of language.

Vocabulary

Refer to your dictionary to define the following words as they are used in this selection. Then use each word in a sentence of your own.

prudence (2)
transient (2)
convulsions (8)
abdicated (25)
conjured (31)
acquiesce (31)
rectitude (32)

Suggested Writing Assignment

Using one of the subjects listed below, develop a thesis and then write an essay in which you argue that thesis.

the Equal Rights Amendment
social security
capital punishment
welfare
separation of church and state
First Amendment rights

GLOSSARY OF USEFUL TERMS

Abstract See *Concrete/Abstract.*

Allusion An allusion is a passing reference to a familiar person, place, or thing often drawn from history, the Bible, mythology, or literature. An allusion is an economical way for a writer to capture the essence of an idea, atmosphere, emotion, or historical era, as in "The scandal was his Watergate," or "He saw himself as a modern Job," or "The campaign ended not with a bang but a whimper." An allusion should be familiar to the reader; if it is not, it will add nothing to the meaning.

Analogy Analogy is a special form of comparison in which the writer explains something unfamiliar by comparing it to something familiar: "A transmission line is simply a pipeline for electricity. In the case of a water pipeline, more water will flow through the pipe as water pressure increases. The same is true of electricity in a transmission line."

Anecdote An anecdote is a short narrative about an amusing or interesting event. Writers often use anecdotes to begin essays as well as to illustrate certain points.

Appropriateness See *Diction.*

Argumentation Argumentation is one of the four basic types of prose. (Narration, description, and exposition are the other three.) To argue is to attempt to persuade a reader to agree with a point of view, to make a given decision, or to pursue a particular course of action. There are two basic types of argumentation: logical and persuasive. See the introduction to Chapter 18 (pp. 298–300) for a detailed discussion of argumentation.

Attitude A writer's attitude reflects his or her opinion of a subject. The writer can think very positively or very negatively about a subject, or somewhere in between. See also *Tone.*

Audience An audience is the intended readership for a piece of writing. For example, the readers of a national weekly newsmagazine come from all walks of life and have diverse interests, opinions, and educational backgrounds.

In contrast, the readership for an organic chemistry journal is made up of people whose interests and education are quite similar. The essays in *Models for Writers* are intended for general readers, intelligent people who may lack specific information about the subject being discussed.

Beginnings See *Beginnings/Endings.*

Beginnings/Endings A *beginning* is that sentence, group of sentences, or section that introduces an essay. Good beginnings usually identify the thesis or controlling idea, attempt to interest readers, and establish a tone. Some effective ways in which writers begin essays include (1) telling an anecdote that illustrates the thesis, (2) providing a controversial statement or opinion which engages the reader's interest, (3) presenting startling facts or statistics, (4) defining a term that is central to the discussion that follows, (5) asking thought-provoking questions, (6) providing a quotation that illustrates the thesis, (7) referring to a current event that helps to establish the thesis, or (8) showing the significance of the subject or stressing its importance to readers.

An *ending* is that sentence or group of sentences which brings an essay to a close. Good endings are purposeful and well planned. They can be a summary, a concluding example, an anecdote, a quotation. Endings satisfy readers when they are the natural outgrowths of the essays themselves and give the readers a sense of finality or completion. Good essays do not simply stop; they conclude.

Cause and Effect Cause-and-effect analysis is a type of exposition that explains the reasons for an occurrence or the consequences of an action. See the introduction to Chapter 17 (pp. 271–272) for a detailed discussion of cause and effect. See also *Exposition.*

Classification See *Division and Classification.*

Cliché A cliché is an expression that has become ineffective through overuse. Expressions such as *quick as a flash, jump for joy,* and *slow as molasses* are clichés. Writers normally avoid such trite expressions and seek instead to express themselves in fresh and forceful language. See also *Diction.*

Coherence Coherence is a quality of good writing that results when all sentences, paragraphs, and longer divisions of an essay are naturally connected. Coherent writing is achieved through (1) a logical sequence of ideas (arranged in chronological order, spatial order, order of importance, or some other appropriate order), (2) the purposeful repetition of key words and ideas, (3) a pace suitable for your topic and your reader, and (4) the use of transitional words and expressions. Coherence should not be confused with unity. (See *Unity*.) See also *Transitions.*

Colloquial Expressions A colloquial expression is characteristic of or appropriate to spoken language or to writing that seeks its effect. Colloquial expressions are informal, as *chem, gym, come up with, be at loose ends, won't,* and *photo* illustrate. See also *Diction.* Thus, colloquial expressions are acceptable in formal writing only if they are used purposefully.

Comparison and Contrast Comparison and contrast is a type of exposition in which the writer points out the similarities and differences between two or more subjects in the same class or category. The function of any comparison and contrast is to clarify—to reach some conclusion about the items being compared and contrasted. See the introduction to Chapter 16 (pp. 253–255) for a detailed discussion of comparison and contrast. See also *Exposition.*

Conclusions See *Beginnings/Endings.*

Concrete See *Concrete/Abstract.*

Concrete/Abstract A concrete word names a specific object, person, place, or action that can be directly perceived by the senses: *car, bread, building, book, John F. Kennedy, Chicago,* or *hiking*. An abstract word, in contrast, refers to general qualities, conditions, ideas, actions, or relationships which cannot be directly perceived by the senses: *bravery, dedication, excellence, anxiety, stress, thinking,* or *hatred*. See also the introduction to Chapter 7 (pp. 95–98).

Connotation See *Connotation/Denotation.*

Connotation/Denotation Both connotation and denotation refer to the meanings of words. Denotation is the dictionary meaning of a word, the literal meaning. Connotation, on the other hand, is the implied or suggested meaning of a word. For example, the denotation of *lamb* is "a young sheep." The connotations of lamb are numerous: *gentle, docile, weak, peaceful, blessed, sacrificial, blood, spring, frisky, pure, innocent,* and so on. See also the introduction to Chapter 7 (pp. 95–98).

Controlling Idea See *Thesis.*

Coordination Coordination is the joining of grammatical constructions of the same rank (e.g., words, phrases, clauses) to indicate that they are of equal importance. For example, *They ate hotdogs,* and *we ate hamburgers.* See the introduction to Chapter 6 (pp. 76–80). See also *Subordination.*

Deduction Deduction is the process of reasoning from stated premises to a conclusion which follows necessarily. This form of reasoning moves from the general to the specific. See the introduction to Chapter 18 (pp. 298–300) for a discussion of deductive reasoning and its relation to argumentation. See also *Syllogism.*

Definition Definition is one of the types of exposition. Definition is a statement of the meaning of a word. A definition may be either brief or extended, part of an essay or an entire essay itself. See the introduction to Chapter 14 (pp. 221–222) for a detailed discussion of definition. See also *Exposition.*

Denotation See *Connotation/Denotation.*

Description Description is one of the four basic types of prose. (Narration, exposition, and argumentation are the other three.) Description tells how a person, place, or thing is perceived by the five senses. See the introduction to Chapter 12 (pp. 190–191) for a detailed discussion of description.

Diction Diction refers to a writer's choice and use of words. Good diction is precise and appropriate—the words mean exactly what the writer intends, and the words are well suited to the writer's subject, intended audience, and purpose in writing. The word-conscious writer knows that there are differences among *aged, old,* and *elderly; blue, navy,* and *azure;* and *disturbed, angry,* and *irritated.* Furthermore, this writer knows in which situation to use each word. See the introduction to Chapter 7 (pp. 95–98) for a detailed discussion of diction. See also *Cliché, Colloquial Expressions, Connotation/Denotation, Jargon, Slang.*

Division and Classification Division and classification is one of the types of exposition. When dividing and classifying the writer first establishes categories and then arranges or sorts people, places, or things into these categories according to their different characteristics, thus making them more manageable for the writer and more understandable and meaningful for the reader. See the introduction to Chapter 15 (pp. 235–237) for a detailed discussion of division and classification. See also *Exposition.*

Dominant Impression A dominant impression is the single mood, atmosphere, or quality a writer emphasizes in a piece of descriptive writing. The dominant impression is created through the careful selection of details and is, of course, influenced by the writer's subject, audience, and purpose. See also the introduction to Chapter 12 (pp. 190–191).

Endings See *Beginnings/Endings.*

Evaluation An evaluation of a piece of writing is an assessment of its effectiveness or merit. In evaluating a piece of writing, one should ask the following questions: What is the writer's purpose? Is it a worthwhile purpose? Does the writer achieve the purpose? Is the writer's information sufficient and accurate? What are the strengths of the essay? What are its weaknesses? Depending on the type of writing and the purpose, more specific questions can also be asked. For example, with an argument one could ask: Does the writer follow the principles of logical thinking? Is the writer's evidence sufficient and convincing?

Evidence Evidence is the information on which a judgment or argument is based or by which proof or probability is established. Evidence usually takes the form of statistics, facts, names, examples or illustrations, and opinions of authorities.

Example An example illustrates a larger idea or represents something of which it is a part. An example is a basic means of developing or clarifying an idea. Furthermore, examples enable writers to show and not simply to tell readers what they mean. See also the introduction to Chapter 10 (pp. 143–145).

Exposition Exposition is one of the four basic types of prose. (Narration, description, and argumentation are the other three.) The purpose of exposition is to clarify, explain, and inform. The methods of exposition presented in *Models for Writers* are process analysis, definition, illustration, classification, comparison and contrast, and cause and effect. For a detailed discussion of these methods of exposition, see the appropriate section introduction.

Fallacy See *Logical Fallacies.*

Figures of Speech Figures of speech are brief, imaginative comparisons which highlight the similarities between things that are basically dissimilar. They make writing vivid, interesting, and memorable. The most common figures of speech are:

Simile: An explicit comparison introduced by *like* or *as.* "The fighter's hands were like stone."
Metaphor: An implied comparison which makes one thing the equivalent of another. "All the world's a stage."
Personification: A special kind of simile or metaphor in which human traits are assigned to an inanimate object. "The engine coughed and then stopped."

See the introduction to Chapter 9 (pp. 127–128) for a detailed discussion of figurative language.

Focus Focus is the limitation that a writer gives his or her subject. The writer's task is to select a manageable topic given the constraints of time, space, and purpose. For example, within the general subject of sports, a writer could focus on government support of amateur athletes or narrow the focus further to government support of Olympic athletes.

General See *Specific/General.*

Idiom An idiom is a word or phrase that is used habitually with special meaning. The meaning of an idiom is not always readily apparent to nonnative speakers of that language. For example, *catch cold, hold a job, make up your mind,* and *give them a hand* are all idioms in English.

Illustration Illustration is the use of examples to explain, elucidate, or corroborate. Writers rely heavily on illustration to make their ideas both clear and concrete. See the introduction to Chapter 10 (pp. 143–145) for a detailed discussion of illustration.

Induction Induction is the process of reasoning to a conclusion about all members of a class through an examination of only a few members of the class. This form of reasoning moves from the particular to the general. See the introduction to Chapter 18 (pp. 298–300) for a discussion of inductive reasoning and its relation to argumentation.

Inductive Leap An inductive leap is the point at which a writer of an argument, having presented sufficient evidence, moves to a generalization or conclusion. See also *Induction.*

Introductions See *Beginnings/Endings.*

Irony The use of words to suggest something different from their literal meaning. For example, when Jonathan Swift proposes in *A Modest Proposal* that Ireland's problems could be solved if the people of Ireland fattened their babies and sold them to the English landlords for food, he meant that almost any other solution would be preferable. A writer can use irony to establish a special relationship with the reader and to add an extra dimension or twist to the meaning. See also the introduction to Chapter 8 (pp. 110–112).

Jargon Jargon, or technical language, is the special vocabulary of a trade, profession, or group. Doctors, construction workers, lawyers, and teachers, for example, all have a specialized vocabulary that they use "on the job." See also *Diction.*

Logical Argumentation See *Argumentation.*

Logical Fallacies A logical fallacy is an error in reasoning that renders an argument invalid. See the introduction to Chapter 18 (pp. 298–300) for a discussion of the more common logical fallacies.

Logical Reasoning See *Deduction* and *Induction.*

Metaphor See *Figures of Speech.*

Narration One of the four basic types of prose. (Description, exposition, and argumentation are the other three.) To narrate is to tell a story, to tell what happened. While narration is most often used in fiction, it is also important in expository writing, either by itself or in conjunction with other types of prose. See the introduction to Chapter 11 (pp. 166–168) for a detailed discussion of narration.

Opinion An opinion is a belief or conclusion, which may or may not be substantiated by positive knowledge or proof. (If not substantiated, an opinion is a prejudice.) Even when based on evidence and sound reasoning, an opinion is personal and can be changed, and is therefore less persuasive than facts and arguments.

Organization Organization is the pattern of order that the writer imposes on his or her material. Some often used patterns of organization include: time order, space order, and order of importance. See the introduction to Chapter 3 (pp. 32–33) for a more detailed discussion of organization.

Paradox A paradox is a seemingly contradictory statement that is nonetheless true. For example, "*we little know what we have until we lose it*" is a paradoxical statement.

Paragraph The paragraph, the single most important unit of thought is an essay, is a series of closely related sentences. These sentences adequately develop the central or controlling idea of the paragraph. This central or controlling idea, usually stated in a topic sentence, is necessarily related to the purpose of the whole composition. A well-written paragraph has several distinguishing characteristics: a clearly stated or implied topic sentence, adequate development, unity, coherence, and an *appropriate organizational* strategy. See the introduction to Chapter 4 (pp. 49–51) for a detailed discussion of paragraphs.

Parallelism Parallel structure is the repetition of word order or grammatical form either within a single sentence or in several sentences that develop the same central idea. As a rhetorical device, parallelism can aid coherence and add emphasis. Roosevelt's statement, "I see one third of the nation ill-housed, ill-clad, and ill-nourished," illustrates effective parallelism.

Personification See *Figures of Speech.*

Persuasive Argumentation See *Argumentation.*

Point of View Point of view refers to the grammatical person in an essay. For example, first-person point of view uses the pronoun *I* and is commonly found in autobiography and the personal essay; third-person point of view uses the pronouns, *he, she,* or *it* and is commonly found in objective writing. See the introduction to Chapter 11 (pp. 166–168) for a discussion of point of view in narration.

Process Analysis Process analysis is a type of exposition. Process analysis answers the question *how* and explains how something works or gives step-by-step directions for doing something. See the introduction to Chapter 13 (pp. 206–207) for a detailed discussion of process analysis. See also *Exposition.*

Purpose Purpose is what the writer wants to accomplish in a particular piece of writing. Purposeful writing seeks to *relate* (narration), to *describe* (description), to *explain* (process analysis, definition, classification, comparison and contrast, and cause and effect), or to *convince* (argumentation).

Rhetorical Question A rhetorical question is asked but requires no answer from the reader. "When will nuclear proliferation end?" is such a question. Writers use rhetorical questions to introduce topics they plan to discuss or to emphasize important points.

Sentence A sentence is a grammatical unit that expresses a complete thought. It consists of at least a subject (a noun) and a predicate (a verb). See the introduction to Chapter 6 (pp. 76–80) for a discussion of effective sentences.

Simile See *Figures of Speech.*

Slang Slang is the unconventional, very informal language of particular subgroups in our culture. Slang, such as *zonk, coke, split, rap, dude,* and *stoned,* is acceptable in formal writing only if it is used selectively for specific purposes.

Specific/General General words name groups or classes of objects, qualities, or actions. Specific words, on the other hand, name individual objects, qualities, or actions within a class or group. To some extent the terms *general* and *specific* are relative. For example, *clothing* is a class of things. *Shirt*, however, is more specific than *clothing* but more general than *T-shirt*. See also *Diction*.

Strategy A strategy is a means by which a writer achieves his or her purpose. Strategy includes the many rhetorical decisions that the writer makes about organization, paragraph structure, sentence structure, and diction. In terms of the whole essay, strategy refers to the principal rhetorical mode that a writer uses. If, for example, a writer wishes to show how to make chocolate chip cookies, the most effective strategy would be process analysis. If it is the writer's purpose to show why sales of American cars have declined in recent years, the most effective strategy would be cause-and-effect analysis.

Style Style is the individual manner in which a writer expresses his or her ideas. Style is created by the author's particular choice of words, construction of sentences, and arrangement of ideas.

Subordination Subordination is the use of grammatical constructions to make one part in a sentence dependent upon rather than equal to another. For example, the italicized clause in the following sentence is subordinate: They all cheered *when I finished the race*. See the introduction to Chapter 6 (pp. 76–80). See also *Coordination*.

Supporting Evidence See *Evidence*.

Syllogism A syllogism is an argument that utilizes deductive reasoning and consists of a major premise, a minor premise, and a conclusion. For example,

> All trees that lose leaves are deciduous. (major premise)
> Maple trees lose their leaves. (minor premise)
> Therefore, maple trees are deciduous. (conclusion)

See also *Deduction*.

Symbol A symbol is a person, place, or thing that represents something beyond itself. For example, the eagle is a symbol of the United States, and the maple leaf, a symbol of Canada.

Syntax Syntax refers to the way in which words are arranged to form phrases, clauses, and sentences, as well as to the grammatical relationship among the words themselves.

Technical Language See *Jargon.*

Thesis A thesis is the main idea of an essay, also known as the controlling idea. A thesis may sometimes be implied rather than stated directly in a thesis statement. See the introduction to Section 1 (pp. 3–4) for a detailed discussion of thesis.

Title A title is a word or phrase set off at the beginning of an essay to identify the subject, to state the main idea of the essay, or to attract the reader's attention. A title may be explicit or suggestive. A subtitle, when used, explains or restricts the meaning of the main title.

Tone Tone is the manner in which a writer relates to an audience, the "tone of voice" used to address readers. Tone may be friendly, serious, distant, angry, cheerful, bitter, cynical, enthusiastic, morbid, resentful, warm, playful, and so forth. A particular tone results from a writer's diction, sentence structure, purpose, and attitude toward the subject. See the introduction to Chapter 8 (pp. 110–112) for several examples that display different tones.

Topic Sentence The topic sentence states the central idea of a paragraph and thus limits the content of the paragraph. Although the topic sentence normally appears at the beginning of the paragraph, it may appear at any other point, particularly if the writer is trying to create a special effect. Not all paragraphs contain topic sentences. See also *Paragraph.*

Transitions Transitions are words or phrases that link sentences, paragraphs, and larger units of a composition in order to achieve coherence. These devices include parallelism, pronoun references, conjunctions, and the repetition of key ideas, as well as the many conventional transitional expressions such as *moreover, on the other hand, in addition, in contrast,* and *therefore.* See the introduction to Chapter 5 (pp. 63–65) for a detailed discussion of transitions. Also see *Coherence.*

Unity Unity is that quality of oneness in an essay that results when all the words, sentences, and paragraphs contribute to the thesis. The elements of a unified essay do not distract the reader. Instead, they all harmoniously support a single idea or purpose. See the introduction to Chapter 2 (pp. 18–19) for a detailed discussion of unity.

Verb Verbs can be classified as either strong verbs (*scream, pierce, gush, ravage,* and *amble*) or weak verbs (*be, has, get,* and *do*). Writers often prefer to use strong verbs in order to make writing more specific or more descriptive.

Voice Verbs can be classified as being in either the active or the passive voice. In the active voice the doer of the action is the subject. In the passive voice the receiver of the action is the grammatical subject:

Active: Glenda questioned all of the children.

Passive: All of the children were questioned by Glenda.

Thematic Table of Contents

Personal Experience

People

The Feminine Experience

The Minority Experience

Nature and Science

Controversies

Language and Thought

Enduring Issues

Places

Ordinary Things

Popular Culture

Education

Health and Medicine

Acknowledgments (continued from page iv)

3. Organization

"Bugs Bunny Says They're Yummy" by Dawn Ann Kurth. © 1972 by The New York Times Company. Reprinted by permission.

"Dust" by Gale Lawrence and reprinted with her permission. Copyright © Gale Lawrence 1980.

4. Paragraphs

"Claude Fetridge's Infuriating Law" by H. Allen Smith. Reprinted with permission from the June, 1963 *Reader's Digest*. Copyright © 1963 by The Reader's Digest Assn., Inc.

"Americans and Physical Fitness" from THE COMPLETE BOOK OF RUNNING by James Fixx. Copyright © 1977 by James Fixx. Reprinted by permission of Random House, Inc.

"What Makes a Leader" by Michael Korda. Copyright © 1981, by Newsweek, Inc. All rights reserved. Reprinted by permission.

5. Transitions

"Walking" from THE MAGIC OF WALKING by Aaron Sussman and Ruth Goode. Copyright © 1967 by Aaron Sussman and Ruth Goode. Reprinted by permission of Simon & Schuster, a Division of Gulf & Western Corporation.

"More Than Meets the Eye" by Leo Rosten from THE STORY BEHIND THE PAINTING. Reprinted by permission of Leo Rosten. © Cowles Magazines, 1961.

"Auto Suggestion" by Russell Baker. © 1979 by The New York Times Company. Reprinted by permission.

6. Effective Sentences

"Terror at Tinker Creek" from pp. 5–6 in PILGRIM AT TINKER CREEK by Annie Dillard. Copyright © 1974 by Annie Dillard. Reprinted by permission of Harper & Row, Publishers, Inc.

"Salvation" from THE BIG SEA by Langston Hughes. Copyright © 1940 by Langston Hughes. Reprinted by permission of Farrar, Straus and Giroux, Inc.

II. The Language of the Essay

7. Diction

"The Flight of the Eagles" from pp. 17–18 in HOUSE MADE OF DAWN by N. Scott Momaday. Copyright © 1966, 1967, 1968 by N. Scott Momaday. Reprinted by permission of Harper & Row, Publishers, Inc.

"On Being 17, Bright and Unable to Read" by David Raymond. © 1976 by The New York Times Company. Reprinted by permission.

8. Tone

"The Language of the Eyes" by Flora Davis. Reprinted with her permission. © Flora Davis. Copyright © 1969 by The Condé Nast Publications Inc.

"How to Fold Soup" by Steve Martin. Reprinted by permission of G. P. Putnam's Sons from CRUEL SHOES by Steve Martin. Copyright © 1977, 1979 by Steve Martin.

"Meet Me at the Rinse Cycle" by Jane O'Reilly. Reprinted by permission of Wallace and Sheil Agency, Inc. Copyright © 1978 by Jane O'Reilly.

"Nobel Prize Acceptance Speech" by William Faulkner from ESSAYS, SPEECHES AND PUBLIC LETTERS by William Faulkner. Courtesy of Random House, Inc.

9. Figurative Language

"The Wilderness" by David Perlman. © San Francisco Chronicle, 1954. Reprinted by permission.

"The Inner Game of Pinball" by J. Anthony Lukas. Copyright © 1979, by The Atlantic Monthly Company, Boston, Mass. 02116. Reprinted with permission of the author and The Atlantic Monthly Co.

"Notes on Punctuation" from THE MEDUSA AND THE SNAIL by Lewis Thomas. Copyright © 1979 by Lewis Thomas. Reprinted by permission of Viking Penguin Inc.

III. Types of Essays

10. Illustration

"That Astounding Creature—Nature" by Jean George. Reprinted with permission from the January 1964 *Reader's Digest.* Copyright © 1964 by The Reader's Digest Assn., Inc.

"One Environment, Many Worlds" from Judith and Herbert Kohl, THE VIEW FROM THE OAK. Copyright © 1977 by Judith and Herbert Kohl. (San Francisco: Sierra Club Books, 1977) Reprinted with the permission of Sierra Club Books.

"At War With the System" (Original title "Businesses Wrong Him") by Enid Nemy. © 1974 by The New York Times Company. Reprinted with permission.

"This Is Progress?" by Alan L. Otten. Reprinted by permission of *The Wall Street Journal.* © Dow Jones & Company, Inc. 1978. All rights reserved.

11. Narration

"Big White" by Skip Rozen. Reprinted by permission of the Author and his Agent, Curtis Brown Associates, Ltd. Copyright © 1975 by Skip Rozen.

"How I Designed an A-Bomb in My Junior Year at Princeton" by John Aristotle Phillips and David Michaelis. Condensed from MUSHROOM as it appeared in *Reader's Digest,* under the title "How I Designed an A-Bomb in My Junior Year at Princeton." Copyright © 1978 by John Aristotle Phillips. By permission of William Morrow and Company.

"Shame" from *nigger: An Autobiography* by Dick Gregory. Copyright ©, 1964 by Dick Gregory Enterprises, Inc. Reprinted by permission of the publisher, E. P. Dutton.

"The Gopher" from CANNERY ROW by John Steinbeck. Copyright © 1945 by John Steinbeck. © renewed by Elaine Steinbeck, John Steinbeck IV, and Thom Steinbeck. Reprinted by permission of Viking Penguin Inc.

12. Description

"Subway Station" from TALENTS AND GENIUSES by Gilbert Highet. Reprinted by permission of Curtis Brown, Ltd. Copyright © 1957 by Gilbert Highet.

"The Sounds of the City" by James Tuite. © 1966 by The New York Times Company. Reprinted by permission.

"My Friend, Albert Einstein" by Banesh Hoffman. Reprinted with permission from the January 1968 *Reader's Digest.* Copyright © 1968 by The Reader's Digest Assn., Inc.

13. Process Analysis

"How to Build a Fire in a Fireplace" by Bernard Gladstone. From *The New York Times Complete Manual of Home Repair.* © 1972 by The New York Times Company. Reprinted with permission.

"How Dictionaries Are Made" from LANGUAGE IN THOUGHT AND ACTION, Fourth Edition, by S. I. Hayakawa, copyright © 1978 by Harcourt Brace Jovanovich, Inc. Reprinted by permission of the publisher.

"How to Take a Job Interview" reprinted from JOB HUNTING: SECRETS AND TACTICS by Kirby W. Stanat with Patrick Reardon by permission of Westwind Press, a division of Raintree Publishers, Limited. Text copyright © 1977, Kirby Stanat and Patrick Reardon.

14. Definition

"A Jerk" by Sydney J. Harris. Copyright © Field Enterprises, Inc. Courtesy of Field Newspaper Syndicate.

"What Is Freedom?" by Jerald M. Jellison and John H. Harvey. (Original title "Give Me Liberty: Why We Like Hard Positive Choices"). Reprinted from *Psychology Today* Magazine. Copyright © 1976 by Ziff-Davis Publishing Company.

"The Barrio" by Robert Ramirez and reprinted with his permission.

15. Division and Classification

"Children's Insults" from WORD PLAY: WHAT HAPPENS WHEN PEOPLE TALK by Peter Farb. Copyright © 1973 by Peter Farb. Reprinted by permission of Alfred A. Knopf, Inc.

"The Ways of Meeting Oppression" from pp. 211–214 in STRIDE TOWARD FREEDOM by Martin Luther King, Jr. Copyright © 1958 by Martin Luther King, Jr. Reprinted by permission of Harper & Row, Publishers, Inc.

"Friends, Good Friends—and Such Good Friends" by Judith Viorst. Copyright © 1977 by Judith Viorst. Reprinted by permission of The Lescher Agency.

16. Comparison and Contrast

"Two Americas" from THE ARROGANCE OF POWER by J. William Fulbright. Copyright © 1966 by J. William Fulbright. Reprinted by permission of Random House, Inc.

"Bing and Elvis" by Russell Baker. © 1977 by The New York Times Company. Reprinted by permission.

"The Bright Child and the Dull Child" from WHY CHILDREN FAIL by John Holt. © 1964 Pitman Publishing Corporation. Reprinted by permission of the author.

"Fable for Tomorrow" from SILENT SPRING by Rachel Carson. Copyright © 1962 by Rachel L. Carson. Reprinted by permission of Houghton Mifflin Company.

17. Cause and Effect

"Never Get Sick in July" by Marilyn Machlowitz. First published in *Esquire* magazine. Reprinted by permission of Marilyn Machlowitz, Ph.D.

"The Collapse of Public Schools" by John C. Sawhill. Copyright © 1979 by *Saturday Review*. All rights reserved. Reprinted with permission.

"When Television Is a School for Criminals" by Grant Hendricks.

Reprinted with permission from *TV Guide* Magazine. Copyright © 1977 by Triangle Publications, Radnor, Pennsylvania.

"Who's Afraid of Math, and Why?" reprinted from OVERCOMING MATH ANXIETY by Sheila Tobias, with the permission of W. W. Norton & Company, Inc. Copyright © 1978 by Sheila Tobias.

18. Argument

"Darkness at Noon" by Harold Krentz. © 1976 by The New York Times Company. Reprinted by permission.

"The Egalitarian Error (Aug. 1962)" in A WAY OF SEEING by Margaret Mead and Rhoda Metraux. Copyright © 1962 by Margaret Mead and Rhoda Metraux. By permission of William Morrow and Company.

"Pain Is Not the Ultimate Enemy" reprinted from ANATOMY OF AN ILLNESS AS PERCEIVED BY THE PATIENT, by Norman Cousins, by permission of W. W. Norton & Company, Inc. Copyright © 1979 by W. W. Norton & Company, Inc.

"Confessions of a Female Chauvinist Sow" by Anne Roiphe. From *New York Magazine*. Copyright © 1972 by Anne Roiphe. Reprinted by permission of Brandt and Brandt Literary Agents, Inc.

"I Wish They'd Do It Right" by Jane Doe. © 1977 by The New York Times Company. Reprinted by permission.

INDEX OF AUTHORS, TITLES, AND RHETORICAL TERMS

9558 027